The Lipstick Chronicles

BOOK ONE

the LIPSTICK *chronicles*

Book One

Kathryn Shay   Fiona Kelly

Vivian Leiber   Lynn Emery

BERKLEY SENSATION, NEW YORK

THE BERKLEY PUBLISHING GROUP
Published by the Penguin Group
Penguin Group (USA) Inc.
375 Hudson Street, New York, New York 10014, USA
Penguin Group (Canada), 90 Eglinton Avenue East, Suite 700, Toronto, Ontario M4P 2Y3, Canada
(a division of Pearson Penguin Canada Inc.)
Penguin Books Ltd., 80 Strand, London WC2R 0RL, England
Penguin Group Ireland, 25 St. Stephen's Green, Dublin 2, Ireland (a division of Penguin Books Ltd.)
Penguin Group (Australia), 250 Camberwell Road, Camberwell, Victoria 3124, Australia
(a division of Pearson Australia Group Pty. Ltd.)
Penguin Books India Pvt. Ltd., 11 Community Centre, Panchsheel Park, New Delhi—110 017, India
Penguin Group (NZ), Cnr. Airborne and Rosedale Roads, Albany, Auckland 1310, New Zealand
(a division of Pearson New Zealand Ltd.)
Penguin Books (South Africa) (Pty.) Ltd., 24 Sturdee Avenue, Rosebank, Johannesburg 2196,
South Africa

Penguin Books Ltd., Registered Offices: 80 Strand, London WC2R 0RL, England

This is a work of fiction. Names, characters, places, and incidents either are the product of the authors' imagination or are used fictitiously, and any resemblance to actual persons, living or dead, business establishments, events, or locales is entirely coincidental. The publisher does not have any control over and does not assume any responsibility for author or third-party websites or their content.

THE LIPSTICK CHRONICLES

A Berkley Sensation Book / published by arrangement with Lark Productions, LLC

PRINTING HISTORY
Berkley trade paperback edition / November 2003
Berkley Sensation mass-market edition / December 2006

Copyright © 2003 by Lark Productions, LLC.
Cover design and illustration by Rita Frangie.
Interior text design by Kristin del Rosario.

ISBN: 0-425-21432-X

BERKLEY SENSATION®
Berkley Sensation Books are published by The Berkley Publishing Group,
a division of Penguin Group (USA) Inc.,
375 Hudson Street, New York, New York 10014.
BERKLEY SENSATION is a registered trademark of Penguin Group (USA) Inc.
The "B" design is a trademark belonging to Penguin Group (USA) Inc.

PRINTED IN THE UNITED STATES OF AMERICA

10 9 8 7 6 5 4 3 2 1

Contents

Prologue

"*To Emma!*" *Elyssa raised her glass of champagne to* toast the imminent birth of her friend's baby.

"To Emma!" The four other women at the table cheered in agreement. Glasses clinked, all filled to the brim (for the third or fourth time, not that anyone was counting) with the sparkling wine. Emma's glass was empty, and so was her seat. The women had gathered to mark their friend and colleague's last day of work and to send her off into the vast and mysterious unknown of motherhood. She was nine months and four days into her first pregnancy and she had long since gone home. Her friends had stayed behind, reluctant to end what had turned out to be a big old girls' night out.

"Here's what I want to know," Elyssa announced to no one in particular. "How can you go from a desk one day to a diaper pail the next?" She waved her glass at the waiter for a fill-up. She removed her earrings and dropped them in her handbag. When her shoes came off, the others would know the party was getting permanent.

"Oh, yeah, I'm sure she's going to miss that desk of hers, all covered with pink message slips and crusty coffee cups and those pesky fires that need putting out every day. Being a mother could seem like a vacation compared to being the company fireman, don't you think?" Dana smiled across the table at her boss.

Elyssa shook her head. "I just don't see it. Emma's been with Allheart since we opened the doors two years ago. I thought she loved her job."

"Elyssa, you shouldn't take it personally that Em decided to leave to have a baby. Lots of people want to have families, you know. It doesn't have anything to do with you or Allheart.com,"

Robyn offered up earnestly. Dressed in a pale peach cotton blouse and hip-hugging slacks just a shade darker, she looked the picture of youthful innocence. Innocent, that is, until you got a look at her chunky metallic sandals and black toenail polish.

The others chortled almost in unison. Only Carole, the office sage, bothered to answer.

"What you can't know yet, young lady, is this: Every day in the life of a woman is a conflict, a mighty battle between what we want and what we get if we leave it up to others to decide. Motherhood for example. It's lovely and I'm all for it. But who was the idiot who started talking about biological clocks ticking? Motherhood should be optional, not a physical imperative. I shouldn't somehow feel failed or unfulfilled because I'm not inclined to become a mother!" Carole folded her arms across her chest in a huff. She had her navy suit jacket off, her tailored pinstriped shirt loosened and her sleeves rolled up; she looked like she was ready to deal the next hand.

"Well, but gee, Carole, why don't you tell us how you really feel?" Elyssa kidded. Everyone around the table laughed and Carole laughed the loudest.

"Okay, then, here's what I want to know," the lovely Alix said when the rumpus died down. "We all love what we do. I know I do. But can anyone imagine meeting a man so captivating, so rapturous, so everything-you-dreamed-of that he could convince you to pick up and move on to be with him?"

"Why do you care? You have Cal at home making you crepes for breakfast and taking you off for weekends here and dinners there." Dana couldn't help rubbing Alix's nose in her own good fortune.

"Hey, I'm not complaining," Alix answered with a grin. "But playing house with Cal is not the same as being knocked off your feet by some guy and being willing to change your whole life in order to be with him."

"Does Cal know that?" Carole joked. Alix made a face at her.

"No, absolutely not." Elyssa pounded the table lightly with her fist. "There's no man in the world who could convince me he was more important than what I've got going on right here, right now."

"How about some time in the future then? Say Allheart's gone public, you've made your millions, you've got a bunch of worker bees doing the heavy lifting. Couldn't you imagine a moment when a perfect man might step up and change your whole agenda?" Alix pressed her point. "Heck, you might even think about having one of those babies yourself!"

Elyssa took a sip of champagne and lolled back in her seat. Her pale blue cashmere sweater was tucked neatly into her short black skirt. Her legs were crossed Hollywood style, and her long, dark hair fell across her face as she peered at the others with a smirk.

"I wouldn't go taking any bets on that happening, ladies. I like a good-looking man as much as the next chick but I just don't have it in me to skid to a stop over a guy. My dream is not to meet a man who'll make me want to change my life. My dream is to meet a man who thinks my life's just great as it is and who wants to play along."

"I think that's true, Elyssa. The goal should be to find a guy who doesn't require turning the tables on your whole life. He should complement your life, not clash with it," said Robyn, pleased to have found a way to describe this truth in fashion terms.

"I guess it's just more romantic—or maybe just more dramatic—to think that Mr. Right is supposed to ride up alongside you, pull you up onto his horse, and ride off into the sunset, leaving life as you know it behind," Carole said with a shrug. "I for one would just be glad to hook up with a man who knew how to do a load of laundry. My laundry."

"Here, here," the women called out, laughing. The table was getting louder, sloppier, and more sprawling. Busboys began appearing to clear the debris, a signal perhaps that it was time to wind down.

"Hold on there, fellas," Elyssa's inimitable tone stopped the busboys in their tracks. "Does anyone want anything else?" she asked around the table. Seeing no takers, she grabbed their waiter by the sleeve. "One more glass of wine for me and the check, my young friend." The clearing resumed and the busboys scurried off to the kitchen.

"Why do you do that, Elyssa?" Carole asked wearily.

"Do what?" she answered with a serene smile.

"Scare the pants off of everyone wearing pants! I mean really. It's like you can't help yourself."

"It's just for sport, silly. I can be nice when I need to."

"Can anyone remember the last time Elyssa was just plain nice to a guy? You know, nice for no good reason. Nice just to be nice. Anyone? Anyone?" Carole looked around the table.

"Well, there was that one time she didn't fire Malcolm the intern for blowing up the microwave," Robyn offered.

"Yeah, that's because Malcolm looks so good in those shorts," Dana snorted.

"Or the time she gave the FedEx man a Christmas tip," Alix added. "Oh, that's right. He's got that shorts thing going on, too." Everyone but Elyssa laughed.

"I am sure I have been nice to Malcolm, but I'm also sure it had nothing to do with his shorts or any other article of clothing in his wardrobe. I mean, come on. What is he? Twelve? Thirteen? What do you take me for?" Her plaints were firm but faintly unconvincing.

"Malcolm is twenty-one and he's cute and you know it." Alix challenged. "For heaven's sake, he's the only male we've hired in the twenty months I've been with Allheart."

"Look, you all can go right ahead and have a pathetic crush on our twelve-year-old intern. I've got a company to run and can't be wasting my time on that sort of nonsense." Elyssa took a last sip of wine, looked at her watch, and began gathering her things. "Meanwhile, as soon as I meet a man worth being nice to, I'll let you know."

Elyssa took care of the bill as the women collected their various bags and wraps and gear and made a group move toward the door, much to the relief of the restaurant staff. Moments later, they all stood in a circle in front of the Georgetown restaurant saying their goodbyes.

"Can I ride with you?" Dana asked, sidling up to Elyssa, who had just summoned a cab out of thin air. This cab trick was one of Elyssa's spookier powers, the others often noted in her absence.

"See you at eight-fifteen sharp tomorrow morning, girlies. Staff meeting, don't forget!" Elyssa called out faux-cheerily as she ducked into the cab beside Dana. The car tore off, making Elyssa deaf to their groans.

"That's just cruel," Robyn griped. "She keeps us out misbehaving til midnight then expects us to turn up at work at the crack of dawn?"

"Only you think of the eight o'clock hour as the crack of

dawn, Robyn," Carole teased. "The rest of us have worked out, showered, dressed, eaten breakfast, and read the newspaper before you've even thought about getting out of bed."

"I make no apologies for my sleep requirements," Robyn answered. "It's who I am. Love me or leave me." A few short blocks from her apartment, she headed off down the sidewalk, swinging her bag at her side.

"Oh, we love you alright. You sure you don't want a ride?" Carole called after her.

Robyn responded with a wave as she turned the corner at the end of the block. The Allheart women called Robyn "That Girl," the happy young thing looking for love in the big city.

Maybe it's not too late to catch Steve's last set at Dark Blue, Robyn thought as she stood at the corner trying to decide whether to turn right and walk toward her apartment or turn left toward the lights and traffic and music she knew she'd find in the other direction. *I know, I'll just walk by, peek in the window, see if he's playing and then decide. Maybe I'll go in and pretend I'm supposed to meet someone there and then act all surprised to see him playing the piano. Then maybe when his set's over he'll want to do something, go somewhere and get a drink, maybe take a walk down M Street, maybe go to my apartment and grope wildly. Maybe not, though. Maybe he'll see me and think I'm there to see him, think I'm some sort of goober-groupie type he should avoid at all costs. That's me. Wild-eyed groupie to a part-time performer at a piano bar. Oh, yeah, that is me.*

Or maybe I'll just go home and go to bed and trytrytry to get to the staff meeting on time tomorrow morning and then get Dana to go to Dark Blue with me tomorrow night. That's what a smart girl would do. Robyn giggled to herself and turned left toward the bar. *Yes, but smart girls sometimes miss the big fun.*

"I guess it's just you and me, kid," Carole said, hooking her arm in Alix's. "You want a ride? There's no traffic at this hour—it won't take more than ten minutes to get you home."

"No, that's all right, a cab's fine. I don't want you to have to go across town and then double back to get to the bridge. You could give me a ride to Washington Circle, though. I'll catch a cab there in a flash."

Piling their stuff into the back of Carole's dark blue Camry, the women took off into the coolish night.

"So you're not on the baby track, huh Carole?" Alix asked with a laugh, buckling her seat belt over her smart gray pantsuit. Somehow Alix could make a flannel bathrobe look like an important fashion statement.

"Honey, I was married to a baby for thirteen years. A big, mean, selfish baby. So I've done the baby thing. As a mother, I owe the planet nothing," Carole answered emphatically.

"I'm just kidding you. I wonder who's changing Hal's diapers now."

"Ha! For months after the divorce, I wandered around the house not knowing what to do with myself. I knew I wasn't missing him—that would be like missing a migraine headache. It was something else. I felt restless and . . . I don't know . . . disjointed. Then one day I realized it was that I didn't know what to do with all the time I suddenly had on my hands. With Hal, every minute of every day was devoted to the logistics of his life. Feeding him, clothing him, entertaining him. When he left, it was like someone had come through my life with an industrial strength vacuum cleaner, hoovering up all the details. I had to really remind myself of all the things I used to like to do before I got sucked into the Hal vortex. Simple stuff, like reading and painting. Yeah, Hal's diapers. God help whoever's in charge of them now."

"Can you imagine if Elyssa ever got ahold of Hal? She'd shred him like a head of lettuce!" Alix exclaimed. They both laughed out loud at the thought.

"You know, it's funny. In real life, I don't take any crap from men any more than Elyssa does. But in the context of a marriage, I found I settled in to all kinds of patterns that didn't seem very characteristic. I think you can unwittingly compromise lots of things about yourself to keep your marriage a marriage. I think I'm with Elyssa—if I ever hook up with a man again, it'll be because he wants to share my life, not the other way around." Carole fell quiet a moment as she waited for the traffic light to turn green.

"Well, I think Elyssa's ripe to meet the man who'll stop her dead in her tracks. She's got all the telltale signs: She's working too hard, she's not paying attention . . . and she's looking like a million bucks. Some irresistible guy is going to just appear one day and she's not going to know what hit her."

"I'm not worried about her being able to resist the guy; I'm worried that she may never notice he's there at all." Carole pulled over just shy of the circle. "It's you I wonder about, Miss Alix."

"Me? Why?"

"I've known you for almost two years now and I've never once heard you complain about Cal or say you had a fight or anything. Can it be there's a truly happy woman among us?" Carole asked with a kidding smile.

Alix's coffee-colored skin twinged with a blush. "Is there anything wrong with that? I can't help it. Cal is a calm, agreeable person. We've just never had occasion to argue in all the years I've known him."

"Hey, don't apologize. It's just hard for the screwed-up majority of the population—myself included—to imagine it's possible to end up in a happy, healthy relationship with your high-school sweetheart. You got the brass ring, kiddo."

Alix sat for a moment. "You know, Cal is great. I love the guy with all my heart and I know I'm lucky. But sometimes . . ." She paused.

"Don't say it! Whatever you're going to say, don't say it! You'll put the whammy on the whole thing if you do."

Alix laughed. "No, no. I was just going to say sometimes I feel guilty, like I have all the food to myself, while the rest of the world is starving."

"Don't you dare guilt yourself just because you have a satisfying relationship with your mate. You deserve your happiness, we all do," Carole reassured her. "The only thing you're missing is the fun you can have making up after a fight."

Then she thought for a moment and corrected herself. "No, on second thought, the fights add up to more than any amount of good sex can fix. Skip the fights." She shooed her friend out of the car. "There's your cab. Grab it. See you in the morning."

Alix slipped out of Carole's car and hurried over to the cab stopped at the light.

I'm going to get home and Cal will have the teapot ready and the bed all poofed up and an old movie on, Alix thought as she settled into the cab. *Most women would pay cash money to have that sort of attention paid to the dear little details. I am lucky, not that I deserve it or anything, but it's just the way he is. I don't know what I'd do if I had one of those pillow fight relationships where you just go from one conflict to the next.* She wrapped her arms around herself. *I better get home and make sure I'm not dreaming.*

Carole watched until Alix's cab pulled off in the direction of Capitol Hill. She had the streets to herself, save the lone taxi at the odd traffic light. She looked forward to the unusually quick, quiet ride across the river to Old Town Alexandria.

I love this city in the dead of night, when all the government types are off the streets and safe at home and just plain out of my way. I should get one of those simple, quiet, graveyard shift jobs, Carole thought with a smile. She stared at the red light that held her at the entrance to the Fourteenth Street Bridge. *Nah, I like the rat race. I even like the rats! Note to self: pack for Chicago trip. And please, God, don't make me sit next to another talker on that plane tomorrow. If I have to hand over one more business card to a person I have felt like strangling for three hours or more, I'll scream. I'd rather sit next to a crying baby than another talker. Okay, maybe not a crying baby, but still. Who is my dream seatmate anyway? Let's see. An old guy—a small old guy—a sleeper. Yeah, he falls asleep before takeoff and wakes up on landing. I help him with his bag and his coat, just for not talking to me the whole time. I wonder if you can request a small old guy seatmate when you make reservations. Ha.*

"*We're going to* R Street near DuPont Circle, then on to Eighteenth in Adams Morgan. I want you to take Thirtieth Street to P Street, turn left on Twenty-first off of P and drop me at the corner of Twenty-first and R." Elyssa never left a cab ride to chance.

She saw the driver's annoyed look in the rearview mirror and shrugged at Dana. "I don't know why they get so cheesed off. You're making their job easier, making it so they don't have to make any decisions."

"Maybe people like to make decisions, Elyssa. Maybe that's one of the small pleasures a cabdriver has, deciding which route he wants to take to a destination," Dana whispered to her boss.

"Well, maybe he should become an air-traffic controller then and really get some fun out of it. What, you're in charge of people's happiness tonight, Dana?"

"Nah, I just love it when you boss around drivers and waiters and grocery store clerks. They get this caught-in-the-headlights look that cracks me up."

"I don't like this recurring theme tonight, that I'm a megawitch on a broomstick. Is this some sort of intervention you all are staging? Because it's not going to work."

"Nobody thinks you're a witch, E. We like you just the way you are. We just want to be sure you're aware of the way you are. You know, just in case you wanted to make some adjustments." Dana couldn't help giggling.

"I've said it once and I'll say it again: I refuse to conduct my life as if it were some sort of popularity contest. I just don't have time for that. I have work to do!"

"Hey, we all do. Just don't want you to miss life's Allheart moments—you know, where you get to laugh and smile and have a good time—because you're so busy work-work-working."

"I know how to have a good time—I have a good time with you guys, I had a good time tonight! I invented the Allheart moment!" Elyssa was officially on the defensive now.

"I'm not talking about having fun with us. I'm talking about having singular, private, glowing instants, where, say, you're kind to a complete stranger or you're friendly to the dry cleaner."

Elyssa stared at her friend. "What are you talking about? What does this have to do with my dry cleaner?"

Dana laughed. "Nothing. Never mind. You're perfect, don't change."

"Carole tells me my approach to life is just very, very focused. I think that's an accurate description."

"Yes, Carole has got each of our numbers. She told me once that I was like an agitated bee hovering over a sea of sunflowers, unable to decide where to land." Dana frowned. "I haven't been able to get those words out of my head since." She picked an imaginary piece of lint off of her skinny black tee. Her legs were tucked under her and her cropped pants revealed lightly freckled legs.

"Ha. I'm glad to see there's someone else to pick on besides me."

"She wasn't picking on me. She was sitting through yet another of my morning-after diatribes, where I go on and on about some guy I've dallied with the night before and why he's just not a real contender. She's a good listener, I'll give her that."

"True. And she's about as good a judge of human nature as anyone I've met. Makes me wonder why she hung on for so long with that Herb idiot."

"Hal. His name is Hal. I don't know. I think Carole's a fixer-upper. She's so good at reading people and situations, she always knows just the thing to say or do to fix what's broken. So she does. And with Hal, she did it for thirteen years. She was on autopilot, just kept fixing it and fixing it, long after it stopped being worth fixing."

"Sounds like you've learned a thing or two from our Carole. Now how about you turn some of this wisdom into some touching Allheart greeting-card copy? You have the feelings, you write the copy. I have no feelings, I make the deals! We're a great team."

"Aha! You admit you have no feelings! I knew it!" Dana laughed loudly as the cab pulled up to the corner of Twenty-first and R Street, per Elyssa's precise instructions.

Elyssa exited the cab, all long legs and high heels. "I do so have feelings. I just don't have that whole messy rainbow of feelings all you other saps seem to have. Call me lucky," she said with a shrug before slamming the cab door. *Someone's got to keep a hard, level head*, she thought to herself as she slipped a ten-dollar bill through the driver's cracked window. *Hugs don't pay the bills, you know*.

Elyssa began giving the cabdriver elaborate directions to Dana's place off of Eighteenth Street but the car drove off before she could finish. She could see Dana smiling and waving through the cab's back window as she began the block-long walk to her apartment.

Oh, god. What if Carole's right about me? Dana thought as the cab pulled away. *I am getting tired of this, the one-nighters and all. And I really can't commit, not for more than forty-eight hours at a time anyway. Do I have attachment issues? Am I commitment phobic? Or am I just plain shallow and have a lifetime of empty moments to look forward to? I need an inner overhaul. Maybe I should go to church. Or maybe I should go to a shrink. Maybe I should just go home and get some sleep and next time I meet a man try to want to remember his name. That sounds good. I can do that.*

Men at Work

KATHRYN SHAY

Chapter 1

$\mathcal{T}$*he computer pinged loudly in the stillness of the offices of* Allheart.com as Elyssa Wentworth, CEO and all-around mother to the outfit, booted up her machine. Though DC's spring weather struggled to sneak through the slotted blinds of her office, it was eerily gray and quiet on this mid-March morning.

A good time for email.

A poor substitute for intimate talk over coffee with a man.

Damn, she thought as she clicked onto the Net in seconds. Her coworkers had messed with her head last night at the office secretary's going-away dinner. Contrary to their claims, Elyssa *was* happy with Allheart as her significant other and offspring all rolled into one. It was their damn innuendoes that had brought on all those dreams last night and awakened her at five A.M. for good.

"You've got mail!" a way-too-chipper-for-seven-in-the-morning voice proclaimed.

"See, I've got somebody to talk to," Elyssa told the computer. The irony didn't escape her as she sipped her cafe au lait from the corner Java Joe's. She savored the sweet, milky taste as much as the welcome caffeine jolt it gave her.

She had, to be exact, one hundred and sixty *someones* to *talk* to, her counter informed her. Slinking off her Calvin Klein jacket—she loved how the sage green silk felt easing down her arms—and kicking back and forth one of the Manolo Blahnik black slingbacks that she'd gotten for a steal, she scrolled down her screen to see if anything interesting popped up.

Her cursor halted at the address of one of the messages.

"Greetings from Allheart.com." Someone had sent her one of her own cards? In the two years since she'd started the company, she couldn't remember a time when anybody had sent her an Allheart. How unique. It certainly got her attention. She called up the file.

And felt that quick zing course through her—like a shot of good bourbon or the jump-start of sexual attraction—as she saw her own little brainchild etch out onto the screen: Allheart's distinctive logo, *Write from the heart,* in its classy red lettering. A swell of pride.

She concentrated on her card. It was one of their initial offerings, updated by Dana, her writer, and Alix, her graphic designer, several times. On the front was a star-filled, inky black night, with a single star standing out bigger and brighter than the others. The note at the bottom read, "Your star shines the brightest." It had been an amazingly popular series whose success had surprised them all.

Discreet but clear directions—thank you Dana—instructed the receiver on how to open the card. This was also one of the personal lines—where the sender could create his own message. She smiled as she clicked to open. Who had sent this?

The script inside was simple. "I admire what you've done with Allheart.com Online Greeting Service. For a small outfit, your number of hits in two years is noteworthy. Let me introduce myself. I'm Joe Monteigne of Highwire Industries. We specialize in helping companies to create their vision and fulfill their dreams. I need only thirty minutes of your valuable time to discuss a business collaboration. I assure you it is of mutual benefit to us both. I'll telephone you today." It was signed—this personal signature touch had been Robyn's idea—in a bold masculine scrawl, *Joe Monteigne.*

Easing back from her triangular teak desk, she studied the screen and thought of the advice her brother Elliot, a hotshot newspaper writer, had given her a while ago. *It's time to take the plunge, Lyss. You can use a new infusion of money. Expand or be eaten alive.*

She'd been mulling over his words for weeks. Especially since other venture capitalists had been sniffing around her. She'd already met with a few of them, but their cocky, arrogant, help-the-little-lady-out attitude made her want to barf most of the time. Oh, she knew she needed financing. She'd started Allheart on an initial one-time investment from an angel—a backer who only wanted a return on his money and didn't want to get involved in the company. Her burn rate—

the amount of capital needed each month to operate—was high. Now that she'd gone through much of that money, she'd need a capital-intensive firm to back her.

Joe Monteigne's proposal sounded . . . different, somehow, from the other suspender-wearing good ole boys. More thoughtful, more respectful. She laughed out loud in the silent empty office, remembering what she'd said last night at dinner, when her defenses had disappeared along with the Cristal champagne. *My dream is to meet a man who thinks my life's just great as it is and who wants to play along.* Of course, she'd meant the comment about her personal life, but it was true about her business, too. She didn't want to be taken over—personally or professionally. If she had to expand, and deal with the money mongers out there, she wanted someone who'd play her game: one, accept that she insisted on keeping control; two, offer help with business strategies and long-term goals; and three, of course, have gobs of money to invest.

Biting off the raisin-colored lipstick she'd applied just this morning, she reached for the phone. It was almost seven. Like her, Elliot would be in his office by now. She was meeting him for lunch at her favorite bistro here in Georgetown, just a few blocks from her office. Maybe he could get some information about Highwire Industries and this mysterious—and clever— Joe Monteigne by then.

This morning, Elyssa had a staff meeting, and that consult with Parker Industries—a big advertising account Carole Titus, Allheart's whiz salesperson, had been after for months— but in between she would do some of her own web research. She'd be ready when Monteigne called today.

"*Ohmigod, who's the hunk?*" Elyssa's personal assistant, Robyn Barrett, wasn't too bleary-eyed this morning to notice the papers scattered on the teak conference table when she strolled in at eight-thirty. Elyssa had been analyzing her just-compiled folder of web research on Highwire Industries while she waited for her staff to arrive.

"A VC," Elyssa said succinctly. Then she added, "You're late."

Robyn scanned the area. "So are Dana and Alix."

Mothering the young woman like the rest of the crew at

Allheart, Carole smiled at Robyn from across the table. "Traf-fic problems. They both called in on their cell phones, kid."

Shrugging, Robyn sank into a chair next to Carole. "Sorry," she said in that teenage-sister voice that always melted Elyssa's pique. Once Allheart had begun to grow, Elyssa had needed help, and something about the young blonde caught her attention. She'd been right to hire the girl—mostly Robyn was top-notch and on the ball. Men, and nights spent with them, seemed to dull her first thing in the morning. It happened to most women, Elyssa knew from experience.

At least she's not a robot like you, was how one of Elyssa's more disgruntled boyfriends had put it.

"VC as in Viet Cong?" Robyn asked.

"As in Venture Capitalist." Carole reached for the picture Elyssa had printed off her computer.

Robyn stared at it. "Man, in this case, it should stand for Very Cute."

"More like Vicious Cannibal," Elyssa mumbled, "just wait-ing to eat you and your business up."

"I wouldn't mind getting eaten up by this one," Robyn commented. "He's got those Mel Gibson eyes."

Reading the text about Highwire Industries—they had re-ally good copy—Elyssa said absently, "Does he?"

Snickers. She peered up over half glasses that she wore when her eyes got tired. Damn that sleepless night. "What?"

Robyn rolled her eyes.

"Christ, Robyn, you act like a teenager sometimes."

Oblivious, Robyn pointed to the picture Carole held up. "Come on, Elyssa, look. Isn't he yummy?"

From behind them, she heard, "We're here. Sorry we're l—Jesus, who's the sexy stud?" Dana dropped her purse onto a chair and peered over Elyssa's shoulders.

Alix joined in. "Linebacker shoulders. My fave." She smiled at Carole. "I know my Cal's a cutie, too." She referred casually to her live-in boyfriend and shrugged. "But even though I've ordered, I can still look at the menu."

Carole gave her a knowing smile back. "You haven't or-dered, lady. And you know it."

"Am I missing something here?" Elyssa asked.

"Nah." Carole winked at Alix. "Alix and I had a little heart-to-heart last night on the ride home is all."

"All right. We can stop drooling over this perfect stranger and start this meeting now."

"Perfect is right." Robyn sighed. She got that man-dreamy look on her face. "A nice strong, solid stranger."

Realizing she wouldn't get anywhere without throwing a few crumbs, Elyssa blithely outlined his morning email.

"How sweet." Dana's eyes glowed from beneath her fiery red bangs. "I love that he approached you with one of our babies."

So did Elyssa, though she'd be damned if she'd admit it. "In any case, since he's calling today, I've got to decide if I'll talk with him. That's why I was studying the file. *Not* to imagine him in his boxers the way you desperadoes do."

"He's my kind of stranger," Carole put in.

"You, too, Brutus?"

The women laughed.

"Seriously," Carole said. "You know we need more financing." A rare mischievous smile graced her lips. "Consider the advantages of working with Mr. Prime Piece of Beef. All those late nights of due diligence and hacking out business strategies. Might be fun."

"Negotiating with a VC is not my idea of fun." Elyssa shrugged. "But I'll keep this one in the running." She scanned the other women who'd finally seated themselves and opened up their notepads. Though they joked and teased each other, all four women knew when to get down to business. It was just one of the things Elyssa valued about them. "All right, here's the agenda." Elyssa passed around a typed sheet with succinct wording and neat columns. "Reports first on the new graphics software—that's you Alix; brainstorm possibilities for the new line of baby cards—Carole; an analysis of the most frequently used messages from Dana." All things Elyssa knew and felt comfortable with. "Robyn, take notes!"

Elyssa gathered up the file on Highwire, and stuffed the grinning picture of Monteigne back into it. Then she went to work.

After all, this was what she was good at.

From a corner table at Clyde's of Georgetown, Elliot waved to Elyssa. As always, he looked a little rumpled in his somewhat worn suit and the paisley tie she'd bought for him for his last birthday. He ran a hand through his chestnut hair—

hers was shades darker—and smiled as he stood to greet her. After he kissed her cheek, he studied her. He had the same hazel eyes as she did, though hers were a bit more green today, thanks to the suit.

"You okay, kiddo?" Elliot was three years older than Elyssa's thirty-four years, but he had an exaggerated big-brother complex.

"Couldn't be better. You?" she asked as she seated herself.

"Terrific." He held up a folder. "I got you some info." She reached for it, but he drew it out of her grasp. "Not now. Let's catch up first. Like your competitors' cards say, 'Stop and . . .'"

". . . 'smell the roses.' How mundane." Placing her beaded Prada handbag on the floor, she smiled affectionately at him. He was so good for her. Making her slow down. Making her relate to *him*, at least, as a human being, not some corporate cardboard cutout.

"You look good today." She opened her menu. "Is there a woman?"

Elliot gave her a thousand-watt grin. "Nah." He shrugged. "But I got the promotion."

"Oh, Elliot." She reached over and grabbed his hand. "Congratulations. Not that I'm surprised. The newspaper needs you."

"Apparently they think so, too." He smiled at her. "Not bad for a kid from Smalltown, USA, is it?"

She tried to ignore the reference. "Senior reporter at the *Washington Post* is terrific for anyone."

"You still don't like to talk about it, do you?"

"What's there to talk about?" One thing she and Elliot never did was lie to each other. He was the only person she could count on to be straight with her. Always. "We grew up poor, we were smart, we made it big. End of story."

He grinned. "Ah, it sounds so simple. Almost makes me forget the hours of working at Old Ebbitt Grill while I went to Georgetown." He shook his head. "Don't you miss that restaurant kitchen smell sometimes?"

"Vassar girls don't ever smell like the kitchen." She batted her eyelashes. "Anyway, if you're asking if I like to think about what we went through to go to college on a shoestring, scholarships notwithstanding, no I don't. Am I to be penalized for that?"

He held up his palms. "Not at all." When a waitress approached their table with the sparkling waters Elliot had obviously ordered, he said, "You ready to eat?"

After ditto-ing Elliott's order of chicken Caesar salad, Elyssa said, "So, what did you find out?"

For a moment, he looked like he might resist the reversion to business; finally he placed his elbows on the table. His photographic memory clicked almost audibly into work mode. "Highwire Industries is one of the most successful VC firms in the area. They specialize in Internet investments. It's the baby of your card guy; he started the company about ten years ago and he's worth millions now. His investors are the standard pension fund and university endowment kinds. He's got an interesting assortment of partners who, rumor has it, depend heavily on his opinions. Word around town is that he thrives on the challenge, and lately he's been after unusual investments."

"Unusual?"

"Smaller, unique boutique businesses, not necessarily the ones that approach him."

"Why?"

"Boredom, probably. He likes the challenge." Elliot's eyes danced. "Just like you, Lyss."

She smiled back. "How old is he?"

"Thirty-eight."

"That's pretty young for so much money and power." The lemon-flavored water felt good on her parched throat. Talking about expanding her business unnerved her as much as it excited her.

"He comes from money. Old Virginia money. He's a Harvard MBA and did his undergrad at Yale."

"How'd you get all this? My web search didn't uncover nearly this much personal information."

Elliot lounged his long, lean frame back in the comfortable chair. Backdropped by the dark wood with Americana on the walls, and surrounded by the friendly, easygoing atmosphere, he looked right at home. "Really, Lyss, you wound me. I'm a *reporter* for heaven's sake." At her pointed look, he shrugged. "The *Post* did a story on him a few years back. They had a file on him."

She nodded. "What are his working relationships like with companies he invests in?"

"No more personal stuff?"

"What do you mean?"

"Don't you want to know if he's married? Gay? What his hobbies are?"

"Why would I?"

"Know thy enemy, Sis."

"So, he's a shark, right, when it comes to investments?"

"Actually, no, he's done some pretty fair negotiating. Most of the companies spoke highly of his light hand and easy manner."

Mel Gibson eyes and linebacker shoulders came to mind. He could afford to be light and easy, she guessed.

In business and with women.

Shit. She scowled to herself. She was going to murder Robyn, Carole and all of them.

"What is it?"

Their salads arrived and Elliot dug in; Elyssa pushed the lightly dressed romaine around her plate. "The women at the office behaved like schoolgirls over his file this morning."

"So?" Elliot crunched happily on his salad. "Don't you think he's attractive?"

"I guess. I'm more concerned with the size of his portfolio than the size of his—" The waitress returned with hot, crusty bread, cutting Elyssa off. Elliot gave the waitress a flirty nod and thanked her.

Breaking off a bit of bread and nibbling on it, Elyssa said thoughtfully, "You should get married again, Elliot."

"Maybe. But that would require meeting someone I'd want to marry, Lyss."

"It's been a long time since Sally died."

Elliot had met a wonderful woman when he'd first started working at the *Post*. She was killed two years after their marriage in a freak Metro accident; that had been almost a decade ago. He'd been wandering from woman to woman ever since.

"And you, dear sister, should dip your feet in the marriage pool, too. You're not getting any younger, you know."

"Please don't start." She patted her mouth with the napkin. "Now, finish up your report on Monteigne."

Elliot scowled. "Oh, no you don't. Not another word until you eat every bite of that salad."

She arched a brow. "You mean I have to clean my plate before I can leave the table?"

"That's right. You don't eat *or* sleep enough."

"I don't have time."

"Eat!" he said implacably. "Then I'll tell you the rest about your hunky hotshot."

Hmm. A decent deal. Elyssa picked up her fork.

At dusk, the streets of Georgetown were just busy enough to make driving a challenge. Which was fine with Joe Monteigne. He liked nothing better than formidable Washington traffic, high-risk business deals, and women who believed they couldn't be seduced.

It's part of your problem, son, his still-young, sixty-five-year-old father had told him that weekend as they'd run along the pond on their Virginia property. *Nothing's a challenge anymore. You need something in your life.*

And since Joe loved and respected J. Lance Monteigne, Sr., more than anybody in the world, he'd noted his advice.

Swerving into a tiny parking spot, Joe edged his impeccably restored Mach I yellow Mustang into an impossibly tight space that had already been passed up by two drivers. He admitted to himself that his father's insights were why he was here tonight, instead of at the racquetball game he'd canceled with a senator from Oklahoma. When he'd called Elyssa Wentworth, aka the Queen of Hearts—also known less kindly as the Ice Queen— he'd told her he was indeed free at seven, since she didn't have another open spot in her schedule this whole week.

He believed it. He'd researched her scrupulously. From the Net and in print, he'd read everything available about her personally and professionally, but he still had a feeling there was something more to her that as yet had not been unearthed. And discreetly, he'd talked to those in the know around town about her, too. She'd gotten the Ice Queen nickname from other money types who'd tried to woo her.

Slamming shut the door, he straightened his tie, threw on his Hugo Boss suit jacket and headed to the door of her building. For a minute, he let himself breathe in the warm night air. Like all the other cherry-blossom buffs in DC, he'd always loved Washington in the spring; he'd returned to be near his family after his divorce and a brief sojourn in Boston, and never regretted it.

As he entered the remodeled brick warehouse and took the

elevator to the offices on the second floor, he caught his reflection in the highly polished aluminum wall. What he saw staring back at him was exactly what his ex had called him: too handsome and too rich for his own good. Bethany had remarried someone just as handsome and rich, which had irked Joe a bit, though he took full responsibility for their breakup. Again, his dad had been right. He'd been bored in his marriage. He only got a slight twinge now and again when he thought about her, like when he heard she'd had a kid—a girl—a few years back.

The elevator opened up to a suite of offices. On the oak door facing him, tastefully scripted on a brass plate, was All-heart.com, Inc. He pushed on the heavy door. Inside, he found a foyer with an empty desk to the left. A secretary/receptionist nameplate told him the help had gone home for the night. He rapped heavy knuckles on the door he'd opened, but no one answered and he let it close. In a glance, he took in the framed cards—obviously their stock—gracing the walls, the thick Berber carpeting, the grasscloth wallpaper and the gleaming wood. Nice digs. Since the foyer opened into an oak archway, he felt comfortable following it through. Inside, he found offices to the left and right; straight ahead was Oz, where the wizardess herself dwelt. He knocked on the ajar door, which simply read, Elyssa Wentworth.

"Hel-lo," he called out.

A rustle inside. She was probably shrugging into one of those suit jackets she favored. Maybe putting on those four-hundred-dollar shoes. Or tidying that dark hair that not a single picture had caught loose. He remembered thinking, as he viewed one photo, about what that mane would look like out of its prissy uptwist. The door was pulled open.

"Hello." She matched her voice. Lush. Rich. And, surprisingly, very sexy.

He stuck out his hand. "I'm Joe Monteigne."

For a second she scrutinized him carefully. She nodded as she shook his hand, but didn't smile. "Elyssa Wentworth." She stepped aside. He noticed she was tall, about five-eight or -nine. Though who could tell with those deliciously high heels. What stilettos did to a female's legs sent his pulse spinning as much as a good takeover.

"You're right on time," she said.

"I wouldn't dream of wasting one of my thirty minutes, Ms. Wentworth."

She glanced at a slim gold watch on a delicate wrist. "And I'm afraid that's all you have. I have to leave for an engagement at seven-thirty."

"As do I." He smiled at the show-of-power comments they exchanged.

She stopped before a couch and indicated that he sit. She took a chair opposite him, and crossed her spectacular legs. "Would you like something to drink?"

Her tone clearly implied he should say no. "Sure. A mineral water if you have it, thanks."

Elyssa gave him a little bit of a Look as she walked past him on the way to the small bar tray on her credenza. She filled a glass with Pellegrino and handed it to him.

"What exactly *do* you want, Mr. Monteigne?"

Joe was shocked to find a personal answer battering to get out of the male portion of his brain. He shook off the unusual urge to flirt with a client. "I want to talk about you and your company."

"Really?" She arched a raven brow at him. "I assume you know all about my company."

He smiled. "I do. And"—he leaned forward, tugging back the sleeves of his suit coat—"I expect that you know as much about mine as I do about yours. So no need for preliminaries." He cocked his head. "What I want to hear is what you expect to do now with your burgeoning business."

"So you can tell me how you can help?"

"Exactly."

"What if I said I was happy with our growth rate? That I didn't want investors at this point?"

"I'd tell you that you were very foolish."

She didn't take offense. Instead, she lazed back in the chair, which notched up her green skirt an inch. Somehow, he knew it wasn't intentional. "Okay, shoot. Obviously you're not the first to have contacted me. I am likely to be choosing someone to back me again soon. So tell me what you think you can do for me."

"Think of Highwire Industries as a facilitator. We bring together the necessary capital, business experience and direction to succeed."

She interrupted. "Which means you want some control of the company."

"We choose to look at it as offering our considerable expertise for the benefit of your company. We have years of business acumen at our fingertips that we're just itching to use to help you make the right decisions for Allheart."

"I've made the right decisions all by myself so far."

"Yes you have, or I wouldn't be here talking to you right now."

"So why do I need you instead of an investment banker or another angel?"

"Because the bigger greeting-card companies are going to gobble you up like turkey on Thanksgiving if you don't move on, branch out and forge ahead into related areas. That's what you need my help to do."

Her hazel eyes deepened to the color of grass in the morning. She was intrigued, he could tell.

Still leaning forward, his hands linked between his knees now, he said, "Let me ask you three questions that will show what I can do for you that the others can't." He gave her a killer grin. "Or can't do as well."

She nodded. Her dark hair was pulled back from her face, but he noticed a few strands escaping down her nape. "First, what's your vision for Allheart? Second, do you have a business plan for it? And finally, what are your personal goals?"

She glanced at the Tiffany clock on her credenza. "I don't think I can tell you that in the time we have remaining."

"Can you tell it to me at all?"

"What do you mean?"

"I mean, as CEO of this successful but vulnerable company, you should have a business plan written in stone."

She studied him, which impressed the hell out of him. She didn't get mad or take his words as an insult. Cool eyes assessed him carefully.

"Look," he said, ready to plunge in. "You've done precisely what you should have done up to now. I'm here to help you go further."

"My vision," she said ignoring his compliment, "is to expand the types of cards we offer, thus expanding our market. I've thought about going into ancillary products, too."

He nodded.

"My business plan consists of a killer concept, first-mover advantage and an annual budget." She watched him. "But that's not what you mean, is it?"

Admiring her savvy, he said, "No, it isn't. I'm talking about a three- to five-year projection that ties your vision to your financing. A vision documents your goals. A business plan outlines tactics, revenues, and cash flow and defines how to implement those goals."

"Yes, and why don't you tell me something I don't already know?"

"You do *know* it, but you're not *doing* it. This is what Highwire does best. And I have the personal expertise to make it happen. We turbocharge the process for you."

She nodded. Her teeth worried her bottom lip as she assimilated what he said.

"And what are your personal goals, Ms. Wentworth?"

Again, the quizzical look.

"For instance, let's talk about your use of time in relation to money. Are you going to have the time and money in the future to do all you dreamed about? Do you want a house and kids or do you want to jet set to Morocco and Tahiti? Do you want a Lexus or a Beetle?"

"I have a Lexus," she said with a mocking tone.

He grinned. "I know. I was making a point."

She smiled back. "I know. So was I. But I get what you mean."

"How your company performs means how much you get to fulfill your dreams."

"I am fulfilling my dreams, right here, right now," she reiterated.

"There's a big difference between immediate dreams and real, long-term success. Hallmark and American Greetings aren't going to let you outdistance them much longer with your cleverness, appeal to modern audiences and innovative product lines."

"So, I need you to help me compete with them."

"Exactly."

This time *he* checked the clock. "All right, here's the deal. We'll work with you on your vision and business plan. Creating those two things isn't easy; it'll take about two weeks of your time and three weeks to a month of ours. We'll come back with a document you feel comfortable with. Concurrently we'll be talking about what's going to make you happy and tailor that vision and happiness to coincide."

He watched to see her reaction. She didn't blink one of those pretty eyelashes. "Interesting," she finally said.

"If you like what I give you, we do a due diligence," referring to the process of gathering information to assess the founders, the market opportunity, the technology and the competition. "Then, when all the data's compiled, I'll bring it to my partners, solicit the necessary capital and we'll form a partnership."

Both brows raised this time. "Let's just say we get that far. What I want to know is how much control of my company will you end up with?"

Smart girl. "That part of the equation is worked out when we decide how much money you need from us, and how much of our business experience you require." Leaning back, he crossed an ankle over his knee. "Having us help run your company is a good thing, not a bad one, Ms. Wentworth. We have the experience you lack. We've brought dozens of companies into full, actual green money-making bloom. Our skill can only help you."

"Sounds like I'd lose a great deal of control."

"No, you'd have help directing the company."

She laughed then. "Semantics, Mr. Monteigne. But, all right. Say I do this with you. When you make me more profitable, you'd want to do an IPO or sell off to a larger company, right?" She knew from her research that Highwire specialized in initial public offerings and sell-offs.

He arched a brow. "What happens after our investment depends on how successful you are. Allheart would have several choices if you were good enough."

From the many deals he'd orchestrated, he sensed he had her interest and maybe an edge on his competitors. Most clients at this point couldn't resist the lure. Now, it was his job to reel her in. "What do you have to lose, Ms. Wentworth?"

"Three weeks of my time."

He stood then. "A small price to pay for ending up with a valuation in the hundreds of millions, don't you think? Look, we both know you're going to need some type of investment soon. Ours will be the best." The little clock chimed once. "My half hour's up." He reached into his suit coat pocket and took out a card. "Call me in a few days and let me know what you decide."

She rose too, accepted the card and slipped it into her pocket without breaking eye contact. Then she held out her hand. He grasped it firmly. Hers was slender and strong, just like the woman she was. Now that the rush of adrenaline that shot through him every time he commenced a deal hummed in his blood, he allowed himself to indulge the thought of how pretty she was—long lean lines, with some interesting curves and angles. It'd be . . . a pleasure to work with her for a while.

"I'll call you either way, Mr. Monteigne."

"Fine." Releasing her hand, he turned and walked to the door. He knew if he pivoted around she'd be staring at him. Unaccountably, he wondered what she'd see.

He didn't pivot. He stared straight ahead as he left, though what *he* saw was crystal clear—a bright-eyed beauty with a mind like a steel trap.

Being all male, he liked the combination.

Chapter 2

"*Are there any men working at Allheart?* The look of male bemusement on Joe Monteigne's handsome face charmed Dana, Alix and Robyn right down to their gleaming leather pumps and high-heeled sandals. Even Carole grinned at his teasing.

It pissed Elyssa off big-time. One of the things she'd agonized over in the two weeks she'd taken to make her decision on financing the next phase of Allheart was, ironically, Monteigne's attractiveness. The last thing she needed was a Lothario hanging around the office, disrupting her staff. However, in the end, he'd made—as the saying goes—an offer she couldn't refuse.

With half an ear she listened to the women fill him in. ". . . There's Malcolm the intern," Robyn practically fawned.

". . . We consult with outside designers occasionally. My favorite is Jonathan, the guy who does . . ." Alix's voice was uncharacteristically breathy.

"One of my field associates is a hotshot named Derrick . . ." Carole's smile was warm and welcoming, if not downright flirty.

As Elyssa took it all in, she thought about what had led to this meeting between her executive staff and Highwire Industries' favorite son.

First, she'd firmly decided that now was the time to seek financing. Then she'd called Monteigne and told him she was planning to meet with other investors and would have a decision about whom she was going to pursue in two weeks.

Thoughts of those meetings caused her to shudder.

The first guy had been a barrel-bellied Texan, who treated her like a Southern belle. A *stupid* Southern belle. She'd turned him down flat.

The second had been another angel. Having had success with the one-shot local type of investor she'd used her first time around, she thought she might try another. The man had all the earmarks of becoming gum on her shoe, though, and afforded no help in forming a business plan and implementing it. She scratched him off her mental list without a second thought.

The last had been an octopus. Aware that many people believed that entrepreneurial women flirted their way to the top with a modicum of business sense and great legs, she was wary of presenting that image. So on the day of their meeting, she'd dressed in a dull gray suit and crisp starched shirt. The furtive little man wasn't daunted by her nun's-habit dress and Elyssa, uncharacteristically, had lost her cool; though it was an anatomical impossibility, she'd told him what he could do with his inappropriate touches, his innuendoes and his money.

All in all, from a business standpoint, the man seated across from her, effortlessly charming her staff, was the best choice. She would give him the three weeks he asked for, let him come up with a plan, and then, if all went well with his proposal, she'd go with Highwire Industries.

"Elyssa?"

Dragging her mind back to business, she raised her brows at Robyn's query.

"Joe asked if there's anything else you think he should discuss with us."

She glanced at the clock. For two hours, they'd been having that *informal little chat with the staff* he'd requested. "No, none." She focused in on him coolly. "You?"

He graced her with a megawatt smile that would give a meteor shower competition and shook his head. "Having been bossed around by three sisters all my life, I think I'm going to feel right at home here."

Whoa, buster, nothing definite's been decided yet. But keeping her mouth shut and being nice to the guy were two concessions she *had* to make, so she bit back her words. Elliot had helped her see that most founders would strip naked and beg for the kind of offer Joe proposed. Given her experiences the week previous, she believed it.

Monteigne flashed his pearly whites at Elyssa again, closed his butter-soft leather notebook, and stood. The suit

he'd worn today showed nary a wrinkle and his shirt held all
its crisp starchiness. As she rose too, she noted how the slate
color of the tailored jacket lightened his eyes.

"Are you ready for our meeting, Elyssa?" Her name rolled
off his tongue easily, sometimes carrying a flavor of the South.
Its tone was a combination of warm honey and thick molasses.

"Of course."

"I'm going for provisions at Java Joe's," Robyn announced
to the group. "Can I get you something, Joe?"

"Please, cafe au lait, heavy on the lait."

"Just like Miss E here."

His eyes darted to her. She gave him a weak smile as the
other women told Robyn their preference. With him behind her,
she headed out of the conference room, strode pointedly into
her office, and took a seat on the couch. Expecting him to
choose a chair, she was surprised when he dropped down beside
her. He wasn't close enough to invade her personal space, but
he was near enough to send a whiff of woodsy, male cologne
her way. It made her picture tangled sheets and a dim bedroom.

"So, what did you think of my executive staff?"

"I can see why Allheart's so hot."

"Hot, huh?"

"Popular. Your ladies are brilliant and talented. It's clear
how you've managed to make Allheart the clever, hip, web
greeting card of choice."

Elyssa chuckled, feeling like a teacher who'd just gotten
complimented on her class. "I'm not sure anyone's ever applied those two adjectives to Robyn."

His brows furrowed. "She reminds me of my younger sister
Carrie. They're both what, about twenty-four?" Elyssa nodded. "She has depth and ability behind that odd little veneer."

"Most people don't see that in her."

"You did."

"Yes, I did." She shifted uncomfortably, and tugged down
the aubergine skirt she wore with a beige cashmere shell and
matching sweater. Toying with the long strand of faux pearls
around her neck, she asked, "So what do we do now?"

She could practically see him rubbing his hands together
mentally, and recognized the kindred spirit in him. He loved
his work, just as she did. "Now, we discuss your vision for Allheart." He opened his notebook. "Unfortunately, I have an en-

gagement at noon but we can talk for an hour or so, and I can be back by two to finish up this section of my research."

She nodded her acceptance.

"Then we can get into your personal history."

"Excuse me?"

"I need to know about you," he said, rolling his black Waterman between his palms. She'd noticed the gesture this morning, with her staff, when he was intrigued by a point being made.

"You mean you need to know my history in terms of the company?"

"Well, yes, of course. But also your personal background, to help us understand your vision and your goals."

Her brows drew together.

"Remember my three questions?"

"How could I forget?"

"How indeed." He lazed back. "So, Ms. Queen of Hearts, how would you deal out this deck of cards, pardon the pun, if you had all the capital you wanted?"

Though she tried not to take the bait, his lure was irresistible. Laying her head back on the leather couch, she closed her eyes momentarily and smiled. "Well, I really want to . . ."

By seven that night, Joe was exhausted and enervated at the same time. And surprised as hell! All day he'd peeled back the layers of Elyssa Wentworth, CEO. During the morning he'd listened to her spin her dreams with a voice that got even more hoarse as her passion for her work peaked. It was a passion he understood, the same kind he experienced with his own business dealings.

When he'd left her at noon, he'd had lunch with one of his partners and found himself in the highly unusual position of being unable to concentrate on Harold's newest endeavor. Instead, he kept picturing hazel eyes that fired up like a hotly beating sun as she talked about taking a baby business from infancy to toddlerhood. Her porcelain skin had glowed with plans and hopes and dreams that, he assured her, he could help make come true.

Now, standing by the window, staring out at the canal path, her shoulders drooped.

"Tired?"

She circled around. Backdropped by the setting sun, the slight breeze tugging at loose tendrils of hair, she shook her head. "No. It's just that I missed my usual workout today so I'm a little low on energy."

"When do you work out?"

"Sometimes mornings or noon—" The clock chimed seven beats. "—or right now."

"You didn't do it at lunch?"

"No, I had to shoehorn in my other work then."

He nodded to the open window. "Want to finish this up over a walk?"

"Really?" Her response was so girlish it stopped him for a second. It was remarkably at odds with the keen, hardened business acumen she'd demonstrated all day.

"Don't get much chance for fresh air, Madame CEO?"

She shook her head, dislodging a few strands around her ears. "It's going to be a gorgeous night. We've got another hour, right, before you're done with me?"

The phrasing interested him. Done with her? Not hardly. He took a quick tour of her legs, which ended at another pair of mile-high shoes—three-and-a-half-inchers today, in creamy brown leather. "Can't walk in those, though."

She took her own stroll down his body. It made him . . . tense. "No, unfortunately your Italian loafers are much more practical than my Ombelines."

Grinning, he stood. "So what will you do?"

She crossed elegantly to the closet by the bathroom. The Ombelines might be impractical, but they sure suited her. From inside she drew out sneakers with socks stuffed in them. "Be prepared," she quipped. "I keep a workout bag here all the time." She sat down on a chair, tugged on short socks and donned her Nikes in record time. Standing, she whipped off her sweater, revealing long, lightly tanned arms, graced by a gold watch and a pearl bracelet to match her necklace.

"Ready?"

As efficiently as she, he shrugged out of his suit coat, dispensed with his tie, unbuttoned his collar and rolled up the sleeves of his shirt. "Ready."

She grinned innocently.

He smiled back; seeing her in this bit of dishabille intrigued him, and his grin was *not* so ingenuous. He followed her out of the office and into the elevator. In minutes they were on the canal path.

Like her, he took great pleasure in the warm April air. It closed around them like a light blanket; he watched her snuggle into it and relax. Joggers had come out, and passed them as they kept a leisurely pace. Lifting her face, she relished the warm breeze for a few seconds, then finally turned to him. "All right, let's get on with it. What do you want to talk about now?"

"Tell me about where you grew up."

The sun died in her eyes. "Must we go into all that?"

"How can I understand where you want to go if I don't know where you've been?"

Her eyes sharpened on him. "Do you do this with all your clients?"

"Pretty much." At her disbelieving look, he raised his right hand, palm out. "Scout's honor."

"Tell me you were a Boy Scout."

"I was. My father insisted."

"Why?"

"He was an ambassador. He knew the value of the four H's."

"The four H's?"

"Health, honesty, hard work and heroism."

"What's he like?"

Joe held up his palms, enjoying the repartee. "Hey, this is supposed to be about you."

She got that corporate I'm-gonna-win gleam in her eye. "I'll make you a deal. I'll tell you about me, if you agree to switch gears and tell me about you, too."

No prospective client had ever asked that. "Why?"

"I don't know." One of her shoulders lifted gently under the tan cashmere. They were more slender than he'd imagined they'd be. "Maybe because this feels a lot like taking off my clothes in front of somebody who gets to stay dressed."

He wished she'd chosen another analogy. His mind latched on to her taking off her clothes, piece by lovely piece. "All right," he acquiesced.

She strolled along, her eyes scanning the water. "I grew up in Lockport—upstate New York. My father died when I was four, my mother worked two jobs all my life. Elliot and I pretty much took care of ourselves."

"Your bio said you had a brother, but there wasn't much background on you."

She didn't break stride as she edged closer to him to avoid a bicyclist. "I don't feel the need to advertise my humble beginnings. Poor-girl-makes-good stories bore me."

He angled his head. "So, how'd you get to Vassar?"

"A couple of wonderful high school teachers who recognized potential in both Elliot and me. He got a scholarship to Georgetown, then I got one to Vassar."

Something was familiar. Elliot. Georgetown. Joe hit his head with his hand. "Elliot Wentworth at the *Post*? He's your brother?"

"Yep."

"He's brilliant."

"There's that word again."

"You surround yourself with brilliant people."

"I like smart people. Nothing irks me more than stupidity." She flicked him a sideways glance. "Which is why I'm talking with you. I do need an investor but I've got to pick the right one."

Silently, he basked in the compliment. "Is that why you chose me over Caulkins, Sortino or Camp?"

"You know who I met with last week?"

"Yes. I would've warned you off Camp if I'd known."

She seemed surprised that he knew about creepy Camp's wandering hands. "I handled it."

He laughed. "I would have liked to have seen that."

"So when am I going to find out about you?"

"Just as soon as I'm finished with you."

For a half hour, he was entranced by the picture she painted of a young, naive Elyssa working her way through Vassar, her first job with a greeting card company, her third with a trailblazing high-tech outfit. It all led to how she'd made the contacts that had landed her the money to start Allheart. Somehow he couldn't connect this sophisticated, tough-edged woman with that bright-eyed young girl she described.

"After Lonestar went public—Oh!" Her story was interrupted when a small boy on rollerblades barreled into her.

Joe's hand shot out to grasp her arm. She would have fallen

had he not tugged her to him. Her weight against him did significant things to his pulse rate. His hand closed around a supple waist that testified to those daily workouts she fit in.

"Hey, buddy, watch it," he said to the wide-eyed, freckle-
faced kid.

"Sorry, ma'am."

"You need to be more careful, young man. You could get
hurt." Elyssa's tone was all business. "Or hurt someone else."

A harried mother rushed up behind the boy, a baby in a
knapsack and a toddler on her hip. "Sorry about that. Timmy,
you have to be careful." The mother led the boy off by the arm.

Elyssa stared after the family.

"You don't like kids?"

"No, it's not that." She relaxed again. "Hey, it's your turn,
Monteigne. My lips are sealed until you tell me about *your* big
secrets."

Walking alongside her again, he started talking. "My
childhood was as privileged as yours was a struggle. Dad
made his money before he was an ambassador, but he always
made time to be with me." Joe rolled his eyes. "We guys had
to stick together."

"Was it tough growing up with so many females?"

"The truth?"

"Nothing but."

"I loved it. I love women."

Laughter escaped her mouth, calling attention to her full
lips. "So I've heard."

He stopped.

She went a few feet, then halted too. "Sorry, I didn't mean
it the way it sounded."

"It's all right, I'm just surprised."

"What, that you have a reputation for being a ladies' man?"

"No, that you'd take time to investigate me personally."

"Why shouldn't I? You turned over all the rocks on me!"
she challenged.

He grinned.

She started walking again and, when he caught up to her, she
asked, "Tell me about your schooling. Did you like Harvard?"

"Yes. I had this economics professor. He was a throwback.
There was this time . . ." Joe told her tales of business school
with just a touch of regret. He'd purposely detoured the con-

versation to something safer. The storytelling felt good, but intermingled with a touch of flirting, it also felt dangerous.

Because, after spending only twelve hours with her, he was beginning to *like* Elyssa Wentworth. Considering the many hours together they had ahead of them, and the tough business negotiations that would follow, he was distressed by the thought.

That he was also beginning to find her combination of vulnerability and tough-guy businesswoman attractive wouldn't do at all. It never paid to mix business and pleasure.

Best to keep that in mind, he thought, even as he took her arm to steer her around another jogger, or dragged her over to the vendor selling fried dough and coerced her to eat what she called *that artery-clogging food*.

By the time seven o'clock came along, and they ended up back at her office, he was more in control of his reaction to her.

Or so he told himself.

Elyssa arranged to have her accountant at Allheart give Joe a general picture of the company's finances the morning after their walk by the canal. Joe was busy the rest of that day, but the following afternoon she managed to get Carole to spend a good four hours with him to get him up to snuff on Allheart's marketing strategy. Elyssa had convinced herself that she wasn't avoiding him, as evidenced by how she was seated now in this posh restaurant in the Latham Hotel waiting for him. Thinking about him . . .

This morning, she'd booted up her computer bright and early, and found another Allheart greeting from him.

It was one of the invitation cards they'd added recently. Embossed with a beautiful gilded scroll, its front asked, "Please meet me . . ." Inside, again, was a personal message. "At the Citronelle for dinner at eight? I need some more information from you."

Absently, she looked around at the newly remodeled glass-front kitchen, and the wall that changed color every sixty seconds, and then down to the lace table covering. She had to admit it. The man had class. And charisma. And—

"Happy tonight?" a deep voice rumbled from the side.

She peered up from her Perrier and smiled. He wore a

meticulous suit, tie and shirt again, and his face appeared freshly shaven. His hair was a little damp, darkening it. She wondered if she should have gone home to change out of her work clothes—a four-button black linen jacket, and slacks and black sandals with two straps crisscrossing over her toes. Self-consciously, she reached back to the twist of hair at her nape. "Of course I'm happy. I had a great day."

"I like hearing that," he said sliding into the bench seat across from her.

"Why?"

"I have a big interest in Allheart."

He signaled the waiter, who came immediately to their table. "Mr. Monteigne. Can I get you a drink?"

"A Tanqueray martini, straight up, dry, with olives, Peter. Thanks." He flicked a gaze at her water. "Anything for you?"

She hesitated. "No, thanks."

"Nothing else, then," he said to the waiter, who promptly left. "Don't drink at business dinners?" he asked her.

"No."

"That's smart."

She cocked her head.

"It's smart for everyone but you?" she asked. "You aren't worried about your mind getting clouded?"

"No, I can relax with you." He grinned. "After all, I know your deepest secrets now."

She raised her chin, wondering for a second if there was hidden meaning behind his words. "Is there a reason for this dinner?" Her tone was more curt than she'd intended.

"Don't take offense. I was just teasing." His drink arrived and he sipped it appreciatively. "And yes, since I couldn't get away from my office today, I'd like to wrap up this history business tonight, so we can get on to some goal-setting tomorrow."

Frowning, she drew out her dayplanner and flipped it open. "Let's schedule tomorrow now."

He said, "I've got two meetings, one at eleven and one at four."

"I can cancel my eight o'clock but I hate to miss—no, never mind. I can work around your schedule."

"You hate to miss what?"

"My appointment with my trainer is at six-thirty and I usually come into the office late on those days."

He thought for a minute. "What kind of a gym do you go to? I mean, are there any real men there?"

She smiled. "Oh, I think my gym gets plenty of testosterone traffic."

He picked up the menu. "Fine, then, how about I meet you at your gym at six-thirty sharp. We can talk through the training, have some breakfast and I can make my eleven o'clock."

"Do you always invade people's lives like this?"

He smiled above the rim of the leatherbound booklet. "Yes."

When he got to Grippe's Gym, she was already there warming up on one of the treadmills. He took a minute to watch her from the doorway. She wore black bike shorts and a tank top of purple and black Spandex, both of which left little to the male imagination. Her hair was in a knot on top of her head, but still he couldn't see its length or determine whether it was straight or curly.

Shit, Monteigne, what the hell do you care?

It was the damn dream he'd had about her hair—spread out across his belly for God's sake—that was causing this unfamiliar speculation about a potential client.

A man with considerable brawn approached her. She smiled warmly at him and something inside of Joe shifted. The guy checked the setting on the treadmill. Must be the trainer.

Joe crossed to her.

"Warm up, do thirty-five, increasing the incline, and I'll be back," the trainer told her.

"Hello." Joe's voice was cool.

Elyssa looked up. "Oh, you made it."

"I'm a man of my word."

"Joe Monteigne, this is Spade Carpenter, my trainer. Spade, this is the guest I told you about."

Spade assessed Joe's nylon shorts and T-shirt, over which he wore a warm-up jacket. "Need any help?"

He nodded to the treadmill. "No, I think I can manage." As the trainer left, he hopped on the machine and started slowly. "Don't you sleep?" he asked, glancing at his watch.

"As little as possible." She smiled. "Going to have trouble keeping up with me, Monteigne?"

"Not on your life, lady." He notched up the speed.

"Okay, start your third degree. I've only got thirty-five until Spade comes back for me."

Eyeing her surreptitiously, he noticed her cheeks were red. "It's time for goal defining. What do you really want from your business, Elyssa?"

"In a nutshell?"

"It's a big question. Splurge."

She thought a minute. The pounding of their footsteps and the clank of weights from some other early birds sounded around them. The gym air smelled clean, as it hadn't yet gotten that end-of-the-day ripeness to it.

"I want to make a lot of money, but I want to achieve something, too."

"What?"

"A company that other companies will point to as a model."

"Why?"

"Because that, to me, is success."

"Good answer."

She stiffened. "Meaning?"

"Founders who are only in it for the money don't succeed as well as people who want to make a mark in the world."

"Oh." They both speeded up. "I want to contribute to the world, too. I'd like to have a charitable presence, maybe help kids like I was go to college and achieve like that." She thought again. "And I want a viable company that can provide well for its employees."

He was silent. Nowhere in that description was complete control over her firm. Maybe this was going to be easier than he thought.

They chatted for the duration of their treadmill stint, but just as Spade approached, she said, "Don't forget, Monteigne, I get to hear what you want out of your business before you leave for your eleven o'clock."

He smiled a mental *touché* to her.

Thirty minutes later, he was *not* smiling. From across the room at the weights, he watched her work with her trainer, trying to ignore Spade's beefy hands on her waist, encircling her biceps, giving her fanny a pat as she did some glut work.

His absorption in her was beginning to irk him, so he turned away and dropped down horizontally to lift his two hundred on the bench press. Thought fled as he battled his way through three sets.

Just as he closed in on his final reps, he noticed she was standing over him, arms stretched above her head and leaning against his machine, the Spandex tightening across her very generous breasts. His barbell slipped.

"Well, I'm done," she announced. "I'll shower here, dress and we can have that quick breakfast."

Replacing the weights, he sat up, took the towel from around his neck and wiped the sweat from his face. When he opened his eyes, they widened like a kid's at Christmas. She'd tugged the tie out of her hair; it fell beyond her shoulders like a black waterfall cascading around her. Masses of curls clung to her damp back.

"What?" she said gazing at him from eyes that looked like a lion's framed by gleaming fur.

"Nothing." He managed to say. "Go shower. Good idea."

Shrugging, she turned and headed for the locker room. The rear view of her was as disturbing as the front.

Well, hell, he thought, irritated, *the Queen of Hearts is a fox.*

And for the first time, he began to wonder if this deal was such a hot idea after all.

Chapter 3

"*Come on in,*" *Joe said, pulling open the door to his brown-*stone in Georgetown.

Her reply was tart. "Said the spider to the fly."

He tried not to smile. She was intentionally playing the Ice Queen today, in all her splendid glory. After how he caught himself thinking of her Friday, a little cold war was probably a good idea at this point. He wondered briefly if she might be thinking the same thing—maybe they'd both needed time to regroup and reset priorities.

She'd indicated as much when they'd had breakfast after working out at Grippe's. *Let's just finish this up. Get all the input early next week. My decision on whether or not to go with you could be made within a week.*

"Can I take your jacket?" he'd asked once she was inside. She'd dressed casually today, as had he. They'd decided to do a marathon session on personal goals at his home office on Tuesday, the first day they were both free.

"No thanks." She tugged on the black linen jacket she wore over a white blouse and pinstriped pants. Her black suede mules had stilettos sharp enough to pierce a man's heart.

Ushering her through the town house's foyer, he angled his head to the left. "My office is on this side. I live on the right."

"Nice place." She examined the space, which divided his personal and professional domains, as if she were studying a corporate report. Did she like the light oak floor and staircase leading up to the top level? Were the sponge-painted walls to her taste?

"Thanks."

"Bob Woodward lives in this area, doesn't he?"

Joe opened the French doors to his office and they stepped inside. "Yeah, he's a great guy."

"You know him?"

"Uh-huh."

Carefully, she scanned the thick Oriental rug and raw oak floors and paneling. Her gaze drifted up to the high ceiling.

He tried not to notice the tired circles underneath her eyes. He knew he hadn't slept well since he'd last seen her Friday morning. Hmm. Perhaps, neither had she.

"Have a seat." He indicated one of the two couches angled so they both faced the backyard. A desk area was off to the front of the room. "Can I get you something?"

"Coffee."

At a sidebar, he poured huge mugsful, laced them both with milk and his with sugar, crossed to the couch and handed her one. Close up, her face showed more signs of strain. "Sit down, Elyssa. Before you fall down."

"Excuse me?"

Prickly this morning, was she? Well, he wasn't feeling much like an Allheart greeting card either. He'd had . . . uncomfortable thoughts about her all weekend. What she was doing, who she might be with. Did she have a significant other who'd caused that lack of sleep?

"Rough weekend?"

She smoothed back her tidy little bun. "No, I'm just anxious to move on with all this. You said you were too, so we could wrap it up today."

"Yes." He smiled and took a seat on the leather sofa facing her. Picking up the notepad from the antique oak chest that functioned as a coffee table, he said, "All right. Down to business. I've got a good handle on your staff, your general setup, your business goals and some of your finances. As I told you, the last step is articulating your personal goals. That should help me finalize your vision and create a tentative business plan. We'll have it done in about a week."

"Great."

He knew he should feel the same way, but he liked being with her and would miss their sessions together.

Too much.

Right, so with any luck, today would conclude their private meetings. After this he would conduct the due diligence and then present her an offer, prepared by him and approved by his partners.

"So, Elyssa Wentworth, what do you want out of life that we'll need to consider in the context of this business plan?"

Sipping coffee, she leaned back into the cushy leather, stared out the expanse of doors to the backyard and said, "Well, I've been thinking about it all week. Basically, I want what I have now—I want to be able to keep it, I guess. My apartment in Dupont Circle. My car. My clothes." She held up a slender ankle and dangled her foot. "My shoes, of course." She smiled.

He grinned. "Oh, definitely those shoes have to stay."

"I want to be able to afford to go anywhere I choose on vacation. I want to have enough money to retire on."

It took her about a half-hour before she relaxed a bit, eased back into the couch, uncrossed her legs and let her shoulders soften. He got up once to refresh their coffee and bring over a breakfast snack his housekeeper had left for him. Joe listened attentively as she ticked off the future in terms of monetary things: investments, portfolios, what she planned for retirement.

She stood once and asked to open the double set of French doors and let in the April air. Toward noon, she shucked off her jacket, revealing a sleeveless blouse underneath. He wished she'd buttoned up the top two buttons, as his eyes kept straying to the V of skin it showed. By the time she was done giving him the necessary information, she'd tucked her legs under her and was smiling. "It's sort of fun to talk about these things, isn't it? Like that game we played as kids—you know, what would you do if you won a million dollars?" she said thoughtfully.

"Do you share this kind of thing with your girlfriends?"

"Not much. With Elliot, sometimes."

"I'd like to meet him."

"I'm sure you will, if we decide to go with Highwire."

"*When* you decide." He stood and stretched. "I'm hungry, how about you?"

Her eyes traveled over him and he felt their touch as if it were her hand. "Sure. I could eat. So long as you realize that over lunch, you'll be telling me what *you* want out of *your* future."

He winced. "Didn't forget about that deal, huh?"

"No, I didn't." She stood too. Grabbed for her jacket. "Where are we going?"

"Nowhere."

"What?"

"I thought we'd have lunch here."

Her eyes widened. Today they had more brown than green in them. "Oh, well, if your housekeeper has it ready."

Shaking his head, he motioned to the door. "My housekeeper has the afternoon off. We're going to make lunch ourselves."

"As in cook?" she asked, rooted to the spot.

"Yes."

"Joe, I don't cook."

"Ever?"

"Ever."

"Well," he said urging her to the doorway. "I'll have to put *chef* on the list of needs for your future." Grasping her hand, he said, "Come on, woman. I'll show you what you're missing."

She didn't want to be here, watching him in his kitchen and listening to the low hum of his voice as he effortlessly charmed her. She wanted to get all this personal stuff over with. Though it had been a tough weekend, by yesterday she was back on track.

The morning, however, had dented the wall she'd built up against her attraction to him.

"They call this a heart attack on a plate," she said, indicating the recipe for Fettucine Alfredo he was working from. She perched across from him on a stool at a butcher block, making a salad.

From the stove—over which gleamed a row of brass-bottomed pots and pans—he threw her a withering look. "You know, for someone who doesn't cook, you're a pretty picky chick."

She sputtered. "Chick?"

He shrugged. "Sorry. I can't be PC *and* cook at the same time. Now how about you just finish that salad. I think it's simple enough for a CEO to tackle."

Like she did everything, she assembled it logically just as she imagined it should be. Lettuce first on the bottom, then tomatoes ringing the outside. "Why do you like to cook?" she asked as she sliced carrots.

"Is this part of my disclosure?"

It hadn't been. She'd momentarily forgotten about the deal, drawn to him as a man, in the sunny kitchen with its cozy eating area, long expanse of counter and myriad gadgets. "Of course."

"One of my nannies was Italian. She made us all learn, though the girls teased me unmercifully."

"I bet they don't now," she said absently.

"What?"

"The women in your life. They probably love this." She gestured around the kitchen.

"I guess." His voice was troubled. "How about you? Do the men you date cook?"

She didn't answer.

"Damn!"

She swirled around. The boiling water had splashed onto his hand when he dropped in the noodles. "You okay?"

"Just careless." He crossed to the sink below windows facing the outdoors and ran his fingers under cold water. "So, what about those men in your life?"

She watched him for a moment. "Are we covering the rest of the personal stuff we have to get out of the way today?"

He pivoted. The sun glinted off his dark hair. The heather blue sports shirt he wore with khakis accented the gleam of interest in his eyes. "No. Just person to person, not VC to exec, tell me why there aren't men swarming you, Elyssa."

"Who says they don't swarm?"

He sighed in frustration, and folded his arms over his chest. "All right, then why don't you follow up on their interest?"

"How do you know I don't?"

"Do you?"

"Well, I went with someone to the Kennedy Center Friday night."

"Did you?" His tone was odd.

"Yes, with my lawyer, Patrick."

He was silent a moment. "Is it serious?"

She shrugged. "No." He waited. "I don't have the time, really, to be serious about anyone."

"Come on, fess up. It's got to be more than that."

"All right. Most men don't want to accept the life I have. I work too hard. I don't have enough time or energy for them. Eventually, it's not worth the hassle."

Before he turned back to the food, his look said, *That's sad.*

It irked her. "I don't see anybody barefoot and pregnant around here, either, Monteigne. What's holding you back?"

She watched as he drained the noodles, poured on the cheesy sauce, and stirred the pungent mixture. Sliding it onto plates, he nodded to the salad. "Bring that on out and I'll tell you." He indicated the patio off the breakfast nook.

Her face brightened. "We're eating outside?"

"Yeah, Fresh-Air Girl, we are."

Two hours later they were still out there, basking in the sun, though shaded by a big umbrella. By then they'd talked about wanting a spouse and kids, but the difficulty of combining that with their lifestyles. She was disturbed by how much they had in common.

"More wine?" he asked, holding up a bottle of Muscadet.

"No, I shouldn't have even had this."

"That's right, you don't drink during business."

"Right." She shifted uncomfortably. "We're pretty much done, aren't we?"

"Yes, I know enough about you to crack out the best business plan I've ever done."

"You know enough about me to plan my wedding," she said dryly.

He didn't smile. She wondered why.

"I've enjoyed it, Elyssa. I'm kind of sorry to see it end."

"Yeah, but now the good stuff starts. If I go with Highwire, you get to hammer out a deal with me."

He just stared at her.

"After all, that was the goal of this whole thing, wasn't it?"

"Yes, of course."

Abruptly, she stood and held out her hand. "It's been nice getting to know you, Joe Monteigne. I'll be anxious to see the vision and business plan."

Standing too, he grasped her hand in a firm shake, but didn't let go. "I hope this works out, Elyssa." He covered their clenched hands with his other one. He looked like he was about to say more, but then let go. "I'll show you out."

* * *

"So, was it a fun week?" Carole asked from a corner table at the Georgetown pub, J. Paul's. Occasionally, Elyssa went out on Friday night with the women from work, but tonight she was glad Robyn and Dana had chosen to go to Dark Blue, the club where Robyn's current heartthrob played the piano; she and Carole had picked a quieter spot.

"Fun? I wouldn't exactly say that."

"No?" Carole stirred her rye and soda. "You seemed different these last few weeks."

"Different?"

"Yeah, like you were having a good time. Usually you work harder than Scrooge at Christmas, with the same somber attitude."

"Selling out *isn't* what I'd call a good time."

"You aren't selling out, Elyssa. You're going to lead this company to a new and wonderful frontier."

"Where no woman has gone before?"

"Maybe."

Elyssa looked serious. "I'm afraid of losing control."

"Of?"

"The company, of course."

A long silence. Then Carole asked, "Just the company?"

Elyssa sighed. She'd been struggling since Tuesday with something. Choosing to let it remain nebulous, she'd made no headway in dealing with her feelings. It was so unlike her normal take-charge attitude.

Reaching over, Carole squeezed her hand. "If you want to talk, I'm here. And it'll stay between us."

Elyssa smiled. "Am I that obvious?"

"Well you *have* been different for a couple of weeks. And taking on venture capital is a big step for you." She smiled warmly. "I thought you might want to vent a little."

Quiet, Elyssa scanned the room, noting the young, professional crowd at the bar and registering soft jazz from a discreet stereo system. "I know it is. And I'm going to go ahead because this is the only way to proceed now. It's not that."

"Is it Joe Monteigne?"

"Yes." She eyed her friend. "I don't need to be kidded about it, Carole."

"All right."

She stirred her Manhattan. "It *was* fun these few weeks. He got me to talk about my dreams for the business and had me spinning fairy tales about what I thought I could do."

"And he's the fairy godfather who can help you?"

"He says he is."

"What's he like?"

"He's a great listener, though I managed to get him to talk too."

"Know thy enemy?"

"That's the same thing Elliot said, but yes, partly." She smiled. "And partly out of curiosity. I wanted to know what makes him tick."

"There's nothing wrong with that. You're considering giving over some control of your baby to him."

Her hand went to her hair, and she remembered how he'd stared at it.

"There *is* something wrong here, though." She sighed. "I'm attracted to him." Her eyes locked with Carole's. Because of the empathy she saw there, she added, "And I think the feeling's mutual."

"Well, I'm not surprised. He's not only easy on the eyes, but he's a charmer. Everyone at Allheart thinks so."

"Everyone in *DC* thinks so."

Carole traced the rim of her glass thoughtfully. "Not a good thing, though, is it, to mix business and pleasure?"

Elyssa snorted. "It's professional suicide. You know, it's so ironic. I've always hated the accusation that female entrepreneurs sleep their way into money. I've worked my ass off for every penny I've got. I'd never compromise my integrity."

"Being attracted to Mr. Looks-Like-a-Male-Model isn't compromising yourself, Elyssa."

"No, it isn't. But I can't afford to let it go any further. It's driven me nuts to be having these feelings, and to see them mirrored in those *Mel Gibson* eyes."

"What are you going to do?"

"Nothing. We're done with the day-to-day stuff. If I like his vision for Allheart and his business plan, I'll encourage him to present it to his partners for financing."

"Elyssa, if you go ahead and let Highwire finance us, it's

bound to be an active investment. They'll want a seat on the board, and it's likely to be Joe. Can you resist long term?"

"I have to. I'm not going to take on a less competent investor for Allheart just because I can't control my hormones." She slapped the table with her hand. "I *will* control them."

Carole glanced over Elyssa's shoulder. "Oh, dear, well you better start now. Mr. Downright Sexy just walked in the door."

"Oh, shit." Elyssa was careful not to turn toward him.

Carole's face darkened.

"What is it?"

"He's, um, got this gorgeous blonde on his arm."

Elyssa straightened in her seat. "Well, that's good."

Carole looked at her askance.

"No, it *is*. It's just what the doctor ordered." She drained her glass and signaled the waiter. When he came over, she said, "I'll have another Manhattan."

"Do you know those women?" Jeanine Connors, with her razor-cut blond hair, high cheekbones and lithe body was one of the most striking women Joe dated. In the doorway to J. Paul's, she clasped his arm and leaned into him intimately. Funny, he'd never found her so . . . cloying before.

"Yes. I'm wooing one of them."

"Excuse me?"

"On a deal." Just a deal, damn it. He scowled. "Let's sit." Taking her by the arm, he led Jeanine to a table across the room from Elyssa and Carole. Unfortunately, his chair faced the two women. Before he seated himself, he said, "Order me a double martini, will you, Jeanine? I have to say hello."

Really, he did. It was the proper thing to do. He headed toward them, straightening his tie, tugging at his shirt cuffs. Christ, was he nervous?

Both women looked up when he approached. Something flashed in Elyssa's hazel eyes that intrigued him. That hint of vulnerability he'd seen before, as rare as it was appealing. It was gone in an instant, making him wonder if he imagined it. "Hello, ladies."

"Hello, Joe." Carole fidgeted with her drink. She glanced at Jeanine. "Out for the evening?"

He nodded and faced Elyssa. "How are you tonight?" He noticed the cocktail in front of her.

"I couldn't be better."

Well, she couldn't *look* better. Her cheeks bloomed with color like they had during her workout last week. Tonight, her porcelain complexion was healthy and glowing.

And she had that damn hair down again. Seeing it curling around her face, sliding down her back did uncomfortable things to his body. "Did you get caught up on all your work? I hope I didn't keep you to myself too long." He practically winced at his own wording.

Her faced colored even more. When she didn't speak, Carole filled in the embarrassing gap. "Our friend E here's a whirlwind. She runs circles around all of us."

"I'm sure she does."

Elyssa's eyes traveled across the room. "Your date looks restless, Joe."

Ah, his cue to leave. "Well, I just wanted to say hello." He smiled at Carole and turned his gaze back to Elyssa.

She'd taken the lemon slice out of her Manhattan and bitten if off. His own lips parted fractionally, and his mouth went dry at the sensuous movement; he could almost taste the tartness of the wedge, smell its fruity scent. His gaze riveted on her mouth. He *wanted* to taste *that*. "I'll, um . . ." Goddamn it, he hadn't stuttered like this since puberty. "I'll see you next week."

He made his escape, cursing himself all the way back to Jeanine. Who was indeed restless. Her usual cool demeanor was closer to frosty now. As he sat down, he thought of Elyssa's nickname. The Ice Queen. Well, whoever tagged her with that was certainly a moron. She was pretty hot when she talked about her business on Tuesday, and last week when she'd worked out and flirted with Spade. What the hell kind of name was *Spade* anyway?

"Joe? I asked you a question." Jeanine's voice was pouty.

"I'm sorry. I'm a little distracted tonight."

Jeanine shot Elyssa an icicle gaze. "So I see."

Disinterested in her pique, he peered down at the appetizer menu. "What does that mean?"

"She's very attractive."

Yes, she is. "Who's attractive?"

"Your potential client."

He glanced up and over. Elyssa was laughing at something Carole had said. He realized he hadn't heard her laugh nearly enough. "I suppose she is." If you liked sultry, sexy, dark good looks. Which he never realized he did.

Annoyed with himself, he drew in a deep breath. "Let's order some food. I haven't had anything since breakfast."

An hour later, bored out of his mind with conversation about the people he and Jeanine knew in common, the refurbishing of some Georgetown buildings and a long, tedious discussion about raising capital for an arts organization Jeanine dabbled in, Joe smoothly let it be known he'd like to leave. It had nothing to do with the fact that Elyssa had gone a half hour before.

Sparing him not even a backward glance.

Not that he'd noticed.

When they stood to exit, Jeanine smiled at him coyly. "Come back to my place, Joey." She ran her red manicured nails down his sleeve.

Did Elyssa paint her nails? He didn't think so.

"It's been a long time," Jeanine purred.

Had it? He couldn't remember.

In fact, he wondered *when* the last time was he'd made love with a woman. His eyes strayed to where Elyssa and Carole had sat.

Damn it. Too long. Way too long!

A week later, Elyssa received a messengered package from Highwire Industries. Inside was the most complete, astute vision statement and business plan she'd ever seen. It thrilled her professionally to see what she'd told him developed into such an articulate, concise plan as to where her baby could go. Joe had been right. Finding out about her, digging through the surface that few had penetrated, he knew exactly what she wanted and where she should go. From what she saw, her choice was clear.

Then why, she thought as she set aside the document and turned to her computer, wasn't she more happy? Why, after reading his report, did she think about the Sharon Stone look-alike he was with last Friday night? Angry at her own reaction, she scrolled through her email, and stopped at yet another missive from Allheart Greetings! He'd sent her another card. With a frown, she brought it up.

On the front was a tree in the winter. Bare of its leaves, it had a small figure creeping out on a branch. The caption read, "Don't hesitate to go out on a limb sometime."

She opened the card, knew what was coming. A picture of the same tree in the late summer, beautifully leafed, with succulent apples dotting the foliage. The figure had inched out farther. The text read, "After all, that's where the fruit is."

For a minute she let her head rest on her palm. He was something else. Then she shook off her weakness. Ruthlessly, she went to delete the card. Just like she'd delete him from her thoughts as soon as she could. That she was unable to bring herself to erase the card just yet stilled her for a moment.

Determined, she picked up the envelope from Highwire and stared at the report. She'd call and tell him she was accepting the proposal. And they'd be back on track. Ignoring the sinking feeling in her chest, she reached for the phone.

"*I'll fire him.*"

From across Elyssa's teak desk, Robyn stared at her as if she'd grown another head. "What?"

"I said I'll fire Malcolm. First the microwave, now the fridge. That man's a menace."

"At least he's not been the Wicked Witch of the West for days."

Elyssa leaned forward in her chair. "What's that supposed to mean?"

"That we've been walking on eggshells ever since you decided to go pursue Highwire as an investor."

"You have *not*." She gave her assistant a stern look. "Now call that boy and ask him to come up here."

"I'm not calling poor Malcolm so you can fire him. If you want it done, call him yourself."

"That's insubordination."

Robyn arched a brow. "Are you going to fire me too?"

"Of course she's not." The deep male rumble came from the doorway. Elyssa cringed at the sound of his voice. It was bad enough to have withstood it over the phone for five days. It took no more than hearing his sexy baritone and lazy drawl to send shivers down her spine. He was here today to discuss the due diligence, and set up appointments for the last information gathering. It would take place while he worked up a deal with his partners. Joe smiled at Robyn. "She won't fire you because her business plan is dependent on all the brilliant people who work here."

Elyssa bristled. "Is this how it's going to be if I accept Highwire's offer?"

His brow furrowed. "Meaning?"

"Will you interfere like this in personnel decisions?"

Giving Joe a sympathetic glance, Robyn scooted out. She closed the door behind her.

"No, I said that as a friend." He studied her carefully. "You're stressed."

"I'm changing the whole future of my company. Of course I'm stressed."

"It'll be a good change."

"A necessary one, at least."

"Are you having second thoughts?"

"Yes, and thirds and fourths."

"That's normal, Elyssa."

She leaned back in the chair. "I know." Sighing, she said, "Did you bring your calendar? We can set up times for your people to come in."

They worked for nearly an hour on the schedule. When they were done, he eyed her again. "Got plans tonight?"

She nodded to a stack of files on the desk. "Are you kidding? After all the time I spent with you these last weeks, I've got a mountain of work to catch up on."

"You need a break."

Just then the phone buzzed. "Carole and Dana are going home," Robyn said, her pout registering over the intercom. "They're afraid to come in and say good night. So am I. Is it all right if I leave?"

Elyssa sighed. "Yes." She cast a glance at Joe. "Look, Robyn, I'm sorry. I shouldn't have snapped at you."

"Does this mean I have a job to come to tomorrow morning?"

"Of course."

"And Malcolm?" Robyn asked, sniffing a bit.

A smile escaped Elyssa's lips. Joe returned it. "And Malcolm."

"Neat. Have a good night, E." She was about to click off. Then Robyn added, "Night, Joe."

"Good night, Robyn."

As she switched off, Elyssa watched Joe give her a long perusal, then rise from the chair and go to her closet, open it up and drag out her gym bag. It seemed like light years ago that she'd shown him where she kept it when they walked by the canal that day.

"What are you doing?"

He tossed the soft leather bag onto her desk. "I'm saving you from a bad case of the very understandable jitters. Come on."

"Where to?"

"I'm going to teach you how to play racquetball."

"Racquetball?"

"Yes. I have standing court time on Wednesdays at my club, but my partner canceled."

"And you think I'm going to fill in?"

"Well, you're going to be my new partner, of sorts. And since you'll be *playing* with the big boys, I thought maybe I'd start showing you the ropes."

It wasn't a good idea, she knew that. But she *was* stressed, alienating even Carole, and . . . he wanted to show her the ropes, huh? It might be fun to show Mr. In-Perfect-Shape a few things herself. He needed to learn he couldn't take her for granted. It might start their business relationship off on the right foot.

She stood. "Well . . . I guess I can handle it."

With the skill of an Olympic athlete, she drew back her arm, snapped the paddle forward and arced the little blue ball into the corner; it bounced toward them past the floor line with the force of a bullet. Joe got a piece of it, and slammed it into the front wall.

She went up close, surprising him. He was too far in the back court to compensate when she graced the damn thing a gentle tap and it whimped to the floor.

Turning, she gave at him the same stuff-it grin she'd been giving him for the past forty minutes. "Game point."

He'd been had.

Who would have thought she'd know how to play racquetball? Hell, she not only played, she was a contender. He wasn't giving her any points, and they were tied one set each.

What the hell is going on here? he'd asked after the first game.

Well, you never asked if I knew how to play.

My mistake.

You shouldn't underestimate me, Mr. Monteigne.

I won't, Miss Wentworth, ever again.

As she took her position in the serving box, he hid a smile. In reality, his plan had worked. The stress lines around her eyes and mouth had disappeared after the first set. After the second, she'd gotten an unholy gleam in her eye. He thought about letting her win just to make her happy. But she wouldn't want that. So he headed to the back of the court again, determined to beat her.

He'd been elated when she'd called to tell him she liked the vision and business plan he'd created—probably a little too elated. But he was distressed to see her so unhappy today. He'd thought about her all week after seeing her at J. Paul's, where he'd *also* been distressed that Jeanine's classic blond looks had seemed like plain grits next to Elyssa's dark beauty.

That was never more obvious than right now; she filled out just fine the short white skirt and red top that skimmed her waist and, every once in a while, revealed a patch of skin. Damn, he had to concentrate on the game.

The advantage went back and forth as they volleyed their way through another ten minutes. Finally he held up his hand. "Let's call it a draw."

She turned to him. "Tired, old man?"

"Yes." He saw her shoulders sag. "So are you. I'm just smart enough to admit it."

Confidently she glanced at the big clock up high near the ceiling. "We have a few more minutes."

He crossed to the door where they'd left their bags in a small recess carved out of the wall to store gear. "I'm done. If you want, I'll concede your victory." Bending over, he took a towel out of his bag and wiped his face. His white shirt was soaked through and he was dripping wet.

As she came toward him, he noticed her face was covered with a fine sheen of perspiration, and her cheeks were rosy. But her eyes danced. And she was strutting. She'd make it in the business world all right. She was a competitor through and through.

"Who taught you the game?" he asked as he fished out a bottle of water and uncapped it. He took a long swig.

"Elliot. He plays all the time."

He handed the water to her and she took a few sips. "So do you, I'll wager."

Playfully, she let the bottle rest against her smiling lips. "Maybe." She took another gulp, then gave it back to him. Their eyes locked as they simultaneously realized what an intimate gesture drinking out of the same bottle was.

And they'd done it unconsciously.

She stared down at the bottle, then looked at his face again. Without breaking eye contact, he dribbled some water on his towel, capped the bottle and dropped it to the floor. Its thud sounded loudly in the big room. The big *private* room. A racquetball court was sealed up tight. With the door shut behind them, they were insulated from the world.

Holding her gaze, he stepped toward her. She backed up to the wall. Her eyes were big and wary—but there was something in them, a keen interest that drew him to her inexorably. Raising his hand, he blotted her cheek with the wet towel.

She gave a little jolt at the sting of the water on her heated face. He tended to her other cheek, then her forehead.

Sighing, she closed her eyes. Savoring the coolness? Or his touch? He brought the coarse terry to her lips, which parted and expelled another soft breath as she opened her eyes.

Abruptly he threw the towel to the floor.

She was flat against the wall now, her arms braced on it. In her sneakers, she was several inches shorter than he. Tipping her chin, he rubbed his thumb across her bottom lip. His eyes dropped from hers to her mouth.

He stepped in closer. Her breasts brushed his chest, electrifying him. Raising his other hand, he tugged out the tie that kept her hair back. Skeins of silk fell around her face. He wasted no time in tunneling his fingers through it.

Their gazes were locked. He could see her pupils dilate. Could feel her chest rise and fall faster, in counterpoint to his.

"Joe." She breathed finally. "This isn't a good idea."

"I know." He lowered his head anyway.

When their mouths met, the world tilted. He kept his touch light . . . for all of two seconds. She tasted unique, so like *Elyssa* that he pressed his lips into hers, parted them and invaded her mouth with the greatest of need. One hand stayed in her hair, but his other banded around her back and yanked her close.

He was caught off guard by the feel of her body aligning with his. She was all angles and curves and supple flesh that pulsed underneath his fingers. It made him dizzy.

His hand dropped lower. Flirted with her waist. Cupped her bottom. And drew her into intimate contact. It was then, when they were totally meshed, that she melted into him.

Elyssa could feel him hard and hot against her. It dissolved something inside her, a vigilance she didn't even know she'd kept with men, with her response to them. Her arms slid up to wrap around his neck. Her fingers caressed his nape, sifted into his hair. It was thick and damp and felt like wet silk.

His mouth plundered hers with delicious abandonment, which she allowed generously, took greedily, met willingly with her own need. Someone moaned—him? her?—and she pressed closer.

She went on her toes to fit him better and their contours met in exquisite harmony. His whole body was taut with white-hot sexual need. He pressed her back against the wall and his hands dropped lower to grasp her legs. The feel of his slick fingers on her bare thighs was like lightning striking. She jolted into him, and his grip tightened.

His chest crushed her as he lifted her up. "Wrap your legs around me," he demanded hoarsely against her mouth.

She did.

Since she was locked around him, his hands were free to probe underneath her top. Wet skin met wet skin and he explored her back, finding every nook and cranny of her waist, her hips, her shoulders.

After several seconds of decadent feasting, he dragged his mouth away and buried his face in her neck. She felt him take love bites there, and it inflamed her. Her mouth found the skin inside his shirt and her teeth closed over it.

His groan was primitive and incoherent.

"Lyss," he murmured harshly.

"J—"

Her words were cut off by pounding on the door at his back. They both froze.

More pounding. Louder.

Joe's body sagged and his forehead dropped to hers. "It's . . ." He cleared his throat. "It's the players for the next court time." He drew back and looked down at her.

His whole face was flushed. His mouth was red. His eyes were hazy with desire. She knew her own face would mirror his. Her legs still encircled him.

"Our time's up," he said.

Though spoken softly, the words echoed with meaning in the cavernous room.

Chapter 4

"*Invite me up.*"

"That's not a good idea."

"Do it anyway."

Joe had pulled his Beemer into a just-vacated parking spot in front of Elyssa's prewar apartment building on R Street in Dupont Circle. He shut the motor off; tension—thick and heavy—hummed between them like another presence in the car, as it had all the way from his club. The only sound was the *pat-pat-pat* of the soft night rain on the roof.

For the entire drive home, Elyssa had sat stiffly beside him as he'd negotiated the heavy Friday evening traffic, waiting for him to say something, praying he wouldn't. Now, to avoid looking at his all-male, sweat-soaked body, she leaned back against the plush interior and closed her eyes. "I won't sleep with you to get financing for Allheart. I've never done it before and I won't start now."

Joe let loose a vicious curse, then another. The words made Elyssa cringe.

After a meaningful silence, he spat, "What exactly have I said or done to make you think so little of me?"

Another very long pause. "I'm sorry. I'm just used to being cautious."

"Cautious? This is miles beyond cautious. It's damned *paranoid*." He waited. "And insulting."

"All right, I'm paranoid." She felt as if someone had drained all the blood out of her. She wanted nothing more than to go inside, soak in a long bath and curl up in her bed.

Well, *almost* nothing more. She could still feel his muscles strain under her fingers, still feel his body arch into hers. It was one of the most exquisite sensations she'd ever experienced in her life. And she yearned for it again.

"Why, Elyssa?" No answer. "Why are you so suspicious?" he demanded.

"Oh, come on, Joe. You've been around. You know the rumors."

He gripped the steering wheel. She tried not to notice his hand now—solid and irresistibly sexy. She wanted that hand on her again. "You've heard that in regard to *me*? That I sleep with Highwire's female clients?"

"No, not specifically you."

"I see. I get lumped with the Jackson Camps of the industry because I'm part of it."

She threaded her hair off her face. He'd reveled in the unruly mane when he'd tugged out the tie, taking sensual pleasure in touching it. "In any case, it's not a good idea. Sleeping together could compromise both our positions. Call our integrity into question."

He drank that in along with a deep, cleansing breath.

"It was just a kiss," she said, exasperated.

"It was more than a kiss." The husky tenor of his voice wrapped around her as his body had. Reaching out, he laid his hand palm up on the console between them, behind the stick shift. Hesitating only for a minute, she placed hers on top of his, and he linked their fingers. The contact was startlingly intimate.

He waited.

"All right. It was more than a kiss."

"I can't help how I feel," he said quickly. "Hell, I don't *want* to help it."

Holding tightly to his hand, she squeezed it hard. "It's just physical attraction." Even to her own ears, the words were hollow.

He squeezed back. "What are we going to do about it, Lyss?" The nickname recalled the moment he'd uttered it harshly against her lips. Intuitively, she knew that's what he'd call her when he was inside her.

"Nothing. We're going to do *nothing* about this. It'll go away." In a million years. "I have to go in." She wrenched her hand out of his and threw open the car door.

"Wait—"

"Good night, Joe."

Stumbling out into the night, she strode to the front steps. The rain beat heavily down on her, chilling her almost as much as the disconnection between them had. Without looking back, Elyssa hurried inside.

Located smack in the middle of Dupont Circle, Kramer Books and Afterwords Cafe was a haven to some, a watering hole to others and a temporary antidote to loneliness for yet another group. It was an intriguing combination of bookstore, indoor/outdoor cafe, coffee bar, and folk club. At night, it was rumored to be a singles hangout, though Elyssa had never frequented it for that reason. Today, she wandered into the store like a nomad, sightlessly staring at the books, indolently bumping into customers until Elliot took her arm. "Come on, kiddo. You're a bull in a china shop today."

She felt like the biggest klutz in the world. She'd handled the situation with Joe two nights ago like some naive teenager he'd put the moves on. Or worse yet, some Victorian maiden whose sensibilities he'd offended.

Before she realized it, Elliot had steered her outside to snag a table in the cafe that overlooked Nineteenth Street. She sank down onto a padded wrought-iron chair and stared out at Dupont Circle unfolding around her.

"It's such a cliché," she'd said without preamble. Throughout most of the day with Elliot, she'd been dropping in and out of conversations about Joe.

Elliot signaled a waitress and ordered two cappuccinos. "Is it?" he asked his sister.

She nodded. "Of course. I won't become a statistic, Elliot."

"You think he's done this before?"

"He got royally pissed off when I implied as much."

"At least he's got some sense."

She peered at Elliot quizzically.

"Look," he said. "I don't know if you should let this go further or not. But . . ." His words trailed off as he watched the Sunday afternoon crowd pass them by.

Elyssa waited for him to continue.

". . . I've never seen you like this," he finished.

" 'Like this'?"

"So affected by a man." He sighed. "Sexual attraction is a pretty powerful pull."

She closed her eyes, trying to shut out the smell of sweat and aftershave and the unique scent of the man she couldn't stop thinking about. For two nights running she'd had startlingly erotic dreams of him. And her. Together.

"It's awful."

"Is it?"

"It *feels* awful."

Elliot chuckled. "Love hurts, Lyss."

"I am not in love with him."

"Do you *like* him?"

Their cappuccinos were delivered and Elyssa sipped hers absently. "I do like him, that's the problem. We have a lot in common, he's got a great sense of humor, he's basically kind and though he flirts with all the women at the office, it seems innocuous enough."

"So you don't think this is his usual MO?"

Lifting a shoulder, she tossed her head back. "I guess not, but what does it matter? I can't compromise this deal."

She could almost see her brother's analytical mind clicking into gear. "Seems like you have two choices here, kiddo. Stick to your decision to keep it solely professional. Or kill the deal."

"What?"

"Kill the deal. Find another investor and then you can go to bed with Joe Monteigne and see where it leads."

"I'd never sacrifice the business for personal reasons." She thought for a minute. "Besides, this isn't anything long term we're talking about. It's just a strong case of chemistry."

"You wouldn't *be* sacrificing the business. You'd find another investor. Tons are sniffing after you."

"No. Highwire's the best for Allheart, I'm sure of it. We need their expertise. And the particular way they deal with the companies they invest in. I can't sacrifice what's best for my business because of some temporary hormonal imbalance that's bound to burn itself out quickly, anyway. I *won't* do that."

Her brother looked sad. "I felt that kind of attraction to Sally, and it never burned itself out." He shook his head. "This thing between you and Monteigne could lead somewhere good."

"It won't. I don't want it to." She stared out at the street. "The only thing that will kill this deal is if their offer is unacceptable."

Elliot looked intrigued. "What could make it unacceptable?"

"Basically it'll all boil down to the amount and kind of control they'll want."

"For instance?"

"I'd never give them more than a fifty percent share, mainly."

"What are the chances of that being a requirement?"

"Nil. Joe knows I wouldn't even consider that."

"Then it's a dead end."

"Yes, and so is the relationship."

Reaching over, Elliot covered her hand with his. "I'm sorry, Lyss."

Elyssa nodded. She never cried, but for some reason she felt emotion clog her throat like cotton candy. "Hey, that's life," she said lightly. "I'll get over it."

"I know you will."

She gave Elliot a smile she didn't feel, hoping to convince him of something she didn't believe, about a planned course of action she didn't want to take.

"*Welcome to Camden Yards. Please stand for the* singing of the National Anthem."

In their box seats, Joe struggled to his feet, stood up straight next to his father and scanned the stadium. The huge circular field sat below thousands of seats, sunlight peeking in from openings between the two levels, as well as shining down from above them like a benevolent deity. The structure was made of brick and steel and looked solid and sturdy. It was built on the site of a saloon once owned by Babe Ruth's father and was the arena where Cal Ripken had broken Lou Gehrig's record for most consecutive games played. It cost one hundred and six million dollars and Joe wished he'd gotten in on the initial financing.

Stop thinking about work and enjoy the game. He'd been looking forward to this night with his father; every year, they attended as many Orioles games as they could together. The sun glinted off Lance Monteigne's salt-and-pepper hair and Joe wondered idly when his own would turn gray.

He wouldn't be surprised if he got a few white strands this weekend. He felt like he'd aged a decade in less than forty-eight hours. Yanking on his Orioles cap, he pulled the visor down over bloodshot eyes and stuck his fingers in his jeans pockets. His shoulders were so weary he knew they sagged.

After the anthem, his father said, "Sit down, son. You don't look so good."

Dropping to his seat, Joe watched the players take the field. "Think José Mercedes will be any good this year?"

His father rolled his program into a cylinder and watched the lineup. "Yes. Your mother clipped an article on him from *Sports Illustrated* the other day for me. I'll fax it to you."

Did Elyssa like baseball? Joe wondered. They'd never gotten to discuss hobbies or anything like that. Hmph. She probably didn't have *time* for any.

"Joe?" His father's quietly uttered word had him straightening.

"Yeah, Dad?"

"You should talk about it."

He didn't try to bluff as he had with his mother and two of his sisters early that morning at brunch when they'd asked him what was wrong. "It won't change anything to talk about it."

"What would you like to change?"

Joe linked his hands between his jean-clad knees. His eyes lowered to the peanut shells dotting the ground and he moved them around with his sneaker. "I met someone."

"A woman?"

"Yes."

"That's good news."

He angled his head to his father. "No, it isn't. She's the most frustrating, stubborn . . . oh, hell. It's doomed, Dad."

"Why?"

"I'm about to make an offer to finance her company."

His father cringed slightly. Outside of his family, there was nothing Lance valued more than integrity. "Ouch."

"I know."

"How did this happen? You've never gotten involved with a client before, have you?"

Joe shook his head. He wasn't sure when he started to feel that white-hot need to have Elyssa. He knew when he started to like her, had admitted the attraction as soon as it had begun, but somewhere along the way his feelings for her had gotten away from him. Like the Frankenstein monster that turned on its creator, Joe felt as if he'd been ambushed by his own emotions. As the Orioles took the lead against Detroit, Joe explained his relationship with Elyssa Wentworth for his father.

When he was done, he quipped, "I can't believe I've only known her for four weeks."

His father didn't answer for a moment. Then he said, "There's something you don't know, Joe, that I'd like to tell you."

Joe studied his father's somber expression. Eyes just as blue as his own peered back at him. "What?"

"What your mother did before we married."

"She worked in the state department, I thought. That's where you two met."

"Your mother was on her way to being a specialist in diplomatic law. She, um, worked for me as an intern."

"Mom?"

"Yes." His father's voice was melancholy.

"I had the impression she dabbled in a career before you got married, but quit to have kids."

"She did quit. But she didn't have a lot of choice."

"Meaning?"

"Washington was different in those days. It was long before scandals like Watergate and the Clinton affair. What passed for scandal then would look like kindergarten stuff now. As soon as your mother and I got involved—and we tried to fight it— one of us was going to lose his or, in this case, her job."

"Wow. I never knew." Joe thought of his still-beautiful sixty-three-year-old mother, who was smart and savvy about politics and had stood by his father's side for his whole illustrious career. "Mom seemed happy all her life, Dad."

"I think she was. And neither of us has regretted the choices we were forced to make."

"So how does this relate to me and Elyssa?"

"You could back out of the deal."

His objection was automatic. "I'd really be shortchanging Highwire if I did that. Allheart could make us millions."

"Life's a tradeoff. You'd lose money but have a chance with a woman you care about."

"You misunderstand. I like her. And I'm attracted to her big-time, but I'm not thinking about June weddings here or anything, Dad."

"Well then, best you let her go and not compromise either of your positions. You could damage this woman's reputation by behaving incautiously. Especially since it's just a fleeting thing."

Joe nodded. He needed his father's sober advice today because he didn't feel that he was thinking clearly. And he didn't feel strong. It took all his willpower not to storm over to her apartment and just wear her down—which he suspected he could do if he tried.

As the crowd around him stood for an Oriole double play, Joe remained seated and sighed. He couldn't pursue this with Elyssa. It wasn't right for either of them.

In the harsh Monday morning light, Joe looked only a little better than she did. Standing in her office doorway, his wide shoulders nearly spanned the entry. Shoulders she'd clutched last Friday night, practically *gnawed* on, for God's sake. "Good morning." Her voice was smoky husky.

"Good morning." He scanned the office, then glanced behind him. "No one's here yet?"

"No." She fidgeted with the pockets of the stark black suit she wore today. The skirt was tightly pleated, hitting just above the knee. She'd taken great pains with her appearance this morning, and chosen one of her favorite outfits to make herself feel in control. She knew the soft teal blue shirt underneath highlighted her coloring. She needed all the help she could get to not look like something from a creature double feature today. The weekend had been rough.

"How are you?" he asked when he'd discovered they were alone.

Horrible. "Fine. You?"

He stuck his hands in the pockets of a suit she'd never seen before. But she'd recognized the material as sharkskin, from Hong Kong. "Great." Finally crossing into the office, he stood before her desk. "Good weekend?"

She busied herself with files, unable to look at him. "It was . . ." *Shitty*. ". . . fun. Elliot and I had some time together." Elliot, who'd told her to choose a relationship over money. Elliot, who'd lost the love of his life and suffered, still, from it.

"Oh, good." He glanced at the clock. "The auditors should be here by now."

Please, let them come. "Would you like to go over the schedule for the week while we wait?"

Seating himself on a chair in front of her desk, he crossed an ankle over his knee and said, "Sure."

"We've got the audit today." She made sure her tone was all business, though she felt more awkward than a high-school freshman at her first dance. "And tomorrow you'll take a look at our current contracts."

"Yes. Did you get the list of customers to contact as references?"

Reaching over, she handed him a paper. Their fingers brushed. Her intake of breath was audible despite the sound of traffic filtering in from the window. He read the list as if he hadn't noticed either the touch or her reaction. "This looks good." He raised his eyes. "I'll let you know who else we decide to contact this afternoon."

His comment momentarily distracted her from the exhaustion in his blue eyes. "I don't understand," she said.

"During due diligence, we contact the customers you give us as references as well as some others not on your list."

"Why?"

"To get a bigger picture."

"Meaning you don't trust me to give names of people who would present an accurate portrayal of Allheart?"

Joe watched her pretty mouth form a thin line. Though dressed meticulously, she looked very tired and very stressed. Her hair was clipped back off her face, but not in its usual bun. Instead it fell down her back in a disarray of curls. He wondered if she did it on purpose. To make him remember how those strands had wound around his fingers as if they wanted to attach themselves permanently. As if they belonged there.

But they didn't. Any more than the troubled woman before him belonged with him in any way but the professional one.

Goddamn it!

"Joe, I'm talking to you. Why didn't you tell me about this maneuver?"

"What good would it do us if I told you we were going to check out customers you might not want us to talk to?"

"I'm not afraid to have you see my missteps as well as my successes."

"I'm sure there haven't been that many."

She lifted that chin. He remembered what it felt like burrowing into his chest. "There haven't."

"So what's the problem?"

Weary, she leaned her head back on her seat. "Nothing! Nothing's the problem." The gesture pulled aside the collar of her blue shirt.

His words were backstopped in his throat by what he saw. Red marks. On her neck. That his mouth had put there.

The sight made him instantly hard. He remembered exactly how she tasted there—a little salty, very sexy. His finger went to the inside of his own shirt collar. He had little black and blue marks from her teeth just below his neck.

And just as four suits appeared at her doorway, her eyes widened at his gesture and her hand flew to her throat. In that moment he knew she knew exactly what he was thinking.

On Friday of the final week Joe would be at Allheart, Elyssa hurried into the office foyer at nine thirty A.M. Gathered around Robyn's desk was her executive staff.

"Really Robyn, if he's that shallow . . ." Carole was saying.

Alix shook her head. "He's not. I think it's all in Robyn's mind."

Dana sipped coffee. "Yeah, and he plays a mean piano." Over the rim of her cup she said, "Oh, here's our fearless leader."

Elyssa dropped her Prada bag on Robyn's desk. "What? Is work optional today?"

"Hey, this day goes down in Allheart history." Robyn lifted her cup in salute. "We're celebrating."

"Very funny," she said picking up her phone messages.

"It *does*." Dana joined in the fun. "We've never known you to oversleep in the twenty months we've been open. We almost had a group faint when you called in."

Her heart pounding, Elyssa said, "Everybody's entitled."

Carole blocked her view of the women. Elyssa knew she was hushing the others. Though she hadn't confided in Carole since the night at J. Paul's, Elyssa was sure Carole could guess why she looked and acted like such a hag these days. Dana, Robyn and Alix disappeared into Dana's office to the left. Carole tugged lightly at her sleeve as Elyssa started for her office. "Elyssa, are you all right?"

Her back to her friend, she said, "I'm just trying to get through today."

"It's his last day for the due diligence, isn't it?"

Nodding, still facing away from Carole, she said, "Yes. He'll do his own market research next week from his offices." Thank God. No longer would she have to see that handsome face, smell that sexy cologne, wait to hear the strong timbre of his voice when he made a comment.

"I'm here if you want to talk."

Elyssa circled around. Carole smiled sadly at her. "You are obviously suffering, E."

In one of the more bald-faced lies Elyssa had ever told, she shook her head. "I'll be fine. As soon as he's out of here."

But a little voice taunted her, all the way to her computer. *You'll still have to see him.*

Not every day.

Big deal. It's the nights that are no picnic.

She wouldn't think about the dreams.

Dropping into her chair, she booted up her computer and idly called up her email. Just as disinterestedly she scrolled down the contents.

"Jesus Christ! What's he trying to do to me?" The question, put to the computer, echoed in the silent room. The unopened, unread Allheart card stared back at her.

Delete it. Don't even look at it.

Ignoring her own admonitions, she double-clicked on it.

On the screen appeared a card from what Dana had informally called their Buck Up series. It was a line that sent messages of encouragement, confidence, you-can-cope sentiments. This one had a beautiful bouquet of pink roses on the front. One stood out from the rest, tinted darker than the others. The tag line read, "You," bold-faced on the *you*, "can do what you

have to do. And because you're so special, you can do it far
better than you think you can."

Elyssa felt her eyes mist as she clicked open the card. Inside, was the same rose. All by itself. Underneath it, Joe had
added his own message. "Thank you for getting us through
this week. Your strength and determination have given me
willpower too. I'll never forget it, Lyss."

Lyss. She rubbed the heels of her hands over her eyes. She
could do this. She knew she could. Just one more day.

Harold Malone, Joe's partner at Highwire, raised bushy
gray eyebrows at Joe when he entered one of Washington's
popular cigar clubs almost an hour late for their appointment.
"Joe." He nodded to the young man across from him. "This is
Tom Carrington. He's a prospective client."

Smoothly Joe reached out his hand. "Tom. Sorry I'm late.
At the last minute, I got a phone call I couldn't postpone."
Usually Joe didn't lie. But what could he say? That he'd been
staring out his office window, remembering how Elyssa's legs
felt wrapped around him like a pretzel last week and lost track
of time wallowing in the memory. Damn it to hell. What he
was *losing* was his *mind* over this situation. And it was so unlike him.

"Must have been pretty important for our Boy Wonder
here to be delayed." Harold pulled out a cigar. "I don't think
I've ever known you to be late for a meeting."

Joe forced a smile. "I'm sure that's an exaggeration." He
faced the young man. The *eager* young man. He'd seen the
syndrome many times lately in people seeking funding. They
were so young, so inexperienced, they practically bubbled
with an ingratiating naiveté.

Not Elyssa. She was as cool as a cucumber.

Just think about work, Monteigne.

"So tell us about this T-shirt business of yours," Joe said,
redirecting his thoughts. "Do you really think there's a market
for custom teenage slogan T-shirts online?"

The skinny young man pulled some papers out of a briefcase. "The market research I've done shows that of the per-
centages of people who use the Internet, teenagers create . . ."

Joe missed the statistic. Instead, his mind drifted to Elyssa and how she'd thrown her all into the racquetball game she'd conned him on. He had wondered then if she'd show the same passion during sex.

Now he knew.

Her hands had clutched at him with a desire that sucked him in like a sexual whirlpool. If she was that torrid about a kiss, she'd wring him dry when they made love.

Damn it to hell, he had to stop thinking about this. *Where's your concentration, Monteigne? Your focus? Hello?*

Tuning back in, he forced himself to listen to young Tom's pitch. When the hour was up, and the boy had left, Harold sat back in his chair and puffed on his cigar. "Want one?"

"Sure." Joe took the cigar and lit it. Drawing on it calmed him.

"What do you think?" Harold asked.

"His proposition doesn't interest me much."

Harold frowned. "Why?" He puffed some more. "Not that I'm questioning your judgment. You're almost always right about these things."

"There's something missing in his vision."

"Usually, you get a little more information before you decide. Get to know their backgrounds and aspirations."

"I know." He stared after the young man. "I'm not interested this time. You can do it if you want."

Harold didn't answer.

"What?" Joe asked when the silence was prolonged.

"I repeat, this isn't like you."

After inhaling on his cigar, he studied it. "I know. I'm preoccupied with this Allheart deal."

"Is it going well?"

Yeah, if I could forget what her mouth felt like on mine, the scrape of her teeth on my skin, her hands . . . damn it! "Yes, it's going well. Things are about ready to wrap up."

"Good." Harold studied him. "Have you liked working with Elyssa Wentworth?"

"Yes. She's brilliant." *And beautiful, and so sexy it makes me want to punch something.*

"I thought maybe she was giving you a hard time."

A thousand puns came to mind, bringing a smile to his lips. "No, she isn't. But I've been spending a lot of hours with her. It'll be good to be freed up again, when this is over."

"How long before that happens?"

"Just one more day ought to do it, then I can write my proposal."

"Good. We're looking forward to seeing it."

"I'm looking forward to being done with all of it."

He *was*.

And once he was finished with Allheart's analysis, it would be easy to forget about what Elyssa Wentworth felt like pressed hard against him.

It *would*.

"Carole and I are done with Allheart's market research analysis." Once again, Joe stood in Elyssa's doorway, afraid to enter the office.

She was at the window, and he smiled at how she breathed in the fresh air. Sometimes, he thought—rather whimsically— that she should have been an outdoor camp counselor. She pivoted at the sound of his voice. He'd watched her get progressively more somber as the week went on and knew her sadness mirrored his own. It was why he sent her the card today. She needed a boost. She needed to know she could do this.

They both did.

He gripped the doorjamb. "Well, I'm off."

"Fine." She glanced at the clock.

Something made him ask, "Do you have plans?" *Oh God, please don't let her say she has a date. With her lawyer. Or anybody.*

She shook her head. "You?" she asked hoarsely.

"No, not tonight."

It seemed to calm her. Lord, how had this gone so far? That they would be relieved neither had a date. He felt a little as if he were going under for the third time and couldn't gain purchase on the ship's wreckage.

She turned back to the window. "You'd better go."

"I know."

He stayed rooted to the ground.

Her head bent and she rubbed her eyes.

"I'll, um, call you next week," he told her. "When we've finished our information gathering."

"Fine." He could hear the unspoken *Just go.*

"I'll talk to you then."

She nodded.

He turned.

Took a step toward the outer door.

Took another one. Two.

And then something snapped inside of him. His willpower. His self-control. His belief that he could direct his emotions and his feelings like he directed board meetings or corporate takeovers.

He simply couldn't do this.

Freed by the admission, he circled back around, strode across the threshold of her office and slammed the door.

She startled, then stiffened, but didn't face him. He was behind her in seconds.

His hands grasped her shoulders gently. His mouth was in her hair. "I can't do it, Lyss. I just can't."

She drew in a deep breath. Let it out. "Neither can I," she said simply.

"I'll kill the deal."

She whirled around. "No! I won't let you do that."

"What then?"

She faced him squarely. "Take me home, Joe."

Joe knew that once he touched her — really touched her — he wouldn't be able to stop. So they were careful not to bump against each other as they hurried out of the office, careful to take opposite sides of the elevator, careful to remain distanced when he opened the car door for her. They didn't hold hands on the way home.

They didn't even speak. Afraid, he guessed, to break the fragile threads of their control.

He took little notice of the entry to the building where she lived. Instead he kept his eyes fixed on something ahead of him, willing his mind to blank, to *not* think about all the reasons he shouldn't be doing this.

But once the door closed in the large, airy living room of her home, he was on her. With no finesse, with no tender wooing, he crushed her to him and took her mouth. It was willing, *she* was willing, and he ruthlessly took what she had to give.

He plundered her. With his lips and with his hands. They

raced everywhere, tearing off the jacket she wore, ripping at
the buttons of her pretty shirt. He had a quick conscious
recognition of black lace and overflowing cups before he released the catch on her bra and she spilled into his hands. "Oh,
my God," he said as he held her full and hot in his palms for
the very first time.

His head lowered and she cried out, "Joe!" when he took a
nipple into his mouth.

"What, baby? Tell me what you want."

She moaned, once, twice, three times; his hands continued
their exploration. He worked his way down her body, kissing
each rib, tonguing her navel. Her skirt unzipped and he
dragged it and the scrap of black lace that passed for panties
off her in one fell swoop. Then he buried his face in her stomach. "Lyss," he murmured again.

The room spun around her. The feel of his hands and his
mouth—everywhere—thrilled her to an almost unconscious
state, where, paradoxically, she became aware of every single
detail. He braced her against the wall and she felt the hard
wood of the door against her bare back. On his knees, his
mouth took love bites out of her stomach. She continued the
sexual chorus, a whimper when he nuzzled the damp curls at
her thighs, a long low groan when he closed his lips over her,
and then, quickly, too quickly, a series of screams when he
sent her over the edge.

She would have fallen had his hands not gripped her hips
tightly. Her fingers scraped through his hair and she tried to
pull him up to face her. He wouldn't be budged. He began
again, and she knew she should protest. It should be them together, but she came too quickly, like a pot bubbling over fast
and furiously. This time she *did* begin to slide down to the
floor. Still holding onto her, he rose.

Dimly she was aware that he was clothed. She started to
speak, but he kissed her quiet. She melted into him bonelessly.
"I like you like this," he whispered in her ear as he picked her
up. Never before had she been carried by a man but it felt right
pressed against his shiny suit, arms draped around his neck.

"Which way?" He wasn't in control. His voice held a desperate edge that she reveled in; his limbs were shaky too.

"Upstairs, to the right."

He catapulted up the steps, kicked open the door and stumbled unsteadily to the bed. He sat her down and she wrapped herself around him, burying her face in his waist. Her hand came up and cupped him through his trousers.

His moan echoed in the spacious room.

"Off," she said almost incoherently. She yanked at his belt. Though her fingers fumbled, she tore open the buckle, tugged down his zipper and slid her hands inside.

"Hmm," she whispered, her lips against the skin of his abdomen. He felt all male and smelled all musky and it made her mouth more urgent. From her vantage point, she saw his suit coat drop, then heard his buttons pop, but she was busy fondling him, caressing him, drawing out a groan here, a curse there.

"Oh. Shit. Lyss. God. Don't. Please." His shirt and tie fell to the floor; he drew away, briefly bent over to remove his shoes and socks and the pile of clothes at his feet.

And then he slid her back on the dark blue silk duvet and covered her.

Joe had never, in his entire life, felt like he felt when their bodies met for the first time, unclothed and without barriers— especially the emotional ones. Every curve, every angle of her found a place to meld with him. He fisted his hands in her hair and took her mouth again, ravenous for her. His heart pounded in his chest as her passion rose again, even after the two times out in the living room, he thought with primitive male satisfaction.

"I want you," he whispered against her mouth. "I want to have you. Possess you. Just me. Nobody else." He knew it was brutish, and somewhere in his mind he realized that Elyssa Wentworth, CEO, would balk at his words. But tonight she was just Lyss, the woman he'd craved for days, weeks. He didn't care how he sounded, how much control he'd lost.

"I want you too." Her hand slid between them and grasped him firmly. He jolted back. "Now."

Now was all he could think as he parted her thighs and slid into her. His body merged with hers, was consumed by hers, assimilated into hers. And nothing had ever been as good. Without conscious thought, surely not of his own volition, he began to thrust. She arched against him, sheathed him inside, then locked her legs around him.

He started to come, just before she did. The cataclysm hit them hard, and they both cried out together as his mouth closed over hers.

*She looked like a pagan goddess propped against the head*board, her hair flowing over her shoulders and curling around barely-concealed breasts. He'd wrapped her up in the sheets, after he'd stroked her back silently for more than a half an hour as they lay together in bed.

And now for the piéce de résistance.

From where he sat at the foot of the bed, he held her gaze and picked up her foot. He started with the arch. Her eyes turned a slumberous green before they closed. "Ohhhhh."

He kissed her toes, and kneaded a little harder. "Did I ever tell you how much I like the way these feet look in those shoes you wear?"

An eye opened. "Do you?"

His fingers moved to her heel. "If you keep wearing them, I'll do this for you every day."

"Hmmm. It's a deal."

He put his mouth on her ankle. "Easily persuaded, aren't you?"

"You could make me do anything." The words slipped out past defenses lowered by the intimacy of sex and the gentleness that came afterward.

He continued to massage. "Me too, baby, you can make me do anything too."

Her mouth curved up. He noticed her lips were swollen and it gave him a small sexual jolt. "You're going to have to stop calling me that. It isn't, well, right."

"I'll stop. But later."

He rubbed each toe, taking his time, watching her bask in the almost-carnal pleasure it gave her.

Intent on her foot, he didn't see that she'd opened her eyes again and was staring at him until he glanced up. "God, you look good," she said, eyeing his nudity and probably the chaotic state of his hair.

He'd never cared too much about his looks. They were always there, and mostly admired. But tonight, he cared, if for only the pleasure they gave her. He cocked an arrogant brow. "You like what you see?"

Her laugh was husky. "Can't you tell?"

He kissed her instep. "I can tell," he murmured and reached for her.

She had him against the headboard, now. He looked like a sultan, lounging amidst navy pillows, a blue and white striped sheet barely draping his hips.

And she felt a little like a harem girl who would, as she'd said, do whatever he asked. Because the thought scared her, she banished it. "Open up."

He opened his mouth. She shoveled sushi from a tin container and into his mouth. After chewing, he asked, "Where did you learn how to use chopsticks?"

Maybe geisha was a better analogy, given the takeout they'd finally ordered at midnight. Scooping up rice, she fed herself some, then him. "I'm a woman of many talents."

He laughed. By tacit agreement, the problems caused by what they'd done tonight—and probably would do again—were shelved. "I know, I've got your fingerprints all over me, sweetheart."

Sweetheart? Had anyone ever called her that? Her heart beat double time at the small endearment. Seductively she scanned his body. "Good."

"Give me more food, then. I'm famished." She fed them both for a few minutes, the silence broken only by the "mmms . . ." Then she reached over and picked up the glass of champagne they'd been sharing. She sipped it, put it to his lips. His blue eyes darkened to match the pillows as he placed his lips over where she'd drunk from. When she set the glass down, picked up the container and reached for the chopsticks, he took her hand.

Gently he held it in his. Raised it. Kissed it in the tenderest of gestures that clogged her breath and stole her heart. "Do you know how happy I am right now?"

She thought about joking, about indicating his state of semi-arousal and making some sexual tease. But his eyes were serious. They said, *Don't spoil it, at least for tonight. Let me have your heart too.*

So she whispered softly, "Me, too. I'm happy too."

Without releasing her gaze, he took the container from her and returned it to the nightstand.

Then he lowered her to the bed.

Chapter 5

"*Studies show there are three favorite things in life: a martini before* and a nap *after*. Thanks for giving me my three favorite things, Joe."

In keeping with their Jekyll and Hyde personas the past week, he sent Elyssa the card on her home computer late Sunday night after spending the entire weekend with her. From the Subtly Sexy line which had been Carole's brainchild, the greeting was snappy and sexy enough to make her toes tingle as she read it, thinking about the weekend they'd shared . . .

Saturday morning had dawned bright and beautiful in the nation's capital. And in Elyssa's bedroom. After declaring that their lovemaking should go down in the *Guinness Book of Records*—Joe Monteigne didn't suffer from a lack of confidence, that was for sure—he'd suggested they shower together. It had been a decadent experience that would cause Elyssa never to view the small stall in quite the same way again. Then they'd dressed and headed to his place so he could change into clean clothes. There, they were detoured for an hour, at Joe's insistence that they see if it was as good in *his* bed. It was. Then he'd driven them out to Virginia in his third car—a sleek black Mercedes—and they stopped about an hour from where his parents lived, for one of the ubiquitous spring festivals occurring in the areas outside of the city. It was the choice of location that got them talking . . .

"Here you go, girl," he said, presenting her with a double scoop of pistachio ice cream with chocolate sprinkles on top.

She gave his dish a withering look. "Sorry, but lemon ice is not my idea of a treat." Scanning the area, she took in the vendors—in addition to food stalls, there were upscale outlets of beautiful lithographs, batik scarves and custom-made jewelry. Elyssa licked her cone unself-consciously. "This is a great place, Joe."

"My sisters love it. They dragged me here every year and taught me how to buy gifts for women."

"Hmm, a skill all men should cultivate."

Reaching over, he squeezed her hand. They sat under a leafy oak tree, on a two-person bench, separated from the crowd. She'd never seen him in jeans before, and they looked like a million bucks with the blue polo shirt that made his eyes the color of the sky. "I figured you'd want to be outside, but you wouldn't want to see anyone you knew. So I thought of this place."

She held his gaze. "We're going to have to talk about it, aren't we?"

He stared ahead at a set of parents with twins in a stroller. The father had his arm around the mother, and she him, as they each pushed the sleeping children in the pram. "Yes. I just don't want to spoil anything." He stared at her earnestly. "Last night was . . . the best, Lyss."

A shy smile breached her lips. "For me too."

"I think we can separate it."

"Sex and work?"

He shifted uncomfortably. "Let's call it our personal relationship and our business one."

So, as the spring air surrounded them, bathing them in its warmth, they discussed how they might keep work and their personal lives apart: no touching when they were together in the office—and no goofy looks, Elyssa had said, embarrassed by the longing she'd felt for him the weeks before. They would try to avoid each other during working hours for a while too, and pledged not to argue over whatever went on at the office. And, much to his dismay, she insisted that on weeknights, they not stay overnight with each other. Joe hadn't liked that, but he'd reluctantly agreed to her suggestion.

The following Wednesday morning was the first test of their separation of church and state, as she'd come to think of it. His voice had rumbled over the phone; its sexy baritone caused her to shiver, though she'd just seen him the night before. Maybe *because* she'd seen him the night before. "I'd like to meet with you today about Allheart's references."

References? Could there be a problem with the company's customers? "Fine. What time?"

"About ten is good for me. Can you ask Carole to be there?"

"Sure. See you then."

Elyssa willed herself not to worry as the morning progressed. When he arrived, punctual as a school bell, she was working with Carole in the conference room on a new account.

He strode in, all business. Today he wore a lightweight navy jacket and khaki pants, with a navy silk T-shirt underneath. His outfit made her mouth water. She'd seen him naked, and dressed in thousand-dollar suits, and then in jeans, but this particular casual look sent her pulse spinning. "Hi," she said hoarsely.

"Hi." He smiled blankly at her. "Morning, Carole."

"Hello, Joe."

Tossing a folder on the table, he sat down without invitation. "Want coffee?" Elyssa asked.

"No, thanks. I'm short on time."

She straightened in her chair. "Then let's get to the point."

He nodded to the file. "I have questions on two accounts that you didn't sign up to advertise on your website. That's why I wanted you here, Carole." He drew out the papers. "The Griffith Perfume account and Bancroft Cosmetics." He zeroed in on the sales manager. "Why didn't you snag them?"

Carole rolled her eyes. "We suffered over those," she said succinctly. "Griffith wanted ads that were a little too sexy for our market segmentation."

A dark eyebrow arched. "Why couldn't you use it on the sexier lines?"

"Elyssa suggested that. Griffith wouldn't go for it. He wanted all or nothing."

"Hmm." Joe scowled. "How about Bancroft?"

"We dropped the ball on it." Elyssa jumped in, trying not to sound defensive. "It was a simple matter of bad timing. He went with someone else."

Joe asked, "Were efforts made to woo him back?"

Elyssa stiffened. At the time, they'd been knee-deep in advertisers clamoring for spots. "We didn't need to."

"You should have," he said matter-of-factly. "If we make this deal, I'd like you to go back and pursue both of these accounts."

Neither woman spoke. Carole finally broke the silence.
"I'm game."

After a long pause, Elyssa agreed.

Abruptly Joe stood. "Good. The rest of the references
check out. The names you gave us, as well as the others we
picked on our own. I'm almost done with my research. I plan
to meet with my partners next week and have an offer ASAP."

"Good," Elyssa said, watching him walk to the door.

"Have a nice day, ladies," he called out, his back to them.
He gave a negligent wave over his shoulder and disappeared
out the door.

Carole stared after him. "Is it?"

"What?"

"Good that we'll have an offer from Highwire?"

"Yes." Elyssa's gaze was locked on the doorway, thinking
Joe was like a tornado who breezed into your life and wreaked
havoc in a matter of minutes.

But only if she let him.

"Elyssa, are you going to be able to handle this kind of in-
terference?" Carole asked.

"I don't honestly know."

"For what it's worth, so far, in my opinion, his ideas are
pretty sound."

"Yes, they are. I'm just concerned he's going to blow in
here like this when the spirit moves him and try to run the
place."

"If you have controlling shares, he can't, can he?"

"He can try, I guess, but finally, no." She tapped her pen on
the desk and bobbed her slingback shoe up and down.
"Though we'd be stupid not to seek his advice. He's a brilliant
strategist. It's why I thought we should go with Highwire."

"It'd be a battle, but it would be worth it, right?"

"Maybe," she said, ignoring the knot in her stomach his
visit had caused. "But we'll work it out."

"How's the other?"

Rotely gathering up her material, Elyssa purposely didn't
make eye contact with her friend. "The other?"

"You know, what's really going on between you two. All
that electricity in the air."

She stood. "It's not an issue," she said succinctly and
walked out of the room.

* * *

"Stay." Joe was poised over her, his arms braced on either side of her head. He was still inside her, his body thrumming from the physical roller-coaster ride she'd taken him on for the past half-hour. His heart thudded in his chest.

Smiling up at him, she brushed back his hair and linked her hands at his neck. "I can't. It's Thursday. We have jobs to go to tomorrow morning."

"You don't have a meeting until nine. Plenty of time to scoot home and dress."

Her pretty brow furrowed. He soothed the lines on her forehead with his thumbs. "We agreed," she said, seeming a little irritated.

He wondered if it had anything to do with his constructive criticism yesterday. Of course they hadn't talked about that. Discussion of work on personal time would breach their professional Mason-Dixon line.

He drew in a breath. "I know."

"We decided not even a week ago."

His forehead met hers. "I realize that. But the best executives reevaluate their decisions occasionally."

"We're not executives in the bedroom."

Tension crept into his body. He wasn't exactly sure why. She hadn't said anything he hadn't already agreed on. Perhaps he was unhappy because, as the days passed, he wanted more from her.

Which wasn't good at all.

So he rolled off of her. "Fine." He picked up the TV remote and clicked the television on. "I'll call you a cab when you're ready."

He surfed the channels, not really watching anything as he became absorbed in his own thoughts. Sure, he was getting involved. Fast. His defenses had been lowered by six straight nights with her in his bed, and as many days with her occupying his mind. He didn't like it, but it wasn't a big deal. When their relationship ended, he'd be just fine, like always.

She seemed perfectly happy being the corporate Dr. Jekyll during the day and turning into a sexual Mr. Hyde at night.

You agreed too, asshole. He kicked off the covers.

"Is something wrong?" she asked.

"No, why?"

"You seem restless."

He glanced at the clock. "Actually I'm tired."

"Oh. Sure." She threw back the sheets. "I'll leave, then."

Watching her tug on underwear, then slacks and a shirt, he felt anger surge inside him. He *really* didn't want her to leave, but was powerless to stop her.

Shit. Their relationship was only a few days old. This was *not* good. He reached for the phone to call the damn taxi.

In the entryway to her apartment, Joe scowled down at her feet.

"What's wrong?" she asked at his frown.

"We're going to The National Gallery for that outdoor cocktail party."

"Yes, I know." Her brows raised. "Am I not dressed right?" She eyed his casual off-white blazer, matching T-shirt and doe-skin pants. Then she looked down at her own steel-gray shantung pantsuit and strappy Valentino sandals.

"It isn't that," he said, taking a quick tour of her body.

"What is it then?"

He jammed his hands in his pockets, a gesture she noticed he affected when he was unhappy with something. "Nothing."

"Joe?"

Casually, he shrugged. "I was just thinking that those shoes aren't going to be comfortable, um, standing in them all night. You might want to change."

She smiled sexily. "You said you loved what these kind of shoes do to my legs."

"I do."

"And if I'd wear them every day, you'd—"

"I know what I said," he snapped.

Angling her head, she watched him. He looked angry. "What's going on, Joe?"

Raking a hand through his hair, he stared over her shoulder, as if he were considering confessing to a crime. "I don't like what's happening here."

Her heartbeat escalated. She'd told herself a thousand times what was between them was temporary. She just hadn't thought it would end so soon. It had only been little over a week. Her self-protective nature told her to pull back into her shell, seek armor against the emotional battering she was going to take, but that wasn't her style. Elyssa the CEO was tougher than that.

But Elyssa the woman was turning into Jell-O, and fast losing her defenses against the troubled man before her.

That notion made *her* angry. "Look," she said, exasperated by her weak knees and pounding heart. "If you have something to say, just say it." She folded her arms across her chest. "After all, it won't affect our business deal."

"Ah, the all-important business deal."

"I'm confused."

"So am I! That's the problem." He started to pace—leaving the foyer and covering the length of the living room rug a couple of times.

Elyssa watched him, appreciating his long strides and masculine grace even as she told herself she could let him go at any time.

"Aw, shit," he finally said, turning back to her. "I'm worried about the shoes you're wearing, Elyssa. A week ago, all that mattered was that they turned me on." He gave her a little-boy smile and shrugged all-male shoulders. "Now, I'm more concerned that you're comfortable tonight."

It took her a minute to understand what he was saying to her. And, against her better judgment—she would have willed the feeling away if she could—a tiny bud of warmth blossomed inside her and spread through every internal organ and out to every limb and nerve ending in her body. "I see. You're worried about my *comfort*. And that bothers you, doesn't it?" she asked.

He looked forlorn. Embarrassed. "Yeah. Go ahead and laugh."

She *should* joke; she should tease him about turning into an old fogey. It would keep things light between them.

But nobody except Elliot ever worried about her. So instead of sloughing off his words, and what they meant about the direction their relationship was taking, she stared down at her feet.

And kicked off her sandals.

When she looked back up, his brows were raised.

When she launched herself at him, he caught her firmly to his chest.

When she whispered in his ear, "Forget the art show," he shook his head, laughed into her hair, picked her up and headed for the bedroom.

Neither spoke again for a long time. Enough had been said, with and without words.

"*Ah . . . choo!*"

Seated across from him at the restaurant in the Four Seasons Hotel, Elyssa glanced up from the menu to Joe. Surrounded by the elegant atmosphere, listening to the piano music, she looked terrific in her sleek white suit and gold necklace disappearing into the low neckline of the one-button jacket. "Bless you."

"Thanks." He shook his head; he'd been fighting the cold for days and it had won. Between late nights with her, and finishing up the plan he was going to present to his partners tomorrow, he'd been burning the proverbial candle at both ends and his resistance was down.

"Are you all right?"

"Yes, of course."

Cocking her head, she studied him carefully. "You don't look so hot."

"Be careful, all that flattery will go to my head." He sneezed again.

"Your head's too filled with a cold to make room for flattery. Why didn't you just say you didn't feel well? We didn't have to go out tonight."

But he'd wanted to go out. He'd needed to see her. To assure himself they were going to weather the next few weeks. Together.

Taking another long look at him, she straightened, turned and signaled the waiter.

"What are you doing?"

The waiter hustled over. "We'd like our check, please."

"Is something wrong?" the man asked.

"No, the drinks were fine. This gentleman isn't feeling well." She handed the guy a credit card. "Thank you."

"Elyssa, why did you do that?"

"Tell me honestly, do you really feel like eating duck à l'orange tonight?"

"I *really* feel like a bowl of chicken broth."

She chuckled. "Even *I* can handle that," she said, rising. "Come on, I'm taking you home."

It seemed as if she'd given the cold permission to rage. His symptoms worsened as she negotiated the streets of Georgetown in his BMW. By the time they were at his town house, his skin was clammy and he felt light-headed.

She stepped inside behind him and closed the door.

"I've got to lie down," he said, weaving a bit.

"Come on."

His weight was too heavy as he leaned on her and stumbled up the steps. Once in the bedroom, he batted her hands away and shucked his own clothes.

"Well, that's a first," she quipped as he tugged off boxers and she turned down the bed.

"What?" He climbed into the sheets and she covered him with a light blanket.

"You wouldn't let me undress you."

"Oh, man, I feel awful."

Her brow furrowed and she laid her palm against his cheek. "You're hot. Should I call a doctor or something?"

"It's a cold, honey. And I'm exhausted. I'll be fine in the morning." He grasped her hand. "I hope you don't get it."

"I never get sick."

"The germs wouldn't dare get near you."

She smiled.

And tended to him. She brought him nighttime cold medicine guaranteed to make him sleep, along with chicken soup she'd fixed from a can. When he balked at eating, she threatened to force-feed him. He downed most of the broth, ate a couple crackers, then his eyes drooped. "I need to go to sleep." His words were slurry.

"Yes," she said dryly, "I can tell."

"Lock up when you leave."

She kissed his forehead. "Don't worry, I'll take care of everything."

His eyes closed. "Lyss?"

"Hmm?"

"Thanks."

The last thing he heard was her soft chuckle.

The morning light woke him. His head was clear. And his limbs were back to normal. He rolled over in the bed. And froze.

She was on the couch across the room, curled up in one of his light blue shirts. Her long lean legs had kicked off the blankets and her hands rested lightly under her head. Her hair fell in tangles around her face. She looked so sexy, it made him ache.

That he wanted to cherish her and ravish her at the same time immobilized him for a minute.

She'd stayed the night because he was ill, he acknowledged soberly. *How the mighty have fallen,* he thought, watching her. But he was grateful she had stayed.

This was not good. He lay on his back and stared up at the ceiling fan. Especially not today. He had to give a presentation to his partners, and he shouldn't be feeling all these soft and fuzzy things for the CEO of the company he was making million-dollar decisions for.

But in two short weeks, everything had changed. Linking his hands behind his neck, he hoped he could balance the two separate parts of his life. Of their lives.

Determined, he threw off the covers, bolted off the mattress, crossed to the couch and scooped her up in his arms. She snuggled up to him and he carried her to his bed where he awakened her with hot kisses full of promise.

The next night Elyssa rolled over in bed —alone— annoyed by the slide of satin on her skin. Everything was annoying tonight. Darkness, invaded only by the sliver of moon sneaking though her blinds, allowed her to admit her restlessness was because of Joe.

It was becoming increasingly harder to leave him at night, or to let him go when they were together at her house. And she was worried about tomorrow, when he'd present his offer to his partners, then submit it to her.

Though she believed in her heart his proposal would be fair, and acceptable—she'd come to know and trust Joe, after all—something nagged at her. He'd been preoccupied at dinner, and they'd gone their separate ways afterward without making love. Which was all right. It was only yesterday morning, after she'd stayed because he was ill the night before, that he'd made her soar in his bed. Their lovemaking had been tender, almost painfully so, and a deeper, more intimate connection had been established. Maybe that was it. The *quality* it had taken on was disturbing.

Sighing, she turned over yet again. *Go to sleep. You need your wits about you tomorrow.*

She was counting sheep when the doorbell rang. Glancing at the clock—it read two A.M.—she bolted out of bed. Elliot? Someone from work? Her heart pounding, she raced down the stairs to the foyer.

She peered through the peephole and her worry dissipated, but not the pounding of her heart. It was Joe on the other side. She whipped off the locks and threw open the door. He stood there, in a rumpled, light blue chambray shirt, khaki pants and Topsiders. His hair was mussed. A growth of beard shadowed his jaw. But it was his eyes that drew her. They were a deep and dangerous blue.

He scanned her tiny black nightgown. He took a long perusal of her bare legs. Gooseflesh raised all over her.

"Did I wake you?" Even his voice was dark and gravelly.

"No."

Without invitation, he stepped across the threshold. "Then you're having the same problem as I am." His back was still to her when she closed the door and circled around. He stretched his arm out for her hand. "Come on."

Meekly—God, what had gotten into her?—she clasped his hand with hers, only minimally calmed by the linking of their fingers. She let him lead her to her bedroom. Once there, he sat on the edge of the mussed mattress and tangled sheets. She stood before him, like a gift waiting to be unwrapped. He raked her with a heated gaze. "Take it off."

She was startled by his arrogant command, but found she felt a spark of excitement flicker inside her. Slowly she slid the strap off one shoulder.

His hands fisted.

Off the second.

His eyes narrowed. She let the slip fall, revealing the tops of her breasts.

He swallowed hard.

Crossing her hands at her waist, she lifted the garment by the hem and drew it slowly over her head, making chaos of her hair.

He exhaled a ragged breath.

She bit back a smile and his eyes darkened when he saw it. "The rest." He was not amused.

Smooth black silk slithered down her legs. She stepped out of her negligee.

Unable to remember if she'd ever in her life posed naked like this before anyone, she knew she should be embarrassed. Maybe even scared. But she wasn't. She straightened her shoulders and tossed back her hair.

Joe thought he might swallow his tongue when she stood before him undressed like this. He didn't know exactly what had brought him here tonight, or what goaded him to play tough guy and demand that she strip for him. All he knew was that the desire to possess her, totally and without restraint, pounded through his body and had driven him out into the night to find her.

Slowly he stood.

She didn't move. He unbuttoned his shirt without unlocking his gaze from hers. She held it—no flinching, no blushing, not even a glimmer of reservation in her eyes.

The shirt dropped to the floor. With his pants. She noticed he hadn't bothered with underwear. Kicking out of his shoes and clothes, he straightened.

They eyed each other like animals. "Come," he said hoarsely.

She stepped toward him. When she was close enough, he tunneled his fingers through her tangle of hair. She winced, and he lightened his grasp. "Do you want me?"

"Yes."

"How much?"

She melded their lower bodies. "As much as you want me."

"Impossible," he said against her lips.

In seconds they were on the bed.

Covering her, pressing his weight into her, he ravaged her mouth; then he devoured her breasts. His hands gripped her hips.

They rolled over and she sat astride him and began working her hands down the length of his body. He moaned, groaned, and whispered a curse when her fingers closed around him. Then her mouth.

He let the torture go on for only seconds, then pulled her to him and turned her onto her back. Unable to control himself or the desire gushing out of him, he thrust inside her.

She cried out.

He grunted, groaned, couldn't keep back the sounds of passion. Words eluded him, but he claimed her as surely as if vows had been spoken.

She was his. Tonight. And tomorrow.

With his body, he strove to ensure that nothing that happened from here on out would ever make her doubt it.

Highwire Industries was located in Georgetown, not far from the Allheart offices. An old brownstone that had been refurbished in what they'd called *brass and glass*, it sported spacious offices and a conference room with sleek lines and smooth cold wood. As Joe sat across from his four partners, he assured himself everything was going to go as planned.

He'd stayed true to his principles and presented the offer as it should be, without bias.

Maybe *too much* without bias.

The thought had struck him as he'd outlined his ideas. Had he not been involved with Elyssa, and afraid of making concessions because of that, would he have hedged the deal some, asked for less because he knew the founder wouldn't go for what he proposed? Had he overcompensated for the sake of his integrity?

No, he didn't think so.

Jesus Christ, he hoped not.

Martin Stanton commented first. Having waited until everyone finished reading the proposal, he said, "As usual, you've done a remarkable job, Joe." The president of a large university, he was one of Joe's biggest supporters and had backed Joe on numerous presentations.

"Thank you, Martin."

"I have a couple of questions; should I propose them now?"

"Fine by me."

"Will you sit on their board of directors?"

That's probably not a good idea. "Yes, I'd like to."

"How apt is the founder to go with your percentage split?"

"In all truth, I think she'll balk. But we're prepared to go for broke and back off only a little if necessary."

A cigar-smoking lawyer who managed some union pension funds snorted. "I know about this chick. She'll try to get you by the balls, Monteigne."

She already has. An image of Elyssa kneeling between his legs swept through his mind. He banished the thought.

"I think I can hold my own with her, but thanks for the warning, Howard. I am assuming I have the authority to renegotiate—throw her a bone or two if I have to."

"Yes, but you're prepared to play hardball, if necessary, aren't you? Even if it means walking away?" This from a female partner, Mary Lou Lawrence, who Joe respected and admired.

Without blinking an eye, he said, "Definitely."

For another hour he answered questions, and they discussed alternatives if indeed the Queen of Hearts balked at their offer. At noon, when they had a backup plan, he stood. "If I have the go-ahead, I'll try to meet with her today." For some reason he felt the need to get this over with. They'd made plans to go to Annapolis this weekend, had rented a cottage and were going to spend some time at the famous City Dock and take in the commercial boat show. He wanted to have this behind him.

"You have the go-ahead," Martin said. "You've done a good job," he repeated.

Joe's smile was thin. "Thanks. I'll be in touch." As he left the conference room, he struggled not to feel so . . . compromised.

He and Elyssa Wentworth, CEO, had agreed that business was business.

They had agreed to not let their personal relationship interfere with this deal.

But as he headed to her office, the picture of *Lyss*, all warm in his bed—where he'd carried her this morning and awakened her with hot kisses—remained with him. He wasn't looking forward to meeting with her alter ego today.

Elyssa's hands were unsteady as she opened the proposal folder. Joe stood by the window in her office and she had the uneasy feeling he was bracing himself for something. Once again, he was in a crisp navy Armani today—a power suit, she noticed. She tried not to read into the way he was dressed. She too, wore Armani, a favorite outfit of muted gray and white.

Taking a deep breath, she began to read his outline. About halfway down the page, her heartbeat kicked up. Two-thirds of the way through the document, her stomach clenched. By the time she finished reading, it was churning like a washer on spin cycle.

Setting the paper down, she looked up at him. He was watching her carefully.

No wonder.

To still them, she clasped her hands in front of her and willed herself to remain calm. "Well, it's obvious that our personal relationship didn't affect your decisions here at all."

"That's what we agreed on."

"Yes, we did. Tell me, where in all our *business* discussions did you get even the slightest inkling that I'd go for a sixty-forty deal with Highwire in control of Allheart?"

"For the many millions of dollars we're talking about here it's a given."

"Clearly, somewhere along the line, you've misunderstood. Under no circumstances will I ever concede to relinquishing control of Allheart to Highwire."

His hands jammed into his pockets. "Don't be rash, Elyssa. Take time to consider this."

"Don't you *dare* condescend to me. You've known from the start I wouldn't give up control. It was the first thing I told you, day one."

"*You* didn't realize we were talking about so much money."

Though she knew the answer to her question—she'd done her own research—she asked it anyway. "Does Highwire ever make deals where the split is in favor of the founder?"

"Occasionally. But I repeat, *not* for that much money."

"I don't want that much money."

"You need it to follow the business plan."

"Alter the business plan."

"That's not in our best interest, nor yours."

"I don't care."

"Damn it, you *should* care. A good CEO *would* care."

She glanced at the document with visible disgust. "How could you include those untenable conditions?"

He looked genuinely puzzled. "What's untenable about them?"

Rapping impatiently on the proposal with her knuckles, she said, "Not only does Highwire get more shares than I do, but you want to be a part of all board-level decisions, have a say in who I hire to work directly for me, get *monthly* reports against my goals and *bimonthly* reports on implementation and financial results. This is crazy. I'd spend all my time reporting to you."

He faced her squarely. "It's the way business is done."

"Screw the way business is done. You knew from all our long, intimate *chats* that I'd never accept this." A snake of suspicion reared its ugly head and she was too upset to ignore it. "Which makes me wonder *why* you'd even propose this."

"I proposed this because it's my *objective* assessment of the best deal for Highwire." He arched an insufferable brow. "And for Allheart."

Which meant, of course, he did not have *her* best interest in mind. Which, ironically, was exactly what she'd asked for—no bias because of their personal relationship.

Elliot always said, *Be careful what you wish for, you just might get it.*

Because all of it stung so badly, she spoke without censoring her words. "Are you so sure of that, Joe?"

"What do you mean?"

"Are you sure you've proposed what you have—something you know absolutely I wouldn't accept—because it's best for Highwire? Or did you propose it because you thought you could sway me by having slept with me?"

His whole body tightened. His eyes went stone-cold. "I can't believe you'd suggest something like that."

"What else am I supposed to think?" Her voice rose a notch involuntarily. "It doesn't make sense any other way."

"It makes perfect sense; either you're more naive about business than I realized, or you're unaccountably insecure as a woman."

She sucked in a breath. "That's a low blow."

"No lower than the one you just delivered to me."

The words echoed ominously in the room.

Her spine stiffened. "I refuse your offer."

He raised his chin. "Don't you think you should consider it for a while?"

"No."

He stared her down. "Then I'm authorized to negotiate."

"Of course you are." She wasn't so naive after all.

"I'd like to do it today, if you can afford the afternoon."

Neither mentioned they'd planned, as they were wrapped around each other this morning, to take the afternoon off, drive up to Annapolis and spend the weekend.

"My afternoon is completely free." *Now.*

"Then roll up your sleeves, Ms. Wentworth. We've got work to do."

Hours later, they had a deal. Joe had spent the first ninety minutes biting an imaginary bullet to keep from railing on her about her accusation. By mid-afternoon, when the agreement began to gel, a kernel of doubt formed—*had* he asked for too much to begin with? Was he so afraid of succumbing that he'd gone for overkill? No, he wouldn't allow himself to think that way. He pushed aside the thought.

Finally the last *t* was crossed and the last *i* dotted. He stared coldly at the document. "Well, this looks hopeful. I'll have to meet with the board, of course." His eyes narrowed on her. "I can't say they'll accept all of it, but I can recommend it in good conscience."

"Fine. We wouldn't want your conscience to suffer."

"What's that supposed to mean?"

"Nothing."

"Damn her. He didn't need this crap right now. His nerves were stretched like a tightrope. "Are we done, workwise?"

"Yes."

Symbolically, he folded up the documents and put them in his briefcase; then he stood. He glanced out the window to where dusk had fallen. When he looked back at her, he saw mirrored in her face what he felt.

He said, "We won't be going to Annapolis this weekend." It wasn't a question.

"No."

They both knew too much had been said.

He picked up his briefcase. "I'll be in touch."

"You do that."

And, much as he had that first time he'd come to see her six weeks ago, he walked out of the office without a backward glance. He should feel good that he'd concluded the business deal he'd begun then.

It was what had ended, along with the negotiations, that threatened to level him. He strode out before that had a chance to happen.

"*Here's to our new partnership. One I'm sure will benefit* all of us." Martin Stanton raised his glass of Dom Perignon and toasted Elyssa, who stood across from him in Highwire's stunning offices.

Surrounding him were his lawyers, who'd just sealed a megabucks deal with Allheart.com's lawyer, Patrick O'Hare. Behind Martin hovered his partners, just as behind Elyssa, Carole, Alix, Dana and Robyn had accompanied her, dressed, like she, to the nines to celebrate this momentous occasion.

"To a long and prosperous partnership." Elyssa's words were strong and forceful, betraying none of the butterflies that were circling around her stomach like planes waiting to land. This was a great moment for her. She vowed to enjoy it and ignore the sinking feeling inside her.

Not because of the deal. She'd hammered out a good compromise eight days ago in her office with Joe. No, the stomach jitters were caused by the fact that this was the first time she'd see him. If he ever bothered to show up. When she'd arrived at the Highwire complex at seven, she'd been shocked to find him missing.

"Let's mingle and get to know each other," Martin continued. "And please, no champagne or hors d'oeuvres are to be left over." He patted his stomach. "My wife keeps me on a strict diet."

People began to mill around and talk. Elyssa turned to her coworkers, grateful for their professional expertise, but more so at the moment, that they were there as moral support and to celebrate with her.

"Congratulations, Elyssa," Dana said with a big hug.

"Great outfit," Robyn told her.

Elyssa had dressed impeccably, as had all the others. She wore a deep navy silk jersey wrap dress, the color of midnight, really. It crisscrossed her chest to reveal just the appropriate amount of skin and fell softly to a dangerous spot just above her knees. Together with the elegant black patent leather slingbacks she wore, her outfit very subtly, but very effectively forced every person in the room to acknowledge her stunning legs. Carole liked to call this Elyssa's "take no prisoners" look.

"Geez, too bad Mr. Hot-and-Hunky isn't here to see this." Robyn scanned the conference room with big, anticipating eyes.

Elyssa cringed inwardly but forced a smile. "I find it very odd that after all his work on the deal he missed the signing of the contract."

From behind her, she heard, "Elyssa, my dear, didn't anyone tell you?"

Pivoting, she found Martin Stanton had come up to her. "Tell me?"

"Joe's plane's been held up. He's called several times about the delay; he should be here . . ."

"Right about now," Alix said breathlessly. All eyes tracked her gaze to the door.

Framed in the high oak archway, Elyssa admitted silently that Joe Monteigne was well-deserving of all the epithets her office staff had attributed to him: hunky hotshot, sexy as sin. Tonight, he was drop-dead gorgeous. His eyes scanned the room and then lit on her. Startlingly blue, standing out even more from a well-tanned face, they raked her from head to toe with a harsh gaze.

"Joe," Martin called out, motioning him over.

Joe approached them with long, masculine strides. Elyssa tried not to notice the slate blue shirt—with a few buttons undone—that he wore with jeans and a deep blue blazer. "Sorry I'm late," he said running a hand through his hair. "I couldn't believe the delays." He addressed Martin.

Then turned to her. "Elyssa, accept my apology. For my lateness and my dress. I came right from the airport." He held out his hand. She had no recourse but to shake it. Just that mere touch, after days of not seeing him or talking to him, made her heart thunder in her chest. She swallowed hard and smiled. A pulse leaped in his throat as he held her gaze for a long moment.

"These things happen, son," Martin said clapping Joe on the back. "How was the cruise?"

Joe greeted all the women warmly, then smiled at Martin. "It was great."

"Wish I had your stamina, Monteigne," a cigar-smoking man said from behind them. "Just after he finalized the deal with you, Elyssa, he booked a last-minute passage on the infamous SunSeas Singles Cruise and jumped on a plane."

How nice for him, Elyssa thought, her heart crumbling. She'd had a horrendous weekend after that Friday afternoon session, a horrible *week,* and he'd been partying with sun bunnies.

"Yeah? I read about those cruises, they're supposed to be so hot!" Robyn said sipping heartily from her glass. Elyssa made a mental note to cut off the champagne for her young assistant.

"Well, he needed a vacation." Martin smiled fondly at Elyssa. "Your boss here kept him hopping for weeks."

"That she did." Joe accepted a glass of champagne from a passing waiter and stared at her over the rim as he sipped. She was reminded of the champagne she'd served him on the bed that first night they'd made love.

"So, will you celebrate tonight with your friends, Elyssa?" Martin asked her.

"No, she has a date." This from Carole, whose eyes had been ping-ponging between her and Joe since his arrival.

A drop of champagne sloshed over the rim onto Joe's hand and his gaze hardened.

"Ah, there you are." Patrick O'Hare joined the crowd. The collective gaze of the women shifted as they took in his classic blond good looks. Joe's eyes narrowed on the man's hand as he rested it at the small of Elyssa's back. "We have reservations at nine, so we need to leave shortly."

She smiled up at her lawyer and let the ruse pass. A date for dinner was no match for SunSeas and a breathtaking tan, but it did allow her to save some face. And it would get her out of there, away from the cologne she never quite forgot the smell of, away from shoulders that dwarfed her. Joe looked so relaxed and content tonight, so tanned and fit. She would *not* think of what he'd done to stay fit on the ship.

"E, Joe asked you a question."

Her puzzled gaze focused on him. "I'm sorry, what was that?"

"I asked if we're still meeting tomorrow?"

She nodded, swallowing the lump in her throat at the coldness of his tone. He turned away from her to talk to someone who'd approached him, and she listened to the chatter among her coworkers and Highwire's best.

His coldness was deserved. She'd insulted him hugely, and considering how important his integrity was to him, she should have known better. In the eight days since their explosive meeting, she'd come to realize she'd overreacted. She should have seen that he had a responsibility to make the best deal for the firm, that in truth, his actions didn't reflect anything personal at all. And though the agreement they'd hammered out was more than satisfactory—she got her controlling shares, freedom to hire the executive staff and other concessions, while he got input into some major decisions—it seemed so sad that it was at the expense of their relationship.

After a few days, it had hit her that in trying so hard to separate their personal lives from their professional lives, they'd done exactly what they both had striven not to do. Let one affect the other.

"Excuse me," she said to the group. "I'd like to freshen up before I leave." With a phony smile pasted on her face, she headed for the powder room.

Feeling his eyes on her back, she held her chin high, nodded to people along the way and strode confidently out the door. Once inside the rest room, she repaired her lipstick and gave herself a pep talk; she felt better as she exited.

He was leaning indolently against the wall across from the bathroom, sipping champagne and waiting for her. Her heart leaped to her throat at the sight. He seemed bigger tonight, more male than ever before. Maybe it was the contrast of his casual clothes to everyone else's evening attire.

Lifting his glass, he saluted her. "To the Queen of Hearts," he said, a definite edge to his tone. "I'd offer you a sip to toast, but we're past that, aren't we?"

So, he remembered that night too.

Damn her, Joe thought, forcefully controlling his spontaneous reaction to her. She looked so beautiful in that dress.

Her hair was loose, styled as he liked it, in a mass of curls tumbling down her back. Her eyes were the color of a forest in the fall.

"Yes, we're past that," she said quietly. He expected pique, maybe sarcasm. Since *he* still felt that burning in his gut, he assumed she did too. Instead, she seemed a little vulnerable tonight.

It softened him. "You look wonderful."

"So do you." She swallowed hard.

He angled his head. "It's all done, then, signing the contracts, closing the deal."

"Yes." She smiled sadly. "It's all over but the shouting, as they say."

"Sorry I missed the big finale."

"Well, SunSeas beckoned." Ah, there was the sarcasm. He could handle that. "Did you have a good time?"

"Hey, as the slogan goes, everybody has fun with SunSeas."

She bit off some of the raspberry lipstick she'd just applied. "You didn't waste any time," she said tightly. "Martin said you left right after our meeting."

"Elyssa, there you are," her fancy lawyer called out from down the hall; he was dressed in a tux befitting her outfit. Joe remembered that she'd dated O'Hare before he and she had gotten together. His fist tightened at the thought.

Pushing off the wall, he inclined his head to the guy. "Neither did you," he spat out with a lethal glare just before O'Hare arrived. He blithely shook hands with the man.

"Are you ready, dear?"

Dear. How pompous.

"I'll just say good-bye to the partners." She stole a glance at Joe. "Then I'd very much like to get out of here."

Startled a bit by her curtness, O'Hare coughed to cover the tense silence.

"See you at the office tomorrow," Joe said silkily.

"Yes. Would you like to make it later?" She scanned his outfit and then rolled her eyes just the slightest bit. "Jet lag and all?"

"Nah," he said. "I spent a lot of time in bed on the cruise." With one last look at her and a final nod to her lawyer, Joe strode into the men's bathroom.

Once there, he kicked the wastebasket from one end of the room to the other.

* * *

"*You don't look good, Lyss,*" *Elliot said from beside her as* they walked along the canal.

Lyss. She had dreams about that name, and how Joe harshly uttered it, almost against his will, when he was making love to her.

Or when he whispered it in a tender moment. Those were worse to relive.

"Please, don't call me that."

Elliot strolled calmly beside her. They'd had dinner in Georgetown and were taking a short walk afterward. "It's not going so well?"

"It's torture." They moved closer to the canal and watched the ducks that had been quacking loudly; she remembered another stroll along here eons ago.

Tell me about where you grew up. How can I understand where you want to go if I don't know where you've been?

Elliot dragged out some bread he'd brought from the restaurant and fed it to the mallards. "Well, you got what you wanted, kiddo."

So, Elyssa Wentworth, what do you want out of life?

Basically, I want what I have now—I want to be able to keep it, I guess. My condo . . . My car. My clothes . . . My shoes, of course.

Oh, definitely those shoes have to stay.

"I got what I needed." She grabbed some bread and tossed it into the water. "So, fill me in on what's happening with you. We've concentrated on my life entirely too much lately."

Elliot smiled. "Well, my new position at the paper has garnered a lot of attention in the past several weeks."

"I've heard good reports from everybody." She reached over and squeezed his shoulder "And I've read all your stuff. It's great."

"The *New York Times* has approached me, Lyss."

"Approached you?"

"For a job."

Elyssa felt her insides go cold. She'd come to DC after college because Elliot was here. He'd settled here. She thought he'd always be here. "So you might leave DC?"

Abandoning the bread, he hugged her close and stared out

over the water thoughtfully. "I'm thinking about it. I don't know. I love Washington, but I'm stuck in a rut, probably because Sally was here. Emotionally, I wonder if a change isn't good."

Be there for him, she told herself. *Don't be selfish about this.*

"Then, tell me about the job. Let's discuss all the angles."

He stared down at her. "I thought you'd be upset. That you wouldn't want me to leave the area."

"I don't want you to leave. But I love you and I want what's best for you. Let's hear about it."

By the time Elyssa returned to her office, it was dark outside. Elliot had left her with a thank-you for helping him analyze his options, and with an admonishment to go home and not work late tonight, as she'd done consistently for the past two weeks. Instead of following his directive, she stumbled her way up to her office and made it inside before she reacted. Sinking down onto the couch, in the dark, in the utter stillness of the empty office, she let the emotion come.

Elliot might be leaving. Her rock. Her best friend.

One tear slipped out and she brushed it away impatiently. Another followed, then another. *It's your own fault, Elyssa. Elliot shouldn't be your best friend. Someone else should. A man you can love and build a life with.*

Joe's tanned face appeared in her mind's eye. Yesterday, meeting with him and the web designers had been excruciating. Her resistance had been lowered by fatigue because she'd dreamed all night about him frolicking on the cruise ship with bikini-clad nymphs.

I spent a lot of time in bed on the cruise.

Women would have fallen all over him, he looked so good with his tan. She'd never seen him in a bathing suit, but she had seen him good and naked. His powerful muscles and washboard flat stomach would beckon any woman's touch.

How many women had touched him since she had?

How many more would?

The notion drove her crazy.

Abruptly, she stood and crossed to the computer. Booted it up. And called up all the greeting cards he'd sent her in the past six weeks. Like a patient with a sore tooth that she kept probing with her tongue and making the pain worse, Elyssa read each one again.

She'd lost so much.

He was so clever. So insightful. So interesting.

And because of her obsession with Allheart, she'd blown it. *Allheart.* She scanned the room. The offices were beautiful. Her clothes were beautiful. As was her apartment, and her car, even her stock portfolio. Especially her stock portfolio. She had everything she ever wanted, and even if her brother did move, she'd still have him, though he wouldn't be the weekly company he'd been for years.

It isn't enough, Lyss. You know it isn't.

Depressed, she shut off her computer and watched the screen fade from brightly lit to dark. Standing, she trudged to the closet and pulled out a sweatsuit and a pillow and blanket.

She couldn't go home tonight, she thought as she changed into the sweats and sank onto the couch. There were too many memories there, too much to deal with. Sometimes she actually thought her bed still smelled like him. Always, she saw him wet and sexy in the shower. Or naked on her couch. Or in the kitchen. Wherever they'd made love.

No, tonight she'd sleep here at Allheart. It looked like this was all she had left.

Climbing into the makeshift bed, and just before her eyes closed, she thought, *How sad.*

"*Slow down, son. I can't keep up with you.*"

Joe cut his pace in half and glanced over at his father, who was indeed breathing too hard. "Sorry, Dad."

"You're running like one of the Furies is after you."

"Yeah, and her name's Elyssa." Joe smiled. It made him feel good to think of her as an ancient Greek shrew. It was better than the erotic dreams, or worse yet, the tender images that came to him in his waking hours. He was going crazy missing her.

"Didn't the cruise help?"

"Nope," he said breathing steadily. "It made things worse. All I could think about was her."

"I take it no one else caught your fancy."

Joe snorted remembering the blond bombshell who was all over him in the pool one day, the redhead who put the moves on him at the casino. But the worst was when he found himself checking out all the brunettes, and deciding one didn't have

Elyssa's graceful height, one's hair was too limp, one's eyes didn't sparkle like cat-eye marbles turning green or brown depending on the day.

But it was when he'd found himself searching for a pair of dynamite legs in designer shoes that he really got disgusted with himself. He would have flown home two days into the cruise if he could have gotten off the damn ship.

"Have you seen her since you got back?"

He nodded. "A few times. At the contract signing." Where he'd wanted to gobble her up, she looked so good. "And when we worked on the new website." Where she looked so stressed he'd wanted to take her home, massage her, and then make love to her until she promised she'd trust him, and herself, to make their relationship work.

"Have you tried to contact her personally?"

"Once." His blood ran cold just thinking about it. He'd called her last night, after hours of pacing and frustration. "She wasn't home. At nine," he said. Then waited. "Or at eleven. Or even at four A.M."

His father slowed to a walk. "Ah. So that's how it is."

"I guess." The knowledge that she was probably with another man twisted in his gut like a giant fist squeezing the life out of his emotions.

"Well, I guess you'd better get used to it."

Joe halted abruptly. "Huh?"

"You let her go, son. She's a beautiful woman. Did you think she'd live her life pining away for you?"

"No, of course not."

"You've admitted it's over, haven't you?"

"Yeah. Sure." He began to walk again. "It is."

A few paces down the road, his father said, "Joe?"

"Hmm?"

"You never could lie very well to me."

Joe chuckled.

"You still can't."

"Dad, it's hopeless."

Used to handling delicate situations, Ambassador J. Lance Monteigne socked his son on the arm and steered him toward a bench on their property. "Not if you don't let it be. Now, let's see what we can do about all this."

* * *

*E*lyssa removed her glasses and rubbed the bridge of her nose. "The line's pretty sappy, Dana," she said indicating the computer monitor that blinked before them.

"I know. That's why it'll be a success."

Studying her office staff, Elyssa smiled. "We have a pretty good market segment here. Let's see what everybody else thinks of it." She nodded to Dana, the writer. "All right, you're twenty-seven, relatively savvy with men, although I think you're ready for a new challenge. And you like this line. Why?"

"Because it lets you make up or compromise without groveling. It'll really appeal to men."

All men? Elyssa wondered, thinking of one in particular.

"I see." She smiled at her graphic designer. "How about the lovely Alix? Twenty-nine, lives with the love of her life. If you and Cal had a fight, would you use these cards?"

"Cal and I never fight!" Everybody snickered. "But, yes, I would. As Dana said, the words and the graphics convey a desire to compromise, not capitulate. Young moderns want this."

Maybe. Elyssa felt as old as Methuselah now, so perhaps that was why she couldn't see it.

"Robyn. You're the baby. Would you send these Allhearts?"

Robyn rolled her eyes. "I'd send *anything* to get, or get back, the man who makes me melt."

"You're no help," Elyssa told her affectionately. She turned to Carole.

"Well, being the elder stateswoman of the group at thirty-seven, I think it'll fly. The rest of you are right. It keeps the sender from being subservient, about which I know a great deal, and still lets him"—here she smiled at Elyssa pointedly—"or *her* ask for a second chance."

Sighing, Elyssa closed her notebook. "Fine. Can you send this to my office computer, Robyn? I'd like to look at it more carefully. But we'll go ahead and test the line."

Everybody cheered as she stood.

"E?" Robyn said.

"Yes?"

"Maybe we should ask Joe. He has a good sense of these things. And he's certainly another segment of the market."

Elyssa swallowed hard. "Sure. When's he due in again?"

"Next week."

"Fine."

"You could, um, send him one. See what he thinks." This from Alix.

"Great idea," Dana added enthusiastically. A little too enthusiastically.

"What's going on here?" Elyssa asked. Her eyes zeroed in on Carole.

Carole shrugged. "Maybe we've all just picked up on some tension between you and our new partner." She gave Elyssa an innocent look. "Maybe for both your sakes, a little humble pie is in order."

Elyssa's shoulders sagged. She was tired. So tired of feeling sad. Of missing Joe. Of being by herself. Shaking her head, she mumbled, "Maybe," and walked into her office.

At four that afternoon, as she made notes on each card, she thought about her staff's comments.

It lets you make up or compromise without groveling.

About Elliot's advice.

Life's so short . . . I've never seen you like this . . . this thing between you and Monteigne could lead somewhere good.

The last card of the group came up on her computer screen. It was the most romantic of the line. On the front were silhouettes of a broad-shouldered man and a long haired woman, walking along a beach, their hands outstretched and almost touching. Underneath the couple was the message, "If it weren't for the obstacles, we'd never know whether we really want something or merely think we do."

The inside was blank.

Just waiting for a message.

Of apology.

Of compromise.

Of trust.

Elyssa's fingers crept to the keyboard. Inside the pretty card, she typed, "Recent *obstacles* have taught me what I *really* want. It's *you*. In my life. Personally and professionally. Lyss."

Not great poetry. Not a declaration of love. But clearly, a *Let's try again* plea if she ever saw one.

She sighed. Stared at it.

Oh, maybe this wasn't such a good idea. Maybe this was stupid. Maybe she should wait until tomorrow. Think about it more.

Over the very long night ahead. And very long weekend after that.

What the hell! She called up Joe's email address, and, taking a deep breath, lifted her finger and pressed *Send*.

There! It was done. The ball, so to speak, was in his court.

Feeling better, she decided to walk home. It was still daylight out and the weather promised a beautiful night. Yes, a walk was definitely in order.

She headed to her closet for her sneakers, and for the first time in exactly two weeks and four days, there was a spring in her step.

Joe leaned against his car watching the Friday afternoon antics of Dupont Circle unfold around him. He drank in the day like a man just released from prison. It felt good to be outside, here, especially. He'd called Elyssa's office an hour ago, and Carole had told him that for the first time since anyone could remember, the boss had left early and was walking home. She'd added that Elyssa said she was going straight back to her place, so if he wanted to catch her there, he could.

He saw her coming toward him and his breath caught in his throat. She wore a little sleeveless brown dress that made her look seventeen. Her hair was loose and free around her shoulders, down her back. She carried her jacket, purse and her trademark high shoes in one hand. There were sneakers on her feet. Her face, sporting sunglasses, was lifted to the sun.

She'd come up even with him before she saw him. "Oh, Joe!" Tugging off her glasses, she stared at him wide-eyed. God she looked tired.

He stuck his hands in the pockets of his khaki pants. "Hi."

Was she blushing or was it from the sun? "You, um," she looked down and kicked the loose stones on the sidewalk. "You got the card already?"

"Card? What card?"

Angling her head, she faced him squarely. The dress deepened the color of her eyes to chestnut. "I sent you an Allheart greeting card."

"You did?" He tried to sound blasé, but he couldn't pull it off. Where had all his sophistication gone in the past few months?

"Yes." She glanced at her watch. "About an hour ago."

"I haven't checked my email today."

"I see."

"What did it say?"

She sighed. Then smiled shyly at him. "Tell me why you're here first."

He straightened. Stared down at her, amazed again at how much shorter she was without her heels. "I came here because I've been miserable."

"Oh, Joe, I've been miserable too."

"You mean that?" He shuddered a little. "I tried to call you Tuesday night. All night long, Elyssa. There was no answer."

"I slept on the couch at the office."

How could that mean so much to him? "Thank God. It felt rotten to think you were with another man."

"I feel the same about your little SunSeas adventure."

"SunSeas was a bust."

"Really?"

He stepped closer. Reached out and slid a lock of her hair between his fingers. "All I kept thinking about was how this hair felt in my fingers, on my stomach, across my pillow. You ruined me, Lyss, for other women."

She blinked, but not before he saw the slightest hint of a tear in her eyes.

"And I need you to know something else. I didn't draw up the deal thinking you'd accept it because we'd been sleeping together. But I believe now that I *did* overreact to the situation. If we weren't sleeping together, I probably would have compromised. I went too far the other way."

"And I should have seen that you had a responsibility to make the best deal for the firm," she told him honestly. "That, in truth, it wasn't anything personal."

They stared at each other.

Then he reached out his hand. "Invite me inside. We need to talk. We need to touch."

She grasped his hand in hers. "Yes," was all she said.

* * *

Hours later, Elyssa awoke pressed closely against hard male flesh, nestled among the green sheets. She smiled against his chest, relishing the feel of him.

"What's the smile for?" he asked. The words rumbled in his chest beneath her ear.

"You're awake?"

"Yep." He stroked her naked back. "I've already been up once. I checked my email from your computer." He kissed the top of her head. "I know what I *really* want too, Lyss."

She digested the words, very happily. "We'll fight. Both here and at the office."

"I know. As a matter of fact, I have some questions about this new line."

She tugged on his chest hair and he grabbed her hands.

"But we'll work at it," he said, chuckling. "See where all this goes, where it takes us."

She didn't say anything.

"It's what you want, isn't it?" he asked.

She was once again thrilled that she could make this strong vibrant man's voice shake a bit.

Climbing on top of him, she stretched out the full length of his body and peered meaningfully into blue eyes that were ocean deep. "Yes. It's what I want. Now, shut up and kiss me."

"Whatever you say, Madam CEO." He dragged her down to his mouth and mumbled against her lips, "For now, anyway."

By a Nose

FIONA KELLY

Chapter 1

How'd that song go again? Robyn stopped humming to rummage through her brain. *Something about turning, turn, turn. Oh yeah! A time to work, a time to play.* She sighed. On this particular Friday afternoon as she sat in the posh offices of Allheart.com, Robyn Barrett was definitely in the mood to play.

Robyn's gaze slid longingly to the corner of her computer screen where the time glared mockingly at her.

Four o'clock.

Would this day *ever* end?

She drummed her neatly manicured nails on her desk as she flipped through the pages of *Vogue*.

How on earth was she going to make it to five o'clock?

All morning after she'd stumbled in nearly an hour late for work—again—she hadn't exactly been Miss Productivity. And then after her two-hour lunch her motivation to do even the tiniest lick of work had taken a massive nosedive into oblivion. No amount of anything could resuscitate it.

The day was a complete wash.

For a moment she considered telling Elyssa she had developed the stomach flu, but if she used that excuse one more time her boss might call in a specialist.

Nope, she was stuck for the day with no way out.

Damn!

Leaning her cheek against her fist, Robyn glanced up as Alix Harris sauntered by, holding a super-industrial-sized coffee mug.

Robyn loved the crisp, black Armani suit Alix wore. It was elegant and chic with just a bold touch of her sheer leopard print blouse peering out of the neckline. The entire ensemble really set off the rich, creamy coffee color of Alix's skin.

"You know what I want, Alix?" Robyn asked.

Alix paused with her left brow arched in that not-another-one-of-your-crazy-notions-Robyn look. "I can't imagine."

Robyn turned the copy of *Vogue* she'd been reading to face her friend and pointed to the model wearing a slip dress that showed her thin, angular frame off to perfection. "I want to meet the man who can look at this ad and think what I think."

Alix looked at the ad. "And that is?"

"Someone throw that woman a cheeseburger and make her eat it before she dies of starvation."

Alix laughed. But as Elyssa Wentworth stuck her head out of the door of her office, Alix sobered and snapped to attention like a soldier facing her commanding officer. And indeed, that was exactly how Elyssa ran Allheart.com.

"Tell me, Robyn," Elyssa asked in her usual distemper. "Is work optional today?"

"It is for what you pay me," Robyn mumbled as she tucked the magazine into her desk drawer and switched off the radio.

Elyssa stiffened, but by the puzzled frown on her face, Robyn could tell she hadn't quite caught her words. "What was that?" Elyssa snapped.

"What was what?" Robyn asked, blinking her eyes in an innocent expression.

Elyssa's eyes narrowed. "What did you just say?"

"When?"

Elyssa gave a half-evil glare, then returned to her office.

Alix leaned over Robyn's desk a step forward and lowered her voice to a whisper. "Girl, one day you are going to get fired for doing that."

And Robyn probably would too, knowing her luck. As the old song went, if it weren't for bad luck, she'd have no luck at all. A particular brand of agony rained on her.

But she couldn't seem to help herself.

She loved Elyssa and all the women at Allheart. They were more her family than the people who really were her family. But the devil in Robyn made it hard to keep her little remarks to herself. Then again, the devil in her made her do a lot of things she knew better than to do.

Maybe what she really needed was a good old-fashioned spanking.

Shaking her head, she met Alix's concerned gaze. "I'm going to behave today," she whispered, more for her own benefit than Alix's.

"*That* would be a meaningful gesture," Alix said before heading back to her office.

Robyn turned in her chair to face the computer monitor.

Work, Robyn, work.

Sigh. Who could work on such a wonderful summer day?

Robyn's attention drifted to the windows where the bright sun tempted her. And Robyn had never been one to deny temptation.

At least not for long anyway.

It was one of those languorous summer afternoons in DC where she'd like nothing better than to peel off her work clothes and pull on a pair of cutoffs and a tank top and walk in flip-flops around the cool, dry Smithsonian.

Closing her eyes, she could picture herself sitting down on the lawn by Capitol Hill, eating one of the scrumptious hot dogs from a vendor's cart and watching the tourists flit by.

And if she *really* wanted to make it perfect, Steve Rood would be there as well.

A smile curved her lips as she imagined him sprawled next to her on the lawn swigging a Coke and munching a dog.

"Don't I wish," Robyn breathed, savoring the thought.

Steve Rood was an enigma. His dark good looks were not obvious in a movie-star kind of way. Sure, he was good-looking enough that you'd notice him across a room. But it wasn't until you got good and close that you felt the peculiar pull of his orbit.

He wore his straight black hair almost to his shoulders in a careless style that always looked as if he'd just brushed his long, lean fingers through it. His light blue eyes were a stark contrast to black eyelashes that were sinfully long and lush. And his chiseled features were almost more than Robyn could take.

Robyn sighed as she wondered what he did during the day-light hours.

In her mind, she pictured him like some seductive vampire who camped out during the day waiting for night to fall. Then, he would come alive and work his sexy spell on her.

How she wished for the courage to walk up to him one night at Dark Blue, the club where he played piano, and seize his lips in a hot, passionate kiss. Then, of course, she'd press him against his shiny black piano, and have her wicked, wicked way with him.

Robyn bit her lip as she savored the dream. If only she had the guts. But for some reason when it came to Steve, Robyn was as nervous as a long-tailed cat in a room full of rocking chairs.

Normally, she had no problem at all walking up to a guy and getting right to the bottom of him.

Not so with Steve. He was different. *Very* different.

"You still here?" Dana Boyle asked, breaking Robyn out of her daze.

"What?" Robyn asked as she shook off her daydream and focused on Dana's face.

Dana pointed to the watch on her wrist. "It's five-forty, Robyn. Normally you bust through the door like you're on fire at five-to-five."

Robyn started, then glanced to the clock on her computer screen which read 4:30. Times like this, she wished she wore a watch. Then again, if she did that, she'd have no excuse for being late from lunch every afternoon.

"All right," Robyn said in a loud voice, "which one of you smart-asses reset my clock?"

"I'm only a smart-ass if you want to draw unemployment," Elyssa said as she swept out of her office and closed the door behind her.

Robyn smiled her sweetest smile, which normally caused Elyssa to forgive her anything. "I didn't mean *you*, Elyssa. I would never have said anything like that had I known you did it."

"Uh-hm," Elyssa said suspiciously as she dug through her briefcase for her keys. "I'm *sure* you wouldn't."

Robyn laughed. "I still love you, even if you did trick me."

"Consider it penance for the fact that you've been at least forty-five minutes late every day this week."

Robyn clicked out of her word processing programs and shut down her computer.

"What can I say?" Robyn asked. "I'm just a little too friendly with the snooze button. Frankly, I'm surprised it still works given how much wear and tear it goes through every morning."

Elyssa rolled her eyes. "Go on and get out of here. And for

God's sake, Robyn, try not to get into any trouble this week-end. No police, no riot gear, no near-death experiences. And for once, leave the strays wherever you find them."

Robyn collected her purse and gave Elyssa a military salute. "Yes, ma'am. I promise, I'll be *real* good this weekend."

Elyssa left and Robyn quickly gathered her things in order to do likewise. She swept out the door, leaving the sound of her coworkers razzing in her own wake. Finding all the energy and motivation she'd been missing all day, she rushed to her red Mustang, which was parked behind the brownstone office building.

She got in and checked the car clock. It was five forty-five and she was supposed to meet her best friend, Rachel, in less than an hour.

"Oh well," she said as she switched the ignition on. "Rach would die of shock if I ever got there on time anyway."

Backing up, she peeled out of the lot and headed toward the town house apartment in Georgetown that Daddy had arranged for when he found out she'd been living with Gun Club because she couldn't afford rent on anything decent in the city.

Yup, good old Daddy could always be depended on to throw money after any problem.

As for Gun Club, well, he had let her bunk with him and he'd been fairly decent in a he-man, belch-and-fart sort of way. Mostly her father couldn't stand the thought of his daughter wasting her charms, as he put it, on a fellow who clearly was more brawn than brains.

Robyn smiled at the memory of Gun Club—his moniker had been one of her better ones. As far back as she could re-member, she nicknamed her boyfriends.

So far there had been Duh-man, Boor, Sprinter, Tightwad, and Mullet. The six-foot tall, macho Marine, Gun Club had just been another in a long line of guys who were fun to hang with, but weren't the type of guy a woman settled down with unless she'd just plain run out of options.

And Robyn wasn't even close to running out of options.

She knew what she wanted when it came to men. A nice, ever-so-slightly-dangerous-in-a-good-way guy who could make her feel what she'd never felt before—unconditionally loved.

Robyn was plenty smart enough to know that what she
sought in a man was what she'd never had in her own family
as a child. Her parents had never had a minute to spare for her.
Mom had always been the busy social queen while Daddy
was so caught up running his company he barely noticed he
had a daughter. Except for when he observed yet another trait
of Robyn's that he could not abide. Then he'd weigh in like
the 800-pound gorilla that he was, barking orders, pulling
strings, doing everything he needed to do to make things turn
out his way.

Her parents weren't necessarily bad people, they just
weren't at all close to each other or to her, and she found little
comfort in their relationship.

The girls at work were good friends, but they were always
tsk-tsking her behavior, and what Robyn needed was someone who could love her just for being her. Someone who
could appreciate—no, cherish—her unique view of the
world.

It was the only thing in life she had ever wanted. And it
seemed to be the thing she might spend a lifetime looking for.

Well, that and a high-paying job.

Shifting down into third gear, Robyn drove around
Dupont Circle and changed her destination. Forget about going back to her place, she needed to cut loose tonight and the
sooner she picked up Rachel, the sooner she could set herself free.

Growling low in her throat, Robyn pulled up in front of
her building and hit the steering wheel with the heel of her
hand. "Of all the lame things to do!"

Okay, so the guy had been cute but not cute enough to
leave Robyn in a lonely lurch over.

*You won't mind if I cut out early, Robyn? I know we were
talking, but Jason has a Range Rover,* Robyn said to herself,
mocking Rachel's words.

Letting go of her anger, Robyn sighed. She should probably hate her friend, but that would be like hating a leopard for
having spots.

It wasn't Rachel's fault she had been blessed with great

genes. The two of them couldn't go any place that guys didn't embarrass themselves trying to impress Rachel.

That's what I get for letting her take me to The Pub House on a Friday night.

Of course, Rachel wouldn't stick with her friend while a gob of men were salivating for the model-thin brunette.

Slamming the car door, Robyn caught sight of herself in the window. It didn't help that the streetlights behind her reflected poorly against the bright colors of her summery dress.

Jeez, she thought, *I look like a troll.*

Lifting herself up on her tiptoes, she sucked her stomach in. It didn't help. She was short and curvy, a little handful of a woman, with a chic, tousled mop of light-brown hair and gray eyes with just the barest hint of color to them. She didn't usually have trouble hooking up with an interesting prospect when they went out together, but sometimes, compared to Rachel's statuesque beauty, Robyn felt like the B-Team.

She placed her fingertip against the tip of her upturned nose and forced the flesh down into the semblance of an elegant, aquiline nose like her mother had. How many times had her mother pinched the tip of her nose and lamented on the fact that poor Robyn had been cursed with Grandma Barrett's?

Maybe a nose job would help?

Robyn scoffed at her reflection as she released her nose. *On second thought, maybe I should arrange for a full head transplant.*

Ah heck, what was she worried about anyway? She was cute. Granted she didn't get as many guys as Rachel, but she had more than her share. And there was nothing wrong with her nose. It was unconventional, just like her, and unlike her prim and proper mother, Robyn loved her more unconventional ways.

She grabbed her small purse and started for her front door.

Robyn had only taken a step when she decided she didn't want to go in right away.

No, not when she felt like this. Alone. Tired. Discouraged. For a woman of twenty-four, she felt ancient.

If only she knew what she wanted to do with her life, perhaps that would help. Alix, Elyssa, Carole and even Dana had always known what they wanted, and they had headed straight for it.

But not Robyn.

All through college she had changed majors repeatedly, seeking something new, something exciting. Something fulfilling.

Flitted from one guy to the next, all the while searching for . . .

"A *raison d'etre*," she whispered.

She wanted her life to mean something, but she was completely clueless as to what that something was. And she was so easily distracted by her own amusements, it was hard for her to concentrate on figuring out what her life should mean.

Robyn rubbed her hands over her eyebrows and shook her head. "Stop it, Robyn, and I mean now! No more pity-party. What is wrong with you?"

No more moping. Moping was for wimps.

Pivoting on her feet, she headed back toward the street.

There were things to see and men to do, and right now she was going to head off toward Dark Blue and see if Steve was playing tonight.

Life was too short to be miserable and alone, and she was finally in the mood to corner Steve once and for all.

*It was only a short jaunt to the club, but the place was com*pletely packed. And worse than the exorbitant ten dollar cover charge they had on Friday nights was the fact that Steve wasn't even playing.

"Just perfect," Robyn mumbled. "A perfect end to a perfect day."

What would happen next? Would Gorbechev drop the bomb on the city?

Robyn blinked. *Was Gorbechev still in power?*

Was he even still alive? Dang, I never could keep my current events current. Anyway, who cares? Alive or dead, he's probably having more fun tonight than I am.

Deflated and ready to give up on the night, she turned to leave and walked straight into a wall of hard muscle. Robyn opened her mouth to apologize as she looked up the tall, lean body and into the electric blue eyes she'd been longing for.

"Hi," Steve said, cracking that half smile that made her legs weak.

Robyn realized her hands were pressed against wonderfully hard pecs. She wondered for a second how long would be too long to linger like this.

Reluctantly, she pulled her hand away and returned his smile. "Hi," she repeated, too awed by the feel of him just millimeters away to come up with anything more brilliant to say.

She'd never before been this close to him. So close that she could actually feel the heat of his body. Smell the faint scent of soap on his skin, and see the light stubble on his angular cheeks and jawline.

She stared longingly at his stubble, wanting desperately to run her hand over the skin and feel it tickle her fingertips.

How she loved the prickly feel of a man's whiskers on her lips. And she had a hunch Steve's skin would taste better than most.

He glanced around the crowded bar, then focused that probing stare of his directly on her. An indefinable light flickered in his pupils when he spoke, and his deep voice resonated with strength and warmth. "If you're looking for your friend, she left about an hour ago."

"My friend?"

"The redhead—what's her name? Dana?"

It took her a minute before Robyn caught his meaning. Seizing it, she nodded. "Oh yeah, Dana. Darn," she said snapping her fingers. "I was hoping to catch her."

And he's a gentleman too! she thought. *Letting me avoid admitting I'd come here only on the freckle of a chance I might see him.*

For that matter, she was finding it awfully hard not to take a step forward and just breathe in the musky smell of him.

If the truth were known, there was nothing that would please her more than to just cut to the chase and get naked with this guy.

"Darn?" Steve repeated with a short laugh. "Now there's a word I haven't heard in a while."

Robyn shrugged as her gaze dipped to his tanned neck where his hair brushed up against it.

"Hang around me, pal, and you're bound to hear lots of words no one else uses."

One corner of his mouth drew back in amusement. "Is that an invitation?"

For the first time in forever, she actually felt heat creep up her cheeks. Nervous, hot and flustered, she couldn't think of anything else to say.

C'mon, Robyn, where are your clever retorts?

Probably hiding in the same place where my common sense lives most of the time.

She tried to think of something to say. But for her life, nothing came to mind.

Nothing.

Nothing except images of how good Steve would look with that sleek hair wet and his lean hips wrapped in a damp, clinging towel.

"I guess I should be going," she said, edging away from him.

Coward.

"You here alone?" he asked before she could make good her escape.

"Yeah," she said.

"How far's your car?"

"It's at my place down the street. I walked over."

He gave her that incredulous look that everyone she knew gave her sooner or later—as if he couldn't believe what she'd just said.

"You did what?"

"It's not that far," Robyn said defensively. "I only live a few minutes away."

"What are you thinking walking down a DC street at midnight looking like you do? You really expect to arrive home safe and sound?"

Robyn folded her arms over her chest. His words both flattered and irritated her.

At first she thought the flattery would win, but the more she thought about it, the more irritated she became.

Was there no one on the planet who would credit her with even a modicum of sense?

"You know, *Dad*, I think I have everything under control, but thanks for your concern. Look, it's not as if I'm alone out there." She pointed out the club's front window to the sidewalk fairly teeming with people. No place was busier than G-town on a Friday night—she couldn't be alone on the street if she wanted to.

He glanced at a man a few feet away who was gesturing toward the piano. Steve nodded, then looked back at her. "Maybe so. Still. Tell you what. I have one more set to play and then I'm done for the night. How 'bout you wait here and when I'm done, I'll walk you home?"

Like she was going to say no?

"You want to walk me home?" she asked around the nervous lump in her throat.

His gaze dipped to her lips and quickly back to her eyes. She smiled to herself as she realized he was mulling his attraction to her. When his eyes narrowed an instant before he looked away, she knew there was a *thing* happening.

Well, if he walked her home, she might actually get a chance to try out some of her daydreams of him *on* him. Go for it, girl.

"Sure," she said with a nonchalance she definitely didn't feel.

Steve nodded, then headed for the piano and sat down.

Robyn managed to grab a table within sight of him as soon as a couple got up and left. She ordered a Long Island Iced Tea while a few loudmouths in the crowd shouted requests at Steve.

"Give us a song, piano man!" a drunk man slurred from the bar.

By the look on Steve's face she could tell the request went over about as well as Monica jokes to Hillary. He didn't even try to hide his disdain for this audience.

Steve took a deep breath before he started to play. Then he broke into a horrendous lounge lizard version of the familiar Billy Joel tune.

The entire audience laughed.

"Any other favorites you'd like to hear?" Steve asked the crowd when he finished the savage parody.

Wisely, no one said a word.

Robyn smiled. *Clever and cute*, she thought.

As Steve worked his way through a few jazz tunes, Robyn couldn't take her eyes off of his slender, muscular hands. They flew over the keys as if he and the piano were one. She'd never been one to think of a pianist as hot—in her mind they were all Elton John types. Over-the-top, key-pounding showmen.

But Steve wasn't like that at all. Dressed in a pair of jeans, a slouchy black linen blazer and gray T-shirt, he was ultra–low-key; to her he was the epitome of raw masculinity. Maybe she was drawn to the air of confident authority in him.

Whatever. All she knew was the irrational way her body screamed for his.

Robyn sipped her drink as she watched him longingly. She hated to admit it, but in the past few months, Steve had become an obsession for her.

The only thing that even came close to this was the insane infatuation she'd had for Sebastian Bach of Skid Row when she was in junior high school. Just like she'd done back then, she could get lost in her daydreams of Steve. It's probably not a good thing to still have a lot in common with your junior high self, but there it was.

"Take me home," she whispered to no one in particular, yearning for five minutes alone with him.

An hour later, she finally got her wish.

Steve finished his set with his rendition of "I Can't Help Falling in Love With You"—the same song he always played at the end of the night.

Then rising from the piano, he said his good-byes, tapped her on the shoulder and gestured toward the door. She took a last sip of her drink, grabbed her handbag and followed him through the winding path he cut through the still-crowded bar.

Steve led her to the front door and held it open for her.

Once outside in the muggy heat, they walked in silence with only the traffic and pedestrian chatter interrupting the calm summer breeze.

"You know, I love the night," Steve said, finally breaking the silence.

"In a vampire kind of way?" Robyn immediately wished she'd given a thought before she'd spoken. How could she let that silly vampire notion she'd had of him earlier that day just fall out of her mouth like that?

He laughed at her.

Even though he seemed amused, she felt foolish. Looking down at her feet, she sought to redeem herself. "I do know what you mean, though. Even as a kid I used to see how late I could stay up."

"We had this huge . . ." she gestured with her hands to show how huge and ended up whacking Steve in the hard pecs again with her hand. He didn't seem to notice. If she didn't knock it off he was going to think she had some freaky thing

for his chest, which of course she did but . . . she balled her
fist up and dropped her arms to her sides.

". . . plate-glass window in the living room," she continued, hoping to distract herself with the story. "And I'd curl up
on the sofa and just watch the moon creep across the sky until
I finally fell asleep."

"Ah," Steve said, shrugging his jacket off. With a graceful
arc, he slung it casually over his shoulder, then tucked one
hand into his jeans pocket.

Robyn's breath caught at the sight of his sculpted biceps.
And of course her eyes couldn't help taking in his lean, hard
stomach.

"So you're a moon goddess."

"I guess," she said, liking the thought. "What about you?"

"I'm definitely not a moon goddess," he said, with a little
smile.

She laughed. "I figured that much."

Steve cut his eyes toward her and she noted the mischievous curl to his sensuous lips. "Well, I for one didn't look out
the windows much after dark."

"Why?"

"When we were kids, my brother told me that if you
looked out the window after dark you'd see the devil."

"Really?" she asked. "And you believed him?"

"Of course not. I knew what a liar my brother was," he
said. "But stupid me, I opened the window to prove him
wrong, and son-of-a-bitch if the devil himself wasn't there
staring eyeball to eyeball with me."

Robyn missed a step. "He what?"

"I swear it. The devil was there in all his evil glory. His
face all streaky orange as he laughed maniacally at me. I
screamed and woke my parents and then I found out my
brother had talked his best friend into dressing up and hiding
in the bushes as a practical joke."

"No, he didn't!"

"Oh yeah, but that's not as bad as the time he set the house
on fire."

Robyn was aghast. "Your brother set the house on fire?"

"When I was eight. I woke up hearing someone whispering, 'I am the devil, I am the devil.' Before I realized it was my

brother, he lit a match and scared the shit out of me so badly that I decked him. He dropped the match and it caught my bed on fire."

"Oh my God!" she said, cupping her hand over her mouth. "What did your parents do?"

"Let's just say they beat the devil out of him."

She laughed until her eyes teared.

Steve's low chuckle sounded good. Too good, in fact.

"I guess the devil never came back to your house after that, huh?" Robyn asked.

"If he did, Sam didn't have anything to do with it."

"So what does your brother do now?"

"He's a fireman."

She burst out laughing again until she noticed he was serious. "Really?"

"Yup. Sammy found a way to turn pyromania into a respectable career. It was either fireman or arsonist. At least my parents think he chose wisely."

"But not you?"

He shrugged. "To each his own is my motto."

Robyn smiled.

"What?" he asked.

"That's my motto too. I'm just not used to hearing someone else say it."

"Yeah, I guess we need more of us in the world."

"I don't know," Robyn said in a low tone. "The women I work with would say one of me is plenty."

"Now why would they say that?"

She shrugged. "I guess because they think I'm all over the place, too individualistic for my own good."

"And are you all over the place?"

"It depends on who you ask."

Steve stopped walking and stared at her. "What, were you a philosophy major in college?"

"Why do you ask?"

"Because the last time I heard someone dance around me so skillfully with circular arguments was the one semester I was stupid enough to take rhetoric and logic."

Robyn frowned as they resumed walking. "Why on earth would you take that?"

"It sounded easier than calculus."

"Was it?"

"Since I ended up dropping out of R and L after four weeks with a D average and ended up getting an A in calculus, I'd have to say no."

"Ah," she said in understanding. "I did a lot of that."

"Getting A's in calculus?"

"Hardly. Dropping classes. My advisor called me Bounce-Around Barrett."

"Bounce-Around Barrett?" Steve asked.

"What can I say? I switched majors eleven times in three years. So—to answer your question—yeah, I guess I am all over the place."

"Eleven majors? Jeez, my dad would have *loved* you. I switched mine fifteen times."

Robyn couldn't believe her ears. Never before had she met anyone who equaled her record, let alone surpassed it. "You did not!"

"I did. Let's see if I can name them. There was art, CAD, history, English, classics, drama, music, business for about three days, marketing for about an hour—"

"Now you're joking," Robyn said, interrupting him.

"Serious as hell. My dad pushed me into the business school. I took one marketing class, sat down and before the professor finished going over the syllabus I knew I couldn't stand two years of that crap, so I dodged out the door and headed straight for drop-add."

"So you ended up a musician?"

He snorted. "Only the very lucky end up as musicians. If I had to live off what I make playing the piano, I'd be one of those panhandlers who spends the night on a grate at the mall."

Robyn frowned. Drat, the man was bursting her dream of him being some sleek, seductive vampire. "You have a day job then?"

"Yep."

She waited for him to elaborate. When he didn't, she prodded him. "And that is?"

"Steal cars, run drugs. Whatever I can to make a spare dime."

Robyn blinked, not sure if he was kidding or not.

"Relax," Steve said, nudging her gently. "It's a joke."

Still a little suspicious, she glanced askance at him. "Then what *do* you do?"

"I do undercover work for the FBI."

Robyn stopped dead in her tracks. "Now I know you're pulling my leg."

She took a step toward him. "Aren't you?"

His smile warmed her. "Yeah, I'm pulling it. I'm actually a programmer for a local ISP. But I've found that telling women that isn't the way to pick them up. They get this really glazed look over their eyes like they'd rather watch Junior Samples on *Hee-Haw* than spend another five seconds with me."

Now *that* she had a hard time believing.

What woman could resist being around a guy so incredibly hot?

"Are you really a web programmer?" Robyn asked.

He nodded. "Computer geek all the way."

"Really?" she asked, still unable to see him as a pocket protector type hunched over a keyboard.

"Why do you think I was so interested in what you guys are up to over there at Allheart the night I met you? I was conducting a little industrial espionage."

"Oh Lord, I hope you're joking for real now or Elyssa will cook my goose and eat it with relish."

"I'm kidding about the espionage part, but I really am a web programmer."

She shook her head as they neared her door. "I would never have pegged you for one."

"Yeah, well, me either, but a guy's gotta eat."

"And for what they pay programmers, I would say you're eating pretty well."

"First class all the way, babe," Steve said with a wink.

Robyn bit her lip as they paused in front of the steps leading to the front door of her place. "Thanks for walking me home," she whispered, as if she were afraid of waking up Mom and Dad.

Steve leaned forward and whispered in her ear. "My pleasure."

His warm breath tickled her neck and the scent of him made her stomach jump. He smelled good enough to eat.

"I guess I better be going," he said.

Steve took her hand and placed a gentlemanly kiss on the back of her knuckles. His soft lips felt cool against her skin.

Robyn swallowed. No guy had ever done that before and it touched her far more deeply than she cared to admit.

He held on to her hand and looked at her squarely. Robyn trembled ever so slightly. The moment felt surreal. She'd been secretly fixated on Steve for months, since the first night she saw him play at Dark Blue, that night the Allheart gang went out and got so sloppy. She'd made her way back to the club several times since then, just to steal a look at this man, his hands, his face haunting all of her daydreams and most of her nightdreams. She'd been sure all this while that he didn't even know she existed and now, here they were, all alone, face-to-face in the summer darkness. Darn, if she hadn't spent so much time daydreaming she'd have had an opening maneuver planned for this moment. She'd have to wing it.

"Would you like to come in for coffee?" she asked, her voice sounding hoarse and strange to her.

"Depends. Do you ask every guy who walks you to your door to come inside?"

"I don't know," she answered honestly. "I've never had a guy walk me to my door like this."

"Something tells me you're not telling me the whole truth about that."

Robyn quirked an eyebrow at him. "Are you insulting me?"

He shook his head. "Not a chance. I'm just trying to read you."

"Do you try to read every girl you walk home?"

He laughed. "I don't know. I've never walked a girl home like this."

"Now who's talking in circles!" She laughed back, pulling her keys out and climbing the steps to her door.

"Look, you're welcome to come in. But don't take too long to think about it." She turned the key and opened the door. "You got a curfew?"

"Why, is there some time limit here?" He looked at her quizzically.

"No, but I do have air-conditioning and it's all being sucked out the door as we stand here discussing whether you're coming in or not. So?" She turned to go in, pretending not to care whether he followed.

"AC? Why didn't you say that to begin with! No man in his right mind would turn down an invitation that involved air-conditioning on a hot summer night in Washington." He fairly bounded up the steps to her door.

"Whatever turns you on," she quipped with a shrug as they stepped inside.

Chapter 2

Robyn bit her lip to keep from smiling as Steve followed her into her house. It had been a long, long time since she'd felt so giddy and nervous over the presence of a man.

Then again, she couldn't remember the last time she'd been quite so keen for a guy as she was for this one.

It was those gorgeous eyes, she decided. Deep, blue and moody. They were calling to her.

She cast a quick glance around the living room, making sure there wasn't anything embarrassing strewn about. No bras or half-eaten cups of yogurt.

Not that she was a slob, far from it. There were just times when she didn't feel like picking up after herself and since she lived alone, there was no one else to complain.

Steve bypassed her white and pink striped sofa and headed for the far corner where she had a Gibson acoustic guitar on a stand.

He reminded her of a kid at Christmas as he pulled the guitar up and examined it.

"You play?" he asked.

She closed the door and locked it. "I've been known to torture it from time to time."

He dragged his hand over the strings, then grimaced at the discord. "Needs tuning."

"I know," she said, tossing her keys and purse on the table in the foyer before walking into the living room. "It never would hold one worth spit. I have a tuner behind the plant on the end table if you need it."

He shook his head as he took it to the sofa and sat down.

"How do you like your coffee?" she asked as she headed to the kitchen.

"Hot and lots of cream," he mumbled as she entered the kitchen.

"What was that?" Robyn asked, sticking her head back around the corner.

"What was what?"

"What did you just say?" Robyn asked again.

"When?"

Robyn laughed as she remembered doing the same thing to Elyssa just that afternoon. "Never mind."

While she started the coffee, he tuned the guitar then began to play "She Talks to Angels." Robyn listened to his beautiful voice, impressed by his talent.

She set two cups down on the counter and returned to the living room. "You are incredible."

He shrugged nonchalantly. "Thanks, but good guitarists are a dime a dozen."

"No," she said sincerely. "Not like that they're not. And I should know."

"How's that?"

"I've dated a dozen of them and none could play half as well as you do. You must have been at it a long time."

He strummed a careless, yet harmonious G chord, and she stared at the way his long fingers wrapped around the neck with a skill that was only surpassed by his gift at the piano. "I started when I was at Julliard."

"*The* Julliard?"

He nodded. "But don't be too impressed. I only went for a few weeks."

"Why?"

"Stuff came up."

"Stuff?"

He set the guitar aside and rose to his feet like some sleek, hungry beast. Robyn loved the casual, loose-limbed walk he had. It was raw and masculine. Beguiling even.

He stopped in front of her and gazed down into her eyes. "Your hair's different than it was the last time I saw you. Blonder I think."

"I had it chunked."

Steve reached up and fingered a streak of blonde next to her face. The heat of his fingers was almost blistering. "It becomes you. Makes your eyes stand out more. I love your eyes by the way. They remind me a lot of someone but I can't think who."

Uncomfortably warm, Robyn stared up at him.

Kiss me, she silently tried to stop herself from begging, even while wondering what he would taste like.

He must have heard her unconscious plea, for he bent his head down and captured her lips with his own.

Robyn closed her eyes at the gentle, titillating pressure as she tasted him for the first time. His mouth was hot and he tasted like salt and beer.

Their breath mingled together as he lifted his hand up and cupped the back of her head, raising chills all over her.

Her head spun in pleasure.

"I have thought about what it would be like to kiss you." He breathed against her lips, and then he kissed her even deeper.

Robyn trembled. "You have?" she answered weakly. If this was another of her nutty dreams, then she definitely didn't want the alarm clock to buzz and tell her she was late for work again.

Steve reached his arms around her and pulled her tight against his chest to where she could feel the taut muscles of his body flexing against her breasts.

She sighed as he deepened his kiss and explored her mouth with his own.

Oh, he was delicious. Even better than she had suspected.

His hard, lean body felt so good in her arms.

Teasing his lips with her own, she wanted to taste more of him. She wanted to taste every single inch of him.

Inhaling his warm scent, she laced her fingers through his sleek hair, delighting in the silk sliding through her fingers.

Her body became consumed with her own urgent, bitter-sweet need for him.

Steve pulled back from her lips, then kissed a hot trail along her jawbone.

Robyn ground her teeth in pleasure as Steve gently nipped her skin with his perfect, white teeth. Her breasts swelled and instinctively, she leaned closer to him.

He groaned as her hip collided with his erection. Robyn felt a rush of excitement at the proof that at least for the moment he was every bit as attracted to her as she was to him.

Running her hands down his back, she savored the feel of his taut muscles.

"You feel wonderful," he murmured as he explored her back as well, massaging and stroking, stoking the need in her to a furious level.

Robyn intensified her kiss, teasing his tongue with her own.

Steve cupped her buttocks and pressed her against him. He gave her one long, hard kiss before pulling back.

His lips were swollen and his eyes dark and somber, and unmistakably filled with passion.

"Say the word, Robyn, and I'll leave," he whispered. "Because if I don't stop now, I'm not sure I'll be able to stop myself later. I want you."

Robyn answered him by untucking his T-shirt and running her hands over the hard muscles of his abdomen, ribs and then to his back. Oh, but he felt so good. So hard and firm, and warm and sleek.

Steve gave a strange half laugh, half groan before taking her back into his arms.

Robyn explored the planes of his back, delighting in the feel of his muscles flexing beneath her palms.

She couldn't stand it anymore. She had to have him—now!

Pulling away, she silently took his hand and led him upstairs to her bedroom.

As she led him inside her room, she didn't know what he thought of her sprawling bed with its Indian silk spread or if he liked the sort of faux hippie décor she had going on. He didn't seem to notice anything except her.

She liked that most of all.

He licked his lips as he lifted her up and sat her on the bed. Spreading her legs apart a bit, he kneeled down in front of her with his hands resting lightly on her thighs. "You are hot," he said as he massaged her thighs with his thumbs.

She gave a deep, throaty laugh as she traced a finger over his chest. "I could definitely say the same of you."

Slowly, Steve reached for the buttons down the front of her dress and undid them one by one.

Robyn held her breath as he exposed her aubergine silk bra to his gaze.

Steve toyed with the lace edge of it as if wanting to savor the moment.

His fingers burned her as he casually explored the outer edge of it, then traced the underwire and ribbon. Her entire body throbbed and she ached to feel his hand against her flesh.

Instead, he tortured her with the careful, small circles he made over the thin material, and then just as she was about to beg him, he cupped her breast in his hand and gave a tight squeeze.

Robyn hissed with pleasure as her body melted.

Steve smiled at her, before he leaned his head down and kissed the top of her breast. Robyn winced, silently, hating the fabric that kept her from feeling his lips against her nipple.

He stood and wrapped an arm around her firmly as he took her lips once again while his hands reached beneath her and cupped her buttocks.

With one tug, Robyn pulled his shirt from over his head an instant before he released the front catch on her bra. She writhed in ecstasy as he cupped her breasts in his hands and when he leaned forward to gently suckle her right breast, she thought she might pass out.

He sucked his breath in sharply between his teeth. "You taste so good," he said as he slipped her dress and bra off her shoulders.

Robyn trembled, feeling exposed and vulnerable to him. Steve toed his shoes off, then laid her back against the mattress.

She kicked off her sandals as he lay down next to her.

Her entire body throbbing, Robyn watched as he pulled her dress down, tugging it gently over her hips and off, dropping it in a pile on the floor.

He crawled up her body then, kissing a blazing path before he returned to suckle on her ear. She groaned with need.

His breath scorched her as his tongue tortured her with pleasure. Robyn lifted her hips, desperate for him to soothe the ache at the center of her body.

To her relief, he took the hint and gently moved his hand into her panties. He rubbed his hand between her legs until she thought she was going to scream.

Robyn pulled away from him and took possession of his lips in a fierce kiss. She wanted him more than she'd ever wanted anything.

And right then, she wanted him naked.

"Hey," she said, as she tugged at his jeans. "Let's get rid of these things."

Seizing the waistband, she undid the button and then realized he wore button-fly jeans.

"My, my." She breathed. *"C'est chic."*

"Mais oui," he purred.

Robyn undid the buttons as fast as she could.

She couldn't help noticing the male part of him that was swollen and straining against the stark white cotton of his undershorts. The part of him she couldn't wait to get better acquainted with.

"I would have pegged you as one of those guys who wore colored briefs or something."

Steve snorted. "Those things look like girl's panties. No thanks."

"No?" Robyn asked, hooking her finger in the waistband of her own panties. "Do you have something against panties?"

"Yeah," he said, his gaze eyeing her hungrily. "They're in my way."

And before she could blink, he peeled her panties from her and placed a tender kiss at the juncture of her thighs.

Robyn bit her lip as pleasure assailed her. Steve's breath tickled her as he trailed kisses up her body until he again returned to her lips.

She rid him of his underwear and reached down to take him in her hand as his own fingers worked magic between her legs.

"Ah damn," he growled in her ear. "I don't have a condom."

"It's okay," Robyn said. "I think I have one in the bathroom."

At least she hoped she did!

He let her up and she sprinted to the bathroom.

Robyn cursed her luck as she rummaged through drawers trying to find one.

C'mon, Robyn, she snarled at herself. *There has to be one someplace!*

Of all the rotten times not to have one in the house!

She was just about to give up when she finally found one hiding behind the cleanser.

Seizing it, she returned to where Steve lay on the bed.

"We appear to be in luck," she said triumphantly as she fairly skipped back to the bed.

Steve smiled and accepted her timely offering.

Moments later, Steve pulled her up to straddle his hips. Reaching up, he held her face in his hands and pulled her down to his lips.

Robyn sighed as he kissed her tenderly.

Unable to stand any more, she took him inside her and they moaned in unison.

Steve lifted his hips, driving himself deeper inside her.

Robyn leaned forward, bracing her hands on his shoulders. Oh, but he felt so good under and inside her.

"You are lovely," he said as he cupped her breasts. "And you feel even better than you look."

After a few leisurely minutes, he turned serious on her. Rolling her over, he took control of the matter.

Robyn didn't mind. Indeed, she wanted more and faster.

Tilting her hips, she drew him deeper inside, wanting to feel him all around her.

She reached to stroke the small of his back. He sucked his breath in sharply between his teeth as Robyn nibbled his salty throat.

Time seemed suspended as they gave each other pleasure, and all too soon Robyn had reached the precipice. She leaned her head back and cried out as her body spasmed and burst.

Steve buried his face in her neck as he quickened his strokes. Robyn felt him tremble and his grip tightened around her.

And then she felt him shiver as he found his own release.

Steve collapsed on top of her and Robyn gently stroked his back.

"Now *that* was fun," she said impishly to him.

He kissed the tip of the upturned nose she so despised, then rolled off her. "Glad you enjoyed it. I know I did."

He stretched like a lean, languid cat.

Robyn noted the satisfaction in his eyes as he propped the pillows up and leaned back against them.

She laid her head against his stomach and listened to him breathe as he idly played with her hair. She brushed her fingers through the short, prickly hairs beneath his belly button.

Wasn't this man wonderful to the touch? she thought.

"I have never seen hair so soft," Steve whispered as he brushed his fingers through her short mop.

"It's the Infusium. That's the leave-in treatment I believe in."

Steve laughed at her words as he lifted her bangs back from her forehead and gently touched her face. "You are something else, you know that?"

"Yeah, and thank God they broke the mold when they made me."

"Now why would you say that?" he asked with a quizzical smile.

"Why not? It's only what everyone thinks about me."

"Well I can't think what they mean by that but . . ."

Before he could finish, a pager went off.

Robyn frowned at the piercing beeps. "Who would be paging you at two A.M. on a Friday night?"

"One of my wigged-out, drug-addicted clients needing a quick fix."

Robyn arched a brow as she reluctantly rose up from his stomach and covered herself with the sheet.

Was he serious?

Steve tossed the blanket aside and went to his pants. He pulled the beeper from his pocket and silenced it.

"The server must have gone down again. Rick quit last week and I'm the only other guy who lives in town. Mind if I use the phone?"

Robyn pulled her cordless phone from the nightstand. She tossed it to him and he caught it in one hand. "Be my guest."

Unabashed by his state of undress, he sat down beside her and dialed.

She heard a deep rumbly voice pick up on the other end.

"Yeah, Mark, what's up?" Steve leaned back and braced his arm over her hips. He laced his fingers with hers while he listened.

Robyn delighted in the feel of his hand in hers, as well as at the sight of him naked in her bed. His dark, tan body looked good against her white sheets, and as her gaze dipped back to his belly button, she saw him start to grow aroused again.

Now this could be interesting, she thought wickedly as her own desire rekindled.

"Yeah," he said to the voice on the other end. "That's what I figured. How long's it been down?"

"All right," Steve said after a long pause. "I'll get right on it."

He hung up the phone, then set it back on her nightstand.

He braced his arms on each side of her and leaned down to give her a hot kiss on her lips, her cheek, her breasts.

Then he sat up. "Looks like I have to cut the night short."

"No way! We're not even close to being done!" Robyn pulled him to her.

"I know. But I've got to go deal with this situation. It can't be helped."

Steve left the bed and pulled his clothes on. "I'll give you a call tomorrow."

Robyn barely caught herself before she scoffed at him. *Here we go again. "I'll give you a call." I'll try not to hold my breath for it.*

Worst part was, she knew she would spend the whole day waiting for him to call, meanwhile he'd be back to his life, which didn't include her in it.

As soon as he dressed, he headed for the door. "Later?"

"Sure," she said with a phony nonchalance.

And he walked out.

Stupid, stupid, stupid! she snapped at herself. When would she learn? She was hopeless.

No, she corrected herself. She was hope-*ful*. That was the problem. Every time she met a man, she kept thinking that she might mean something more to him than a bit of fun.

"Oh, whatever." She sighed, getting up to take a shower. "I didn't need him anyway."

It was true. Steve had been a *want*. A want she had fulfilled, and now they could go their separate ways.

And at least this time, the guy didn't steal anything on his way out of her life.

Robyn took a quick shower, then dressed in a long, oversized T-shirt. She went to the kitchen to turn off the coffeemaker, then heard someone at the door.

"Yes?" she asked, crossing the room to look through the peephole.

Her heart stopped as she saw Steve on the other side.

"Hey, how about you let me back in?"

Chapter 3

Robyn was startled to see Steve standing outside. The bright moonlight played on the dark strands of his hair as he appeared to wait patiently for her to answer the door.

What could he possibly want?

Did he want her to go with him?

Her heart leapt at the thought that he might not want to actually leave her.

Fumbling with the lock, she opened the door.

"Hey. I left my keys," he said. "They must have fallen out of my pocket in the bedroom."

"Oh," she said, trying not to look as disappointed as she felt.

Robyn followed him up the stairs and watched as he grabbed the keys from where they lay on the floor in front of her nightstand.

"Sorry you had to come back for them," she said from the doorway.

"I didn't mind really." He hesitated by her. "You okay?"

"I'm all right. Just tired."

"You sure?"

She nodded.

"Well, I hate that you got dressed for bed. I was going to ask if you wanted to come along with me to the office."

Robyn's heart stilled. So he wasn't trying to scrape her off the bottom of his shoe.

"Really?"

He smiled. "Yeah. I hate going up there this time of night by myself. It's way too quiet. Like a tomb."

"Sure," she said trying desperately to sound nonchalant. "I'll come."

"You sure you're not too tired?"

Was he kidding? All she had dreamed of since the night she first saw him was spending time with him.

Making love to him.

The last thing she wanted was for the night to end so soon.

"No, you just gave me my second wind," she said.

Boy, had he ever!

Steve laughed at her exuberance. "Okay. I'll go get my car while you dress. I'll be back for you in a few minutes."

Thrilled, Robyn dashed to her closet to dig out a pair of jeans and a T-shirt while Steve let himself out.

In no time, she was dressed and waiting for him by the door.

After a few minutes, a white Mustang pulled up in front and stopped. The passenger window rolled down and she saw Steve looking for her.

Smiling at yet another thing they had in common, she locked the door and went to meet him.

"We're car twins!" she said as she got in his car.

"What do you mean?" Steve asked as he rolled up the window.

She pointed to her car just a few yards away. "I have a Mustang identical to yours. Except mine's red."

"V8 or V6?"

"V8. I feel the need for speed."

"Ha," he said draping his arm over her headrest.

Robyn leaned back in the brown leather seat and watched the streetlights drift by. The inside of the car smelled like Steve.

"Where's your office?" she asked.

"Two blocks from the Lincoln Memorial."

"Not a bad neighborhood to work in."

Steve nodded. "Yeah, so long as you don't have to pull nine to five or even eight to four. Getting to the office during rush hour is almost impossible."

"Are those your normal hours?"

He shook his head. "Nah. As long as the work gets done on time, he doesn't care when I work."

"That must be nice. I hate having to be at work for set hours. Elyssa has a conniption every time I'm five minutes late. Wait," she corrected herself. "She has a conniption every time I'm five *seconds* late."

"Well as far as I'm concerned work is highly overrated. I only do this job thing to pay the rent."

"Oh, it can't be all that bad," she said lightly.

"Really? Don't you think a pianist should be playing the piano for a living, Robyn?"

Steve's mood had changed completely and his face was dark and angry. Robyn was startled by this sudden shift and didn't quite know what to say. "Um, I guess, I mean . . ."

"Okay, I'll help you. Yes, Steve, of course a pianist should be playing the piano for a living." He practically snarled at her.

"So why don't you? Play I mean." *Dumb question*, Robyn thought the minute the words fell out of her mouth. Steve's face went stone cold and his right hand tensed into a fist on his lap.

"That's a great question, Robyn, one I ask myself every single day." His lips were a tight straight line as they fell into an uncomfortable silence.

Let me out of this car, Robyn thought. *What the hell kind of hornets' nest have I stirred up this time? And who is this guy anyway?* She folded her hands in her lap and wished she'd stayed home in her cozy bed and missed this little explosion.

She stared straight ahead, not wanting to see his angry, unfamiliar face. After another five traffic lights or so, Robyn decided she didn't want to play Steve's silent game.

"Look, Steve, I hardly know you, so I can't even begin to guess what's behind all this . . . whatever it is . . . rage, you've got going on. But I'm a big believer in just doing what you feel like doing, so I ask again, why don't you play full-time if that's what you want to do?" She folded her arms across her chest as if to protect herself from his response.

Steve said nothing for more than a minute. Then he let out a deep, long sigh and pulled his car over to the side of the nearly empty road. He cut the engine and turned to Robyn.

"You seem like a nice person so I'm not going to torture you with my whole sordid life story." He spoke in a careful, measured tone. "I *meant* to be a professional musician. My parents *meant* for me to be one too. Which'd be why they took out a second mortgage on their house to send me to Juilliard." He stopped talking for a moment and stared at the steering wheel.

"Not long after I started I had an accident—a pretty bad one. I broke a wrist and badly sliced a tendon in the other hand, among many other lovely results of this accident. I was in the hospital for weeks.

"When I got out the doctors told me it'd take a while for

my hand to heal and that I'd have some numbness. Turns out I had all kinds of complications and it's never completely healed and so my days as a classical musician were ended before they even began." He flashed a creepy, phony smile at Robyn. "Tragic, isn't it?"

Robyn was once again at a loss for words. "Well that explains a lot. I'm sorry." She looked down at her hands.

"Don't be. These are the cards I was dealt. Actually they're the cards I dealt myself. I did a stupid thing and I get to pay for it every single day." He looked at Robyn and shrugged his shoulders. The grimness and anger was almost gone from his face, but he looked tired . . . and resigned. "Lucky for me I can still do the easy stuff I play at Dark Blue. If I couldn't play a little I'd go crazy." He started up the car. "Anyway, I guess we better get on to our little crisis at my office." He pulled out into traffic and turned on the radio.

Robyn cringed at the classical music that came on.

"Sorry," Steve said as he switched stations. "I forget not everyone loves Greig as much as I do."

"It's okay," she said. *Why does he torture himself listening to classical music?* she wondered.

He flipped to a rock station. After a few minutes, Elvis came on with "Can't Help Falling in Love with You."

When it was over, she asked, "Why do you always end your gigs with that song?"

Steve shrugged. "It was the first song I ever learned to play on the piano. My teacher was a huge Elvis fan and she had sheet music for all his hits and for some reason, she chose it to start me out."

"Ah, you play it to remember her."

"Sort of. It also reminds me of this big ironic thing about life. Kind of like what comes around goes around."

In no time, they pulled up to an unexceptional white building that looked like any of a dozen other federal buildings all over Washington.

He parked the car at the empty curb in front of the building.

He ran his I.D. card through the scanner and the front door of the building clicked open.

"So how'd you get into this business anyway?" She asked casually, hoping they were safely past the tense conversation they'd had in the car.

"Actually one of the surgeons who worked on my hand suggested I take a beginner's programming class because the keyboard work would be good physical therapy. I liked the class so I took another, then another, and before long people were waving money around, trying to get me to work for them. I guess you could say I have an aptitude for it, which is fortunate because otherwise I'd be just another unemployed musician."

"It looks so official," she said as she followed him to a suite of elevators.

"It is," Steve said as they stepped into the elevator and he pressed the button for the ninth floor. "There are several government offices in this building."

"I'm surprised they'd share."

Steve nodded his head. "Well, we don't take up much room and, given what we pay for rent, I'd say they're glad to have us."

Steve led her through a second set of double glass doors to a guard station where he signed them in under the scrutiny of a huge uniformed guy who looked a lot like Rocky Balboa.

"Server go down again?" the guard asked.

"I think so. Mark told me to come check it."

"Man." The guard breathed. "He can't even leave you alone long enough to finish your date."

"Tell me about it," Steve said as he led her to a lobby of elevators.

They didn't say anything on the ride up.

When the door opened, she immediately saw the glass-walled office of SunSurf Access Solutions.

"Good old SAS," Steve said sarcastically as he pulled another card out of his wallet and slid it through the magnetic lock on the door. "I like to say we're the golden glow on the dark cyber highway."

Robyn chuckled.

"Yeah, I know," he said as he opened the door and held it for her. "It sucks as a motto. But the investors thought it was clever. I guess to someone over forty it is."

Robyn walked into the cozy office. It appeared like any other office with a receptionist's desk and a couple of waiting room chairs.

A dark brown door stood in front of them. Steve stopped in front of it and swiped his card again.

"Jeez, how many doors do you have to swipe in the morning?" Robyn asked as he led her through it.

"Four."

She shook her head incredulously. "You guys have more security than Fort Knox, you know that?"

"Well when you're responsible for several *million* dollars of hardware and software, they tend to get a little paranoid about who has access to what."

"What happens if you lose your card?" she asked.

"They take me out back and have the FBI shoot me."

"That's a joke, right?"

"God, I hope so," he said with a nervous laugh. "But Mark swears his kid brother who works for the Bureau would do it if he asked him to. Personally, I'm not willing to find out."

"I can't say I blame you."

Steve stopped in front of a door that had his name on it.

He unlocked the door to his office, then held it open for her. Robyn stepped in while he flipped on a halogen lamp in the corner.

"Are the lights broken?" she asked as he bypassed the switch.

"Nah," he said, stepping to his desk and wiggling the mouse. "Fluorescent lights put a nasty glare on a computer screen. It's a lot easier on your eyes if you use a low-watt bulb instead."

"Hey, I wonder if Elyssa would let me try that. On second thought, she'd probably accuse me of trying to dim the lights for a quick nap."

Steve began entering commands on his keyboard.

Robyn stared at the monitor that was broken into three small panes. One box had a light-green marbled background, another had a burgundy landscape and one was a dark blue ocean-looking thing.

She had no idea what any of it meant, but Steve hammered out commands and seemed to have no problem making out the bizarre lines of type.

"So, is the server down after all?"

Steve nodded. "I'll go reboot her and see what happens."

"Want me to stay here?"

He draped his arm around her shoulders and gave a light squeeze. "You've come this far, you might as well see Ground Zero."

He led her the rest of the way down the hallway to another magnetically locked door. He swiped the card and when the door opened, the coldness of the room took her breath.

"Holy Christmas Tree, Batman! Could it be any colder in here?"

Steve moved to one of the huge machines on a wire rack of machines and again entered commands on a keyboard. "For an obvious reason, we call it the cold room. We need to keep the servers from overheating."

"It's a wonder they don't have frostbite."

Steve laughed as he shut the computer down and restarted it.

Robyn looked around at the room full of servers and computers that hummed like a hive of mad bees. "These suckers are huge."

"Hercules over here," he said, pointing to the computer to his left, "is a full terabyte."

"What's a terabyte?"

"A thousand gigs."

"What do you use it for?"

"It's our mail and newsgroups server."

Robyn shook her head, amazed by the size of the computer. "No wonder you call him Hercules."

Steve smiled. "Our sys-admin has this cartoon, fantasy, fetish thing going on with the equipment. The Cold Fusion server is called Stimpy. We also have Mickey, Spaceghost, Mojo, Bugs and Roadrunner. My computer is named Scooby."

Robyn rolled her eyes at the bizarre names. "At Allheart, we're pretty boring. Our computers are named one, two, three and so on."

"That would make them infinitely easier to keep straight. When I first started working here, it took me forever to remember which server did what."

Robyn counted about thirty servers in the room. "So how much does one of these go for?"

"Stimpy, the Real Audio server to your right, came in at a cool seventy grand."

Robyn choked. She had no idea they cost so much. "Are you serious?"

"And it was a bargain price."

"Baby, let's toss a few of these things into the car and head to the border!"

He laughed. "No thanks. I make way more than that and it doesn't require any heavy lifting."

"So are you going to become one of those Internet million-aires, you have stock options and all that? I might want to go take a few computer classes if it pays enough."

"Oh it does," he said sincerely. "I'm a six-figure guy and I'm not even trying that hard."

"That must be nice," she said. She'd *kill* just to make over twenty-four thousand a year.

"It's okay, I guess. Still, as I believe I mentioned earlier, I'd rather be playing the piano. Which I'd do for peanuts." He turned back to his work.

"*What are you doing now?* Robyn asked, following him back to his office.

"Making sure the authentication works."

After a second, he smiled. "Okay, you can kiss me, baby. Crisis averted!"

Robyn kissed him, but she was completely unprepared for the reception she got.

Before she knew it, they were lying on the floor, half under the desk and completely entwined. Hungry for him, she pulled his shirt off.

Robyn ran her hands over him, delighting in the heat of his kiss, the feel of his warm skin under the palms of her hands.

Just as Steve started to return the favor and pulled her shirt up over her head, they heard someone in the hallway.

"Yo, Steve, you here?"

He froze.

"Oh shit," he mumbled in her ear. "What the hell is Mark doing here?"

Steve gave her a panicked look. "If he comes in here and catches us like this, I'm dead meat."

"Steve?" Mark called as he paused in front of the door. "Where are you?"

Robyn heard the door handle turn.

Now fresh agony was raining down on poor Steve!

Chapter 4

Robyn scrambled from under Steve and handed him his T-shirt. "Get dressed," she whispered as she pulled her shirt down, then she climbed under the desk.

"What are you doing?" he asked.

"I don't want you to lose your job."

"Yeah, but—"

Before he could protest, the door swung open. "There you are," Mark said.

Robyn pressed herself farther up under the desk, hoping Steve's boss didn't look down and see her there.

"Man, I must have caught you at a bad time," Mark said.

"What?" Steve asked as Robyn held her breath.

"You look like you just crawled out of the bowels of hell, buddy. What, were you sleeping when I called?"

"Oh, yeah, I was tired. *Really* tired."

"Well, you probably want to turn your shirt right-side-out and around before you head home."

Robyn glanced up and had to stifle a laugh as she saw the tags of Steve's T-shirt sticking out at his throat.

Steve sent a flash of a grimace her way before he whipped the shirt off over his head and fixed it. "Sorry. I was trying to get here as fast as I could."

"Did you get it fixed?"

Steve nodded. "Yep. We're good to go."

"Great. Then let's go."

Oh shit! Robyn thought, her heart hammering.

"Oh, you go on ahead," Steve said nervously, and she noted the tenseness of his body. "I have a couple of things I still have to noodle with before I can leave."

"Yeah," Mark said with a strange note in his voice. "Like

getting whoever you have hidden under your desk out the door without me seeing her?"

Robyn covered her face with her hands as she heard Steve curse under his breath.

"I can explain," Steve said.

"I'm sure you can, first thing Monday morning. In my office."

She heard the door shut.

Feeling terrible, she crawled out from under the desk. "I'm so sorry, Steve. I didn't mean to get you into trouble with your boss."

He shrugged it off. "Forget about it. It's my fault anyway."

"Is he going to fire you?"

"Well, if he didn't fire me for leasing a Porsche on the company card for the trade show in Chicago last month, I doubt he'll fire me for this. He'll just chew me a new one and send out a memo to everyone about fraternizing on company property."

"I'm sorry. That'll be so embarrassing."

"Nah, not really. Memo-man sends out so many a day, most of us never read them anyway."

He held his hand out to her. "C'mon, let's get out of here before we get me into any more trouble."

"Okay."

Instead of taking her home, Steve drove her to his place. Robyn didn't really want to go home and once he suggested she stay with him, she wasn't about to say no.

Steve's apartment was fascinating to her. It was dark and not very spacious, pretty much consisting of a large square living area, a little bedroom off to one side, and a kitchen area and bath off to the other. But however modest the size, the place was filled with tantalizing and intimate details. There were books everywhere, in stacks on the floor, on tables, windowsills and shelves. There were luscious floor pillows—they looked to Robyn to be Moroccan or something equally exotic. The couch was huge and covered with the broken-in leather of an old valise. Across the couch was draped an old Navaho blanket, and there were odd little musical instruments, obviously from all over the world, carefully arranged in the nooks and crannies of his living room. There were a couple of Arts and Crafts glass lamps in opposite corners of the room, which, when he clicked them on, shed an otherworldly glow on the fabulous baby grand piano that obviously owned the room.

"It's gorgeous," she said as he came up behind her.

"Thanks. I used to play it late at night, but the neighbors started complaining. Now I can only play it between nine A.M. and eight P.M."

"Are you serious?"

He nodded.

"Who could possibly complain about the way you play?"

"I dunno. Maybe they just don't have an appreciation for the finer points of a Phil Collins composition."

She shot a quick look at him, afraid his mood might be about to veer again. He just smiled and shrugged his shoulders.

Before she could say anything more, and without saying a word himself, he lifted her up in his arms and carried her to his bedroom.

When Robyn woke up the next morning, she was alone. Her disappointment faded as she smelled the warm aroma of bacon and coffee.

Leaning back into the soft pillows, she remembered the wonder of last night.

Steve was amazing. She had suspected it before, but after last night, she knew it for truth. Even now her skin burned with the memory of his touch. He was so tender and thoughtful. The last of the real gentlemen?

Oh, how she hated for the morning to come. Now she'd have to go face the awkward "morning after" before making an exit, after which they'd no doubt go their own ways.

"I hate this," she mumbled as she got up and pulled on her clothes. Once dressed, she headed toward the good smells of morning.

Steve stood with his back to her. He was engrossed in the song he was humming until he turned toward the fridge and caught sight of her.

"Good morning," he said cheerfully. "Did you sleep well?"

"Like a baby."

"Great. I was just about to bring you breakfast in bed."

"I can go back there if you want."

"If it weren't two in the afternoon, I might take you up on it."

"Is it really?"

He pointed to the clock behind her.

Robyn turned. "God, I had no idea." A tremor of nervousness shook her. "I guess I better get going before I wear out my welcome."

"Wear it out? You kidding? I was kind of hoping we could go find more trouble today."

"What kind of trouble?" she asked, intrigued. Robyn loved trouble like a duck loved a clear pond.

Steve set a plate on the small breakfast table for her. "I heard there's a great exhibit up at the Smithsonian. You interested?"

"Am I?" she said, taking a seat. "That is my number-one place to hang out on weekends."

He winked. "I knew you were a woman after my own heart."

They ate their food in a hurry, then headed out to brave the wave of summer tourists they knew they'd meet.

As expected, the Mall was mobbed. There were the locals lounging about, some flying kites with kids; folks walking their dogs; and there were a million and one tourists gawking and taking photos.

After three passes without finding a parking space, Steve pulled up to one of the reserved parking spaces in front of the National Air and Space Museum.

"What are you doing?" Robyn asked. "They'll tow your car."

"No, they won't," he said confidently, then pointed to the baseball cap in his back window that bore an official FBI emblem. "The police have a courtesy arrangement. So long as they think I'm one of them, they'll leave my car alone."

"Where did you get that hat?"

"I borrowed it from Mark when we went to a trade show last fall."

"You are such a criminal," Robyn said teasingly.

He leaned over the gearshift and gave her a quick kiss, then opened her door for her. Robyn got out while he locked the doors and got out on his side.

Hand in hand, they walked across the Mall and headed to the National Museum of Natural History.

The day went by all too fast for Robyn. They laughed like kids as they explored the exhibits she had visited a thousand times, but never before had she enjoyed them more.

After a couple of hours, they left the museum and went to pass time in the Mall. The crowd had thinned out a bit and Steve led her toward one of the vendors.

"I'm hungry. You?" he asked.

"I could go for a hot dog."

Steve laughed, then kissed her.

Robyn savored the feel of him, until she heard his stomach rumble. "You are hungry, aren't you?"

"Yeah, food and sex are all I think about."

"And music?"

"Oh yeah, that too."

He let go of one hand and led her to a cart where he ordered hot dogs for both of them.

As they ate, they wandered toward the Vietnam War Memorial. Robyn stared at the names of all the faceless men who had died before she'd been born in a war no one had ever mentioned in any of her history classes.

She could feel a change in Steve's personality as they walked along the walls.

"It's so sad, isn't it?" she said.

"Yeah." He breathed. He paused by one plaque and reached out to finger one of the names.

Robyn looked closer and read the name, James Alexander Rood.

"My dad," he said quietly.

"Oh Steve, I'm sorry." Robyn touched his arm.

Steve placed his hand over hers and gave a light squeeze. "Thanks. I never knew him. My mother didn't know she was pregnant with me when he left and he died just a few weeks before I was born."

"That must have been terrible for her."

"Yeah, it was. She told me once that she was talking to this woman in the doctor's waiting room, and when she told the woman her husband had been killed over there, the woman asked her how it felt to carry a dead man's child."

Robyn's throat constricted in sympathetic pain. She couldn't imagine anything worse. "Some people are so thoughtless."

"Yes, they are," he agreed. "Or as my stepdad always says, 'Everywhere I go, there's always an asshole.'"

Robyn laughed half-heartedly. "I'm glad your mother found someone else."

"Yeah. She married Jim when I was three. My brother and I used to pretend Mom was normal, but as we got older it became more and more obvious that my father's death had taken a heavy toll on her."

"How do you mean?"

"I don't know. She just got increasingly withdrawn and moody over the years. We spent all of high school tiptoeing around her, trying not to set her off. She perked up a little when I got into Juilliard but ever since my accident, she's completely pulled back into herself."

"It's okay," she said, rubbing his arm. "My mother is no picnic either."

"Yeah, but is she certifiable?"

"She would be if there were a pedigree in it."

"Huh?"

"My mother—bless her heart—is one of those pretentious snobs who would jump out of a window if it became the vogue thing to do. I don't think she's ever had a thought that someone else didn't give her."

"So how'd you turn out to be so . . . different?"

"Ha! Different—I like that. I don't know, I've been in the business of bucking the norm since I was about six. Maybe it's who I am; maybe it's been a lifelong quest to get my parents' goat. Whatever. We've reached a point where we understand each other—at least enough to know what to expect from one another."

"I find it hard to believe they know what to expect of you—aren't you kind of making it up as you go along?" Steve asked with a chuckle.

"Oh, they know to expect phone calls from strangers in the middle of the night, telling them to come make bail for me!" She grinned at Steve as she watched his eyebrows go up just a little.

"I'm just kidding," she reassured him. "I mean they know to expect the unexpected. Let's just put it this way—I know where to find them, and for the most part, they know where to find me. We try to keep it simple like that."

"Simple would be nice. My mom is hard work." Steve sighed.

"What about your stepdad?" Robyn asked. "Does he take care of her?"

Steve shook his head. "He divorced her a few years back. He still keeps up with us though. His philosophy is we may not be his by blood, but we are his by the sweat and time he put into raising us."

"That's nice," she said, lacing her arm with his. "Most men wouldn't feel that way."

"Yeah, he's been a good dad. I can't complain on that side. Sam and I are lucky my mom didn't start slipping until we got older." He removed his arm from her grasp, then draped it over her shoulders. "What about your dad?"

"Let's see. It's summer so he's living in his New York penthouse with wife number five, at least I think it's number five. I've sort of lost count and I can't remember if her name is Brandy or Mandy. His former wife was one and this one is the other, but I can't keep it straight. Not that it matters. Since it's an even-numbered year I figure he's due for another divorce sometime this fall."

Steve drew a deep breath. "How do you stand it?"

"Well, at least he makes sure I have a place to live. Unlike my mother, when he does remember me, he comes bearing gifts. My mother just comes bearing heavy amounts of guilt and criticism."

"You know, I don't get it. If you go to the SPCA to adopt a pet, they screen you carefully, and ask you all kinds of questions such as if your dog whizzes on the rug what will you do? But they'll let anyone leave the hospital with a baby. Man, people have some seriously screwed-up priorities."

"It's true."

They walked around the Washington Monument in silence. Robyn thought about what Steve had said. There was a lot of depth to him, much more than she had suspected when she first started obsessing over him all those months ago at Dark Blue. He was sort of serious, and not the type of man she'd spent much time around. He was a whole person, with life experience, opinions, and moods. He wasn't easy to get, the way most of the guys she'd known had been. Those guys were paint-by-numbers guys. Steve was a Monet.

What was it about him that made her so breathless?

Nine thirty Sunday night found her still with him as he played a set at Dark Blue. She sat at a table in the back drinking a beer.

"I thought I'd find you here."

Robyn looked up to see Dana Boyle standing to her right.

"Hey chick!" she greeted with a smile. "What brings you out here on a Sunday?"

Dana took the chair by Robyn and set her glass of wine on the table. "Big fat boredom, baby, and a need to get out of my sublet before I scream."

"Bad weekend?"

"Let's just say a season in hell would have brightened my afternoon."

"Ouch."

Dana sighed as she draped one arm over the back of her chair. "Where have you been all weekend? I kept trying to call. Brewster-Mills just got a whole bunch of new earrings and I thought you'd like to go fishing with me."

Robyn smiled knowingly as her gaze inadvertently went to Steve. "I was busy."

"Busy?"

Robyn felt heat creep over her face. *Oh jeez. Am I blushing? Me?*

"Who was he?" Dana teased.

"You wouldn't believe me if I told you."

"Oh lord, not the president?"

Robyn tossed a handful of peanuts at Dana. "I was with Steve."

"Steve?" Dana repeated. "Not *the* Steve."

Robyn nodded.

Dana turned around to look at where Steve played. "Steve?" she asked again.

"I told you you wouldn't believe it."

"Da-mn!" she drawled. "How'd you manage that?"

"I have no idea. Call it kismet."

"So did you have fun?"

"Um, yes?"

"Oh, it must have been great if you're not coughing up the details." Dana laughed. "Well I see old Steve is finishing up his song. I guess I better motor so as not to interfere with you two."

"You sure?" Robyn asked with a frown. "I mean you just got here."

"Actually, I've been here for over an hour and unlike you, I like getting to work on time. If I don't head home soon, Elyssa will get to chew on us both come morning."

"Yeah, yeah, rub it in."

Dana drank the last of her wine. "Ciao, babes."

"Yeah, adigo."

"Adigo?" Steve asked as he came up behind Robyn's back.

Robyn turned with a smile. "When I was a kid, I thought they were saying 'adigo,' so I still say it instead of adios."

"Okay," he said slowly as he took Dana's vacated chair. "So where did your friend run off to?"

"Home."

"Ah." He reached over and took a drink of her beer. "I have one more set and then I'm free to go as well."

"So, what are you going to do when you finish?"

He flashed her a grin. "I was kind of hoping to nibble on some more of your flesh. I kind of like the way your skin tastes just behind your ear. And behind your knees and your—"

Robyn shushed him quiet. "I suppose that could be arranged," she said in a low whisper.

"Good," he said, taking another swig of her beer. "Cause I'm feeling hungry."

Morning came too soon for Robyn. She woke up as Steve pulled away from her.

"You leaving?" she asked.

He nodded. "I've got to go to work and let Mark chew me out, remember?"

She trailed a hand over the muscles of his back as he pulled his undershorts on. "I'm sorry."

"Don't be. If I have to get yelled at, I can't think of a better reason." He stood up and pulled on his pants. "I had a great time this weekend."

"Me too."

Steve stared at her with an expression she couldn't read. "I really like you, Robyn."

"I'm glad." And she was too—much more than she should be.

Steve pulled his shirt on over his head. "I'll give you a call later."

You better.

"Okay."

He gave her one last long kiss before pulling away. "Later?"

"Later," she said, hoping this time the guy actually meant it.

By noon, Robyn had stared at the phone so much, she thought she might be going blind.

"What are you doing?" Carole asked as she dropped a contract on top of Robyn's desk.

Absently, Robyn stuck it in Elyssa's incoming box without breaking eye contact with the phone. "I'm waiting on a call."

"From?"

"Steve."

"Steve?" Carole asked in a vague way that let Robyn know she was searching her mind for whom Robyn meant. "Piano Steve?" she asked after a brief pause.

"Yes."

"Why?"

Robyn looked up, blinked, then stared back at the phone. "He told me he would call me later."

"Call you later when?"

"I don't know. That's why I'm staring at the phone."

Carole snapped her fingers in front of Robyn's face, until Robyn looked up and met her gaze. "Could you please elaborate?"

"We spent the weekend together."

"Oh Robyn, you didn't sleep with him, did you?"

"Duh! Of course I did."

Carole rolled her eyes. "Will you never learn? You don't just hop in bed with a guy then expect him to call. Really Robyn, you have to take time and develop a relationship first. Didn't your mother ever tell you a man won't buy a cow when he gets the milk for free?"

"I'm not a cow and when was my mom supposed to say that to me? Before or after her Junior League meetings, tennis lessons, pedicures, facials and lunch appointments?"

Carole folded her arms across her chest as she looked askance at Robyn. "God, you're really bummed."

"I'm getting there," Robyn murmured, looking back at the phone.

"Then call him."

"What?" Robyn asked, stunned that Carole would suggest such a thing.

"Call him. Do you know his number?"

"Yeah."

"Then call him."

Robyn sat there debating. "Will you stand here while I do it?"

"Why?"

"I need moral support."

"Okay. If it'll make you feel better, I'll stand here until you two get mushy."

Robyn dialed Steve's work number. "Um, yeah, can I speak to Steve Rood please?"

"I'm sorry," the receptionist said. "He's not in."

"Oh? When will he be back?"

"I don't know," the woman said peevishly. "He just took off this morning and didn't say anything. Oh wait, yes he did. He left me a message to tell Donna that he'd be late for dinner tonight so keep it warm and be ready for him. Are you Donna?"

Chapter 5

Robyn couldn't answer the woman on the phone.

"Ma'am?" the receptionist asked. "Are you Donna?"

Numbly, she hung up the phone.

"Robyn?" Carole asked. "You okay?"

She still couldn't speak. It was all she could do to just sit there and not scream.

Who the hell was Donna anyway?

His girlfriend?

His *wife?*

For a moment, Robyn felt like a character in a soap opera, and she half-expected to discover that this Donna was his evil twin, out to wreck his life, or something stupid like that.

But this wasn't a soap. This was real and Steve had been two-timing them both.

Tears gathered in her eyes and Robyn struggled to hold them back. Steve had toyed with her feelings, lied to her, used her, and then left without a word. Damn him! Damn his sorry, rotten hide.

"That rank, no-good, sorry bastard!" Robyn snarled.

Carole frowned. "Who?"

"Steve."

"Steve?"

Blinking back tears, Robyn looked up at her. "He's not at work. He went to see someone named Donna."

"Oh Robyn, I'm so sorry."

"Don't be," she said angrily as she grabbed a stack of papers off her desk, lifted them up and organized them as if nothing was wrong. "You were right. I *am* a cow. A big, dumb, stupid heifer cow with the common sense of a lump of cud."

"Don't be so hard on yourself."

"Yeah right," she said bitterly as she shoved the papers into a folder.

She had to get out of here. She needed time to think. Time to . . . Oh, she didn't know what she needed other than a break from staring at the crisp, pristine walls of Allheart.

Carole sighed. "Robyn—"

"Tell Elyssa I'm taking my lunch."

"Robyn—"

Robyn ignored Carole as she snatched up her purse and headed for the door.

"Robyn!"

Still she didn't stop. She didn't want to talk right now, she just wanted to be left alone to sort through her conflicting emotions.

What she needed was a long lunch at Neiman Marcus!

Robyn headed to her Mustang, which she now despised, and decided the mall was just what she needed.

For an hour and a half, she scoured the stores, charging like a bull rhino on steroids.

Yeah, she'd have a time paying for it, but right now she just wanted to pamper herself. Dammit, she worked hard for her money and it was hers to spend.

Pushing off her buyer's remorse, Robyn only vaguely considered the fact that she had gone through over five hundred dollars since she'd left her desk.

She'd dwell on that later.

By the time she got back to the office three hours later, she felt a little better.

But Steve was still a pig. A big, hairy, nasty, three-toed, tree pig. With warts.

"Hey kid," Elyssa greeted as she came through the door and headed for her teakwood desk. "Carole said something was bothering you. You okay?"

"Fine," Robyn said as she sat back down at her desk and shoved her purse in her desk drawer. At least her depression kept Elyssa from chewing her out over taking such a long lunch break. "I'm just peachy."

"Did you do something to your hair at lunch?"

"I got it spiked. What do you think?"

"It's cute."

"But it makes my nose stand out, right?" Robyn asked as

she began clicking for her email. "I thought so too. So I made an appointment with Dr. Briley."

"That lunatic who advertises his plastic surgery clinic on the radio?"

"The same," Robyn replied. "They're having a special two-for-one thing. I figured I could get my nose fixed and have him suck some fat out of my a—"

"Robyn! Don't be an idiot."

"Why not? My stepmonkey had her thighs done last year. She said it didn't hurt a bit."

Elyssa narrowed a cold glare on her. "Your stepmother is twenty years older than you."

"Ten," Robyn amended. "My father wouldn't be caught dead with a forty-year-old wife."

By the irritated look on Elyssa's face she could tell her boss didn't think much of her glibness. "You're being ridiculous."

"No, I'm not. I'm being *practical*."

"What's going on?" Alix asked as she joined them.

"Robyn is going to have her nose done," Elyssa explained in a disgusted tone.

"Not this again?" Alix asked with a sigh. "Good Lord, Robyn, when are you going to quit thinking—"

"She's not thinking about it," Elyssa interrupted. "She made an appointment for it."

"Why?"

Robyn didn't say anything. She couldn't. How could she tell them what was inside her? Never had she been good enough. Her father had wanted a son and got stuck with a daughter. Her mother had wanted a beautiful, graceful, *pliable* daughter and got stuck with the awkward, freewheeling nut with mousy-brown hair.

Robyn was tired of being Robyn. She wanted to be someone else for awhile. Maybe if she changed her hair, her style, and got a new face, she'd feel better.

Perhaps if she were really different, then she could do like Carole suggested. Push the men away and take her time finding that one special man.

Anything would be an improvement at this point.

And at any rate, she couldn't feel any worse about herself than she felt at this moment. A nose job could only be a step up.

"Whose green Escort is that outside?" Dana asked as she came in the front door.

"Mine," Robyn said.

"You got a new car?" Elyssa asked. "When?"

"At lunch. I traded my Mustang for it."

"Why?" the three of them asked in unison.

"It's part of the new me," Robyn said. "I'm now practical Robyn Barrett."

"A practical person wouldn't get plastic surgery done off the cuff," Elyssa said.

"Who says it's off the cuff?" Robyn asked testily. "All of you know how long I've been thinking about it. Why, I've been putting away five percent of my salary since I started working here for the day I would have it done."

"I thought you were joking about that," Dana said.

"Well, I wasn't."

Feeling suddenly trapped by them, Robyn got up. "Now if you'll all excuse me, I have work to do."

They followed her to the copy room.

"What?" Robyn asked as they squeezed into the little room behind her. "Are you all going to follow me to the bathroom next?"

"Until you tell us what's going on, we are." Elyssa folded her arms over her chest and took that stubborn pose that didn't bode well for whomever she confronted. "What is going on?"

"Steve two-timed her."

Robyn stiffened at Carole's voice coming from the hallway.

"Steve the piano player?" Elyssa asked. "She barely knows him."

"Not after this weekend," Carole explained. "Seems Mr. Rood spent the whole weekend with our little Robyn, then skipped out on her with someone named Donna."

"Well, that sucks." Dana humphed.

"How dare he!" Alix added.

As her friends' indignation broke out on her behalf, Robyn felt overwhelmed by their loyalty and love, and before she knew it, she was crying.

Elyssa hugged her as she sobbed out the pain inside her heart.

"It's okay, Robyn. You take your time," Elyssa said gently.

Robyn patted Elyssa on the back as she pulled away. "I'm sorry. But for some reason I thought Steve was different."

Dana handed her a tissue. "We all fall victim to it at one time or another. We see what we want to see, not what really is. I think it's something chemical in a guy that enables them to slip past our best defenses."

Robyn smiled tenuously. "Actually I always thought it was how cute their butts looked in jeans."

"Well," Dana said, giving her a pat as she wiped her eyes. "I think we should declare an official wienie-roast tonight. What say you, ladies?"

"Here, here," Carole concurred. "A wienie-roast for the Steve Wienie himself."

"I'll pick up the hot dogs and stuff after work," Dana said.

"And I'll bring the wine," Alix volunteered.

"You up to it, Robyn?" Elyssa asked.

Robyn sniffed and tossed the tissue in the trash can. "I'll bring the buns."

"That a girl!"

Dinner that night was interesting, more like a twelve-step meeting than a dinner party. They grilled their wienies at Robyn's house, and each one barbecued a man in her past who had done her wrong.

It was amazing just how long the list of men was. But Robyn was surprised to learn her list wasn't as long as some of her friends'.

"Now you know why I've sworn off men," Carole said as she swirled her wine around in her glass. "May they all roast in their own male juices."

"Amen," Dana said, taking a huge bite of hot dog. "If it weren't for jars and bugs, we'd have no use for them."

"Yeah well, that's why God invented can openers and Orkin," Elyssa said.

Robyn laughed, but inside she didn't really feel that much better. It still hurt.

Worse, she kept seeing Steve as he'd been the past weekend. Kind, considerate, by turns serious and funny. And she knew he was still being all those things tonight, only he was doing it with Donna.

By eight thirty, the party was over and her friends were heading out.

Alone, she walked around the living room. She tried to sit on the couch, but all she could do was see Steve sitting there playing her guitar. So she headed to bed, but that was even worse.

By nine fifteen she knew she had to go out or go crazy. As quickly as she could, she dressed herself all in black—her uniform for anonymous night-crawling—and headed off to the Black Cat. Yup, tonight she wanted to get as far from old Steve's haunt as she could and the alternative dive on T Street was just what she needed.

An hour later, she ended up parking less than a block from Dana's Adams-Morgan sublet and walking down U Street to reach the club. It was one of those nights where the club featured lesser-known bands so the management had pulled the curtain down the center of the room and set up a stage in the back corner. Robyn entered through the Red Room in the bar area where the red walls were covered in murals.

She scanned the occupants, looking for a familiar face in the crowd of punks and townies, but tonight there wasn't a soul she recognized except for the bartender, Thorn. He was cute enough. Not much taller than she, he was probably only a year or two older. His dark brown hair was short and spiked and he wore one of those goatees that she really didn't care for.

Who was the idiot who had told the guys that women liked those anyway? Whoever it was, she'd like to corner them and give them a piece of her mind.

"Hey Robyn!" Thorn called as she stopped at the bar and ordered a beer. "I haven't seen you here in a while."

"Yeah," she shouted over the music. "I've been busy." A small fib, really. She'd been spending most of her nights for the past few months sighing over Steve at Dark Blue.

What a solid waste of time *that* had been.

When she went to pay Thorn for the beer, he pushed her money back at her. "You look like you could use it," he said with a wink.

"Thanks," she said, then headed off into the crowd.

A few minutes later while she stood off to the side listening to the thrash band, someone came up and touched her on the arm. Robyn turned to see Thorn standing behind her. "I'm on break," he said. "And I thought you might like another beer."

"Thanks," she said, taking it from him. She still had half of her first beer to go, so she set it aside discreetly.

"You know, you look really hot tonight," Thorn said, leaning forward to talk into her ear.

A wave of coldness went up her spine as tears gathered in her throat. She didn't want to hear that from him. Not tonight.

"Well, it's the middle of summer in Washington, DC. Of course I'm hot," Robyn said sarcastically.

"Not that kind of hot. Hot-hot." Thorn gave her a half smile.

She was determined to swallow the pain. To hell with Steve. If he didn't want her, that was fine. Thorn was good-looking. Granted he couldn't play anything other than the radio, and he wasn't quite the stunningly handsome guy Steve was, that didn't mean she should just shut him out.

"You look hot too," she said.

"You know, I get off at eleven. You want go get a cup of coffee or something?"

She fought the urge to say no. If Steve could go off with another woman, she could go off with another man. "Sure."

Thorn smiled. "Great. If you get bored, head on back to the bar and we can talk while I serve."

Robyn followed after him, and within fifteen minutes she realized he wasn't nearly as engaging as Steve.

Not that I care, she said to herself. Tonight Thorn wasn't Steve and that made him plenty attractive to her.

Besides, she had no intention of sleeping with Thorn. She just needed to be around someone tonight who could distract her from thoughts she didn't want to have.

By the time Thorn got off work, Robyn knew she was making a mistake by going anywhere with him. She had no interest in Thorn.

"You know, Thorn," she said once they were outside. "It's getting late and I have to work in the morning. I probably should just go on home."

"C'mon Robyn," he said, smiling a charming smile at her. "Don't be such a nervous Nellie. I'm not asking you to have sex with me. Let's just go grab a decent bite to eat and I'll bring you back to your car."

She should probably say no, but he did look a little

adorable. He gave her a hopeful grin. "Please?" he begged. "I'll behave myself. I promise."

How could she say no to that?

"Okay," she said with a smile she almost meant.

Thorn led her behind the club where he parked his Honda Nighthawk. He handed her a black helmet.

Robyn strapped it on, then climbed on behind him.

Thorn kick-started it, then they were off.

As usual, the streets were bustling as they made their way through the rushing traffic.

Robyn was just about to shout at Thorn to slow down when she heard brakes shrieking. One moment, her worst problem was Steve dumping her and in the next, it was the fact that she was flying through the air with nothing to hold on to.

"Robyn? Can you hear me?"

Robyn came awake slowly to the sound of Elyssa's commanding, somewhat irritated voice. At first she thought she had fallen asleep at her desk again.

Until she tried to move and couldn't.

Panicking, she opened her eyes and met Elyssa's concerned gaze. Her throat was so sore that she could barely swallow and the back of her right hand stung from the IV buried in it. The pungent odor of antiseptic stung her nose and she heard the beeps from a monitor over her right shoulder.

Looking around, she took in the small hospital room as well as the faces of Carole, Alix and Dana, who were crowded around her bed to see her.

"Oh thank God." Dana breathed as she took Robyn's left hand in hers. "We were scared to death you were in a coma or something."

In that instant everything came rushing back. Robyn remembered the car that had cut them off and Thorn yelling as he swerved into traffic. Worst of all, she remembered the bike skidding and falling and her body tumbling through the air, then across pavement that seemed to shred her skin like a grater.

The last thing she remembered was coming to rest beneath the front end of a car. Of staring up at an engine and feeling the heat of it on her face as sirens blared in the background. And then everything had gone black.

"Thorn?" Robyn asked, her voice sounding strange and muffled to her ears.

"The guy you were with is okay," Carole told her. "He banged up his leg, but they sent him home a little while ago."

Since Robyn was still hooked to the monitors, and judging by the concern on her friends' faces, she could tell she hadn't been so lucky.

"When can I leave?" Robyn asked.

Her friends exchanged panicked looks.

Once more Robyn tried to move and couldn't. "Oh God, I'm paralyzed!" she shrieked in panic.

"No, no," Elyssa said, touching her arm to comfort her. "You just took a bad tumble. The doctor said you won't have any trouble walking or moving about in a few days. They just have you drugged right now to keep you put and let your body heal itself."

Robyn calmed a little as she realized if she could feel Elyssa's and Dana's touch, that was a good thing. If she could feel them, she wasn't paralyzed and Elyssa wasn't lying to make her feel better. Taking deep breaths, Robyn leaned her head back and relaxed a little.

"Did I break anything?" she asked.

Elyssa shook her head. "You have a concussion and hit your head pretty hard on the street. The doctor wants to keep you here for a few days and just see how you're doing before you go home alone."

"Did you call my parents?" Robyn asked.

"I did. Your dad wasn't home, so I left a message with his answering service and your mother's housekeeper said that she's in France for two weeks. The housekeeper has been in touch with her, and she said she'd call you when she gets back in the States."

It figured. God forbid her mother should be concerned about her only child being in the hospital.

Well, at least she had her friends.

"My body's okay, right?" Robyn asked again, needing to be reassured.

"Yes. Your body's fine. You just hurt your head."

It wasn't until the next morning that Robyn fully understood Elyssa's words. It wasn't just her head that had been hurt. It was her face.

"We can do a nice job, though you won't quite look the way you did before the wreck," the doctor had explained breezily.

As his words filtered through her mind, Robyn could feel the tears seeping again from the corner of her eyes.

And she couldn't even wipe them! Something that was hard for a woman who prided herself on being self-sufficient.

Robyn tried to sniff, but her bandaged nose just burned, reminding her of the damage she must have done to it. No one would let her see what she looked like and in her mind she figured she must be truly hideous.

It's what I get, she thought wryly. *I always joked about plastic surgery and looking like someone else. Well, I got what I wanted. Only I wanted to look like Catherine Deneuve not Boris Karloff.*

"Hey kiddo," Dana said as she came through the door. "How you feeling?"

Robyn drew a trembling breath. "Not so good. Tell me the truth, Dana. How bad is it?"

Dana gave a nervous glance to the door. "I know the doctor said not to, but I can't let you lie there without knowing." She fished in her purse and pulled out a small black powder compact. Opening it, Dana held it up to where she could see.

Robyn's heart stopped as she saw herself bandaged up like a mummy. There was still a nose, but she could tell by the shape of the bandage that her little pug nose would never be the same again.

Sobbing, she closed her eyes and wished herself anywhere but here.

Chapter 6

*Steve came off the stage feeling invigorated. He couldn't re-*member the last time he had felt this good about a performance.

They had actually liked him!

No, not just liked, they had *loved* him. Three curtain calls and they still were applauding.

Man, a guy could get used to this.

The only thing was Robyn. If he could just have her here to share it, it would be even better.

He paused at the pay phone in the hallway and for the millionth time, tried to call.

The phone rang four times.

Hey there, sorry you got the machine. But hey, I'm a busy woman and am probably out having a great time. Do me a fave and leave a message at the tone. Ciao.

Steve clenched his teeth. "I swear, if I get that message one more time I'm going to go to her house and rip the damn machine out of the wall."

Whatever. He'd try again later.

Steve paused. Then again, maybe Robyn was trying to give him the brush-off . . .

Nah, not possible. She was just a busy woman like she said and sooner or later, he would catch her at home.

"*Am I ever going home again?* Robyn asked as she*watched the doctor examine her face.

"Of course you will, Robyn. You just need time to heal."

Time to heal. Robyn rolled her eyes. She was tired of hearing that. All she wanted was to escape from here and go home where she could at least be around things that reminded her of her. Especially since her face no longer looked like her.

If only Steve had shown some interest, then maybe it wouldn't be so bad. But with each day that came and went with no word from him, she felt worse and worse.

Did no one care about her?

It was two weeks before they let her go home. Her parents still hadn't bothered to do anything more than send flowers and phone. Her father promised her the best plastic surgeon money could buy, but when it came to him actually coming for a visit, well, he had more excuses than a convict on death row.

Thorn had stopped by a few times and brought flowers as well. He felt terrible about the wreck and told her repeatedly that if she needed anything at all to give him a call and he'd come running.

But what she needed, neither Thorn nor her girlfriends could provide.

She needed someone to really take care of her. Someone who could make her feel whole again.

Unfortunately, that someone was her and in the mood she was in, she knew it would be a long, long time before the huge empty hole in her chest went away.

Worse, she had no way to distract herself from the hurt she felt over Steve's abandonment. Had anyone told him about the wreck?

If they had, he must not have cared at all, because she hadn't heard a single word from him. And that hurt even more than the knowledge that it would be a year before she had a normal face again.

Doom, despair, rain agony on me.

And so the days went. Each one more painful than the one before and it seemed like forever before the doctor finally let her go home.

Rachel drove her home that evening and stayed over, then left for work.

To celebrate her first morning back in her town house, Robyn stared at her face in the bathroom mirror. Most of the bandages were gone, except for the one over the bridge of her mangled nose. She still had ugly, dark-purple and yellow bruises under her eyes and a large cut across her chin and left cheek.

"Ooh babe," she whispered bitterly to herself. "You are one hot mama."

Her nose would never be the same again. The bone had been crushed and it was turned at a strange angle. Maybe she should consider taking up boxing? At least she wouldn't have to worry about being punch-drunk.

"Ha, ha," she muttered sarcastically, leaving the bathroom and heading downstairs to the kitchen.

She choked down a few bites of cereal, but that was all she could manage. What she needed was to get out of here and do something.

She'd even begged Elyssa to let her come back to work, but Elyssa refused. She wanted her to recuperate.

Robyn just wanted her life back the way it had been three weeks ago. Funny, she'd never appreciated how wonderful the mundane was until now.

She left the kitchen and flopped down on her sofa. Picking up the remote, she flipped channels.

Heck, she'd even show up for work on time if Elyssa would just let her back in the office.

The phone rang.

Robyn glanced at it, but decided to let the answering machine have it. She didn't want to talk to anyone at the moment. All she wanted was to wallow in her misery.

Leaning her head back, she continued to flip channels on the television.

Just as she became halfway interested in Ronco's latest infomercial a knock sounded on her door. Robyn pushed herself off her couch and walked to the peephole. A man around the age of fifty stood on the stoop holding two dozen roses.

Robyn rolled her eyes. Great, just great, another bunch of freaking flowers she didn't feel like putting in water. Her father had always been a florist's best friend.

Why couldn't he just come see her? Whoever had told him that flowers would make everything okay with a woman should be shot.

Worse, she knew he wasn't really sending them himself, but was having his secretary do it for him.

Opening the door, she smiled at the older gentleman. "Hi," she said.

"I have a delivery for Robyn Barrett," he said, handing them to her.

Robyn signed for them, thanked him and closed the door.

These were prettier than the last batch. Robyn took her roses to the kitchen sink and set them aside as she opened the card.

Hi, Honey. Hope today is better than the last. Keep your chin up.

"Thanks, Dad," she muttered. "If I still had a chin, I would do that for you."

She tossed the roses into the garbage disposal.

By the time Steve made it back to his apartment, he was exhausted. Man, how did rock bands manage such tours? It was hell on the body.

He flopped down on his sofa and dialed Robyn's number. The one good thing was that he had finally learned it by heart. Again it rang and the answering machine picked up.

"Oh, screw this," he snapped, tossing the phone away. He was an attractive man, he didn't need to waste his time on some chick who couldn't be bothered to even phone him once in a while.

He had more important things to do. Leaning back, he closed his eyes and pushed Robyn completely out of his thoughts.

Two weeks later, Robyn sighed as she sat in her old desk chair. "At last," she said, smiling. "I'm finally getting back into my old routine."

"Robyn?" Dana gaped as she came through the door. "You're here before I am? Holy shit! Is the world coming to an end?"

"Yeah, babe. It's Armageddon and you missed it."

"Ha-ha." Dana laughed as she made her way to her office. "But just in case the holocaust does come today, please take a message and tell the four horsemen to get back to me. I have way too much to do today to be bothered."

"Will do," she shouted as she pulled up Elyssa's schedule and emailed her a list of appointments for the day.

An hour later, Elyssa stuck her head out of the office. "Wow, Robyn, you're really on the ball today."

"I know. Having a wreck was great for my work ethic. Maybe you guys should hire someone to run me over on a regular basis."

"You're not funny."

"Sure I am. Besides, I saw you laugh."

"I did not."

"Did too."

Elyssa rolled her eyes, then vanished back into her office.

Robyn got up and grabbed the stack of contracts Dana had left on her desk earlier and took them into the copy room where Malcolm was fighting the Xerox machine again.

"Toner?" she asked.

"Nah, I think it ate a wad of paper."

Robyn cocked her brow as Malcolm took his shoe off and hammered the side of the copier, trying to move one of the switches.

"You better be careful, if Elyssa catches you doing that she'll flip."

Before he could answer, Robyn heard the door open. She peeked around the corner to see Steve coming in, removing his sunglasses.

"Oh my God," she breathed, dodging behind the door to keep him from seeing her.

"What?" Malcolm asked.

"The guy who just came in. You have to go out there and tell him I died or something ok? Hell, tell him I no longer work here."

Malcolm frowned. "What?"

"Just do it, Malcolm, or I'm going to tell Elyssa what you were just doing."

Grumbling, Malcolm went to greet Steve.

Steve stared blankly at the nerdy little guy in front of him. "What do you mean she went to the Ukraine?"

The guy shrugged. "She said she needed a major vacation and took off."

Locking his jaw, Steve nodded. Fine, he knew a brush-off when he heard one.

"Well, tell Miss Barrett—"

"Steve?"

He looked around to see Dana coming through the door behind him.

"What are you doing here?" she asked.

"I came to see Robyn, but this guy said she quit and took off to the Ukraine for a vacation."

Dana burst out laughing. "That sounds like Robyn, doesn't it?"

"Actually," he said, "it does."

She nodded. "Well, she didn't jump the country. She's here."

"And she's avoiding me."

Dana shook her head. "Do you blame her?"

"Hell yes, I blame her."

Dana raised a censorious brow at him. "My that's some ego you have there. You play around on her and then—"

"I do what?"

"Play around on her, bucko. Your secretary told her you were off with your other lover for a tryst."

"My what?"

"Just like a man to deny it," she said to the guy behind him. "Isn't it Malcolm?"

"If I agree with you, do I get a pay raise?" the kid asked before he took off into the back of the office.

Miffed, Steve glared at her. "Look, I don't know what you heard, but I don't have another lover."

Dana shrugged. "Well, if that's true, then you have a lot of explaining to do to Robyn."

"Well, I'd be happy to if I could ever find her."

"Have you tried her house?"

"Yes. I went there before I came here, but no one's home."

"Then keep trying."

Angry, Steve glared at her. "You know, I'm too old to be playing these high school games. Tell Robyn to call me when she grows up. I might still be around then, but most likely not."

And with that, he headed out the door. To hell with her, he thought. He really didn't need this shit.

Robyn rushed out to Dana. "Well?" she demanded. "What did he say?"

"He said he didn't have a girlfriend."

"Oh, bullshit."

"I know."

"And?"

"He said to tell you to call him when you grow up. He might be around."

"What the hell is that supposed to mean?"

"I don't know. You're the one who slept with him. I'm just telling you what he said."

Robyn glared out the door wishing she hadn't stayed in the back after all. What she needed was to give the two-timing dog a piece of her mind.

Oh to hell with that. She didn't need the stress of it. She could do just fine by herself. She was a strong woman, with a strong mind. The last thing she needed was a moody, woman-izing musician.

Almost a month later, Robyn was feeling a little better. Her face had started to heal more and some of the scars had already faded. Still, there was a large bruise under one eye and her nose had that odd twist to it.

But she was beginning to see a light at the end of the tunnel.

And better still, she hadn't needed a man to help her. She had done it all on her own.

Yup, she was feeling better than she had in a long, long time.

Steve finished up his gig and wended his way through the crowd. Since he'd come back, things just hadn't been the same. He was even more jaded than he had been before. Something he would have thought impossible had he not been experiencing it.

"What's wrong with me?" he whispered as he neared the bar and ordered a straight vodka.

But then he knew.

He missed Robyn. Even though she was only one step away from an asylum, he missed her craziness. She had such a *je ne sais quoi* about her.

He laughed as he remembered them getting caught in his office.

Now *that* had been fun.

Tossing back his drink, he realized how much he missed her. *You don't need this crap*, he told himself.

No, he didn't. He was a big boy with a big-boy job and big-boy dreams. The last thing he needed was some half-baked woman screwing up his life.

But then, when had life ever been about what he needed? He was an artist living a life of dreams.

Nope, his life was all about what he wanted. And right then, he wanted Robyn.

Robyn woke up to a lazy Saturday. Scratching her head, she poked around the kitchen looking for food. She poured her cereal into a large tumbler, then added milk and drank the mixture while her coffee percolated.

Sitting down at the table, she skimmed the paper. Nothing but crime and corruption about.

And a long, boring weekend ahead. Yee-friggin-hah. She couldn't wait.

She yawned as someone knocked on the door.

"Come on, Dad," she groused. "Not again."

Plodding down the hallway, she saw Fred, the delivery-man. By now, they were on a first-name basis.

"Hi Fred," she said, as she opened the door. "How's the wife and kids?"

"Fine," he said with a smile as he handed her another bunch of roses. "You doing all right at work?"

"Yes, sir," she said, taking them from him. "It's a real peach."

He laughed. "Well, you have a great weekend."

"You too."

Robyn closed the door and headed back to the kitchen. She was just about to send them to the same place as the past four million roses her dad had sent when something made her stop.

A strange sensation prickled the back of her neck and before she could stop herself, she looked at the small card.

I hope you get these. I've called a million times and either the phone is busy or no one answers. Call me! Steve.

For a full minute, she didn't move. All she could do was stare at the note.

Just who the hell did he think he was?

Anger ripped through her.

Call me?

Hah!

Furious, she tossed the flowers in the trash and ground the card up in the garbage disposal.

"Rot in hell," she snarled, heading to the living room.

What an insufferable jerk!

The phone rang.

Without thinking, Robyn picked it up. "Hello?"

"Well it's about—"

She slammed the phone down as soon as she heard Steve's voice.

The phone rang again.

She answered it.

"Robyn?" Steve asked timidly.

"Bite me." This time, she turned the ringer off and tossed the phone to the coffee table.

Forty-five minutes later, there was another knock on the door. Still seething, she didn't bother to look through the peephole. This time, she was sure it was flowers from her dad.

Opening the door, she froze as she saw Steve standing in front of her.

Oh but he looked good. He'd gotten some sun on his face and the warm breeze ruffled his dark hair. He had circles under his eyes as if he hadn't slept much and that damn musky scent of his wafted toward her, reminding her just how good he had felt in her arms.

Robyn let out a curse, then she slammed the door shut. Or at least she tried to. Unfortunately, Steve had put his foot in the way.

Furious, she leaned her weight against the door and struggled to close it with or without his foot there to block it.

"Lay off the freaking door before you break my foot," Steve snarled, forcing her to open it wider. He entered her house limping. "You know, they make it look easy in the movies."

"Get out!" Robyn yelled, looking around for a weapon.

"Look, we need to— What happened to your face?"

"Get out!" she screamed again, picking up one of her father's bouquets off the table in her foyer and hurling it at him.

Steve ducked as flowers went flying all over his head.

"Don't!" he shouted as she picked up another one. "You'll just have to clean up the mess when I leave."

Robyn paused. But only for an instant before she hurled it as well. At least cleaning up the mess would give her *something* to do.

Before she could grab another batch of flowers, Steve caught her arms. "What is wrong with you?"

"You unbelievable bastard!" she snarled. "You run off with some sleaze named Donna and then just show up here like—"

"Donna?" he asked, blinking. "Who's Donna?"

The confusion on his face was too real to be feigned. "Isn't she your wife or girlfriend?"

His frown deepened. "Hell, no. The only Donna I know is my sister-in-law."

Robyn's jaw dropped. "Your sister-in-law? You mean you sleep with your sister-in-law? Oh God, you're even more disgusting than I thought."

He scoffed. "I don't sleep with my sister-in-law. Just what the hell is all this about anyway?"

Robyn twisted out of his hold. Crossing her arms over her chest, she glared at him. "When you didn't call me on Monday, I called your office, and the woman I spoke to said you left town. She said you left a message for Donna to keep your bed warm for you, you slimeball."

To her amazement, he laughed.

Robyn growled at him, but still he laughed.

"Robyn," he said after a minute. "Terri, our receptionist, is such an idiot. You can't listen to half of what she says. When I got to work that Monday, I had a message from my agent. He had me booked at a concert hall in Seattle for two weeks."

"What?" she asked suspiciously, not sure if she should believe him.

Steve reached out to touch her, but she stepped back. Sighing at her withdrawal, he tucked his hands in his pockets. "They had some other pianist, but he had to cancel at the last minute. I didn't even get a chance to pack. My agent ordered me out the door and even drove me to the airport. I tried to call you right before I boarded the plane but no one was here and they told me at Allheart that you hadn't got there yet."

Okay, so that was plausible. It still didn't explain away the Donna issue.

"What about Donna keeping your bed warm?"

"Remember, I told you Sammy and his wife lived in Seat-tle?"

Vaguely she recalled him mentioning it.

Steve continued. "As soon as my agent told me I had to go to Seattle, I called Donna and Sam to tell them I was coming. Sammy was on duty and wasn't home so I told Donna I'd be in around five. It wasn't until we were en route to Dulles that I found out I wouldn't be able to get to their house until nine or so. I knew Donna would panic and call out the National Guard to look for me if I didn't get to her house by five thirty so I tried to call her back, but she'd already left for work.

"I then left a message for her to call my cell number. I was afraid either she would call it or you would while I was on the plane so I had the number forwarded to work. I told Terri to tell Donna I would be late and to make sure I could get to the bed. They've got four kids and the guest room is usually piled to the ceiling with toys." He shook his head. "I should have known Terri would screw it up."

Robyn bit her lip as she absorbed his excuse. Did she dare believe him?

Was it true?

Could it really have been something so stupid?

He touched her cheek. "You must have gone crazy when she told you that."

"You have no idea." Robyn punched his arm.

"Ow!" he said, rubbing his biceps.

"Why didn't you call me?" she asked, still not sure if she should trust him.

"I tried at least four times a day. I never could get through."

"Well, I was in the hospital," Robyn said sarcastically.

"So I see. What happened?"

"A wreck."

Concern darkened his eyes as he gently traced the healing scar on her cheek. "Why didn't you call to tell me?"

"Because I thought you were with Donna."

"I'm going to kill Terri."

It was then she knew he wasn't lying. There was too much anger in his voice. Too much care in his eyes.

He meant it. And in that moment, she felt as if she could fly.

Steve cared! For some reason, she actually meant something to him.

He laced his hand through her hair. "I want you to know that had I known about your accident I would have hopped the next plane home. I can't believe I wasn't here. God, you look like you barely survived it."

"It's all right. Actually, it's kind of funny in retrospect."

"I don't find it funny," he said. "I wish I'd known."

"Yeah well, I guess there are just some things we have to go through on our own."

"Maybe, but I promise you this, Little Red Riding Hood, the Big Bad Wolf is *very* sorry he didn't come by sooner."

"You're here now," she said with a smile. "That's better than not being here at all."

Steve took her hand and placed a tender kiss on the back of her knuckles. "You had breakfast yet?"

She shook her head. "Not really."

"C'mon, let me show you the great Rood Omelet."

Robyn pulled back from him. "I don't need you to take care of me."

"I know you don't," he said sincerely. "You can definitely take care of yourself. But you're hurt and I *want* to take care of you."

"What about work?"

"Work, *schmerk,* they owe me about a year's worth of comp time. Besides, all I need is a computer and a connection and I can work from anywhere."

Robyn hesitated. "What about my scars?"

He traced the one across her chin. "Remember I told you how much I loved old horror movies?"

"Yeah?"

"Well, I never confessed that I always had the hots for Elsa Lancaster in the Bride of Frankenstein."

"You're not funny."

"Not even a little?" he asked with a boyish grin that took her breath.

How on earth could she stay mad at him? Especially when he looked like that?

"Maybe a little," she conceded.

And before she could move, he leaned down and kissed her

tenderly on the lips. "I told you before, Robyn-egg, I like you and it'll take more than an idiot receptionist and a car wreck to make me go away."

"Really?"

"Really."

And for the first time since she could remember, she let herself believe a man's words.

Steve led her into the kitchen where he set about making her breakfast. While she waited, Robyn sat down at her kitchen table and starting flipping through the latest *Cosmo* magazine, which Elyssa had given her in the hospital.

Steve poured her a glass of juice and brought it to the table.

Feeling the hair on the back of her neck rise, Robyn looked up to see Steve staring at the ad with a frown on his handsome face.

"What?" she asked.

He shook his head as he set her glass down in front of her. "Man, someone needs to give that woman a cheeseburger and make her eat it."

Robyn smiled. Yep, it was definitely love she was feeling this morning.

Here I go again, she thought with a sigh. But something deep inside told her *this* time it might be different.

Landslide

VIVIAN LEIBER

Chapter 1

Herbert Kolkey, vice president of sales and marketing for Madam's Closet, lined up the edges of the notebook paper with the reverence normally reserved for peace treaties and papal encyclicals. He cleared his throat, jiggled his glasses on his bulbous nose and sighed. His two assistant veeps leaned forward expectantly.

"Miz Titus, we certainly are impressed by what your company has to offer," he said. "And I can't tell you how appreciative we are of the time and effort you have put into making us aware of our possibilities. We're an old-fashioned firm and we often don't understand the newfangled ways of the Internet."

Carole Titus Life Lesson Number One: Whenever there's an I Love You, a But is sure to follow. Men, potential clients, people who wanted to sell you something, didn't matter—every time the words I Love You passed through someone's lips, you knew a But was coming. Totally infallible rule.

She had endured too much—a hideous flight out from Washington, a hotel room a mere tissue-paper wall apart from a raucous bachelor party, a two-hour presentation to these three clowns who didn't notice that every business in America was either hooked up or passed up. Too much and that was saying a lot, because she was a 24/7 saleswoman. She would not, would not, would not return home without a contract.

But (there's that word) because she had been in sales since the day she discovered that a bachelor's degree in Art History qualified her for a job at the reception desk of one of the SoHo galleries of forgettable modern artists, she did not give in to her desire to whack the shiny red top of Herb Kolkey's head or at least tell him he was an idiot.

Her smile remained friendly, expectant, as if only good

news could be coming. She did not move, though her long espresso-colored hair begged to be flipped away from the warm, moist skin on the back of her neck. Her left hand— ringless, with fingernails polished a pale tea-rose shade—lay relaxed on the faux leather armrests of her chair. Her right hand worked a pen on a leather bound notebook that she had propped up against the side of the conference table so that the execs couldn't be privy to her notes.

Important Notes on This Wasted Exercise of a Meeting: a drawing of Herb Kolkey as a recalcitrant mule being led to water by a stern cowgirl who bore a striking resemblance to herself.

"Miz Titus, I hope you won't lose patience with us."

She had spent a lot of time working on Herb. Phone calls. Reports. Projections. When she had signed the papers on the deal with the chocolate company in California, she had taken a layover in Chicago just so she could take Herb and his wife to dinner at the Everest Room, the most expensive restaurant outside of New York. She had thought then that they were making progress. When Herb's wife mentioned that she grew up in DC, where Allheart.com was based, Carole made a point of sending the Kolkeys a box of locally manufactured saltwater taffy that had been Mrs. Kolkey's favorite childhood treat.

This trip was supposed to be the closer trip.

Some closer.

Carole Titus Life Lesson Number Two: It ain't closed until everybody signs and then initials every page with the date and three witnesses. If one of the gals in the office is a notary public, tell her to get out her seal and glue a few ribbons and gold embossments on the last page just to give the contract an official feel.

"Please, Herb, call me Carole."

"Okay, Carole, I just gotta say, we really appreciate this offer, it looks great, but . . ."

There was the but.

"But we have to, well, we have to . . ."

Lesson Number Two Corollary: It ain't no—a real no— until they throw you out of the office and slam the door on the back of your feet.

His two colleagues, vice president of this, division manager of that, nodded solemnly. Double bad sign when underlings figure out that the kiss-off is coming. Carole drew a small mosquito buzzing threateningly above the mule's rump.

"I'm going to have to take this to our president," Herb concluded.

There. Said. Out in the open. Carole shifted her legs. With just the barest tug of her navy gabardine skirt, she was suitable again. She glanced up and caught the appraising gaze of the doofus on Herb's right. She liked a little admiration from the opposite sex—what woman didn't—but she found this guy unaccountably revolting. Maybe it was the band of gold on his left ring finger . . .

"So what you're saying is that you're taking a pass on this," she said, feeling a little more like the mosquito than the cowgirl. Her flight left in an hour and a half. A cab out of Chicago's Loop at the beginning of afternoon rush hour would take a good forty-five minutes. O'Hare airport was huge and if the plane was in the B concourse, there'd be the dash. In heels. Herb Kolkey couldn't have timed a rejection better. "In other words, you're saying no."

"Not at all," Herb protested. His underlings shook their heads. No, the boss sure ain't sayin' no. "We just don't have any authority to enter into this contract. Call it a maybe."

Whoa, no authority? Herb was in charge of sales, marketing and advertising ventures. His older brother, who had started the lingerie firm when his trucking company went belly-up, was the one who liked to paw the merchandise at the designer's studio.

"Then let's get your brother in here."

Herb startled. A row of sweat beads appeared on his upper lip. He stammered unintelligibly and tugged at his lunch-stained tie.

"How about it, Herb? Shall we?"

"Joey's not in the office today."

"So this is a no."

"It's a maybe."

"It's a no."

Her ex-husband, Hal, had said she could turn into a bitch when she wanted to. Like when she told him he had to stop drinking or the marriage was over. Like telling him he had to get a job and playing in the band didn't count. Like telling him that the marriage was over the day after he bolted out of rehab.

She didn't think there was any wanting to being a bitch. Desperation was a great makeover.

She had no doubt that she looked like a bitch right now. She felt her lips pressing together in a single, disapproving line. She saw Herb's vague alarm turn to panic.

She should let him off the hook. That was what nice women did. Nice saleswomen. And possibly, eventually, with a great deal more massaging, Madam's Closet would sign on. But, damnit, Allheart.com needed advertisers. Now. Not so much for their revenue, but because it showed the venture capital people where they were headed. And with Hallmark and American Greeting battling over the Internet greeting card market, Allheart.com had to prove it was a player too.

"Herb, I like you and I like Madam's Closet," she said. The trio of suits relaxed visibly. The little lady was going to take it. It was just a matter of letting her talk out her disappointment.

"And we like Allheart," Herb offered.

Carole took a deep, measured breath. "Gentlemen, my business moves at a different pace than yours. If I can't close with Madam's Closet, I will—with great reluctance—have to take this offer elsewhere. I have to catch my plane so I can't say too much," she closed her notebook and glanced at her watch. "I'm flying out to New York, where I'll be meeting with Victoria's Secret. As you know, VS was the first to produce an Internet fashion show. They understand the pace of twenty-first–century business. They have said they want to move on this. Tomorrow morning."

Herb gulped. Carole kept her hands on the table so that she wouldn't give in to the childish impulse to cross her fingers. Because she was, after all, lying. The next time she expected to see Victoria's Secret was as a catalog in her mailbox.

"All right, I guess you have to do what you have to do," Herb said, swallowing hard. "But if you don't sign with Victoria's Secret, we'd still have a chance, wouldn't we?"

She wasn't done with him, not yet.

"I suppose," she drawled, as if the matter was one she hadn't considered. "But I don't want your president—your brother—coming to me and saying I never offered you this chance. So, just to protect myself"—she raised her hand to silence the three stooges' protest. "Just to protect myself, I want you to sign off on having seen this proposal."

She pushed the contract across the conference table. The men recoiled.

"Just your initials, Herb, and, of course, I'd need your initials as well," she said, nodding to the two assistant veeps. "Just to show you were here and aware of the terms. It's a protection for you too, so that if Allheart.com signs VS, you can show your president that not any one of you rejected this offer—it was all three of you."

Herb pushed his chair away from the table. His assistants exchanged worried glances.

"I'm not saying no," Herb protested. "I'm saying we have to think about it."

Carole regarded him coolly.

"Your title is vice president of sales, right? You're a good salesman. A great one. And you know as well as I do, maybe means no. Take it to my people means this ain't happening. So before I take this proposal to my meeting with VS, I want a clear conscience and no misunderstandings. I offered you the opportunity. You said not today. I will sign Victoria's Secret tomorrow. And every time an Allheart.com customer sends his sweetie a card, he'll be invited to up the ante with a bra and panties set or maybe a sweet little negligee and matching robe. And those scanties won't come in a Madam's Closet box. Now, if you could just put your initials on the margin of each page."

She tapped her Mont Blanc pen on the first page of the contract. Now that she had them by the balls, she had to stop squeezing. So she smiled.

Carole didn't consider herself vain, but she made the absolute most of what she had—moisturized every night, worked out when she had the time, watched what she ate, and wore clothes that accentuated her lean legs without a smidgen of trampiness. She still got the occasional "hey, baby" on the street and she could smile her way out of traffic tickets. She wasn't above using a smile now, especially since she was so close, so close.

"Maybe we could turn that maybe into a yes, Herb," she purred.

Herb Kolkey stood up. Hiked up the waist of his pants, which tended to droop below his immense belly.

"And maybe you could get the hell out of my office."

* * *

The good news: she made her flight—*charging into the* gate just as the doors were being closed. The plane was a 727, her favorite because there were so few bad seats. Five across, aisle between C and D seats. Aisles or windows—either was fine with her. And a full flight like this one didn't faze her. Ticket agents tried to put families with young screamers in front or on the bulkhead. In fact, she waited for several minutes in line at the bulkhead and the screaming baby in row 8 didn't bother her because she knew the acoustics were so terrible that the noise wouldn't reach . . . She pulled her ticket out from her briefcase and checked the folder.

Now the bad news: she was in row 28. In the B seat. The line edged forward as—*thwunk, thwunk*—overhead compartments were slammed shut. Over the tweedy upholstered headrests of aisles 26 and 27, she saw the next two hours of her life.

And they were very squished hours. The man on the window seat had marked out his territory—which included the armrest, his tray table and hers, upon which he had spread out as if he were at a picnic—laptop, cell phone, paper cup with a clear liquid and slice of lime. He had put the fresh *Wall Street Journal* and Palm Pilot on the middle seat—a territorial thing. She had a fleeting sympathy—his sweat-soaked white shirt and loosened tie bespoke someone who, like her, had served valiantly on the field of business and now just wanted to get home in the quickest, least painful way possible.

"I'm afraid this is my seat," she said.

The man sighed as if he were considering whether to let her have it or not. Then he took the *Journal* and the Palm off the seat.

She put her bag and her suit jacket in the overhead compartment and sat down. She opened her briefcase to look for her notebook. She liked the old-fashioned act of writing everything down in a dayplanner—it was more relaxing than a Palm. Her seatmate sighed grievously as he reorganized his belongings.

"If no one is assigned to it," she offered, "I'll move to the aisle seat."

"They always pack this flight pretty full," he warned. The little girl across the aisle announced in a voice that trembled at high C that she didn't want to go. A man in the seat behind

Carole's bumped her backrest over and over. Behind her right shoulder, somewhere, another baby cried.

The not-so-bad news: The flight was only two hours long.

She looked up at her seatmate just as he made the telltale check of her left hand.

"My name's Pete," he said and maneuvered to bring his right hand over his bulky chest to shake hers. "I take this one out of Chicago twice a week at least. It's hell with wings. I'm in sales. Responsible for the entire east coast. Lead brushes. Bet you don't know what a lead brush does."

Oh, no, Carole, don't answer that!

Too late to pretend I can't speak English, she thought. *Too early to pretend to be asleep. Just don't answer the question. If you answer the question it'll start this guy going as surely as winding up a music box. And the music will play all the way to Washington.*

The aisle seat, that was her only hope. A twenty-eight inch barrier between herself and Pete the Lead Brush King. Even if it put her closer to the girl who was whining about not wanting to fly. Oh, joy, there were only two men walking toward row 28 and they both had name tags pinned above their shirt pockets. Flight attendants. She could take the aisle seat, stick her head in her dayplanner and . . .

"Go ahead. Tell me what you think a lead brush does."

She was going to get a wedding ring. A wedding ring at a time like this would be a lifesaver. Why had she thrown hers into the Potomac River, as if mud and carp would appreciate her new freedom?

The aisle seat, if she could just move over to the . . .

The man who cut off her escape was a twentysomething hottie with chocolate-colored hair and a tan that couldn't have come from a bottle or a booth. He wore tight-enough jeans and a white, all-cotton oxford shirt that didn't concede anything to heat, stress, or the grime of everyday life. He glanced at her, smiled to reveal Chiclet-white teeth and then tucked his head forward just enough to acknowledge the lead brush salesman. Then Mr. Gorgeous gave her a look of utter pity— oh, how those warm, dark eyes could make a woman melt.

Must be gay.

Or married.

Or a jerk.

Or all three?

"So what do you think a lead brush does in your automobile engine?" Pete said to her shoulder, obviously prepared to give her a big hint to get her in the game.

The flight attendants walked the aisle, slamming shut the overhead compartments. Carole leaned her head back onto the headrest and closed her eyes.

"Cleans stuff?" she guessed miserably.

"NO! And that's the amazing part."

The amazing part is always the most hideous. And the amazing part always takes up a lot of elbow room. Luckily, Mr. Gorgeous had turned his attention to the girl across the aisle. She had calmed down considerably, at least she wasn't hitting the high notes. Now, if the baby a few rows back would only stop crying and the guy in the seat behind hers would stop crossing and recrossing his legs. Because if she got that kick-in-the-kidneys thing one more time . . .

"Ladies and gentlemen, this is your captain speaking, and welcome to flight 109 to Washington, DC. I've been told by the tower that we're going to have a slight delay getting out of the gate . . ."

Twenty minutes turned into thirty. Getting out onto the runway looked like a good sign until they spent another twenty-five backed up on parade readiness. Pete the lead brush salesman had told her everything about lead brushes, the vehicles in which his brand of brushes are installed, his prowess as a salesman, the jerks who ran the home office—he was starting to repeat himself and it was made worse by the fact that the drink he had brought onboard was what Starbucks would have called Vodka Venti.

As he spoke he leaned farther into the armrest; it wasn't to be helped because twenty-eight inches of seat wasn't made for thirty-eight or -nine inches of Pete. Carole found herself leaning farther into seat C, right into Mr. Gorgeous. But that wasn't much of a problem because 28C was playing gin rummy with the little girl across the aisle. Mr. Gorgeous smelled good, a little like fresh figs and cardamom and, given the close locker-room mustiness of the cabin, she had to stop herself from burying her nose in his shoulder. She concluded he wasn't gay. Gay men were the only ones who wore expensive cologne and this scent wasn't about cologne. Mr. Gorgeous was the kind of man who put the occasional bottle in his medicine chest and forgot about it.

Every once in a while, Mr. Gorgeous glanced at Carole. When their eyes met, his twinkled with intelligence and understanding.

Flying is hell, they both agreed without a word.

The man behind her punched the call button and when a flight attendant appeared, he bellowed a drink order. She said drink service would begin when they were airborne. The man responded with sharp words and some body movements that Carole was sure would cause her permanent kidney problems. Then Mr. Gorgeous removed his seat belt, stood up and had a whispered conference with the flight attendant. She motioned him to follow her up to the first-class section. Almost immediately thereafter, a male flight attendant came to aisle 28 and leaned close to Carole.

"Please gather up your things and come with me. You can just leave anything you've got in the overhead bin. We'll retrieve it later."

What? Leave her seat? Without Pete? Without the lead brushes? Without the guy behind her kicking? Without the baby that wouldn't shut up? Without the kid across the aisle? Where were they taking her? Off the plane? Prison?

Okay!

She scooted out of her seat before Pete could squawk. The flight attendant, slight and boyish as he was, managed to keep Pete at bay.

"I'm sorry, sir, my instructions were to bring this passenger forward. Please buckle up as the captain advised."

First class was nearly full, but one seat was hers. It was an aisle seat, across from the kitchenette. It was faux leather and smelled a little like whiskey. And it was next to Mr. Gorgeous. He smiled broadly, but seemed to direct that smile somewhere just a little off her left shoulder. At the same blonde flight attendant who had refused beverage service to the man in aisle 29.

"I hope you don't mind, Sis," he said to Carole as she sat down. "Cindy here was nice enough to make an in-flight adjustment for us."

Cindy leaned over to put a napkin and crystal flute on the tray table in front of Carole.

"Anything else, Mr. Evans?"

"No, that's all right," Mr. Gorgeous said. "Please call me Mitch. Isn't that the captain?"

The intercom bleated.

"Oh, yes," Cindy said. "But we aren't getting off this runway for at least another hour. So settle in and enjoy yourselves."

Another hour? Carole moaned softly.

Cindy drifted away to attend to another passenger and Mr. Gorgeous—call him Mitch—touched his flute to Carole's.

"Hope you don't mind," he said. "You looked a little frazzled."

"Mind?" Carole sipped the sweet bubbly. "Not at all. Especially if we're . . . did she say another hour?"

"Yeah. Terrible isn't it? And I just got off a plane from Colorado that was two hours late."

"Then thank you. I would have killed the man sitting next to me before this flight was over. Maybe the guy behind me too. How'd you manage that?"

"Introductions first. My name's Mitch Evans."

"I heard. I'm Carole Titus. And I'm very pleased to meet you. This is wonderful champagne. I've had a long day and it tastes just like Brother Perignon said—like stars."

They let the bubbles do their magic.

"Now. You have to tell me—how'd you do it?"

He leaned toward her just a bit so that he could pull out his wallet. He showed her his senate staff identification card. Carole had lived in D.C. long enough that she had seen one before. She glanced at his stats. Six one. One hundred eighty pounds. His hair and eyes were described as brown, which was a word that didn't do his looks justice. And he was coming up on a birthday—with a quick subtraction of years she put him at just shy of thirty. Eight years younger than herself.

At this proximity, she realized he was saved from being unutterably too gorgeous by a small, barely there scar on his chin.

"Wouldn't have figured you for a senator's aide."

"Don't worry, I have the gray suits to prove it. But I'm on my way back from a meeting with the senator's home staff and wanted to be comfortable."

"But I don't get how you used this card to get first class," she said, and she gave him back the card.

"You just have to pick a flight attendant who doesn't know the difference between a senator and his aides."

Chapter 2

Carole laughed. They both knew that aides outnumbered senators by a good twenty-to-one ratio. Senators lived in Middleburg mansions while aides lived in Georgetown sublets. Senators ate at black-tie fund-raisers and swank restaurants, while aides ate Chinese takeout at their desks late at night. Senators ran the country—and aides ran the senators. Good enough reason to put an aide in first class. Professional courtesy.

"So did you say I was a senator too?" Carole asked.

"I told her you were my sister."

Carole arched her brow.

"Sister?" she asked mildly.

"It might not have worked as well if I had said you were my wife or my girlfriend."

Carole chuckled. *Sister*. She was confident about her age. About her appeal to men. Admittedly, she was past the years during which she could reasonably win the Miss America title, pose for a *Vogue* photo shoot or play a Bond girl.

She thought women who dreaded the big four-oh, or who shaved a few years off their total—oh, they were being so silly. The years should be celebrated, because after all, the alternative was dying young, or dying old, but fearing life. So two years from now, she would light up all the candles on her cake with joy and gratitude.

Still, she startled at the recognition of her years—just like the first time the bag boy at the Big Giant called her ma'am instead of miss.

"I hope you don't mind," he said. "You seem to be a patient woman, but that coach section back there was like one of Dante's rings of hell."

"Agreed," she said, absently thinking about how men had a later sell-by date. "Thank you."

"My pleasure."

"To a long, not-so-miserable flight," she said, and touched her glass—real glass, not that breakable plastic stuff—to his.

After a companionable moment, Mitch pulled a folder out from a briefcase at his feet. Carole picked up the dismissal. She had, in fact, pulled out similar folders on other flights in order to put a gentle, polite halt to unwanted conversation. Even if the guy back in row 28 didn't pick up on her hints, she could pick up on Mitch's request for privacy.

She sighed, enjoyed her champagne and nodded a thanks when Cindy came back to top off their glasses. She slipped off her heels, wiggled her toes, wrote a few notes to herself in her dayplanner, and looked ahead at her week.

The shock at being thrown out of Madam's Closet had turned to vague amusement. Especially at the part where the assistant V.P. tossed her briefcase into the elevator. *And the part about being Mitch's sister? If that's how it happened, fine. And besides*, she gave him a sidelong gaze as he read, *he's too young for me.* She wanted a man with maturity, his own business, a proven track record, and that kind of man came with a little more than the fine lines that crisscrossed at the corners of Mitch's eyes when he smiled.

The champagne made her feel quite satisfied with the world.

When the pilot announced that the flight attendants should prepare for takeoff she glanced at her watch and noted that an hour had gone by as quickly as . . . well, as an hour should. Carole put her tray table back up and Cindy took their glasses.

Perhaps once a month she flew out to see clients at their offices. She flew more often than she ever rode on buses or trains. And yet, the few moments as the engines roared to life and the plane catapulted along the runway always made her heart go *thadump! thadump!* If she didn't distract herself quickly, she would start thinking about aerodynamics. How could several tons of aluminum rise up in the air and fly when she couldn't even juggle oranges for her nieces and nephews? Oranges dropped to the ground with a thud, and aluminum? Why shouldn't it drop as well? What kind of deal did the airlines have that they got a pass on the law of gravity?

She consciously relaxed her grip on the armrests. It was silly, really, this fear. It was irrational. It kept her from enjoying herself. It did not fit with her self-image as a strong, confident, independent woman.

Mitch reached over and put his pinky finger through hers. She startled but when her eyes met his, she didn't see any disrespect. She wasn't any different from any other woman—she didn't like unwelcomed physical contact but when it was welcomed, a touch could be of great comfort. And she relaxed, laying her head back against the headrest as the plane began its ascent. His hands were calloused, surprisingly so for a Beltway Boy, but his broad nails were clean and finely buffed. He didn't wear a ring. His watch was a Rolex, but not the diamond-studded oyster—rather, the original, stately model the company had made for decades, long before they became trendy.

"It's only when we go up," she said. "Once we're up it's okay. Did you ever see a television show called *The Flying Nun*?"

"Oh, yeah, I remember. With Sally Field. She wore a habit with a cap that made her look like she had wings on either side of her head."

"Right. Anyhow, maybe you didn't watch the show," she said and he shrugged in a manner that suggested that no, he didn't watch it but he didn't want to stop her from explaining. "Whenever she had to explain why she was able to fly, she would say her brother, the engineer, explained to her the formula thrust plus acceleration must be greater than drag plus inertia. I keep trying to repeat that formula in my head but it doesn't work. I still get nervous."

Telling a virtual stranger your fears, even if you've had a couple of glasses of champagne, makes the social scales feel imbalanced.

She asked, "Do you ever get nervous?"

"About flying? No. Other things."

"What other things?"

He shook his head.

"You know one of mine."

"All right," he said. "I'm afraid of failing."

"Get out. Civilization wouldn't exist without a large segment of the population terrified of failing. It's the fear of failing that makes us succeed!"

The plane made a sudden lurch and she tightened her grip on his finger. He pulled away but only so that he could take her hand anew in a tight, comforting clasp. She peeked at his right hand. He wore a class ring on that hand. West Point. With a large star sapphire.

"I'm not sure I'd call it afraid, but I would get very uncomfortable when I was separated from my unit."

He caught her look.

"Army," he explained. "Peacekeeping mission. I was always very afraid of losing one of my men. So if we were patrolling a food distribution, a funeral or even something as simple as the town's marketplace, I would feel funny even if one of my guys was just on the other side of a civilian. Only for a moment, but it was very intense for me."

"Did you ever lose anybody?"

"Have you ever been in a plane crash?"

"No."

"Then we're even."

The FASTEN SEAT BELT light went off and the pilot made the usual in-flight announcements, adding that he hoped to make up some of the delay time. Cindy poured drinks for the first-class passengers. Mitch let go of Carole's hand and there was a moment of awkwardness.

"Did you need to get back to your work?" Carole offered.

"It's boring. Did you want to get back to your dayplanner?"

"Not particularly," she said.

"I didn't want you to feel like you had to talk to me just because, well, you know."

"Because you saved me? I'm not that easy."

Cindy poured them each a glass of champagne and offered a choice of lobster Creole or chicken cordon bleu. But the in-flight service suddenly didn't seem nearly so friendly.

"I think holding hands might have tipped her off," Carole said when the young woman was out of earshot. "I'm clearly not your sister."

He touched his flute to hers.

"I'm glad you're not. I felt guilty that I flirted with her a little—only to get an upgrade."

"You're a rat," she chided playfully.

"Hey, all's fair in love, war and commercial airlines."

It was flirting, plain and simple. And she didn't mind. So,

she wasn't so old after all? It was just her being overly sensitive. Like getting worked up about a moisturizer commercial or a cover-your-gray hair color ad. Why shouldn't she be happy being herself, a mid-thirties—be honest, nearly forty—executive with her own home, a fully paid-off car, and her own life?

And why shouldn't she flirt, just a little, with a man just because she wanted to?

The rest of the flight passed very quickly. They swapped faint sketches of their lives and unlike most Beltway Boys, he didn't punch up the resume. He was accomplished enough. He had graduated West Point and taken his four years based in or near Bosnia—officially keeping the peace and unofficially just trying to keep himself and his men alive.

"I felt terrible for those guys who joined up thinking they were getting some training, making a living," he said. "I had guys whose wives were back home feeding the kids. And we weren't there to be an Army. We were there to keep the warlords separated. I don't know why the politicians back home didn't consider letting us do our job and take the warlords down. Just a bunch of gangsters with Kalishnikovs and Uzis."

He loved his home state of Colorado and the popular Senator Snyder was a friend of the family. He had taken the job in Washington just two years ago. Because Senator Snyder was an independent Republican, well-liked and respected on both sides of the aisle, Mitch was relieved of much of the partisan bickering and loyalty swapping his fellow aides endured.

She found herself opening to him, and when he asked, she told him about her early years in sales. The stupid jobs—like selling cosmetics and perfumes on the first floor of Bloomingdale's in New York after getting a degree in Art History. And then deciding that if she was going to make decent money, she had to get her hands dirty.

"Lotus computers. Then Apple," she explained as Cindy offered after-dinner coffee. "Some of those businessmen couldn't comprehend how computers were going to help their bottom line. Actually, today I met with a vice president who still doesn't get it."

She told Mitch about her meeting with Madam's Closet.

"That's the company that's one step up from Frederick's of Hollywood?"

"I don't know that there's a scale for this kind of thing,"

she said, but the look on his face confirmed there was. "But it's not quite as elegant as Victoria's Secret or as pricey as La Perla or Cosabella. But the packaging is nice. Every item comes in a cloth-covered box with a satin ribbon and there's a crystal bracelet that is tied into the bow."

"Does anybody wear the bracelet?"

She shrugged her shoulders.

"I wouldn't know."

"But the concept of something extra—a lagniappe—is good."

"Everyone likes that part," Carole agreed and buckled up for the landing. "A little something extra."

"So what'd you say when he said maybe?"

"I said maybe means no," she said. "That's so true in sales."

"Then what happened?"

She described the little contretemps at the conference table. The overturned chair as one of the assistants leapt to his feet. The other assistant spilling his coffee all over his white oxford shirt. The receptionist calling out to ask if they needed security. The briefcase thrown into the elevator. The four letter words. The fire-engine red of Herb's face.

Mitch laughed.

"So you'll never talk to them again."

"We'll talk tomorrow. That's how business is. I'm very persistent."

Within minutes they were at the gate and the pilot was thanking passengers for their patience. Carole gathered her briefcase and purse. A flight attendant helped her with her navy gabardine jacket and soon Carole was swept out of the plane on a tide of weary passengers. When she turned around once she noticed Cindy putting a slip of paper into Mitch's shirt pocket. He was handsome, Carole decided, and decidedly worth flirting with.

She waited in the gate for him so that she could offer him her thanks. When he emerged she teased him about Cindy.

"Do all women react to you that way?"

"Not enough of them," he quipped. "She said she figured out that you aren't my sister."

"Smart."

"But then she noticed no wedding band on your left hand."

"Even smarter."

"I told her maybe."

"Maybe means no."

He nodded ruefully.

"But she insisted on giving me her number in case I changed my mind."

"Which you . . ."

"Won't."

They walked down the nearly empty terminal with the other passengers from the flight. She started to think of ways to say no.

Non! Nyet! Nein!

"So if you're really not having a meeting with Victoria's Secret tomorrow morning," Mitch said.

Sorry, love to, can't.

He readjusted his garment bag over his shoulder.

See, I was in this terrible marriage, but . . .

"How about you spend the day with me?"

There it was.

And a flat-out no felt cold. While a yes was fugeddaboudit!

"Maybe. I don't know. I've got a lot of work to catch up on. Tomorrow? Oh, dear, the office is such a mess . . ." She was babbling, which she hardly ever did, being a woman who ordinarily knew what she wanted to say and said it. "Maybe. Let me think about it. You could call me. Yeah, sometime, sure. Maybe. Definite maybe. But not tomorrow."

A flicker of disappointment and then he recovered.

"A very wise saleswoman once taught me that maybe means no," he said. "And that's okay. It's been a pleasure meeting you. That doesn't change."

He walked away and she could only stare.

Okay, Carole, why'd you do that? Handsome guy, steady job, fun to be with—already that makes him a one-eighty on Hal. And every time you say no to a nice guy you're only increasing the number of creeps and jerks that will catch you in a moment of weakness.

On the other hand . . .

She charged down the terminal, hard to do in heels with a duffel and briefcase to juggle. But the terminal was nearly empty, only a few people from the Chicago flight trudging toward the baggage terminal. Mitch turned around.

"Mitch, I'm sorry, it's just that there's really only two ways this could turn out."

"Only two?"

"We could go out and we'd have a wonderful time and then things would develop," she said, her words coming in a rush. "I'm not a one-night-stand person, but you're handsome and fun and intelligent, and who knows? And then I'd feel guilty and stupid—more stupid than guilty—and you'd feel obligated to call me again. Or maybe you wouldn't. Either I'd want you to call or I'd be happy you didn't. And I'd be miserable. For at least a week. Maybe more."

"And the other option?"

"We could take it slower and then things would . . ."

"Develop."

"Yeah, develop. And when they did, one of us would fall in love and the other one wouldn't. It would be awful for both of us. Because it's like having simultaneous orgasms. Nobody can do it."

He tilted his head just so slightly as to give the impression that simultaneous orgasms had occurred with each and every woman he had bedded—and then he grinned.

"Oh, and that would lead to marriage."

They both paused at the *M*-word. Carole had never, ever met a single man who dared to speak its name—voluntarily anyway.

"Wow," he marveled. "So there are actually three possibilities and all of those sound grim."

"See? So that's why I said maybe. So, you're right. Maybe means no."

"Which option is the worst option? The one-night stand or the one of us falling in love or the married bliss?"

"I don't know."

"Give it some thought. I hadn't actually planned as far as the miserable or married part. I was just thinking of having you show me the Washington Monument."

"The what?"

"The big tall white thing. Honoring our first president and the commander-in-chief of the Revolutionary . . ."

"I know what it is. What made you think of that?"

"That's where I want to go."

For the moment, dire predictions of emotional distress were of secondary importance.

"You can't go there," she said firmly. "It's so . . . so . . . so . . . tourist."

"That's exactly what I am."

"I don't know that I've known anybody in Washington admit to having seen it. Except on the skyline. Better yet, from the helicopter leaving the pad on the White House lawn. I can't tell you how many men have told me they've been on that helicopter. Never once has anyone told me they've actually gone to the monument."

"Last week I went to see the Jefferson rotunda."

His smile was boyish and yet all sex appeal. And there just wasn't any way that a woman couldn't smile back.

"I just want to see the monument," he said, crossing his hand over his heart. "Have you ever been to it?"

"When I'm flying in from somewhere else. And never from the president's helicopter."

"Have you ever been inside?"

"Certainly not."

"So you wouldn't be my tour guide exactly. Still want to go?"

"I didn't say I wanted to go in the first place."

"Hmmm."

She felt a sharp, reflexive intake of breath. Ready to explain everything all over again. He stopped her by lightly touching her shoulder.

"I know. Maybe," he said. "Maybe."

"No. It's not maybe. It's an almost yes."

"Then I'll pick you up at your office. A little after noon. Don't wear heels."

"I didn't say . . ."

"This great saleswoman I was telling you about? She said after the maybe, you turn it around to a yes with persistence."

And then he walked away. She couldn't follow him. *How could he understand her baggage? How could he understand her being so afraid to be with a man? How could he understand Hal? How could he understand that the Washington Monument was the most laughable tourist trap in the entire district?*

When he walked out to the sidewalk cab stand, she mentally kicked herself.

You are a total idiot, Carole. Told him exactly why you couldn't and then turned around and said yes. Or at least, enough of a yes that he thinks you're on board. I should really have my head examined, she thought and then headed for the parking garage.

The next morning, Herb Kolkey was very, very, very contrite.

"I'm very, very, very sorry about our misunderstanding," he opened the phone conversation.

Uncharacteristically, Carole was on a short fuse. And all over a simple pair of sneakers, which she had put on one of two chairs on the other side of her desk. The sneakers—unassumingly white, suitable for tennis—were in sharp contrast to the fashionable leather slides that coordinated with her sleek jersey wrap dress.

"I don't think we had a misunderstanding," she said to the shoes. And then to Herbert. "You said no thanks. I said good-bye. That just about covers it."

"But I'm very, very, very . . ."

"I have to go."

"If it's because of your meeting with Victoria's Secret . . ."

"No, Herb. It's not. You know, you are a dinosaur business. And very soon you are going to find yourself as extinct as the dinosaurs. Women want more from a man than a Madam's Closet box. And nobody, but nobody, wears those crystal bracelets."

Stunned silence on both sides of the connection.

"I accept your apology," Carole said. "Now, good-bye, Herb."

How Not to Succeed in Sales While Really Trying, by Carole Titus.

She stared at the shoes after she hung up. She blew it. She should have let Herb talk himself out. But because of a pair of sneakers—reminding her, taunting her, teasing her—she had lost an account because of a man.

This is ridiculous. I'm not going to turn my work life—hell, my entire life—upside down over a simple date. And a stupid date at that.

She called up the Congressional exchange and asked for Senator Snyder's office. A receptionist cheerily picked up and Carole asked for Mitch.

"He's away for the day," the receptionist said. "Is there someone else on staff who can help you?"

"No, that's all right," Carole said wearily. "Does he pick up his voice mail?"

"Funny thing. This is the first time Mr. Evans has ever done this, but he's asked that no messages be forwarded to him."

"Oh."

"You aren't Carole Titus, are you?"

"Yes."

"He said you'd call and try to cancel. But I've been told to tell you that you can't. He's on his way."

Damn. Damn. Double damn.

Just as Carole hung up, she got an instant message on her screen from Dana the copywriter.

Wow.

Huh? That made no sense. And not just because Dana was the sort who could waste a four-page memo on describing the salad at the building's basement cafeteria. Why would Dana be so pithy all of a sudden?

Before she could unravel that mystery, the phone rang. It was Robyn, who was manning the front desk because the receptionist was on vacation.

"Is Mitch Evans a twin?"

Carole paused. She was often the Monday morning quarterback to Robyn's dating life, but she couldn't imagine having told Robyn about Mitch.

"Uh, no clue. Why do you ask?"

"Just hoping. I guess genetic material like this can't be replicated. He's just so dreamy."

Carole sighed heavily.

"Robyn, is there a point to this?"

"He's in the lobby. He says he wants to see you. Instead of me, and I think that's proof that the world is basically unjust."

Oh, no!

Carole charged down the carpeted hall, uncomfortably aware of how the other women in the office were trotting out for a gander. Carole nearly slammed into the backsides of three colleagues who were poking their heads around the corner to see the lobby. Unobtrusive was the look they were going for. Plain ridiculous is what they ended up with. Alix, being the mischievous one in the office, was the ringleader.

"I wouldn't mind some of that," she whispered, as Carole passed. Carole gave her a stern look but Alix was Alix, and therefore, utterly unfazed.

"Is he a consolation prize from the Madam's Closet suits?" she asked.

"How come I don't ever get business trips?" Robyn demanded as Carole entered the lobby.

Mitch stood at the far end of the foyer, reading the framed original cells of early Allheart.com cards. He did not seem to notice the three women who squirmed and elbowed each other in the doorway of the nearby conference room.

They were shamelessly ogling and Carole was mortified.

Sure, he was handsome. He was strikingly tall, well-built, his pants fit oh so perfectly, his white shirt was tailored and showed off his muscles, his features were strong but not over-powering, his hair was dark with just a smidgen of the sun's help. His eyes, well, his eyes *were* dreamy—no doubt.

As sinfully delicious as a Dove bar. But worth making such a fuss over?

Absolutely!

"Carole!" he said. "I'm so happy you haven't changed your . . ."

Mitch was interrupted at that moment by a wolf whistle.

A wolf whistle? Could this get any worse?

Carole looked beyond his shoulders toward the hall. Three pairs of *Who Me?* eyes met hers.

She had to get Mitch Evans out of this office—fast!

"Mitch, we're out of here," Carole said. "Let's go. You just wait right here. I'm getting my . . ."

As she went back to her office, Elyssa was there.

"I want a memo on this guy," she said. "Where did you find him?"

"On an airplane," Carole said smartly.

"I didn't know. I mean. After Hal, I thought—"

"Well, you thought wrong. Girl's gotta go for it," Carole said, with a bravado she didn't feel. She grabbed her purse, laptop, briefcase, sneakers. "I'll be out for the afternoon."

"Full-blown memo," Elyssa reminded her. "And one other thing, don't take this wrong, but we really need you to pick up more advertisers. The venture guys are on my ass."

"It's Friday afternoon and the last time I took five minutes off from work was to go sign my divorce papers. Get a grip, Elyssa. It's not all about business."

Whew! What a thing to say!

Carole marched past her friend and boss, and picked up speed as she reached the lobby. She grabbed Mitch's sleeve and got a jump on the elevator as the UPS man—the now-dethroned sex god of the office—got out. She had just pushed the button, and Mitch had just asked what the hell that was all about when Robyn yelled after her, "I've got Herb Kolkey on the line."

"Tell him I'm unavailable."

She punched the elevator button.

"When should I tell him you'll be available?!"

The elevator doors started to close.

"Monday morning!" Mitch called out.

Chapter 3

The elevator doors closed on them.

"Mitch, I've been giving this a lot of thought."

"I bet you have."

"I don't think this is a good idea for me."

"I bet you don't."

"I'm thinking . . ."

He shut her up with a kiss. A kiss that was meant to be playful, she was sure, but which carried some kind of charge. Her hands, which first reached up reflexively to push him away, grabbed the front of his shirt and held him steady.

If you're going to kiss me, Carole thought, *then kiss me, damnit!*

And he did. Oh, he did. He kissed her within an inch of her life and when he relinquished her, she didn't want to let go.

"You're some kind of kisser," she said a little woozily. She patted his wrinkled shirt with a sheepish smile.

"Anything to get you to stop thinking so much."

But then there was a distinct throat-clearing. The elevator doors were held open by a small, balding man with an umbrella tucked under his arm.

"Pardon me," he drawled. "Is this elevator . . . uh, working?"

"Of course it's working," Mitch said. "But you have to get your own woman."

"Well, I never!" The gentleman huffed.

"Too bad," Mitch said, and led Carole out onto the atrium floor.

"If you ever wanted to go into sales, you'd be very successful," Carole said, falling into stride with him. "I meant to tell you I wasn't going but now here I am. If you ever ran for office, you'd win by a landslide."

"I'm too young for elected office. Have to be thirty to be a senator, thirty-five to be president. But someday—and when that day comes I'll remember that you said landslide."

His car, a small red Fiat convertible, was parked out front. The security guard opened the passenger door for Carole and told her to have a good time. In the three years that Allheart .com had been in this office building, the security guard had not once broken a smile or said good morning to anyone she knew. But here he was, tossing Mitch his car keys and wishing him a good day.

"Do you know everybody in Washington?" she asked when he settled into the driver's side.

"Yes," he said brazenly.

"I guess that answers that."

"Want to change into your sneakers? Those heels don't look very comfortable."

"They're Manolos. They're not meant to be comfortable."

She took off the red python leather sandals. He pulled out into traffic.

"Why are you still wearing a suit?" she asked, looking him over.

"Seven o'clock breakfast prayer meeting with the Congressional Caucus. Mandatory attendance."

"God watches over our government?"

"But not the lobbyists. Satan watches over the lobbyists."

Her laughter was taken by the wind and they gave up talking over the roar of the engine.

Carole proceeded to spend the afternoon visiting a series of sites she was sure no self-respecting District of Columbia resident would dare be seen at: the Supreme Court, the National Archives, the National Portrait Gallery, and the Library of Congress.

In general, the locals used places like these as landmarks when giving directions. "Take a left just after the Supreme Court, go two blocks and the restaurant's on your right." The Library of Congress was a definite never unless, of course, you had hard-core research to do or you were ushered into the Member's Room, which, of course, was where only the most distinguished academics were. But Mitch only had to say a few whispered words to the circulations manager at the mezzanine and they were shown to the large, elegantly appointed study.

Carole sat down on a moss-green velvet couch in front of the marble fireplace that was decorated with a mosaic depiction of Ancient Greece and scagliola columns. Dust danced in a shaft of sunlight falling from a leaded glass window.

Though she wore her sneakers, her feet throbbed mercilessly.

"How'd you ever manage . . ." She glanced at the elderly man seated at a round tiger-maple table. Outside it was ninety-nine degrees on the furnaces of hell index, inside the air conditioner was set at sweater weather. The scholar peered at her over his glasses. The table before him was covered with textbooks, index cards, legal pads—and he balanced a pen in one hand and another behind his ear. She lowered her voice. "How'd you manage to get in here?"

Mitch sat down beside her, adjusting a cushion.

"The circulation manager's brother is on the staff of the senior Senator from Indiana."

"Nice to have friends in power."

"You say that like it's not a compliment."

"Quite the contrary. After an afternoon tagging along with you, I'm so hot and tired I could happily spend the rest of my life on this very couch."

"That bad?"

"It's just Washington in the summer. I've actually had a lot of fun. I just can't tell anybody about it."

"You're right. And we definitely can't buy any commemorative T-shirts."

"Or snow globes," Carole said, chuckling.

"Or postcards."

The old man cleared his throat. Mitch leaned close. She thought he would kiss her again. This was possibly the only moment she would not have welcomed it because of the scholar's intrusive gaze. She *had* been thinking about the touch of his lips. And she had been feeling the crush of his flesh against her own, frequently touching her own lips just to remember the tingling sensation left in his wake.

Yes, yes, please do that again.

Just not here, not now.

He didn't. He simply whispered in her ear, his breath soft and warm, "We're going to have to clear out. But at least we cooled off a little."

"A brief but welcome respite."

"Indeed. And we've got one more stop."

"The Washington Monument? We can't. It's nearly five o'clock and the Park Service doesn't stay open late for anyone—not even Mitch Evans."

Another throat clearing, this time followed up by a louder cough.

"Pardon me, but this room is strictly for research."

"Sorry," Mitch said, tugging at Carole's hand. "We were just leaving."

Outside the Member's Room, the hall was crowded with a group of seniors on a guided tour of the world's largest library. The air was heavy and suffused with sweat, perfume, cigarettes, and popcorn—it was a smell that permeated the most popular spots in Washington and was made worse by the heat and scent of dead carp rising from the Potomac River.

It was a Friday and while tourists were still milling about, the worker bees were clearing out en masse. Office buildings were emptying as quickly as if the British were repeating their early nineteenth-century invasion of the District. Drivers hung indecorously out the windows of sleek black stretches, taxi drivers slammed on horns at every slight and police officers whistled and gestured at every intersection. The most brazen drivers were those with the diplomatic plates—police were not allowed to give diplomats so much as a speeding ticket.

Mitch pulled into a spot next to the Park Service booth at the Monument and when they got out, a uniformed guard put an orange "Park Service Official Business" slip under the windshield wiper.

"Thanks," Mitch said. "Closed?"

"Absolutely. She's all yours."

The guard escorted Mitch and Carole to an iron door that was tucked under scaffolding from the recently completed restoration.

"By the way, thanks about . . . you know," the guard said, as he waited for Carole and Mitch to pass.

"Please forget it," Mitch said.

"This man is my guardian angel," the guard told Carole.

"Don't embarrass me," Mitch warned.

The guard shrugged.

"Now remember—we'll be down here," he gestured to-

ward two of his colleagues who were sitting on a traffic barrier. "No funny business."

"I am a gentleman," Mitch protested. "Besides, there are
the panic buttons."

"Just remember to show her where they are. Sure you don't
want the elevator?"

The elevator had been installed during the seventies and
the stairs were not open to the public. The chance to use the
stairs? Priceless. But 897 steps?

"Carole?"

"No, stairs are better," Carole said. "It can't be much worse
than a StairMaster."

The guard waved good-bye as Carole and Mitch entered
the narrow, stone-lined stairwell. While the air was humid, it
was pleasantly cool and the stones gave off a fresh, green
scent.

"It's okay if you wanted to go on the elevator," Mitch said.

"Just because you were in the Army doesn't mean the rest
of us are wimps," Carole said.

"I didn't mean . . ." But she was already ten steps ahead
of him.

They didn't speak much the rest of the way, communicat-
ing only by the occasional expression of weariness. The climb
required some concentration, for the stairs were only lit by
small, utilitarian sconces and the marble was worn where so
many feet had trod.

"Maybe worse than the StairMaster," Carole admitted.

They reached the top and the climb was worth it.

They were given a chance few tourists ever have: the place
to themselves and the view . . . *oh, the view*. The sun was the
color of an Hermes shopping bag and it hung low on the hazy
gray-and-pink fluff of gathering clouds. The reflecting pool
glittered like sapphires scattered on a jeweler's cloth. And
while some office lights of the city were being snuffed, Lincoln Memorial's colonnade lights snapped on just as Mitch
pointed it out to Carole. From each of the four walls, two windows allowed a beautiful view—Mitch and Carole enjoyed
every one of them.

"So this is the other side of the view I get every time I fly
back home," Carole said, pointing to a plane making an approach to the Ronald Reagan airfield. It looked so close!

"It's so beautiful, but there's so much," Mitch said. They sat on the cool, blocked marble sill and watched the traffic on K Street. "I'm from Colorado and it's very hard for me to get used to every available inch of land being filled up by something humans built."

"Do you want to go back home?"

"I have to make a decision at some point. My family has traditionally been in politics. My father was governor of Colorado for four years, two of my uncles served in the Roosevelt administration, my grandfather was in the House of Representatives."

"Oh, my God. I had no idea your family was so well-connected. No wonder you know everybody."

"No, I just know *how* to know everybody."

"And how is that?"

He considered what he had said lightly, in jest.

"If someone needs a favor, do it," he said. "Always say hello—to the president, to the security guard at your office building, to the garbage man. And try to remember everybody's name—because everybody's name is important to them."

"Taught that by your parents?"

"By example only. They were never the sort to lecture. And my dad only thought of politics as a service, a duty, never a lifestyle."

"What'd he do in his off-time?"

"Mining and logging. A couple of ski resorts. A ranch. Some real-estate development. All part of a family trust started by my great-grandfather."

"I get the picture. You're loaded."

"Sorta," he conceded.

"And here I was going to pay for dinner, congressional aide salaries being what they are."

"Yeah, well, glad you've reconsidered. I'm terribly old-fashioned about who pays. That and who gets on the lifeboat first. Otherwise, I'm fairly progressive."

"Will you take over the family business, er, businesses?" Carole asked.

"Actually, I think my family expects me to run for Senate someday, but luckily, Senator Snyder is so popular that he'll stay in office for a long time—until I'm fifty or so."

They laughed companionably. Senator Snyder was one of the oldest, best-loved senators in the country, which counted for a lot, allowing for the current state of politics. The press, his political adversaries—no one could think of a bad thing to say about him. He had served for three terms after years in the House and was expected to run again the year after next, most likely unopposed.

"Speaking of the senator, I have a dinner to go to tonight. Didn't know it until this morning, but when a senator asks you to dinner, you have to say yes. Even on a Friday when normal people do everything in their power to get out of town."

"Maybe you could drop me off at the office?"

"No, Carole, I was being clumsy. I'm trying to ask you to go with me and it's coming out all wrong."

"The senator didn't invite me."

"Oh, yes, he did. I told him you'd be coming with me."

She arched a brow.

"Weren't you being a bit presumptuous?"

"Foolhardy is more like it. This morning I was willing to have the senator think I'm a failure at wooing a woman if you said no, but now I think I couldn't stand it."

His words played jester, but his expression—half seen in the twilight—was serious. Carole wished she were more like other women, women who could throw themselves headlong into romance and courtship, and who carried smaller baggage. Trim little carry-on items as opposed to the gigantic steamer trunk known as Hal, her ex-husband.

Still, Mitch was handsome and the mood he had set on this trip was irresistible.

"I guess I have to take pity on you," Carole said, matching his light tone. When he smiled, she knew that he was the sort of man who could persuade a woman to do anything. With or without those kisses. "I need to get back to my house to change. I really can't go like this."

"You look fine."

"Yeah, but I'm dripping with sweat."

And that was true. A day in Washington leaves a woman's outfit a sopping mess.

"Then we'd better go now. Wanna take the elevator?"

"Seems like a good idea to me."

They punched the call button and Mitch reached above the

doors. He placed his index finger on a small black lens which she hadn't noticed—and which she'd guess few tourists noticed either.

"Wide lens. Security," he said. And with his other hand he put his arms around her waist and drew her close. A gesture that expressed both a precarious weakness and surprising strength.

Finally!

When his lips touched hers, she felt a weakening that could have been a sudden dip in blood pressure, an unexpected spike in blood sugar, a plummeting elevation of the entire District, an electrical charge caused by humidity and electrolytes and heaven knew what other forces of nature.

But Carole Titus weak in the knees over a man?

Not in all her life—and so when she swayed and moaned as his kiss deepened, she never once considered the obvious fact that had been proven now twice over:

Mitch Evans was a helluva kisser.

I could get lost in this, she thought with just the tiniest reasoning faculty left—*I could crave this man more than I crave Mint Milano cookies, margaritas on hot summer nights and potato chips once the bag is open. And with far more dangerous results.*

She lost her balance. He steadied her, but in doing so, had to stop kissing her.

And the stopping made her realize just how far gone she was.

But as they took the elevator down, her pulse returned to normal, blood sugar up, pressure down, and electrolytes safely returned to the atmosphere where they might make a wondrous thunderstorm later in the evening.

Outside, the Park Service guys smoked cigarettes and waved desultorily at the mosquitoes. The outside temperature had dramatically plunged from oh, say, 99 to 98 degrees. Mitch took the Official Business sign off his windshield and thanked his benefactor.

"What did you do for the guard, by the way?" Carole asked when they were at the next stoplight.

"A favor," he said.

"Whose friend of a brother or a cousin of an acquaintance is he?"

"He was in the Army stationed in Bosnia at the same time I was."

"And you're not going to tell me what you did for him."

"I'm sorry, no."

"That important, huh?"

Mitch sighed.

"He called me a few days ago, just got this job and wanted me to stop by. Offered to let me in after hours."

"So you could take girls up to the monument?"

"Only this once. Besides, it's good to let someone do something in return. So letting him do this for me made him feel like the scales were evened out. People can sometimes resent someone who has done something for them."

She supposed that might be true. Letting someone do something for her was, come to think of it, an uncomfortable prospect. And maybe Hal had come to resent how she took care of everything.

Carole's home was in a patch of Virginia that might be mistaken for a small town but was actually the end-sprawl of Alexandria. Her house was a two-story cottage, white wood siding and celadon shutters. The playful shade garden in front sported purple violas, nodding astilbes and blue-green hostas. Oak trees and buckthorn formed a parkway border that almost, but not quite, gave the impression of impenetrability. On the porch, Carole picked her mail out of a wicker basket and ushered Mitch into the foyer.

"I'll be just a minute," she promised. "I'm not high maintenance. If you want a drink, feel free to rummage in the refrigerator."

She started up the steps, turning as she felt his bafflement. Okay, this house wasn't what somebody would expect of a—what could she call herself?—vice president of sales of an Internet startup. No, no, this house was an oasis of feminine calm. Hal got the car, the bank accounts, the stocks, the furniture, the—well, be honest—the everything. And when she was left with the divorce attorney's bills and ten thousand in an account Hal somehow hadn't laid claim to, she immediately paid off the lawyer and sunk her remaining money into the foreclosured crackhouse. Hard to believe, but this neighborhood had been tough—real tough.

Over the past year and a half, she had stripped the floors, painting a checkerboard black and white pattern throughout the lower floor of the house. The walls she had determined would be a cheery yellow, even though the salesman at Home Depot insisted the color was too bright. Well, it worked, if she did say so herself. And she had sewn the curtains—finally that home ec class in eighth grade had come in handy. The red-and-yellow gingham fluttering at her windows was just on the right side of charming. Six months of estate sale Sundays provided the furnishings—and there was a dining room set given to her by a woman who had come to the end of the day and her rope selling her grandmother's possessions.

"If you can get this Hepplewhite stuff out of here, you can have it," she had said. "And you can have that ugly ole chandelier too, if you can get it off the ceiling."

That ugly ole chandelier turned out to be a treasure once she sanded it and bleached off decades of grime and dust.

Somehow Carole had managed to make her major fixer-upper into a home. Meanwhile, all around her, gentrification had doubled, tripled, quadrupled, and quintupled the price of real estate.

It was her island, whether surrounded by toughs or by thirtysomething couples with strollers and Saabs. If it veered a little in the Mary Englebreit direction, so be it.

Mitch stood marveling.

"The refrigerator, it's in the kitchen," she prodded.

"This is nice," he said. "Really nice."

And then she realized that he was the first man she had ever invited into her home. Not to say that she hadn't dated since Hal and she divorced. She had had approximately the same range of experiences every woman in her thirties has had—men who boasted of this, that or the other triumph in business or politics; men who had mothers, ex-wives, children and dogs whom they loved or didn't love but definitely wanted to talk about; men who flew in and out of a woman's life with flattery at their arrival and indifference at their passing. All of this conducted in restaurants with unbearably pretentious food, stage productions that were loud and too long, gallery junkets to see art that was meant to provoke and confound.

She had had a number of one-night stands just after her divorce was final. She hadn't liked that about herself, feeling not so much guilty as drained. She had had some relationships—the sort that lasted not much longer than the average high school going-steady.

But after a while, she realized she had less patience than most women, and that she didn't need a man. So what was she doing with Mitch?

"I'll be down in a minute," she said abruptly.

Upstairs, she took a very quick, very cold shower, putting her hair up in two Indonesian bone chopsticks. She spritzed on Angel perfume, which was light, cool and always reminded her of raspberries. She rejected a filmy sundress as too casual and settled on a bias-cut turquoise silk scarf dress with an asymmetrical hem that was up to her kneecaps and down as low as her ankles. When she added a pair of Sabrina-heeled slides and a briolette aquamarine and sterling silver choker, she had to admit it was not bad for ten minutes. She chucked the essentials—cell phone, keys, compact, just-in-case Tums, champagne-colored lipstick—into a white beaded evening bag. She would have taken her hair down, but it was hot and the effect—tousled and yet very proper—was a good one. At the last minute, she added dangly pearl earrings that made her neck look long and lean.

She closed her eyes. Unbidden thoughts and feelings made her weak in the knees. *He would be . . . delicious.*

She startled and scolded her mirror image.

"You wouldn't!" she declared. "You simply wouldn't—not after knowing him just one day!"

Chapter 4

"*Wow*," *he said, when she came down. He was sitting in* the white armchair with Whiskers. Whiskers was the closest thing that a woman could have to a watchdog without actually having a dog. Whiskers sprawled across his lap on her back, enjoying a stomach scratch. That cat is turning into a tramp, Carole thought. She accepted the glass of soda he had prepared for her. The ice was already melting. She supposed she should have turned on the AC but it didn't make sense now if they were leaving.

"Thanks. Were you wearing that shirt all day? Your white shirt looks so remarkably fresh."

"There's a reason. I always pack an extra in the trunk of my car. Which I'm now wearing. Along with a different tie. And suit. And I packed a razor. I hope you don't mind, I used your downstairs guest bathroom."

"You put on aftershave. I can tell."

"You like it? My sister bought it for me—Ferragamo."

"Yeah, it's nice," she said coolly. She crossed her arms over her chest. "What else do you pack in the trunk?"

"Do you think I packed my car because I expected to be asked to stay the night?"

"No, no, I just find it strange for a man to keep all these items in his car."

"It's Washington in the summer. I couldn't go to a dinner in what I was wearing. Besides, what have you got in the trunk of your car?"

Carole opened her mouth to say something about spare tires and jumper cables—and then she remembered.

"A packed garment bag," she conceded. "But only because I don't want to get caught having to make an emergency trip to a client. Oh, Mitch, I'm sorry. It's just . . . I don't know what I want from you. Look, I'm thirty-seven years old, divorced, quite happy with my life and . . ." She tilted her chin up. "And I don't even know where you want this thing to go."

He shrugged. Outstretched palms. Shoulders imperceptibly raised. And that smile. Oh, his smile was simply the most infuriatingly melt-a-woman-at-the-knees smile.

"I want 'this thing' to go to dinner," he said.

The Cosmos Club is set on Embassy Row amid the grand residences and offices of the world's ambassadors to the United States. The building is a four-story federalist brick with white trim and columns, which lend a regal air. Yet the mock orange bushes, hostas, oriental lilies and vinca minor covering the ground all grow so quickly that even the most meticulous landscaper can't keep up. The Cosmos looks like a spot of civilization set in the midst of an omnivorous jungle.

The Cosmos membership, Mitch explained as he managed District traffic, was originally limited to men who could prove they had traveled to at least four of the five continents. Since very few Americans attempted to reach Antarctica in the pre–World War I founding of the Club, members tended to have explored South and North Americas, Europe, Asia and Africa. Members outdid each other bringing back exotic "proofs" of their worthiness to call themselves Cosmopolitans. After Mitch turned over his keys to the Club valet, he escorted Carole into a lobby that looked very much like a museum.

The walls were papered in red and gold duchesse cloth and the floors were covered with expensive but well-worn carpets of Persia, Kashmir and Pakistan. Every heavy-legged table groaned under the weight of Ming vases, Thai ceremonial masks, Ceylonese pottery. Carole studied a display case of Egyptian scarabs given to the Club, according to the yellowed card pinned to the case, by President Theodore Roosevelt himself. She enjoyed looking at the sepia-toned photographs of Roosevelt's adventures as well as an entire case of Peruvian beads.

Mitch signed in at the front desk and was given a stack of messages, which he stuffed into his inside suit jacket pocket without reading.

"We're in the Wilson Room," he said. "It's where President

Woodrow Wilson met with club members to ask their advice on creating the League of Nations."

"You're mighty proud of this place," she said, as he took her arm and led her up the stairs, past a series of sepia-toned photographs. "Are you a member?"

"Absolutely."

"Four continents?"

"Five. But these days, travel conditions are easier."

In the hallway, they were greeted by a crowd of people exiting the lobby. The women were dressed in pale suits and silk dresses. The men were mostly wearing suits, but a few were in dress uniform. Carole couldn't tell the difference between a sergeant and a lieutenant (*and what exactly was a rear admiral?*) but she assumed these men were not the kind who had to peel potatoes or do the dawn marches.

"Mitch! Mitch! Over here!"

A tall, gray-haired man waved heartily from the back of the crowd. Senator Snyder. She noted that the senator's smile and twinkling eyes were every bit as charismatic as on television. Mitch tugged Carole against the tide toward his boss. Several times they were stopped when someone recognized Mitch and he always introduced Carole. When they got to the senator, the hallway had nearly cleared behind them. The party was ready for dinner in the Wilson Room.

"Senator, may I introduce Carole Titus," Mitch said.

"Carole, pleased to meet you," the Senator said. He grabbed her hand and pumped once—strong but not aggressive. Perfect politician's handshake. "So you're the cause of Mitch's mysterious disappearance today."

"I hope he's not in the doghouse for it," Carole parried.

"Oh, not at all. Mitch doesn't take enough time off."

"And thank you for having me, on such short notice."

"In fact, tonight you're doing me a most wonderful favor by dining with us. My wife informs me that it's the cardinal sin of entertaining to have an uneven number of the sexes at a dinner party. Too many men and the talk turns to sports and politics. Too many women and, well, I wouldn't know. Washington has so many more available men than women it's never happened."

"Don't tell the gals from New York," Carole quipped dryly.

The senator roared.

"Is Mrs. Snyder here tonight?" Mitch asked.

Carole could have sworn she saw a flicker of sadness on the senator's face but he cheerily said that the missus had decided to go out to their daughter's home in West Virginia.

Mitch looked a bit puzzled but said nothing.

"We'd better go in," the senator said and he winked at Carole. "The staff here runs the club at their convenience, not the members'. If we tarry in the hall we won't get a bite to eat."

The Wilson Room was a well-appointed maple-paneled study with an ornately carved marble fireplace and leaded eight-pane windows. A damask-covered table set for twenty-four sprawled in the center of the room. Mitch and Carole found their seats near the middle, side by side. A gentleman who introduced himself as the Ambassador of Uruguay held her chair and then seated himself at Carole's right hand. A reporter from the White House Press Corps sat on Mitch's left side.

Uniformed waiters quietly and efficiently served plates of crab cakes with a red pepper sauce.

The conversation was stilted during the first course when Carole was obliged to devote her attention to the Ambassador. When she mentioned that she worked for an Internet startup, the Ambassador proceeded to explain at length his country's troubles maintaining and developing phone lines that would work twenty-four hours a day and would reach the rural areas outside the capital Montevideo.

When the plates were cleared, Mitch concluded his conversation with the reporter and the Uruguayan ambassador and turned his attention to the woman on his right.

"Having fun?" Mitch whispered at her ear.

"You know I'm not," she murmured discreetly. "Not having fun exactly. It's more like . . . education."

"Really?" His breath caressed her neck, sending a shiver down her spine. She struggled to maintain her ladylike posture.

"Ask me any question about Uruguay," she said.

He laughed and then leaned back so that the waiter could serve the plates of sliced steak au poivre, potatoes madelaine and green beans.

"I told my seatmate the senator's position on the race in New York," Mitch whispered. "But only so that she wouldn't quiz me on the senator's position on the new missile system."

"You like politics."

"No, I don't like politics," he said. "I actually hate politics as it's played out in the past fifty years. I think there's a huge difference between the people who go into politics because they believe in doing a duty for others and the people who go into politics because they have an ego to feed."

"There are a lot of egos in Washington."

"And I don't want to be one of them. If I serve in government—even if being the senator's aide is the last job I have here—I want to do so as a service. And I think everybody should take their turn of giving up a few years to serve their community, whether it's chairing the school PTA or ushering at church. I could as easily be a Little League coach as the representative from my district. As long as you're contributing something, you know, giving of the gifts you've been given."

Carole studied her date for a moment. She couldn't remember the last time she'd seen such fine salt-of-the-earth qualities in a man. She considered asking him to pinch her, as she must be dreaming, but then she thought better of it because he just might!

The food was passable, which, in Washington private clubs, was high praise. Mitch discreetly told her about every person seated at the table and there were many Carole recognized from newspaper photographs, TV news programs or the MSNBC.com screen that she sometimes checked out during the day.

As the dinner dishes were cleared, the senator—at the head of the table—stood up and asked that they all join him in toasting the sixtieth birthday of the four-star general at the other end of the table. Waiters scrambled to offer everyone flutes filled with champagne. The general nodded, beaming, as the gentle murmur of here-here was accompanied by the tinkling of crystal glasses touching one another.

Dessert was served, but not five minutes later, guests were making their excuses. Washington is an early evening town, and many were making the trek to countryside farms or weekend waterfront homes. When Mitch rose from his seat, the senator gestured for him to come speak privately. The Uruguayan ambassador had already said good night with a kiss to every lady's hand within his reach and Carole was mildly flattered when the reporter from the press corps moved her plate so that she could sit in Mitch's seat. She brought with her the subtle scent of Chanel.

"He's a hottie," she said, pulling a tube of lipstick out of her minaudiere.

"Pardon me?"

The reporter put on a sharp shade of red, checking her reflection on the blade of an unused knife.

"Mitch Evans. Definite hottie. If I didn't love my husband, I wouldn't mind some of that."

Carole laughed and the press corps reporter joined her.

"My name's Pepper January," she said, extending a right hand that was cluttered with a large aquamarine set in platinum.

"I'm Carole Titus. I recognize you from television. I must say, you always ask the president the most outrageous questions."

Pepper shrugged as if to suggest that what might seem outrageous was normal to her.

"How long have you and Mitch been an item?"

"I met him last night."

"Not quite ready for the golden anniversary party."

"No," Carole conceded. "I'm not even sure it's that kind of thing."

"What do you want it to be?" she queried. Then she saw Carole's slightly startled expression. "Sorry. I'm a reporter. I'm always asking questions, even ones I have no right to ask."

"It's all right. To be honest, I don't know what I want yet."

"At least you're not one of his cowgirls."

"What do you mean, 'cowgirls'?"

"His family's very important in Colorado. Easy to forget because everybody here thinks the only place anybody can mean anything is in the District. So every few months his family sends out a girl from Colorado—the other senate staffers call them cowgirls. Under the guise of 'help her find a job and an apartment' or 'she's starting law school at Georgetown, show her around town,' his parents keep sending him Mrs. Mitch Evans prospects. Any of these girls could smoke the competition at Miss America. In fact, I think one girl was a Miss Colorado. Not that you're not pretty, but you don't have a charge account at a plastic surgeon, and I'll bet your eyelashes are real. And you're from New York—it's still in your voice."

Carole laughed.

"What are you two talking about?" Mitch said, sitting at Carole's other side.

"Cowgirls," Carole said.

"Huh?"

"Forget it," Pepper said. "Just one last thing. Mitch was saying you work in the Internet field. How do your colleagues feel about the Justice Department's suit against . . ."

"I'm sorry," Carole said. "I really don't follow politics. But it was really nice to meet you."

Pepper sighed.

"I guess it's hard for me to stop working."

"But you do it so well," Mitch said. "You're going to call me tomorrow about the senator's reaction to passage of the appropriations package?"

"Absolutely. And will you have a statement about the senator's wife?"

"What about her?"

"There have been some rumors," Pepper said. "But if you don't know anything . . ."

"I don't know anything. What are you talking about?"

"Mitch, I'm the reporter, remember?"

Before Mitch could pursue anything further, Pepper's husband, a magazine publisher who had inherited money and lots of it, appeared to spirit her away.

"Darling, please, the pilot will be furious if we're late again," he said.

Everyone said good night and Mitch asked Carole if she wouldn't mind having a drink with him at the bar before they left. They went down a back stairwell to a cozy little sitting room. They seated themselves on a leather couch in front of a coffee table strewn with antique travelogues. He ordered two snifters of brandy and some coffee. From another room, they heard the sounds of happiness and celebration.

"You look a little out of sorts," Carole said mildly.

"The senator has asked me to go back to Colorado for a three-day meet-and-greet tour. Starting Tuesday."

"Meet-and-greet?"

"It's what we call talking to constituents. Town halls, church basements, YMCAs, Women's League of Voters coffees."

"Why is that a problem?"

"Three things. Usually, he's the one who does them. I only rarely do this for him. Second, they're usually planned months in advance. This is very sudden. I didn't even know about it this morning."

"But you'll go, right?"

"Of course. But I just got back from Denver last night. *He* must not have even known about this trip until this morning, otherwise why not leave me there?"

"And what's the third thing?"

"It's silly. It's my birthday coming up. The senator claims the reason he's sending me is so I can spend my birthday in Colorado, with my family."

"That's wonderful."

"I suppose. But I was hoping I would spend it with you."

"We can celebrate together when you come back," she offered.

He sighed.

"Carole, do you remember how you said there were really only two things that could happen and both of them were going to make at least one of us miserable?"

Carole swallowed. Hard.

"Mitch, we haven't known each other for even..." She looked at her watch. "All right, we've known each other for more than twenty-four hours, but only just barely."

"Carole, we're both old enough to know this might be good. Hours, days, minutes aren't the issue here."

She took a sip of the brandy. It felt good. Strong. Courageous.

"But Mitch, as much as we both think something will develop, we haven't actually, well . . ."

He put his glass on the coffee table.

"My apartment is a block away."

He took her hand in his. It was as intense as taking off in an airplane and just as important to have his strong fingers entwined in hers.

Tempting.

Oh, so very tempting.

He leaned toward her and kissed her, his lips sweet and unbearably soft. Not from the brandy did her belly feel opaline warmth. Not from the leather cushions did she develop a great languor. Instead, in his arms, she felt the great need for surrender, to his desire and to her own. And yet . . .

She pulled away gently.

"Mitch, I don't think I . . ."

He touched his index finger to her lower lip to shush her. For the first time since she had met him, she was unable to meet his eyes.

"I'm sorry, Carole, I've been so brash, I've moved too quickly. I've never had my heart broken, so I don't know the wisdom of taking things slow."

"That's not it," she said, shaking her head. His hand moved to beneath her chin and he tried to get her to look at him but her thoughts and feelings were too intense, too chaotic, for her to share just yet. "Mitch, I've only recently seen my way out of a bad marriage."

"It must have been bad—you don't seem like the kind of woman to take divorce lightly," he said. He leaned back into the leather cushions and waited for her to continue.

"I would be heedlessly ignoring the advice of every women's magazine ever published if I told you about him."

"Why is that?"

"On a first date, you shouldn't unload about first husbands or ex-boyfriends. Makes you sound like a man-hater."

"I'll have to remember that," he said. "I promise not to talk to you about my first husband or my ex-boyfriend. I would not want to be accused of man-hating."

She smiled in spite of herself.

"And the second rule is absolutely no sleeping with a man on the first date."

"Why don't we have you break the first rule before we even talk about the second rule. And only then can you tell me the third rule."

She hesitated.

"Come on," he urged. "He didn't physically abuse you, did he?"

"Oh, no, not at all," Carole replied. "It's just . . ."

"Just?"

"Hal was, well, needy."

"You seem like a person who could help a needy person."

"You're right. I am. Although I've never thought of it quite that way."

"So what did Hal need from you?"

"Everything," Carole said. The words were out loud for the first time, although she had given the matter a lot of thought. "Hal was brilliant, but couldn't finish college. Personable, but couldn't get along with any boss. And so talented, I could just cry wishing I had the talent he had—" She shook her head at his almost interruption. "No, he had talent. Wonderful guitarist. His band nearly got a record deal and played a lot of gigs up and down the east coast. Oh, but he worried so about 'selling out' and then, of course, there was the drinking. And the drugs."

She left out the suspicions of other women.

"And pretty soon you were playing Mom?"

She nodded.

"It was funny, really, because I had raised my three younger sisters after my father left. My mother had a recurring role in a soap opera, didn't make a lot of money but it paid the rent. But she was hopeless at the day-to-day things. You know—making sure the kids got off to school with their lunches, washing the dishes before we ran out of them, that sort of thing. She was a star, even if a very minor one, and couldn't be bothered."

"So you're always the one who takes care of, how should I put this?"

"I'll put it bluntly for you. So far, I'm the one who takes care of the real talented, real smart, real wonderful person."

"But you're real talented, real smart and real wonderful!"

"I'm a thirty-seven-year-old salesperson in a computer company started by a woman who is one of my best friends and who does not need me to take care of anything except the marketplace. Which, as hard as I have to work at it, is a relief."

"Don't you think being a salesperson is a talent?"

"Not really. It's a job anybody can do."

He shook his head.

"Man, you're hopeless," he said. "No talent, no brains . . ."

"And I'm older than you."

"I figured you were going to notice that."

"That means I'm not going to be pushed around. Not going to compromise. I've worked too hard to make my own life."

"This is terrible," he said, a devilish twinkle in his eye. "Next thing I know, you're going to tell me that you're not willing . . ."

". . . and I'm not willing . . ."

". . . to be . . ."

". . . to be . . ."

"The caretaker in this relationship," they said in unison.

She sighed.

"Carole, I'm not looking for a nanny," he said, kissing her lightly on the forehead. "I already have a mom and she's awfully good at being one. Hal might have needed a groupie but I don't play it that way. And I already have a doormat outside my house that says Welcome."

"Then what are you looking for?"

"I'm not looking for anything. And that's always the moment when you find a diamond."

He stood up.

"I'll drive you home," he said. "Much as I don't want to end this night, I should have understood you would want to take things slow. Real slow."

She looked up at his face, which had gained rather than lost a sensual appeal from his distress. The she shocked herself by taking the quickest peek below his waist, where she saw the barest outline of his immediate desire. He wanted her, badly. Suddenly, she had a vivid, yet fleeting image of her hand taking his belt, unclasping it, pulling him down to her. His strong, sure hand would slip under the hem of her dress and make its way up her legs to the center of her own desire. She wanted him. . . . The plush burgundy velvet couch in a staid Washington private club seemed the perfect place for trouble.

Trouble of the very best kind.

Chapter 5

She shook her head to snap out of it, a little like when she went swimming and got water in her ears.

Then she stood up. Splayed her hands on the crisp white cotton of his shirt. Kissed him lightly, but pulled away just as he wanted more. She tugged at his tie and the knot loosened.

"Ooooh, Carole." He sighed. And then, remembering where they were, "Uh, here? Now?"

She laughed at his distress.

"You can drive me home," she said. "But don't plan on driving back into the District."

He sized her up.

"Are you telling me to bring a toothbrush?"

"I'm telling you I don't want to take things quite *that* slow."

They walked arm in arm from the bar into the brightly lit foyer. A group of men and women in formal dress were coming in for dinner. Rain had just started falling, and the women's hairstyles were a bit bedraggled and the shoulders of the men's black dinner jackets were dotted with moisture. The doorman held an umbrella to protect Carole as he saw her to the passenger side of the car.

It was a quieting rain. The kind that muted the horns and stereos and subway gusts. The kind that softened the sodium glow of streetlights. The kind of rain that relieved the day's heat but did not shock the system with thunder and lightning.

He stopped the car in front of a quaint graystone on an off-street in Georgetown. An iron grillwork fence surrounded a tiny potted garden. On the steps were two griffins, made of once-perfect marble. One griffin sat on its haunches, proud and haughty, while the other reared imperiously on hind legs. Gorgeous home.

"You sure you don't want to come up?"

She was firm.

"No, I want you to come home with me."

"I'll be just a minute," he promised.

She waited, listening to the radio. When he came back, a song was just ending. She turned down the volume. They didn't talk much on the drive, but she didn't feel the silence was uncomfortable. She put her hand on top of his while he shifted gears and they both agreed that Peter Gabriel grated on the nerves, mostly because all his songs sounded exactly the same. And the newest boy band was indistinguishable from any other boy band. The rain stopped and they rolled down their windows. The cool, fragrant breeze made conversation impossible.

When they reached her house, she suddenly became aware of her nervousness. She told him, in a tone she hoped was as light as the butterflies in her stomach, that she had invited him here because then she could throw him out in the morning instead of vice versa. In the light reflected off the window to the kitchen, she saw that at first he wanted to respond to her seriously. And then he seemed to know that that was wrong. So he simply shrugged and said, "Well, when you do, could you make sure I'm dressed?"

They got out of the car and he surveyed the backyard, which had not been visible to him in the evening when he had parked on the curb. The clouds had given way to a sparkling sky, with a pale full moon hanging high above the pin oak leaves.

"Wow," he marveled.

"It's my evening garden," she said. "I don't get home much during the day so it doesn't make a lot of sense to put in beautiful dark red roses that I won't see. So I planted the back all in white. I even have moon flowers, which only bloom at night."

She took off her shoes and led him through the back path of granite block, past a trellis covered with sweet autumn clematis, along a border of nodding plantain leaves and plumed astilbe. The grass was cool and wet.

"The challenge is to find plants that can survive drought-like conditions every summer and yet not fall prey to mold and fungal infections of . . ." She turned to face him. "I'm babbling, aren't I?"

"A little," he conceded. He had taken off his suit jacket and pulled loose his tie.

"It's just that it's been a while," she said.

"If you don't mind my asking, how long is 'a while'?"

She came to him, and the scent of flowers gave way to the masculine combination of musk and citrus. She stretched to whisper in his ear. He sighed.

"You're right. That's a while. Maybe we shouldn't . . ."

She kissed him once on the earlobe and he faltered. For such an articulate guy, he was awfully distractible.

"Maybe we shouldn't . . ."

She kissed him on the side of his neck, where the artery pulsed to meet her lips. He said something that sounded like "wuh" and then pulled her closer.

"Carole, you are . . . very hot."

She reached inside his shirt and found, as she would have expected, abs that were firm and taut. But before she could caress him to her satisfaction, he pulled her wrist. Only so he could pick her up as effortlessly as if she were twenty years younger and some pounds lighter. She dropped her shoes and her shriek was followed immediately by laughter.

He walked around the house to the front porch and he only put her down because she couldn't get her keys out of her bag unless he did.

As soon as she opened the door, Whiskers meowed and came to be scratched. Carole picked her up, trotted to the kitchen, and firmly shut the door on the shocked feline.

She came back out to the foyer to find Mitch exactly where she left him. Now, a nice genteel lady entertains her gentleman caller in the living room and only after great courting and some refreshment, invites him up to her bedroom. A full-fledged tramp takes the hottie in question directly upstairs, no offer of a drink necessary or expected. Carole, being in no mood for the pleasantries of the former and still being in possession of enough of her faculties to disapprove of the latter, led him by his tie to the living room couch.

"Carole, I understand that you might feel that you're a little . . ."

Now the complicated part—all those buttons.

"I don't want you to feel things are going tooooo . . ."

She touched her index finger to his lips. Now was not the time for talk. Then she undid one button and then another. She was nothing if not nimble and in just an instant, she had before her his smooth, tanned chest. She pushed aside the starched white shirt so that she could admire him. He stared at her from beneath a strong, masculine brow.

For an instant—an instant so fleeting as to hardly be measurable by stopwatches or egg timers—she thought, *This is what the Madam's Closet people are missing. They don't understand what women want. What women want is what I've got right here. If only those suits in Chicago could understand that.*

Mitch wasn't thinking of Madam's Closet or marketing or selling lingerie—he was staring at her with an unbroken and unyielding concentration that was unlike any that had ever been directed at her. It unnerved her—as did the thoughts about Madam's Closet, which she tucked away in the furthest part of her brain, marked BUSINESS—and so she hesitated. Torn between taking what she wanted, what they both wanted—and doing what was prudent and well thought through.

Oh, the hell with thinking. She picked up the hem of her dress and slipped it over her head. As the silk fluttered to the floor, she felt Mitch's fingers tighten around her hips. Finding just a little thread of lace.

"The whole time we were at dinner . . . ?"

"I'm not big on underwear," she explained. "I don't wear much except during business hours."

"I'm not going to be able to think straight for a while."

"You're not here to think."

He arched and brought her down so that she felt his hardness straining against her. And though he now was in control of her, she felt unafraid, perhaps in part because he had acknowledged how she could hold a little sway over him by, well, by just being.

He caressed her breasts, bringing her nipples to exquisite hardness. Only when she was brought to the brink did he ease her away from himself so that he could unbuckle his belt. She slipped out of the tiny lace thong.

"I brought . . ." he said. She tugged his pants down. "That's why I stopped at my apartment . . ." she pushed the waist band of his boxer briefs low enough so that she could release him . . . "I didn't think you would have any and I didn't want to stop at a drugstore."

Somehow she had the presence of mind to find the small condom packet in his front pants pocket. Thank goodness he'd been thinking ahead! She was successful at opening it but too clumsy to put it on. She was relieved when he took over. When he finished, he leaned back and gently, very gently, eased her onto himself. But no matter how gentle, how slow and measured he made his movements, it could in no way ease the sudden bolt of sensation.

She had just another thought—that this, this was what she wanted and needed and would probably never again be willing to live without. A totally scary thought, the implications alone worth several anxiety attacks, and so she filed that away with BUSINESS right next to Madam's Closet. And then the cerebral cortex—the seat of high-level thinking—was told firmly but nicely to Butt Out.

No, don't think about business or psychology or philosophy for that matter, when a drop-dead gorgeous man was inside of you, caressing every tender, innermost part of your womanhood. No, no, this wasn't rationale, this wasn't something to think about or through or of. This was sensation. And unfortunately, not quite enough of it, because she had barely taken him into her before she felt the falling, falling, falling of orgasm. And moments later, heard his cry as his pulsing grew faster and stronger and then faded.

Oh, lordy. Whiskers was scratching at the kitchen door, yowling in protest. And she was stark naked in the living room, astride a man she hadn't known—and here she checked her watch—thirty-six hours before. She glanced at the windows, with their curtains gaily pulled back—thank goodness she had woods beyond the yard. This was most undignified, certainly unwise, and definitely causing her knee joints to ache. She eased to the side of him, careful not to let the condom slip off him. The joint in her knee popped.

"Maybe we should have tried the bed?" she asked.

He looked at her, smiling lazily.

"I think we should try every piece of furniture in your house."

"Oh, I'm sure I don't have the energy . . . oh, Mitch, that feels good."

Later, as the lazy hands of her bedside clock slid to four thirty, she told him, "If this was a one-night stand, this has been delicious."

He stilled.

"It hasn't been a one-night stand, and you know it."

"Well, if it is, it's been heavenly," she said. She rolled over and set the alarm for seven, make that seven-thirty.

"And if I'm still here?"

"I don't know, Mitch, I honestly don't know."

She fell into a deep and dreamless sleep, punctuated only by the unforgivably cheerful bells of her alarm. She reached and silenced it without opening her eyes. Beyond her windows, the sun poured through wavering leaves of oak and willow, giving the room a faintly golden glow. She became aware of the empty space on the bed beside her and she traced the warmth of his body's absence. Then the bathroom door opened and Mitch came out wearing a towel and a smile.

"I figured I'd better get up early if I wanted a shower," he said.

"How can you look so good in the morning when I feel so tired?" she moaned.

"Part of my training was to wake up good to go after an hour's sleep. I got nearly two."

"I gotta get some coffee," she said. "I think Whiskers is gonna attack me. I left her in the kitchen all night."

"I let her out right after you went to sleep."

"Good thinking."

She roused herself and watched him dress.

"What? I got spinach in my teeth?" he asked, as he righted his cuffs.

"I was just thinking your clothes don't have any wrinkles," she lied. She was actually thinking a lot of things that weren't cool. And a woman should always play it cool the morning after.

"This means I can go directly to work. It might be a Saturday morning, but I've got to get into the office."

"So do I."

The phone rang. Work. Work? Carole thought. Oh, damn, the weekly staff meeting had been moved to Saturday because Elyssa had spent the week working with the venture capital boys. They had scheduled it for . . . she looked at the clock— just an hour and twenty minutes, make that an hour and nineteen minutes.

"Hello?"

"Carole, it's Elyssa. I want to run some numbers past you about the Godiva account."

"Now?"

Mitch slipped downstairs.

"Of course now. Why would I be calling you if I didn't mean now? The staff meeting was rescheduled for this morning and you and I always . . . oh, no, I got it." Long pause. "You little vixen."

"Elyssa."

"Was he every bit as delicious as he looks?"

Carole thought about Mitch. He looked as good with just a towel around his waist as he did in a suit. No, better. And delicious? Hmmmmmm.

"Carole? I asked you a question. Is he every bit . . . ?"

"Absolutely."

A long, cool sigh.

"Damn."

"Listen, seriously, you're getting in this morning, right?" Elyssa said, with uncharacteristic urgency. Staff meetings were supposed to be mandatory. And they were, except in the summer. Carole always thought meetings were a waste of time. And if she had plans with Mitch, she might be inclined to invoke Saturdays, summer and the fact that she hadn't had a day off in months.

But Mitch was going to work, the flowers in the garden were maintenance-free, and besides, Elyssa seemed more insistent than usual. Which was difficult because when Elyssa wanted something, she was usually *very* insistent.

"Of course I'm coming in. Now what did you say you were calling about?"

"You know the Madam's Closet account?"

"I'm sorry about that. I suspect we'll get them on board in

another few months. I jumped the gun thinking I was closing them this past week."

"All right, then what about the Godiva people?"

"The earliest I can get a meeting with their veep is two weeks from now. He's in Switzerland, what can I do?"

"So the numbers are meaningless until you get the face time."

"I think so."

"What about those scented candles people?"

"Colorado Candles? They're close. Very close. We've been crunching numbers. Elyssa, why are you all of a sudden so concerned about my work? Is this because I have one date in . . . ?"

"No, of course not," Elyssa interrupted. "Oh, shit, that's my phone again and Robyn hasn't dragged her butt in here. See you in an hour."

Mitch came into the bedroom with a steaming cup of coffee for her.

"I'm assuming two sugars because that's what you had on the plane."

A man who remembers that sort of thing?

Wow.

After turning on the shower, Carole checked her email while the water got hot. *Fifty-six messages*. She didn't bother reading any of them. Most Friday nights she'd order out Chinese and watch the sitcoms, do a little catch-up on the week's work and call her sisters to hear about the latest achievements of nieces and nephews. Last night was wonderful, no doubt about it. But could she keep her life if Mitch was in it?

She didn't bother with blow-drying and she grabbed the first dress she saw in the closet after remembering that she had a luncheon meeting with one of Elyssa's venture capital boys—a cream-colored St. John knit with a matching cardigan. Add on a spectator slide and that spelled success!

Downstairs, she found Mitch at the kitchen table eating cereal and reading the *Washington Post*. Of course, Whiskers was not holding a grudge against him and, in fact, was his biggest fan.

"Get off the table!" Carole scolded. "She knows she's not supposed to do that."

Whiskers gave her a look and Carole knew that a houseplant would be toppled over or a pillow was going to be clawed to pieces while she was at work.

"Can I see you tonight?"

"Of course, I would love . . . oh, I'm sorry, I just remembered Charlotte, my niece, is coming for a sleepover. My sister and her husband are coming into Washington to see the ballet at the Kennedy, and they wanted me to baby-sit."

"I leave tomorrow."

"I'm sorry," she said. She hoped she wasn't sounding too cool. Another of Hal's pet names for her was Ice Princess. But there was nothing to be done.

"We can see each other when you get back. Next week?"

"That's too far away."

"No, it's not. Oh, shit, I just remembered I have a trip to New York week after next. But it's not for sure. It depends on whether the vice president of Godiva comes in from Switzerland."

Mitch stared at his breakfast.

"This isn't a brush-off, is it?"

"Of course not."

"Then give some thought to coming to Colorado. Is there any part of your work that you can't do from there?"

"Not really."

"Is there any part of your work that would be helped by going?"

"I have one client I could stop in on."

"Then think about it. You can reach me on my cell phone. Call me if you change your mind."

"You've got to understand that if I went with you to Colorado, I still have to work," she said. "It can't all be . . ." she gestured widely.

"What?" he asked.

"Oh, don't look so innocent."

"Honey, that's the only advantage this baby face gives me. I can look convincingly innocent."

She shook her head and growled as if she were frustrated. And she warned him—as they left the house, as they drove in to her office, as they said good-bye in the parking lot—that she couldn't possibly go with him.

When she entered the conference room of Allheart.com, she found all the women gathered around a desk calendar laid out on the conference table.

"Sorry I'm late," she mumbled.

"Yeah, well, close the door," Elyssa said.

"Must have been some date." Robyn giggled.

The other women didn't break a smile.

"What's wrong?" Carole said, sitting down at her usual place at the table.

"We've got cash-flow problems," Alix said soberly. She shoved an inch-thick financial statement across the table. Carole leafed through the pages. A lot of red.

"We need clients," Elyssa said. "Isn't there anybody that you've got that is close to signing on?"

"The candle company," Carole said absently. The figures prepared by the Allheart.com accountant were dire. "And there's that jewelry outfit in Austin, Texas. I could fly out as early as tomorrow."

"Leaving town just as you've got a new man?" Dana asked. "That either means he's gay, a jerk or married."

"None of the above. He happens to be going to Colorado tomorrow too," Carole flipped to the end of the document. She studiously ignored the butterflies in the stomach. Business was supposed to have trouble early on, sure, but not now, please not now. "We could fly out together. He invited me to join him for a week. And I could drop down to Texas on a day trip. Just not on his birthday. He wanted to celebrate his birthday together."

The women hooted. Carole protested they should keep this a business meeting.

"Besides, I didn't say I was going. I just thought maybe . . ."

"Go with him!" Robyn urged.

"This is much more interesting than numbers," Dana said.

"Rocky Mountain High . . ." Robyn sang, sounding so unlike the late John Denver. "Just remember to bring sunblock. The upper altitudes are deceptive. Especially if you're playing nature girl."

Alix hooted.

"Don't bother with sunblock, get your ass down to Spalique. That man looks like he's worth every extra effort. And get a Brazilian wax."

"No!" the women sang out in unison.

"There are some things a woman shouldn't have to do for a man," Dana said.

"Yeah, but I heard that a certain politician—" Alix named a regular guest on *Meet the Press*, "—was so happy with his wife's Brazilian wax that he gave her a diamond ring and sent the woman who did it a dozen roses."

"Maybe he gave her the diamond because of a certain little scandal we all know about," Elyssa observed. "I say a trip to La Perla Boutique would be quite enough. No need for pain."

Carole nodded her gratitude to Robyn, who poured her a cup of coffee from the pushpot. It wasn't in her job description as Elyssa's administrative assistant, but she didn't seem to mind.

"It's kind of good to have Carole get a little ribbing." Robyn giggled. "We've all had our share."

"Why don't guys put this much thought into their undies?" Dana said thoughtfully. She was content queen, writing all the copy for the Allheart greeting cards.

"Oh, damn, I hear another line of cards coming," Alix moaned as Dana started scribbling on her notepad.

"Point is, ladies, we can release Carole for one week to Mr. Good-Looking," Elyssa said. "Alix, you'll have to take the meeting she would have attended with the placement director of American University. We can't take on new employees but we certainly can look into a few interns. And Dana, you'll need to proof the brochure that Carole put together. Robyn, could you be extra careful about directing her correspondence?"

"Will do," Robyn said.

"Wait!" Carole cried. "I was just saying I could go out there. Call it a musing. Or a hypothetical."

"With a man like that, I don't think you wait," Alix observed.

"Actually, Carole, I've decided you're going," Elyssa said abruptly. "I had been counting on the Madam's Closet account and with that gone, I really want the Colorado Candle Company and those Texas folks. You read that report. Or at least got the gist of it. We are going to have serious cash-flow problems if we can't persuade the venture capital boys that we're all about the money. Now, that having been said, let's turn our attention to the other matters on the agenda."

Chapter 6

The staff meeting dragged on a little longer than usual and when Carole returned to her office, she picked up the ringing telephone with a weary hello.

"Good morning, it's Herbert Kolkey," the voice on the other end said. "Carole, I know you sorta think of us as a slowpoke company. And maybe you think of me as the most slowpoke guy you've ever had to deal with."

"You're right, on both counts," Carole said, and then immediately softened. "Herbert, you worry that the greeting-card business is driven by women customers and that's a legitimate concern, but have you ever considered what women might want from your company?"

"Well, sure, I suppose."

"Herbert, I know this is an extremely personal question, but just give it a try."

"Okay."

"Have you ever bought your wife lingerie from Madam's Closet?"

"Oh, absolutely," he boomed. "We have a wonderful product line and some of those things are just the prettiest and my bride of forty-two years, why, she looks just as good as any supermodel when she's wearing something made by our designers."

"Do you think she'd ever want to buy you a little something?"

"'Course not! I'm not that kind of man—I don't dress up in women's clothes."

"No, I'm not saying that."

"You mean, men's . . . unmentionables? That stuff is for guys who play for the other team."

She rubbed her temple, where a headache was forming.

"Herb, you're right. Your company probably can't handle e-commerce. You're an old-fashioned company with an old-fashioned niche. You should stay true to that vision." *And you're welcome to it,* Carole thought but didn't say. Then she remembered the accountants' report. "Did you talk to your brother?"

"No."

"Why don't you do that. See what he thinks."

"W-w-w-w-wait a minute," Herb stammered. "I want to get back to your other point. You're talking about marketing mens' . . . stuff . . . for the ladies to buy?"

"It was just a thought, Herb."

"Oh, dear. It's not really . . . well, I'd have to think about that one a long time."

"Take your time, Herb. Take all the time you need."

Like until the next century, she thought after saying good-bye. Elyssa poked her head in the door and Carole waved her to one of the chairs across from her desk.

"Have a good time in Denver," Elyssa said.

Carole looked up from her intensive search of the bottom right-hand drawer of her desk. Nail polish remover, a box of tissues, Estée Lauder wrinkle cream, a thesaurus, and a half-empty bag of Pepperidge Farm Mint Milano cookies.

No aspirin.

"Thanks," she said cautiously. "Elyssa, you've got something on your mind. Start talking."

"All right. We're approaching a speed bump."

Carole looked under the bag of cookies. Midol. But she wasn't having her period. Besides, there weren't any tablets left.

"We've been in this shape before. Lots of red marks on an accountants' report. The landlord threatening to evict us. Working without a paycheck for a few weeks. We'll get through this."

"That was when we were on our own. When we answered to ourselves. The venture capital guys will want to see serious budget cuts before they give us any more money."

"Okay, so we won't buy the pushpot from Starbucks," Carole suggested. Why did she have a box of Biore nose strips in her desk? "We'll get our coffee from 7-Eleven. Better, we'll make our own. I mean, we play it pretty close to the bone as it is."

"You don't get it. We're talking jobs."

Carole slammed shut the drawer. And looked at her boss—and friend—who bore all the signs of a nervous breakdown.

"Elyssa . . ."

"It's better to go to them with the cuts having already been made."

"I thought you got money from Joe," Carole said. "This was already taken care of."

Joe Monteigne had wooed and won Elyssa's heart. And had brought in money. Bags and bags of money. Where had it all gone?

"You wouldn't be affected," Elyssa said. "Obviously, we can't work without a salesperson hitting the pavement. But we've got to get that Denver account. So go with my blessings but don't forget—business first."

"First I've got to get rid of this headache. Wanna continue this conversation downstairs?"

Downstairs in the lobby was a newspaper kiosk that sold aspirin, candy bars, soda, cigarettes, Tums and anything else an office worker would need. Elyssa and Carole walked through the Allheart halls and as they did, Carole noted that there were quite a number of people at the firm who were recent hires. In fact, one of the conference rooms had been set up with four desks shoved up against each other. Even on a Saturday, the place was humming with activity.

Carole thought about the work that was being farmed out to the pajama gang—she herself had been given an assistant named Molly who worked out of her home in Columbia City, Maryland. Carole had only met Molly once, on the day she was interviewed—but she did great work at evaluating prospective clients and was grateful for the flexibility of the job, as she was a single mother. Carole remembered what it was like to lose a job—she couldn't fail.

"Elyssa, I'll bring in the Denver people," she said, after she bought aspirin and two diet Cokes. They sat down on one of the benches in the tree-filled atrium lobby.

"Good. Now that business is out of the way, tell me all

about him. You know I asked for a written report. What'd you do all day?"

Carole blushed.

"Okay, so you can't tell me what you did."

"We saw the Washington Monument."

"I'd be embarrassed to admit that too. By the way, I told Joe about him. And he said he's from a very old, very wealthy Colorado family. Sorta like the Kennedys, but without Hyannis Port, the drinking and the tragic early-death curse going. They go in for lots of kids."

"It's too early to talk about kids," Carole said.

"But he's younger. His clock is ticking slower than yours is. I know it's unfair, but you're older than him by what?"

"Eight years."

"Eight years. His family's going to put pressure on him at some point. And the other thing is, Joe was telling me that they really believe that public service stuff. Mitch might end up in politics one day or running the family busi—"

"I'm not thinking about the future," Carole insisted. "This isn't that kind of thing. I don't want to get married again, not after Hal. And while I love my nieces and nephews, I'm not sure I want kids—I might not have the strength to do a good job of motherhood. As for Mitch, I'm sure he's not thinking long-term, either. We haven't known each other for very long."

"You've dated other men. You haven't cared one way or another about them—this one you care about."

"You're right. This one I care about."

"Then it's good you're not waiting until next week to see him. Because you know relationships are like sharks."

"They are?"

"Yeah. They have to keep moving or they sink."

When she called Mitch, he couldn't talk because he was in a meeting.

"I'll make the reservations," he said. "Five o'clock flight tomorrow. I could pick you up."

"No, I have to take Charlotte home. I'll meet you there. Bye."

Carole packed her briefcase and called her neighbor to hire their eleven-year-old to feed Whiskers while she was gone.

"Get your mail and newspapers too?" the boy asked.

"Absolutely. And water the garden if it doesn't rain."

"Will do. Thanks a lot, Miz Titus. Did I tell you I want to

buy a Razor scooter from the Sharper Image? They cost a hundred dollars."

With as many trips as I take, Carole thought, *you'll be able to afford one in every color.*

Her sister dropped off Charlotte at the office, and Carole took her to get her nails done, which was their traditional girlie thing and then to the latest Disney pic, which was boring and predictable and still left her in tears at the end. Then they went out for ice cream before coming home.

The next morning, after making Charlotte pancakes, she put on a blue silk wrap dress that was comfortable and cool enough that it wouldn't stick to her skin. It came with a matching sweater that was a godsend in case she got cold on the plane. She threw a pair of sneakers and jeans into her bag because, after all, she was going to Colorado and Mitch might want to go on a nature walk. But she also packed two bias-cut dresses that, she'd be honest, made her look gorgeous. And, for business, a white knit St. John suit with black trim at the pockets and cuffs. She opened her underwear drawer and shook her head.

Bra straps held together with safety pins. Whites grayed from repeated washings. Nothing matching. A cotton Tweetie Bird nightshirt.

Well, there was only one solution. After she dropped off Charlotte at her parents' house, Carole hit the malls.

She met Mitch just before five o'clock at the gate at Ronald Reagan Airport. He was dressed in a well-tailored gray suit, a white shirt and a pale yellow tie. And he looked, in the instant before he saw her, as if he were worried she might not show. She felt a flicker of unease—she didn't want to be responsible for his frown, for his pacing, for his worried glance down the length of the terminal. But then he smiled at her, waved as he thought he was the first to see her, and then she smiled too. And only briefly chided herself—was she really afraid of having somebody else be the architect of her feelings?

In that precise moment, she had the urge to bolt. Walk right out of the airport. Or tell Mitch that she had come to meet him only to tell him that business—yes, that's it, business—kept her back in Washington. That she'd see him sometime when he returned from Colorado. Have a great time. Happy Birthday, while you're at it.

But then he had forged his path through the businessmen and tourists and he took her into his arms for a long, simmering kiss. Her heart surged, her arms clung to his shoulders of their own accord, and she let her briefcase and bag drop to the floor. There was no going back home.

"They're boarding," he said when he relinquished her. "Let me take that."

He picked up her bag by its shoulder strap and slung it on his shoulder with his garment bag. Carole grabbed her briefcase.

On the 727, they found their seats three-quarters of the way back in coach. The plane wasn't full and Carole and Mitch had pulled the aisle and window seat on the three-seat row. Mitch offered her the window. While he put their bags in the overhead compartment, a woman two rows behind them asked for his help. He sat down next to Carole just as the flight attendants closed the overhead bins and started the safety lecture.

"Butterflies?" Mitch asked.

"Yeah, but not so much," Carole said. He had laid his hand palm up on the armrest between them. He remembered that she didn't like takeoffs. The plane lumbered onto the runway. Carole felt her chest squeeze and it was an effort to remember to breathe. In through the nose, out through the mouth, in through the nose . . .

This was a business trip, like any other. But of course, it wasn't like any ordinary business trip at all. She was with Mitch, going to his home state, celebrating his birthday, and—what had he said as they were driving into work this morning?—oh yes, and they would be spending the weekend at his favorite place on earth.

She wasn't so young, in heart or in years, that she hadn't gone on trips with a man. When she first met Hal, there had been weekends away. And after her divorce, there had been one weekend at Hilton Head in South Carolina with an ocular surgeon, who taught her what little she knew about golf. She had been celebrating her new job and had insisted they split the costs fifty-fifty. Boy, had she been surprised at how expensive a weekend away could be!

But this trip seemed more fraught with anxiety. She didn't remember feeling this way on the plane heading out to South Carolina.

She glanced at Mitch, at his strong, lean profile. He had

closed his eyes and his lashes were enviably long, sun-bleached at their tips.

She squeezed his hand as the plane's engines roared. Trust. She had to trust him in Denver.

She chided herself. *Now how is it that you trusted him in your home, in your bed, in your arms last night and suddenly you're worried about being with him in another city, not your own?* She shook her head. Sometimes it was better to listen to other people's worries—they were so much easier to solve.

They began the acceleration, and as always, there was that moment when she thought something was wrong, even though all the odd sounds and chaotic rumblings were the same odd sounds and chaotic rumblings she heard on every flight. For just one instant, she thought she might scream or take off her belt or leap to her feet—and like every flight, the impulse passed.

And after a few drifts that were stomach jarring like roller coasters, they reached cruising altitude. The pilot announced that they could take off seat belts and feel free to move around the cabin.

"You okay?" Mitch asked.

"Absolutely," she lied.

"I should warn you that I have a file I have to read," he said. "I start with a seven A.M. breakfast with the Denver Rotarians and the day just goes on and on from there. I need to read up on them."

"That's fine. I've got a meeting with candle people," Carole said and she reached up under the seat in front of her to get her briefcase. "I've got some catching up to do myself."

She was relieved to pull out the file Molly had written on the Colorado Candle Company and its market profile. In just moments she was engrossed and only pulled herself away long enough to tell the flight attendant that she'd have a glass of white wine. Tasted terrible, but was relaxing.

They put away their work when dinner was brought, a perfectly ghastly tray of chicken l'orange and something rice. But neither had eaten since lunch and both were starving.

"Have you figured out why he's sending you back?" Carole said, gesturing toward the seat pocket where Mitch had stashed his file.

"I haven't a clue. But since I haven't had a weekend off in months, I'm happy to be going. On Friday, I'm going to show you the most beautiful place on earth. And that's where we're going to celebrate my birthday."

"Any clues as to where this place is?"

"Let's put it this way—don't expect to wear your heels."

They got into the hotel after midnight, tired and preoccupied with thoughts about the next morning's work. The Hotel Teatro was a small but quite delectable hotel in Denver's best neighborhood. The penthouse suite they were ushered into boasted a potted garden terrace with a beautiful view of the valley spread out before them, and the mountains beyond.

"Taxpayers pay for this?" Carole asked.

"Absolutely not. I'm paying for this with my money. If I let the senator pay for it, we'd have to stay at the Motel Six."

"This is nicer," Carole mused, and then walked back into the sitting room where Mitch was sorting a sheaf of pink message slips the desk clerk had handed him. He had pulled off his suit jacket, loosened his tie and rolled up his sleeves, revealing tan, muscular forearms with blue veins.

On the tiger-maple desk, a basket of fruit and a bottle of a local vintner's best were waiting—courtesy of the senator's Colorado staff. She accepted a glass from Mitch and walked into the bedroom. The bed was piled high with soft Porhault covered pillows that said, "Come here, you look exhausted." And she was. But when Carole emerged from the bathroom in her tags-just-ripped-off La Perla gown, sleep wasn't what Mitch had in mind.

"I thought you had a meeting in—" Carole glanced at her watch, "five hours."

He kissed her again. Oh, how delicious his lips were.

"Five hours is a long ways away," he said.

And he picked her up, carried her to the bed and deposited her on the bed as if she were the most exquisite treasure.

"No fair, you're still dressed."

He unbuttoned his shirt, slowly, standing before her in a proud masculine pose, his eyes never leaving hers. He let the shirt fall to the ground. He was unrepentantly muscular, but in a way that no gym rat or steroid junkie could master. His chest was warmly tanned and smooth. She leaned back in the pillows, giving him the once over—twice.

"Do you like what you see?" he asked, undoing his belt.

She regarded him appraisingly. She felt a wicked smile come upon her.

"Absolutely," she replied.

"Good, because you'll be seeing a lot of me."

He let his pants fall to the floor. She roused herself to touch his stomach. So hard, so smooth, and yet, the flesh rippled at her touch. She felt so powerful, seeing him respond so utterly and completely to her, and yet, there was such a playful, knowing quality to their lovemaking that power wasn't something one of them had and the other longed for.

"No fair," he said. "You have this little dainty thing . . ."

And he pulled it over her head with a minimum effort. She didn't feel as comfortable in her nakedness as he was but she resisted the urge to turn off the lamp on the night table. Her breasts, she knew, were not as firm and round as they were when she was in her twenties. She worked on her arms sporadically, having admired Linda Hamilton's biceps as much as any other woman who saw *Terminator II*. And the Atkins, Pritikin, Sugar Busters! and Zone diets had worked—but only for a few days at a time. She had soft curves. And plenty of them.

Something in his eyes, the way he hungrily regarded her, made her think he didn't need for her to have ripped muscles or to be a waif. And so she drew him onto the bed with all the confidence of a goddess.

The last thing Carole thought before she went to sleep at four that morning was that Alix was right—a gal should spring for nice lingerie and let nature take care of the rest.

The desk clerk called her at eight o'clock that morning to say that Mitch had thought she would need a wake-up call. And boy, did she ever! She barely got to the Colorado Candle Company in time for her first meeting. But she was as incandescent as their finest creation. The tour of the factory would have normally bored her—but with a diet Coke to energize her, she found herself making small talk with the candle makers and packagers. When she presented sales figures to the five-member marketing group, she felt in command. She remembered names, figures and finances with ease. When she was introduced to the president of the company, she even mentioned a highly flattering piece in *Entrepreneur* magazine that had featured him. She was totally on her game. She was a sexy, sexually satisfied woman and that confidence and power radiated off of her.

Still, she declined an invitation for dinner—not so much because she wanted to get back to Mitch but because she needed rest. Around four o'clock, the high she had experienced had worn off completely. The next day, the real negotiations would begin and she couldn't afford to be dragging then.

Luckily, Mitch was in complete agreement when she explained herself over dinner at the hotel's dining room.

"It's not a problem for me," he said. "But you're never going to forgive me if you don't get this account, so off to bed with you—alone!"

He sat on a couch in the sitting room and read position papers while she went to sleep.

The next day went even better and over dinner with the marketing committee she got the commitment she was looking for. She immediately ordered a bottle of the Vieuve Clicquot for the table. She always did that with clients—harder to wake up with next-morning regret after a saleswoman has bought you the best champagne in the world. It wasn't closed yet, but keep her fingers crossed, the pens would be working tomorrow.

When she returned to the hotel, Mitch was just coming back from a late-night pow-wow with the governor and they should have fallen right to sleep. Instead, they celebrated with a dessert of strawberries, whipped cream, and champagne.

In bed.

"When you come back from Texas, we should go shopping," Mitch said later.

"Shopping. I love it," Carole said. "I've never met a man who liked shopping. I saw a few boutiques in the Lodo neighborhood."

"Not those kind of shoes."

"Shoes? Who said anything about shoes?"

But he was already asleep, sprawled naked across the bed. How had she gotten so lucky? she wondered. She pulled up the sheets around herself, being so much more modest than he was. *Time to thank some lucky stars*, she thought before falling asleep.

The next morning she didn't bother with her hair, just pinned it up in a twist and changed into the only dress she had that the Colorado Candle people hadn't already seen. She suppressed her anxieties until the last flourish of the vice president's signature and then faxed the contract to Elyssa and FedExed the original. She dashed out of the office and picked up her flight to Austin, which was uneventful except for the fact that she missed him.

Goddamnit, she missed him.

It bothered her, yes, it bothered her a lot that one part of her was missing him, even when she negotiated with the jewelry company, admired their delicate turquoise and kunzite creations, crunched numbers for them, played hardball and inevitably softened to a contract that pleased her mightily. The company president, in a celebratory mood, gifted her with a carnelite bracelet. She insisted on buying a pair of cuff links for Mitch since she had not had time to buy him a birthday present.

Mitch met her at the airport in Denver and when they embraced, she thought she'd never want to let him go.

"Come on, darling," he said. "Oh, and we have to get you new shoes. I saw those sneakers you had packed. Pitiful things. That swoop don't mean a thing."

"Oh, I get it now. We're going on a nature hike."

She had visions of pine needle–covered paths in the woods. The sighting of a moose or an eagle—at a distance of course. A picnic basket. A bottle of ice cold Riesling. A river glade. Then back in town for dinner, a nice soak in a hot tub, and . . . well, what else is a gal supposed to think?

"Nature hike," he repeated with ominous good cheer.

Chapter 7

He took her out to the airport's parking garage.

"What's this?" she asked, suspicious.

"It's a loaner from a friend."

"Some friend."

The vehicle had once been a two-door, four-wheel-drive Jeep in good standing. It was now a bit rusty and had lost its side doors. It had a sunroof that stretched from one fender to another—meaning, of course, there was no roof at all. The backseat had been pulled out, as had any upholstery.

It was not the sort of Jeep to inspire confidence, although the Free Tibet and Phish bumper stickers on the back suggested the possibility of some vague spiritual protection for its passengers.

"You got everything you need for the next two days?" Mitch asked.

"What do you mean, two days?"

"Two days in paradise."

"Where exactly is paradise?"

"Gunnison. Small town on the edge of the border with New Mexico. That's where the trail starts. I've gone there nearly every birthday since I was ten. We follow the river for two days."

"Oh, no, you've got the wrong gal. My idea of roughing it is traveling to a city that doesn't have its own Bloomingdale's."

"Do you trust me?"

She swallowed.

"We don't have to go," Mitch said. "There are other things to do in Denver. Hell, the owner of the Rockies invited the two of us to his skybox for tomorrow's game. And then there's opera here and they're doing . . ."

"It's not trust. It's fear."

"Of what?"

This from a man who clearly didn't understand fear.

"Making an absolute ass out of myself," Carole said. "Looking foolish. Stupid. Too tired."

"It's not a test. It's a trip down a river. A river I love. That I want to share with you. It's like sharing everything else of me with you."

An unmistakable reference to their lovemaking.

"Then let's go. How far away is it?" She added as a smile crossed his features.

"Six hours. You have six hours to change your mind."

"And then?"

"It's just like a relationship. Once the river takes us, we can't turn back. We'll stop at the hotel and FedEx everything to Washington that we aren't taking with us."

She tentatively got into the Jeep and strapped herself in. She put a firm hand on the crash bar behind her head. This was a good time to have a talk, the kind of talk about intimacy that every woman needs to have with her man. She was just about to launch her words when he turned the ignition.

The engine roared to life and as the seat vibrated beneath her and the wind whipped her hair this way and that, she figured out that a quiet, heartfelt conversation would have to wait six hours.

At the hotel, she changed into jeans and a T-shirt. She dropped her business clothes, heels, and laptop into the garment bag containing Mitch's suits and papers. At the last minute, she added her filofax.

But her cosmetics case? No way!

"Your bags will be waiting for you at the airport," the concierge assured them. "Have a pleasant trip."

They stopped only once more, at a dusty, tar-shingled shack four hours into the trip. There, Mitch bought her hiking boots, a tank of gas, and a cold soda.

The afternoon temperatures peaked and then began the slow decline. Mitch turned off the three-lane highway onto a two-lane blacktop road and then onto a gravel path that ran into a dirt trail. The dusty yellow of the plains gave way to a rich green of forest.

After a gal got used to the mind-blowing beauty there was nothing left but, well, nothingness.

No billboards, no skyscrapers, no parking lots, no traffic stops, no apartment buildings. Carole was reminded of certain of her New York relatives who got anxiety attacks if they were more than a hundred miles outside of the city. She would never make fun of them again.

Mitch turned off the engine at the bank of a topaz-colored river. Hidden beneath the branches of a cluster of pines was a shed. He got out and pulled his pack out of the back seat.

"We'll leave the Jeep here and take the river up," he said. "Two days. You'll love it."

Two days? Jeep?

"Hey, wait," she said, undoing her seat belt. She scrambled to catch up with him at the shed. He pulled a fiberglass and steel canoe out. "What'll happen to the Jeep?"

"Oh, somebody will take care of that."

"Who?"

He glanced at her.

"It's just I would never leave my car, unlocked, out in the middle of nowhere," Carole said. "It could get stolen. The radio could get . . ."

"The radio's already gone."

"See? My point exactly."

All this was said good-naturedly, but Carole knew herself well enough to know this was trust, pure and simple. Did she trust him?

"We're not in nowhere," he said, standing up. "Don't worry so much. One of the caretakers will come and pick up the Jeep. I'll call him when we get to the plane."

"Caretakers?"

"This is my land. We've been on family property for over an hour. Most of the next two days we'll be on our property, except some of the time we'll cut through into the Blue Mesa National Park. And the airstrip is on our land as well."

She looked around. She had grown up in a rent-controlled two-bedroom apartment in New York. Shared one bedroom with her sisters. Found privacy only in the summers when she could go up on the roof.

Thought her standard-sized lot with the little cottage was the grandest estate.

"You own this?" She gestured at, well, everything. The mountains in the distance. The pine trees towering overhead.

The columbine weed and lupine at her feet. The river flowing into the horizon.

"Yeah, my family does, in a complicated trust," Mitch said. He leaned down and examined the raft for hairline cracks, looking up just once. "Carole, I live in your world. But this is mine. And I hope you'll love it as much as I do."

He inspected the canoe and oars, repacked their packs so that his was heavy while hers was lighter, and found a Ziploc bag for her cell phone.

"Put this in your vest," he said, handing her the phone. "You won't want to get it wet."

"Where exactly are we going to be sleeping?" she asked. Surely there was a cozy little cabin out there . . . somewhere.

"I brought a tent."

"Oh. It's like that."

They cast off just as the sun drooped into the tree line. She had never heard quiet like this. Behind her, Mitch rowed and told her river tales. Camping with his family. Taking his buddies with him when he was a little older. The river widened and on either bank were impenetrable green hills that reached into mountains and mountains that reached to sky. Stars began to dot the tea-rose sky as the sun slipped down below the horizon.

Stars and more stars, so many that Carole felt she had never seen them before. But they threw off no light, and the couple was soon enveloped in a darkness that was blacker than any she had ever known. She felt a nervousness shoot up through her spine.

Carole, what are you doing out here in the middle of nowhere with a man you just met—what?—a week ago? He could be Jack the Ripper, for all you know—except he is a senator's aide, who surely has gone through those infamous background checks.

"Difference between city folks and country folks is that city folks are scared of night and country folks are scared of all the bright lights," Mitch said.

The shadow of him pulled the raft to the shore and tied it to an overhanging branch. He told her to wait, wading onto shore as he pulled the raft near. He lit two Coleman lanterns on either side of a room-sized clearing. Carole slipped out of her life vest and stood up. The raft tilted one way and then jerked back another.

"Here, wait, let me," Mitch said, wading out into the water.

He picked her up and waded to shore, depositing her on the dry, grassy shore. "You might want to stretch out a little."

Boy, did she! Her muscles ached, her butt felt like it was asleep and her knees creaked when she walked. Which she only did enough of to reach a boulder that was sized just right to be her perch.

She would have helped him, but he seemed so completely economical in his movements. Within minutes he had a modest tent assembled, a fire providing light and warmth, and a fold-out stove with stew bubbling in a pot.

He changed into fresh, dry clothes.

"This is my idea of a perfect evening," Mitch said. "The stars, the river, and you and me. But you don't look quite so enthralled."

"The mosquitoes."

"The quiet."

"No restaurants."

"No taxis."

"No people," they said in unison.

She approached the fire and sat down in his arms. He wrapped a blanket around both of them. It had gotten quite cool. They shared a plate of stew he had heated up for them.

"I'm having a wonderful time," she assured him. "But was that a coyote I heard?"

"Maybe, from very far away. Coyotes don't want to get anywhere near humans. And I checked for droppings to make sure we weren't in their territory."

"What about snakes?"

"The fire scares them."

"Bears?"

"Oh, now, bears are a different story. They love to eat humans, especially women."

"Really?"

"Absolutely. And women in the computer industry. Ouch!" he responded to her elbow in his ribs. "Darling, don't worry about nature. Half the animals out there are more scared of you than you are of them."

"That's awfully damned scared. And what about the other half?"

"They're too busy making dinner out of the scaredy-cat half to be thinking about you."

"That's not as comforting as all that."

"Besides, you have me to protect you."

"Well . . ."

"You have trouble letting somebody else be responsible for even a minute."

"Me? No way, I'd love it if people were more responsible. It would mean less pressure on me. Like in the office, if I could hire someone to work in sales who would do half the follow-up that each account requires . . ."

"I'm not talking about work. I'm talking about your personal life. You don't like to rely on anyone else. You want to be in charge because you think that's the only way you'll be safe. Maybe that comes from having the men in your life let you down. But I'm just telling you to let me be in charge of fretting and worrying—just for two days. I'll let you know if things are dire."

The *pop!* of the wet inside the wood and the hooting of an owl on a faraway tree was the only punctuation to the quiet.

"And they're not right now," she said as much as asked.

"They're not," he confirmed.

"I'm just very self-sufficient."

"I know."

"I've had to be."

"I know."

"Maybe a little too self-sufficient."

"Mm-hmm."

"No, just the right amount self-sufficient. I've had to be."

"Mm-hmm."

"Are you listening to me?"

"Mm-hmm. I'm just hoping that at some point you'll shut up and kiss me."

Which she did.

The next morning, she awoke in his arms. The tent's canopy glowed with the buttery yellow sunshine. Outside, a bird chirped madly and the water lapped against the rocky shore. The air smelled of juniper, fresh water and just the barest hint of last night's fire. *This wasn't so bad*, she thought, burrowing further into his embrace. *Not so bad at all.*

After dozing for what seemed like forever but which could only have been a few minutes, she knew she couldn't wait any longer. *Nature calling*. This was the one part of the trip that

she would not get used to. But better while he was still asleep
than after he awoke.

She opened the tent flap and stretched her arms. The day
was just beginning to warm and she had never seen such a
beautiful sight as the water like diamonds laid out in front of
her and the raft sailing on the gathering current.

"MITCH!" she screamed and ran toward the water. The
rocks were slippery but this was no time to put on hiking
boots. As she charged toward the raft, Mitch ran out from behind her, vaulted twenty-odd feet and dove.

His stroke was fierce and powerful, shooting a spray of water in his wake.

Carole would look back later and think that she should
have believed he would overtake the raft. That he didn't need
her help. That he could do a better job if she didn't try. But inaction was something that Carole loathed. And trusting
Mitch—*well, sure, of course, but what if he failed?*

To her later regret, she followed him into the water, wading
out until she was nearly waist deep. The water was so cold it
felt like pine needles jogging her skin.

One mossy rock spelled her undoing. She felt a crackling
pain shoot up her leg and then she was facedown in the water,
and every time she tried to get up, her leg gave way, and she
was gasping and gulping and screaming.

Mitch scooped her up and carried her to shore. He laid her
out on the blanket, whacking her back so that she would cough
up all the water. Then he wrapped the blanket around her. After he pulled on some jeans and dried himself, he inspected
her ankle.

"You might have sprained it," he said.

"Damn. And where's the raft?"

"I had to let it go. When I heard you go down, you
screamed, I couldn't let you . . ."

"Double damn."

"Sorry. I thought I had tied the raft in securely."

"Apparently it wasn't," she said coolly.

"Well, you shouldn't have gone into the water. Those rocks
are slippery."

"I didn't want to just let the raft drift down the river."

"I could have caught up to it," he said.

They stared at each other. And then seemed to reach an uneasy truce. It would do no good to argue. She tried to break the tension.

"Is it time to worry yet?"

"No," he said firmly. "You still have your cell phone. It's in your life vest, remember? We'll call for help."

"Uh, Mitch, there's only one problem."

"What?"

"I left my life vest in the raft."

"Hmmm."

"Time to worry?"

A pause.

"Not yet," he said, forcing a smile. "I'll let you know."

"Who knows where we are?"

"Nobody. But I told the pilot to meet us on Sunday at an airstrip in the Black Canyon. It's just twenty miles."

"Twenty miles?!"

"And we're going to make it," he said confidently. "Now do you want to pee?"

"Yes," she said.

"No, no, don't try to stand on it. Oh, Carole, I told you not to."

She sat back down, humiliated, sopping wet in her dainty Hanro camisole and panties. She was near to crying, whether from anger or fear she couldn't have said.

"I'll carry you into the woods," he said. "And I'll stay with you. Then we'll change your clothes and we'll hike it. We'll make Black Canyon by tomorrow afternoon. I promise."

She looked at him with a pain so raw that he flinched.

"Carole, you're just going to have to depend on me. There's nobody else out here."

She sighed.

"You sure know how to show a girl a good time."

He picked her up and carried her into the woods and he helped her steady herself with a tree branch.

"Get out of here," she said. "I can't do it if you're here."

"I'll come back for you in a few minutes."

"Fine."

It was only when he was out of sight that she let herself cry. *What the hell had happened?* Out in the middle of nowhere. Sprained ankle, can't stand up on her own, let alone walk. No communication possible with the outside world. No bathrooms, no hot showers, no room service, no telephones, no cable access, no flattering shoes and definitely no chocolate.

And for what? Was she so sexually desperate that she had done this for a few good lays?

"I could have bought myself a vibrator," she muttered.

Well, a few good lays and some fun.

"Take the nieces to Disneyworld next time," she said.

A few good lays, some fun, and a feeling that she belonged somewhere, even if that somewhere was wherever Mitch happened to be.

She pulled her panties up.

Next time, pick a guy who likes opera. Or Broadway. Or cozy little bistros in Paris. Better yet, forget the men. You were doing just fine without him.

CAROLE TITUS HITS ROCK BOTTOM: I'd rather be in the middle of nowhere—Colorado, same thing—with a sprained ankle and a raft gone missing just so long as Mitch is there.

That's a deeply disturbing thought for any woman with a smidgen of independence.

When Mitch came back for her a few minutes later, her eyes felt puffy and must have been red but when he asked if she had been crying, she told him she thought she was having trouble with her allergies.

He carried her back to the camp and helped her change into new panties, hiking shorts and a T-shirt. He insisted she take two ibuprofen. Then he ripped his T-shirt into wide strips and wrapped her ankle.

"We'll only take what's essential," he admonished, putting on his camp shirt which, infuriatingly, looked as freshly pressed as if he had just picked it up at the dry cleaner. He had packed one backpack which he would carry in one hand and then another. "Anything in this cosmetic case you can't live without?"

Only an eyelash curler, mascara, powder, blush, six different lipsticks (one of which was a discontinued shade), two Cosabella thongs and a bottle of Angel perfume that had set her back a hundred dollars.

"No," she said.

"Fine. Makes it easier for me. I'm carrying you piggy-back and every extra ounce I'm going to feel."

"You're not."

"I am. The only other possibility is to have me hike ahead alone and come back for you with a raft. It would take two days. You'd be alone."

She considered this.

"I'm a hundred and thirty pounds," she said, optimistically shaving a few pounds.

"I'm not worried."

He cleaned up the campsite and carefully arranged the items they weren't taking, including the tent and the stove, in a pile to be picked up later.

A well-worn path paralleled the river. Mitch didn't seem in the slightest bit undone by the heat, which grew steadily through the morning, or by her weight, which she felt more conscious of every passing minute. He taught her ridiculous marching chants. She taught him the words to Madonna songs.

She felt like a child, asking him nearly every ten minutes if it was time to rest. No, no, and no. He had set for himself a schedule of work and reward so that only after they finished three miles did he allow themselves an hour to lie on a smooth rock overhang and watch the river splay out in front of them.

"You need this," he said, and proceeded to paint zinc oxide on her nose and cheeks. As ridiculous as she was sure she looked, he was just as bad. While it was worth laughing about it didn't make her feelings for him any less intense.

She had to learn, and quickly, to let him lead. To let him shoulder the responsibilities for their journey just as he shouldered her weight. When he said that no, she shouldn't touch those leaves because they were poison oak, she was hardly in a position to disagree. When the path was swallowed up by overhanging leaves, he decided on a different route. How would she know the difference? And when he declared that they would make six more miles before nightfall, how could she protest that she was tired? In fact, as the afternoon wore on and his step seemed to falter ever so slightly, she repeated chants and songs to distract and goad him.

True to his word, as the sun slipped down behind the distant mountains, he brought her into a cool, damp cave on a peak overlooking the river. They hadn't spoken much in the afternoon, hardly a word in the last two hours, all energies spent on the common goal. He helped her settle into a rela-

tively comfortable position on the Tyvek blanket he had
folded into his backpack. Then he made a fire at the mouth of
the cave and groaned as he lay down beside her. He handed
her a PowerBar and a bottled water. Dinner.

"Would you mind very much if I didn't make love to you?"
he asked. "I am too tired to move, but I want to, oh, I want to.
Even with the zinc oxide, you look so beautiful to me."

She laughed. So much for spending all your money at Bar-
neys or Bloomingdale's.

He slipped into drowsy inaction as she took off his boots
and pulled off the blood-soaked socks. The skin on his feet
was puckered pink and covered with blisters.

Then, without the moisturizing cream, the fluffy pillows,
the crisp sheets and the aromatherapy candle she had always
thought were essential, she fell asleep on the floor of the cave,
with just a thin Tyvek blanket. She was happy.

The next morning, he woke her and took her to the river to
soak her ankle in the freezing water. He took off his clothes
and bathed without the slightest self-consciousness. She liked
looking at him. *It's sort of like having your own personal
pinup*, she thought with a smile.

Not a bad weekend, except for the ankle, which felt better
but wasn't going to be of any use for making eight more miles
before nightfall. Funny, if Hal were here, he would have had a
three-Hs attack when the raft drifted away—hysterics,
hypochondria, helplessness.

Mitch waded back to shore.

"Ready to go?" he asked cheerily.

He dried himself in the sun for a few minutes while they
talked about, well, nothing really. They had passed the point
where they felt each conversation had to be about Important
Things That Matter. He pointed out a blue jay in the upper
branches of a spruce. She told him about the time a pigeon
had gotten into her mother's New York apartment.

"I was working in Boston at the time," Carole explained.
"And she said get on the next commuter flight and get this
thing out of here."

"Did you do it?"

"No, but I called the landlord and bitched at him until he
took care of it. The pigeon knocked over a lamp during the

chase and my mother still blames me for it. Thinks if I had just made the extra effort to take care of it myself . . ."

He put on thick white socks while she told a few stories of visiting her mother on the set of the soap opera *The Bad and the Beautiful*. He allowed as how his parents' housekeeper always watched the show.

"Aren't those blisters painful?" she asked as she watched him slip his feet into his boots.

"Yes, but the pain lets me know I'm alive. If I wasn't feeling any pain I'd be more worried. I know it sounds crazy, but it helps my attitude about it. And attitude is going to get us home. Ready?"

He gave the appearance of a man asking his lover to accompany him on a restful little stroll. And Carole admired that.

Especially since, by noon, they were both exhausted and crabby. Carole had started to remember that if he had secured the raft better they wouldn't be in this jam. Hell, if they were having her kind of weekend, this would be about the time for a leisurely brunch at a little sidewalk cafe. It was strange— almost out-of-body—for this city girl to pass two days without once seeing a building, a streetlight, even a street. And as much as she could rationalize it, she didn't like the fact that he was pulling his weight—and hers.

As for Mitch, he seemed to draw inward, perhaps looking for the last push. No more singing, no more chants, no funny anecdotes, no pointing out nature.

When they rested in the afternoon, he asked her to keep an eye on the clock.

"Just give me a half hour," he said, stretching out on a rocky slab warmed by the sun. He covered his face with a T-shirt he had soaked in the river.

"Mitch, what's wrong?"

"Nothing's wrong."

"That's so male."

"All right, I'll tell you what's wrong," he said, sitting up and flinging aside the T-shirt. "I blew it. I absolutely, positively blew it."

"If this is about the raft . . ."

"It's not just the raft! It's not just about your ankle, although God knows, that would be enough. It's about bringing you out here, and not understanding that you couldn't love this as much as I do!" He struggled to put his thoughts into words and what was a sputtering turned into a torrent. "I shouldn't have rushed you into this thing," he said, gesturing at the wilderness around them, "but I just couldn't stand the idea of taking you to dinner on a Friday night and kissing you at your door and then waiting a week to take you to another restaurant and then the next weekend and finding out after a month that your niece is named Charlotte and your ex-husband's a jerk. I wanted you then and I want you now. And I'm going to want you tomorrow. And tomorrow you're going to be in Washington telling your girlfriends what a horrible weekend you had and you won't see me again."

A terrible silence and then:

"I'm not Hal," Mitch said plaintively. "I'm not out to break your heart."

She carefully skittered next to him and put her arms around his neck. He smelled like the outdoors, all of it, and she found the scent of him suddenly irresistible. She kissed him and his hands reached under her sweat-soaked shirt and cupped her naked breasts. She moaned softly. His kisses grew hungrier and fueled her own hunger.

Abruptly, he rolled her over so that she lay on her back on the warm, smooth rock. He tugged open her pants.

"Uh, are you sure we're alone?" she asked.

He laughed.

"Okay, ridiculous question," she admitted.

She lifted her buttocks and he pulled her pants down around her ankles. He kissed the smooth inner flesh of her thighs.

"Uh, Mitch, I forgot. In my cosmetics bag was the only condom we had."

"I know," he murmured at the soft tender place where she should have had the Brazilian wax Alix suggested, if only she could have stood the pain. His tongue found the soft, delicate bud.

He sure knows what he's doing, she thought. She closed her eyes, and for the briefest moment, she lay suspended before ecstasy. Then she heard a moan that was her own.

She absently ran her fingers through his hair as he rested his head on her stomach.

"I think this weekend has been a lot of fun," she mused.

He laughed and raised himself up.

"But I should do something about . . ." she let her words trail off.

"I should be embarrassed to admit this, but I already came."

"What?"

"Hey, I'm an excitable guy. Besides, it was so damn sexy to be between your legs, I feel all better about this weekend too."

They lay together for a few minutes longer before Mitch urged continuing the journey. They were within an hour, he thought. It didn't seem so long, and Carole only felt the faintest worry as she thought about his outburst.

They would stay together, wouldn't they?

She wasn't going to break his heart, was she?

She didn't confuse him with Hal, did she?

Chapter 8

*The landing strip on the Evans ranch was not very im-*pressive. Just a tar-paper shack powered by a generator and a concrete slab a hundred feet long.

But impressive they didn't need. A plane they did, and a plane was there waiting for them. The pilot, introduced by Mitch as Hutch (and apparently so named because of a barely there resemblance to the second member of the television team of *Starsky and Hutch*), was shocked by the details of their ordeal. He called ahead to Denver International to have the airport doctor available to examine Carole's leg. The puddle jump to Denver took just forty minutes. The ringing in Carole's ears from the plane's engine would take an hour to dissipate.

At the airport, a uniformed airline employee met them at the gate with a wheelchair. He then took the couple to a private lounge where they were offered a shower in adjoining locker rooms. Mitch's garment bag was brought to him and a doctor was sitting by the lounge check-in desk chatting with the hostess.

"I'll take a look at your ankle after you've had a chance to freshen up," he said.

"Are you sure you're able to manage?" Mitch asked her, when she got up out of the chair upon discovering that the locker room door was too narrow.

"I think I can," she said, limping timidly. "It's much better than yesterday. But what about you?" She turned to Mitch with a sheepish smile. "Maybe the good doctor should take a look at your raw and blistered feet. You know, the ones you have—thanks to me?"

Mitch shook his head and smiled. "I hardly feel a thing." He shooed her off in the direction of the locker room.

"That's because they're NUMB!" she called over her shoulder.

She was grateful for the shower and the chance to wash her hair. She had a few cuts and bruises and her nose was peeling, but all in all, she was doing okay. She changed into a Fortuny pleated sundress that was supposed to look wrinkled and decided on a pair of flats rather than the coordinating heels she'd brought along. A spritz of perfume, a little blow-dry up under her hair to give some volume, and a bit of the lipstick that hadn't been lost on the river.

She didn't bother with the wheelchair when she came out.

"I'd advise staying off your feet," the doctor said after looking at her ankle. "You've definitely sprained it but I think you'll be good as new in a few days. On the other hand, the Washington flight just got called so maybe you might reconsider using the wheelchair."

"How 'bout a piggyback ride?" Mitch suggested, coming up behind her. "For old time's sake."

The doctor trailed behind them with the garment bag as they stoically managed to cross the terminal to their gate.

Their seats were good ones on a 727 but when the pilot announced a twenty-minute delay as they sat on the runway, Mitch raised an eyebrow.

"Not a chance," Carole said. "You're mine. All mine. No taking advantage of the tendency of flight attendants to fall in lust."

He grinned.

After twenty minutes the pilot announced another delay and a flight attendant came back to whisper to Mitch that as soon as they were airborne, they would be patching him through for a phone call from Senator Snyder. Like it or not, they were upgraded to first class and as soon as they were settled in their seats the engines roared.

As soon as the seat belt sign went off, the attendant brought a cell phone to Mitch. It was impossible not to overhear the senator's every word.

"It's my wife," he said. "We just got back the test results—she's got cancer. Stupid organ, really, nearly useless, and now that it's cancerous, I'm afraid it's going to take her away from me."

A stab of horrified empathy tore through Carole.

"I'm resigning, Mitch, effective this next week. I want every available minute with my wife. But that means we need someone to take over my job, and I don't mind telling you that we have wide-eyed crazies on each side of the spectrum who are ready to tip this senate. We need an independent."

"I'll try to come up with a short list," Mitch said.

"I don't need a short list. I need you. The governor will appoint you tomorrow morning. I don't know where in Sam Hill you were all weekend, but I . . ."

"Sir, I don't think I can do this." Carole saw Mitch's face was grave and his body looked tense, as if it were braced against a strong wind.

"Son, we've been grooming you for this. I thought I would finish my term, take on a next one, all to set you up for taking my seat. We have work that needs to be done. Better pay for our soldiers. The China situation. The national forests. I swear, I won't rest easy if I see a right-wing loony or one of those sell-out liberals take my place."

Strong language from the senator, like nothing Carole had ever heard when he was featured on the network news or cable.

"Sir, I'm not old enough."

"You will be tomorrow. And being thirty years old is all that article I, section two, paren three of our Constitution requires. Please, Mitch, if you won't do it for me, do it for my beloved bride of forty-three years. She wants me. Promise her that last wish, Mitch."

"All right, sir. That I will do."

"Besides, the Kennedys practically get their Congressional seats with their drivers' licenses and I betcha one of them cousins would have moved to Colorado by Wednesday just to claim residency if they thought they could get a spot on the senate floor. I want you there. Someone who's in love with his state, hell, with his country."

"Thank you, Senator," Mitch said softly.

He hung up. Or rather, the senator announced that he had a call on the other line and would talk to him when he got in the next morning.

"I don't know whether to say I'm sorry or congratulations," Carole said.

He looked at her, started to say something, and the phone

rang. He answered. A voice informed him that the vice president of the United States was on the line.

"Oh shit," Mitch whispered, giving Carole a mournful look. "I'm going to be busy for a few hours."

Try a few years, Carole thought.

Over Nebraska, Missouri, Kentucky and the Virginias, Mitch took phone calls and messages from well-wishers and colleagues. The tone was somber, as though people considered the sad and serious prospects for the senator and his wife. The governor called to confirm Mitch's willingness to serve. The press was hungry for details of the senator's wife's illness, of which Mitch had none. And there was insatiable curiosity about the man who would become the youngest living senator. Mitch answered questions about his education, his aspirations, his hobbies, even the name of his dog.

"Yes, I'm single," he said at one point.

Carole stopped filing her nails—the wilderness had not been kind to her manicure—and unabashedly eavesdropped.

"I can't tell you her name but she's very special to me."

He looked at her for approval. She shrugged.

"No, no, I don't think you need to know who she is. How long? Long enough to know how lucky I am to be with her."

The reporter eventually tired of the glib answers and asked more substantive questions about Mitch's position on recent legislation Senator Snyder had sponsored.

Carole understood business, she understood busy, she understood deadline and client time and under the gun. She wasn't looking for a man who didn't have a life. *But a senator? In the pressure cooker called the Capital?*

Complicated at best. At worst? The destruction of her very carefully constructed life, her recovery from a draining marriage and wrenching divorce. Besides—and here a very insidious notion caught hold of her—Mitch needed one of those "cowgirls" his parents sent him. A nice pretty one, one who wanted marriage, babies and ballot boxes. Hadn't Laura Bush told George Dubya that she would only marry him if he promised she'd never have to give a speech on his behalf?

When the plane landed, they were met at the gate by Senator Snyder's driver, reporters from the *Post* and the *Times*, and Mitch's parents, who had flown back from their summer vacation in Europe. Introductions were virtually impossible though Mitch did his best.

"Look, I'm going to take a cab," she said as they trotted through the terminal. The *Post* and *Times* reporters had gotten a little morsel and were satisfied. The driver said the senator had offered his car for Mitch and his parents.

Mitch looked at her sharply, the first time since the phone call with Senator Snyder in which she felt he was giving her his full attention.

"Get in the car with us," he said, gripping her arm. "We need to talk."

"Where can we drop you?" Mitch's mother said. She was impeccably dressed in Chanel and gave not the slightest impression of jet lag after her flight from the Continent.

"Actually, Mother, we'll drop you and Dad at your club and then I'll see Carole home."

His father grunted.

"Where is your family from?" Mrs. Evans asked pleasantly.

"New York," Carole said.

"Titus. Titus. The name sounds familiar."

"Maybe you've heard of my mother. She was in a soap opera—*The Bad and the Beautiful*—before it got canceled. She played Joy Loftus."

"How . . . charming." It occurred to Carole suddenly that there was a whole stratosphere of society that simply didn't tune in to daytime television. And she was in a car with at least two of its residents.

The drive to the University Club was excruciating. Mitch's parents wished her a frosty good night and asked their son to pick them up in plenty of time for the senator's morning press conference.

The car slid away from the curb and Mitch put up the privacy screen so that it was just the two of them. For a moment they sat silently side by side, like a married couple that has so much to say to each other but has long since stopped talking. Mitch reached across what felt like the longest seat in automotive history and entwined his fingers in hers.

"Mitch, I don't think . . ."

"Don't tell me tonight. For the love of God, don't tell me tonight."

"You don't know what I'm going to say."

"I have a pretty good idea," he said, his voice hoarse with emotion. "Carole, this isn't about careers and fulfilling dreams or ambitions. This is about honoring a man who has done his duty and now wants to be with his wife."

"You don't have to do this," Carole said. "He'll resign even if you don't agree."

"And the governor will install who he wants, someone who could single-handedly derail the ten years' worth of the senator's work in the senate. And the next election will be a bloodbath."

"You wanted to be a senator," she said with unaccountable bitterness.

"Yes, I'm guilty as charged. I wanted it later, when I was older, more experienced, but this is the hand I've been dealt. I have to do it."

They rode in silence to her house. She bolted, climbing out before the driver could come around to open the door.

"Good night, Mitch," she called out.

"No, Carole, don't do this," he pleaded, bounding up the steps. His cry was so plaintive she faltered at her front door. "Please, Carole."

Just call me a sucker for a handsome man with a hangdog expression, Carole thought.

She opened the front door, reached for the hall light switch and felt him come up behind her. She turned around, feeling Whiskers thread between their legs. Mitch kicked the front door closed and kissed her, long and deep.

She knew this was their last time together. She knew it deep within her, with a knowledge that had crept upon her as she sat next to him on the plane and now fully possessed her. And his kiss, his touch made such poignant sense, she should send him home so that he would hurt as much as she would.

But she didn't, and she led him up to her bedroom, there turning on the nightstand lamp quite deliberately because she wanted every sense to remember him clearly. The touch of his hand, the ridge of callouses worn on the base of every finger. The smell of Ivory soap and something more basely masculine. The taste of his kisses, long and languorous, and the sound of his lust, a vibrato deep in his throat.

She sat astride him, wanting to see him and feel him and remember him clearly. She reveled in every inch of him as he entered her. She took his hands to cover her breasts. And that he did, until the rhythm of their coupling intensified and he splayed his fingers around her waist and guided her toward the tide of their shuddering orgasms.

Afterwards, they lay spoonwise.

"It's over," Mitch said quietly. "You want to tell me it's over. I could feel it when you came."

"Mitch, remember when I said that there were only two possible outcomes to this?"

"This isn't a one-night stand."

"No, and it isn't that one of us has fallen terribly in love with the other."

"Speak for yourself."

"Then it's all the harder to say this. But I can't be your girl-friend, your lover, your whatever."

"Bill Bradley's wife's ten years older than him."

"It's not age. It's that I don't want to fit myself into . . ."

Mitch abruptly sat up.

"You don't want a man. You want a boy, if you want any-one. You can't handle a man who has a life of his own. A life I'm happy, willing, eager to share with you. Sure, it's going to be rough in the next few months. Hellish would be a good word for it. But it's my life. And I want you to be part of it."

"I have my work. I have my friends. I have my house the way I like it. I like my life the way it is. Exactly the way it is."

"Then live it," he said and quickly gathered up his clothes. He strode out of the bedroom naked and when the door slammed downstairs she peered out of the window. He had put on his pants and was shrugging on his shirt. The driver ditched his cigarette and opened the back passenger door. In mo-ments, the sleek black limousine pulled away.

"It wouldn't have worked out," she said aloud to Whiskers, who had come up for a cuddle. "Better to cut it off now."

Better didn't feel better the next morning.

"Good job on the Madam's Closet deal," Elyssa said when she called. Carole had picked up the phone in her sleep but now looked at the clock. Eight. She had slept in after taking one of those over-the-counter sleep aids. She felt groggy and worn.

"Madam's Closet?"

"Yeah, they signed the contract. Sent it in today. They're putting together a new line. Little bikinis and thongs in boxes for women to buy for their men—with a fun little bead on a leather bracelet. *Tres savage!* Joey said his brother came up with the idea, but I see a little Carole Titus in it. Speaking of which, how was your weekend?"

"Hideous," Carole moaned. "Just hideous."

"Look at the bright side. You picked up three accounts over the weekend. You're a hero."

"I sure don't feel like one."

Carole went back to work, intent on shaking the whole thing off in record time. But days passed and soon she realized a week is a very long time to a broken heart. Especially one belonging to a woman who's done the right thing.

"Call him," Elyssa said, interrupting a full-throttle daydream during the week's staff meeting.

Carole startled.

"I can't call him," she said.

"I've been hearing you say that all week," Alix said. "And that's bullshit. Did you see the report on *20/20*? Asking women on the street what they thought of Mitch Evans?"

"I thought the woman who meowed was a little tacky," Dana said dryly.

"Point is, that man is the IT boy of Washington," Alix exclaimed.

"He's not a boy," Carole said. "He's a man. And I can't call him because eventually we'd have to break up. So just leave it the way it is now."

"Why?" Elyssa asked. "Why would you have to break up? There are plenty of people who stick together through harder stuff than this."

"Some even get married," Robyn said.

"All right, since nobody is interested in talking about market forecasts, I'll tell you why Mitch and I would have to break up."

"Good, because these numbers in your sales report are confusing," Robyn said. "I'm better at relationship talk."

Carole took a deep breath. She had had plenty of time to think this through and her logic was unassailable.

"Mitch is a young man who will eventually want to marry and have children. We meet commitment-phobic men every day . . ." Robyn raised an Amen! . . . "and it's hard to understand but it's true that he wants those things. His family wants those things for him."

"Why wouldn't you make a good wife and mother?" Elyssa probed.

"For one thing, I'm too old. I'd have to have a child soon. Very soon. And I just think the timing for Mitch and me is off. Off enough to make it impossible."

"Rationalization," Alix said firmly. "You are too damn smart for your own good. Why can't you just relax and have a good thing with him?"

"Because I . . ." and here she realized something that a week of pondering hadn't revealed. "Because I love him. I'd get lost making all kinds of adjustments in my life just to be with him. And if we broke up, it would be so hard to put the pieces back together."

"That's what everybody has to do when they fall in love," Dana observed gently.

Carole blinked back tears.

"Now, are we sure that we don't want to see Madam's Closet's new ad campaign?" Elyssa said, correctly sensing her friend's desire to change the subject.

At the end of the table, Elyssa had set up an easel with a cloth-covered poster board. With a dramatic *voila!* she flung off the cloth.

"Holy Toledo," Dana said.

Alix smacked her lips and Robyn started giggling.

"I don't think Herb Kolkey came up with this on his own," Carole said.

The picture was a black-and-white Helmut Newton–style photograph of a dark-haired hottie wearing nothing but a little leopard-print thong. The caption read, *How do you dress yours?*

"I feel a new line of cards coming on," said Dana. And she began scribbling in her notebook.

The meeting broke up with most of the women lingering at the poster board to admire its . . . artistic merit.

Carole slunk back to her office, nearly colliding with a bike messenger dropping off his packages.

"It's just a postcard," he said, holding out his clipboard. "Sign here. It's the Washington Monument. Ever been?"

"Sure, just a few weeks ago," Carole said, turning it over to read the note. *Meet me at 5:00.*

Unsigned, but it didn't need to be.

"I've lived here all my life," the messenger said. "And I've never been to it."

"You should go. It's really quite amazing," Carole said. She glanced at her watch. The meeting had run very late, she had just forty-five minutes. She thanked the messenger, grabbed her purse and charged to the elevator bank.

At the Monument, she saw Mitch's little red sports car parked curbside and she pulled up behind him.

She said hello to the guard who waved her into the stairwell just as he ushered the last tourist group out of the elevator.

Okay, life is not a promise. Love is not a promise, she thought in cadence to her step. But let me just have a little more of this. Just when she thought her lungs would burst and her ankle would split in two, she reached the observatory floor. The sunlight poured through the windows, tossing dust motes this way and that.

Mitch was emblazoned with light—waiting, pacing, anticipating. When he saw her, his face glowed with such delight that Carole could hardly remember what made her send him away.

"Happy birthday, happy birthday!" she cried. "I know it's late, but happy birthday."

They kissed and Carole knew, with hideous and joyful certainty, that she could not send him away again.

When he pulled away, he showed her a bottle of champagne and two glasses he had set aside on the observation bench.

"But the park service guards," she protested.

He pointed out the duct tape with which he had covered the security lens. She laughed, and accepted a glass of the sweet bubbling stars.

"I have a present for you," she said, taking from her purse the subtly elegant cuff links she had bought for him in Dallas. "Ta-da!"

"They're wonderful," he said. She helped him put them on. "They'll remind me of you when we can't be together."

"I hope there's not much of that 'can't be together' stuff."

"Well, let's get to work on that."

Then he proceeded to win her over—by a landslide.

Tumbling Down

LYNN EMERY

Chapter 1

Alix Harris was mighty pleased with herself as she strode into the offices of Allheart.com. The bold company logo in red lettering on the front door—her creation—confirmed that life was good. She had it licked at last.

Her day had started out with her long-time love being his usual sensitive, thoughtful self. She'd mentally kicked herself for doubting him. Sure the man was distracted and tired lately. Cal put in long hours as an architect, "building their future," he'd told her many times. But he'd risen to the occasion at six A.M., in more ways than one. Steamy sex and a delicious breakfast. Yum. Alix smiled to herself.

"Morning all," she said.

"Glad you penciled us in." Elyssa Wentworth, CEO and founder of Allheart, glanced at her watch pointedly. The lithe brunette let her expression say it all.

"Hey, girl. Another hot night with Cal? Excellent excuse!" Robyn Barrett, Elyssa's personal assistant, winked at her.

One of Elyssa's shapely brows went up. "Unlike yours. Your elegant black nail polish didn't dry on time?"

Robyn smiled blithely. She totally missed Elyssa's swipe at two of her habits. Today's outfit, a form-fitting black top, purple flip skirt three inches above the knee and inky black fingernails, proved Elyssa's point.

Alix laughed at them both. "You two sure make coming to the office fun."

"Well I guess I should be glad you show up at all," Elyssa deadpanned. She shook her head in mock resignation.

"It's the traffic, boss." Alix put an arm around Elyssa's shoulder. "And don't I always deliver?"

"That remains to be seen,'" Elyssa folded her arms across her chest.

"Don't mind her, Alix. I'm sure she understands your predicament, whatever it *really* is," Carole Titus offered as she joined them. "And how is oh-so-fine Joe Monteigne?" she gently teased their boss.

"Mr. Monteigne is not the subject of this meeting." Elyssa nipped the lighthearted banter in the bud. "Now get to work. We need to be ready for the Preston and Saks meeting."

"Right. They're good," Carole said.

"We'll see." Elyssa was not easily impressed. She headed for her office.

Dana Boyle emerged from her office just as Alix headed for hers. Dana tilted her head, causing her fiery red bangs to fall into her eyes.

"Well, well. Miss Thang is in the house. Maybe we can finish up the designs for the new Kwanzaa cards?"

"I gotcha covered, don't worry. You supply the brilliant copy and I'll do you right." Alix powered up her Mac and opened PageMaker.

"It's already done. I sent the file to you. Just open it up." She pointed to the computer.

"Fab." Alix beamed at her then turned back to the monitor.

"Stop that!" Dana snapped.

"What?" Alix slid the mouse around. She moved quickly through a set of icons, bringing up the text Dana had written for the cards.

"Your good mood is getting on my nerves. And please don't tell me how blissful everything is at home with Mr. Perfect. I'll toss my bagel and latte." Dana brushed her hair back with one hand.

Alix gazed at a sketch she'd been working on. Then she looked at her colleague. "Dana, dear, sweet Dana. I love that wit."

"Okay, I give up. Be a bitch and rub it in," Dana said with a dramatic sigh.

"So maybe I'm being a little annoying." Alix laughed at Dana's complaints. "But stop trying to screw with my good karma."

Dana held up both hands. "Okay, cease-fire."

Robyn sailed in. "Elyssa sent this over." She dropped a glossy brochure on the desk.

Alix picked it up. "Thanks. Hmm, Preston and Saks Advertising and Public Relations. Swanky stuff. They're really coming after our business." She flipped through several pages of the material and stopped at one picture.

"Elyssa has them on a time-limited contract to see what they can do," Robyn supplied.

"Whoa, who the hell is that?" Dana peered over Alix's shoulder at the picture that held her attention.

"Marcus Preston. Sexy name." Dana leered at the photo.

"Sexy guy. And we get to meet him in a few minutes," Robyn said. "He's coming at ten to meet with the boss."

"Excellent way to end the week. He might even tempt Miss Monogamy here." Dana tapped Alix lightly on the head.

"Not hardly." Still Alix couldn't look away from his arresting eyes.

Marcus Preston had a killer smile and bronze hair cut close. He had the square jaw of a classic jock type. His navy pinstripe suit looked all business. Yet the Fumagalli's silk tie he wore implied a playful side.

"I see you looking," Dana singsonged.

Alix shrugged and handed her the brochure. "Just another pretty face. Let's get down to it."

"Geez, it's okay to look, Alix." Dana flipped back to the page with Marcus Preston's picture. "I mean, he's got it all."

"Yeah. Brains, muscles and his own successful business. What more could a girl want?" Robyn agreed with grin.

"True love," Alix shot back. "Which is what I have with Cal." She recognized the defensive sound in her own voice.

"Give it a rest, you two. Alix is deliriously happy, accept it." Carole interrupted the exchange with a smile and put a hand on Alix's shoulder.

"Yeah, and she's pissing me off." Dana grinned. "Be right back with my notes."

"I better go back to my desk." Robyn glanced at her watch. "The phones should go wild right about . . . now." A double trill sounded at that moment.

"That girl scares me sometimes," Alix quipped as she watched her scurry off.

"So things are better at home?" Carole spoke in a confidential tone now that they were alone.

"Yes, definitely better. I guess every relationship goes through different stages. Thanks for listening, Carole." Alix smiled at her.

"No problem. I'm just glad you're smiling again." Carole was about to say more when Elyssa appeared at the door.

"Carole, Marcus Preston is here. Oh, Alix, I'll probably call you in to meet him at some point," Elyssa said.

"Sure thing," Alix replied.

Elyssa and Carole left, already talking about plans for a new marketing and ad campaign. Dana stood aside to let them pass.

"You lucky dog! Now let's think up a reason for you to drag me along," Dana said as she pulled up a chair and sat down.

"Let's try to concentrate on work. Elyssa will crack the whip if we don't get these new cards done soon. And I don't want it cracked on my butt."

"If we must," Dana said with a dramatic sigh.

In a matter of minutes they plunged into their usual creative give-and-take. They managed to finish two cards before the interoffice line buzzed on Alix's phone.

"Hello. I'm on my way." Alix clicked the save icon and pushed back her desk chair. "I've been summoned."

"I'll start on the set of July Fourth cards while you're gone." Dana moved to Alix's chair. She was tapping the keyboard in seconds.

"Sure, make yourself at home," Alix retorted.

Her remark went unnoticed as Dana concentrated on what she was writing. Alix shook her head with a smile as she went down the hall to Elyssa's office. She passed Robyn on the way in.

"Let me warn you. He's better than the picture!" Robyn whispered with eyes widened.

"My God, we've been working in this all-female office too long. Don't drool, babe."

Alix rolled her eyes and kept going. She paused to tap on Elyssa's door, and then she pushed it open.

"Hi," Alix said before she fell dumbstruck at the sight before her.

Marcus Preston unfolded his six-foot-three form from the chair he sat in. Even at five-foot-seven, Alix had to look up at him. His skin truly was the color of cinnamon, a smooth brown that begged to be touched. He wore a steel gray pinstriped suit cut to fit his broad shoulders and chest. And another Fumagalli's silk tie, not the one in the brochure photo. This one was a deep wine color with a subtle paisley pattern. As if that package weren't enough, beneath the elegant suit lay the hard body of man who worked out. Lord have mercy! He smiled and she blinked again. His even white teeth gleamed, a Crest Kid that would make a mother proud.

"Alix Harris, this is Marcus Preston. Alix is a top graphic design artist, and luckily *our* graphic design artist," Elyssa said.

"I'm glad to meet you. Your designs are fantastic, both classic and funky urban. I like your work," Marcus Preston said, rolling off the combination greeting and compliment with ease.

Alix's heart fluttered at the sound. His baritone voice flowed over her like melted milk chocolate. She shook his hand, still dazed. "Thanks," she managed to get out.

"Uh, you want to sit down?" Elyssa's dark eyebrows arched.

Alix realized she was still pumping his large hand. "What? Oh, yes, of course."

Carole's eyebrows were up, too, but she made no comment. "Mr. Preston—"

"Call me Marc," he cut in smoothly.

"Marc was telling us about some of his ideas to help us increase web traffic," Carole continued.

"Yes, I was just saying that we offer a wide range of contracts for our clients. We can work as a team with Allheart .com. My staff can match its ideas and talents with the creative energy that you obviously have. The result would be an ad program that rules," Marc said. He looked at Elyssa, then Carole, then settled his gaze on Alix.

Alix nodded. "Oh," she said then pressed her lips together.

Elyssa and Carole exchanged a puzzled glance then proceeded with the meeting. Alix cleared her throat and tried to sound a bit more intelligent than a zucchini for the rest of the meeting. Twenty minutes later they wrapped it up. Marc Preston stood and buttoned his jacket.

"I've gotten enough information here to get started. Of course we'll need a series of work sessions before we can make a final presentation to you."

"We look forward to seeing your proposal," Elyssa said. "Alix, would you mind walking Marc out? Carole and I have a conference call in five minutes."

"Sure," Alix said. She smiled at him and led the way.

"Show him some of your design work," Elyssa called out.

"That sounds great," Marc said with a gleam in his eye.

"My office is this way," Alix said trying not to get sucked into that no-man's-land of a smile again.

"I'll follow you anywhere." He grinned widely.

As Alix led him toward her office, she could feel him walking just behind and to her right. It was as if his body heat snaked out to tickle her spine. The man moved with the grace of a panther, each step a liquid motion. They arrived at her office to find Dana still tapping away.

"Oops, I lost track of time. Hello." Dana stood.

"This is Dana Boyle. She writes copy for the cards. Marc Preston," Alix said.

"So you're the talent behind the words. Good to meet you." Marc shook hands with Dana.

"You've read my stuff?" Dana blushed.

"For sure. I've gotten a few Allheart cards myself. Very nice." Marc smiled at her.

"Thanks. Speaking of which, I better get to my own office. Nice meeting you." Dana waved her fingers at them both. When he turned aside, she gave him an appreciative once-over glance and Alix a thumbs-up sign.

"*Goodbye*, Dana." Alix made a face as she waved her out. She returned to a normal expression when he faced her again.

"Your office reflects your artistic nature. Yours?" he said, pointing to one of the prints on the wall.

"These three are mine." Alix pointed to a series of mixed media collages. "Those are by an artist named—"

"Ted Ellis out of Houston, Texas," he finished.

Alix raised her eyebrows in surprise. "How do you know about him?"

"I get catalogs of African-American art. His prints are featured in more than one. I own a couple."

"Good taste," Alix said.

"Thanks. I was about to say the same to you." His full brown lips curved up in a most delicious smile.

The effect was magical. Marc's eyes were deep brown, the

color of coffee with just a hint of cream. His smile streamed over her body. This brother was good. Two seconds alone and his presence was like a hot invitation. Alix took three quick shallow breaths to steady herself.

"Thank you. I'll, uh, give you a quick review of some of the graphics I've created. We try to give Allheart cards a certain look." Alix opened up files saved in various formats on her computer. "For example, these for Mother's Day."

Marc looked at photos and pictures on the monitor for several seconds. "Impressive."

"I use a file of copyright-free pictures as well as create my own. I prefer to use my original images tailored to Allheart."

"To get that certain look," Marc said. He glanced at her from head to toe. "You've got it."

Alix almost got lost in those eyes, but pulled back from the ledge. Imagine this guy thinking all he had to do was pose and she'd melt. Nice try, her cool smile signaled to him. Her tone was all business when she spoke.

"That's about it. How about I give you a collection of our designs? I'll include a banner ad we created for a about fifty top websites." She sat down at her desk. In quick order she called up a new set of images.

Marc leaned over her with one arm resting on the desk, the other hand on the back of her chair. "Great idea. Looks like you've got a slick setup here."

"Yep, I use Adobe Illustrator, Photoshop and three other premium applications. Everything I need is right on this cute little baby." Alix gave her PowerMac G4 a fond pat. "Give me an email address and I'll send these over to your graphic designers."

"Designer, as in one." Marc held up a forefinger and grimaced. "You dot-com folks are luring away all the best people." He stood straight.

"I'm sure you don't have trouble finding the talent you need." Alix closed the file then swiveled the chair around and looked up at him.

"Finding the talent isn't the problem, but can I get who I really want?" Marc stared at her steadily.

Carole stuck her head in the door. "How's it going? I'm sure Alix wowed you."

"She did that for sure." Marc turned his smile on Alix again.

"No surprise." Carole winked at Alix then looked at Marc again. "Here is the marketing report we did on our customer base."

They talked for several minutes about marketing strategy before Carole left. Marc gave Alix his email address as he gathered his things to leave. Walking down the short hall, they chatted easily about her experience in advertising. Once they were in the foyer, he reached into an inside coat pocket and took out a business card.

Marc glanced around before he handed her the card. "I have a confession," he said in a confidential tone.

"Oh?"

Alix knew what was coming. She'd had offers before. So this is the motivation for his seductive act. He was head-hunting. The realization pricked at her female ego for a moment.

"I checked around with a few colleagues. Your reputation precedes you, Alix. I think we can do great things together."

"For Allheart.com you mean," Alix said as she took the elegantly embossed card.

"Where do you see yourself in five years?" Marc put one hand in the pocket of his pants.

"Heading up a kick-butt ad agency," she wisecracked with a cocky smile.

Marc threw back his handsome head and laughed. "You're something else."

Alix tried not to like his mellow baritone voice too much. She briefly imagined a string of women dropping their silk panties at the mere sound of it.

"Seriously, I'm happy where I am right now."

"We'll talk later." His confident manner suggested he was a man used to getting his way.

Alix stuck out her hand and gave him a quick send-off kind of handshake. "Goodbye, Marc. It was good to meet you."

"Pleasure's mine. Goodbye," he said and flashed one last dazzling smile.

Robyn came in just as was leaving. "Bye now." She waved at him merrily.

"Bye, Robyn," Marc said and strolled out the door.

"He remembered my name. What a guy, huh?" Robyn said.

Alix rolled her eyes. "There are only five of us here right now. How hard could it be?"

"Don't tell me you didn't notice that body, that face, those eyes. Whew!" Robyn fanned her face with a handful of envelopes she held.

"No, I didn't." Alix shrugged at the skeptical look Robyn gave her. "Okay, maybe I did for a moment. But why look at ground chuck when you've got prime beef at home?"

"Lucky you. But still, you gotta admire what he's advertising," Robyn quipped.

Dana came in and dropped a few letters in the out tray. "He was checking Alix out too."

"I knew it!" Robyn squealed.

"He may have turned on his brand of charm. Fortunately it was wasted on me." Alix lifted a shoulder with an attitude.

"We know, Cal is all you the man you need." Dana rolled her eyes. "He can cook, clean and he's working on world peace in his spare time."

"Very funny." Alix gave her the finger.

"Admit you looked the man over from head to toe. Be a normal human being for a change," Dana said.

"Marc Preston is a common variety of canine," Alix retorted. She flipped his card into the pocket of her linen jacket. "Now I've got work to do."

She gave them a sassy toss of her long mahogany hair then went off toward her office. Alix mentally filed Marc Preston under "Be polite but watch his hands."

The day buzzed along with no major glitches. It was six-thirty when the five women sat around the conference table in a variety of quitting-time relaxed poses.

"The end of another productive day. I'm outta here." Dana did not move despite her words. Instead she examined her Donna Karan hosiery with a critical eye.

"I, for one, thank God it's Friday," Robyn added with fervor.

"What do you say we go out for drinks and celebrate the passing of another good week. Whaddya say?" Elyssa glanced around at them.

"I say lead on," Carole said and stood.

"I vote for the place with the best music and the cutest waiters!" Robyn added, noting two of her benchmarks by which any establishment was judged.

"I don't know. I'd better check with Cal." Alix reached for the phone in the center of the table.

Dana pressed the button on the phone, cutting off her call. "You've got to be kidding! This is the new millennium, babe. We women don't have to 'check in.'"

"He'll worry if I don't at least leave a message." Alix slapped the back of Dana's hand until she drew back.

"You didn't say, 'I'll let Cal know I'm going out.'" Dana shook a finger at her. "You said you'd have to ask his permission."

"That's not what I said, at least it's not what I meant." Alix frowned at her.

"I think it's sweet the way Cal looks out for her," Carole said.

"Thank you. Now explain the meaning of a stable relationship to *her*." Alix nodded at Dana and punched in her home number again. The phone rang until the machine picked up.

"Ah-ha! I hear that voice-mail cue. He's out doing his thing with friends," Dana said. "Now let's go. I need refreshment after a long hard day."

"Honey, I'm going to be a bit late. Going out for drinks and snakes with the gang," Alix said after the beep. "Love ya, bye." She hung up and gazed at the phone for several seconds.

"I'll get my purse," Robyn said and dashed off.

"I'm going to freshen up for a sec. Five minutes you guys," Dana ordered.

"Right." Elyssa headed for her office.

Carole started to follow her but sat back down next to Alix. She reached over and touched her arm. "Hey, everything okay?"

"Sure," Alix said too quickly.

"He's probably working late. You know how driven he is," Carole said.

"Right. Driven," Alix repeated with a weak smile. "That's what I've been saying for months now. Then there's the one about how we both need our own space sometimes."

"I thought things were better. This morning . . ." Carole's voice trailed off.

Alix wanted to say things were indeed better. Yet the pattern seemed to be still firmly in place. Cal blew hot and cold. Actually it was more like a steady lukewarm lately. For a few days at a time he'd seem his old self. They would meet for dinner at home or at a restaurant. They would talk for hours about news, politics and their work. Or sometimes they would simply sit close together in companionable silence. They'd bring work home and spread papers all over their king-sized bed. More often than not jazz or African music would play softly in the background. Cozy, precious times that seemed fewer and farther between lately.

Alix sighed. "This phase is wearing thin," she said.

Carole rested both elbows on the table and looked at her with sympathy. "When you talked to him about it, what did he say?"

"Well, not much." Alix fidgeted beneath Carole's steady gaze.

"You did talk to him."

"Sort of. I mentioned he was working too hard and we needed more time together." Alix shrugged.

"That's a start. It's a pretty lame one, but a start."

"We're going to have a deep-down discussion. We really will."

"You're going to have to tackle it. I guess you'll know when the time is right." Carole gave her a reassuring pat.

"Yeah, that's it. Before I go through the whole serious talk thing, I'll roll with it for a bit longer. Who knows? This morning could signal the end of the phase." Alix thought about the empty apartment. Somehow she didn't think so.

Dana, Robyn and Elyssa came in together, talking in animated voices. Robyn giggled at something Dana said. Elyssa, tuned in to nuances, glanced from Carole to Alix.

"You okay?" she said.

Alix fixed on a smile. "Just fine. I'm ready." She followed the others, counting on their lively conversation to raise her spirits a little higher that evening than they were right then.

Chapter 2

Elyssa strode up just as Alix came in. Feeling guilty, Alix glanced at her watch. "Sorry I'm late, Boss. I—"

"Later. I need you to meet with Marc Preston this afternoon at his office. Here are some notes." Elyssa handed her a folder with neatly typed pages.

"Marc Preston?" Alix bit her lip as she opened it.

"Haven't had your latte yet? Of course Marc Preston. It's looking like they're going to work with us on an ad push for Allheart." Elyssa's focus was always strictly narrowed to business.

"Marc Preston," Alix repeated in a low voice.

"Alix, will you wake up! Now I want to start off with a humorous kind of thing." Elyssa pointed to a page. "See—"

Robyn broke in. "Elyssa, Mr. Kendall from Jerri's Gift Baskets is on line three."

"Okay, then. Carole will fill you in." Elyssa hurried off.

Carole gazed at Alix with a critical eye. "Is something wrong?"

"Uh, no . . . not really." Alix cleared her throat.

"Elyssa is right. I say a nice latte would be just the thing." Robyn gladly took her cue and scooted off for the coffee shop nearby.

"You have a problem with Marc Preston already? You seem unhappy to hear his name." Carole wore a slight frown.

"Me have a problem with Marc? Of course not."

"Okay." Carole glanced at her once more, a look that said she didn't believe her but wouldn't press it. "Let's go to my office."

Alix followed her yet her mind wasn't on the folder she carried. Marc Preston, Mr. Temptation himself. She shivered at the thought of being close to him again. After their first encounter she'd easily dismissed the bit of electricity between them. But now she felt like a woman desperate for male attention.

For days Cal had been distracted and distant. He spent most evenings studiously ignoring her. At least that's how Alix saw it. Last night had been the worst. She'd spent a restless night lying next to him. His body had been stiff, as though he was afraid she'd touch him. When she tried to talk to him in the morning, he rushed out without breakfast, claiming to have an early meeting. Alix could not shake the strange, lonely feeling she'd been walking around with for weeks. And she was starting to feel a little sex-starved too. Cal hadn't touched her in two weeks. Carole's voice broke into her thoughts.

"The reason Elyssa is so jazzed is because of this new customer—well, potential new customer anyway. Sweet Tooth is a mega candy store with chains across the Midwest. Their new online store has taken off."

"Really?" Alix mumbled and sat down, her mind far away.

"You best believe it. They want proof that we're going to be aggressive when it comes to publicity. I worked like crazy to—" Carole broke off and stared at Alix hard.

Alix blinked at her. "What? I'm listening, go ahead." She pushed aside her personal issues and forced herself to pay attention.

Thus it was that two o'clock found her seated across from Marc Preston in his upscale office on Wisconsin Avenue. She was surprised to find it to be stylish yet functional. His large desk was made of oak. Forest-green leather chairs were arranged in a seating area to her left. The framed prints on the walls were eclectic; some abstracts while others were representational. Yet somehow it all fit. All in all, she liked what she saw. Especially the man across from her. Marc wore a navy suit and pale yellow shirt. His silk Gucci tie was the color of rich, creamy butter flecked with tiny navy diamond shapes. His dark brows were drawn together as he studied the notes she'd given him. Finally, he looked up at her with a gorgeous smile. Alix smiled back automatically, a mental *ahh* sounding in her head.

"We're definitely on the same page." He tapped the typed sheet with a forefinger.

"Good. Elyssa is anxious to see what you'll come up with. So am I. We all are," she added hastily.

He rocked back in his chair and gazed at her. "I look forward to working with you too." Marc made it sound personal.

"I think we can really make this happen." She crossed her long legs.

"I agree totally," his voice deepened.

Alix panicked because she didn't know what to say next or what move to make. All those years in her comfy relationship with Cal had left her seriously deficient at the game of flirtation, innocent or serious.

Subtlety was certainly the key. Something that was provocative yet sufficiently ambiguous. So she lifted a hand slowly, brushed back her thick mane of dark hair and smiled wider. Marc stopped rocking and looked at her for a long minute without speaking. A soft, sensuous hunger seemed to light his eyes. Her body tingled in response as she leaned forward.

Then a voice switched on inside her head. "Shameless hussy!" it hissed. "Is your entire history with Cal so easily forgotten?" Alix sat back abruptly.

"The ad campaign could certainly increase our web traffic. Elyssa is coming up with all kinds of ideas for our retail store line," Alix said in her most formal, all-business tone.

"Alix, have you thought about making our working relationship permanent? I could really use a woman like you." Marc stared at her steadily, a man going straight to the point.

Her pelvis vibrated at the image his words conjured. "I'll bet you could," she murmured, staring at his mouth.

The voice came back again. Her conscience always spoke in the voice of her mother. "Alix René Harris, shame on you!" This heaping helping of self-reproach kicked in to counter his effect on her. Alix studied her copy of the notes.

"Not really. As I said, Allheart means a lot to me."

"Sure it does. But have you considered the possibility?" he pressed.

"Briefly." Alix shifted in her seat. God, first she sinned against Cal, then Elyssa. This man was trouble.

"Good, keep thinking about us," he said simply then switched back to the purpose of their meeting. "Now let me tell you what I can sketch out in, say, three days. I'm confident we can make the Candy King very happy."

They met for another hour. From time to time, Alix would look up to find Marc studying her. He'd look away quickly each time and continue with his train of thought. Two of his staff joined them for another twenty minutes before leaving them alone again. Alix glanced at the brass clock on his desk.

"Wow, we covered a lot of ground. No wonder Preston and Saks is on top," she said.

"Thanks. The advertising business moves like lightning. Think you could handle it?" Marc's dynamite smile came back at her with a vengeance.

Alix bristled at the implication. "Of course I could. I— slick move, Preston." She shook a finger at him.

Marc laughed. "Okay, you caught me."

She relaxed and smiled back at him. "I better keep my eye on you."

"I hope you do," he said quietly, his gaze sweeping down her body like a caress.

"Whoa, I've got to get going. Got tons to do now." Alix stood. "Elyssa will be delighted to hear the good news."

"I aim to please." Marc stood and smoothed down his tie before he came around the desk.

"Goodbye," she said.

Alix made a neat exit before he could incite more of that tingling. Too late, she thought, as she tingled during the entire cab ride back to Allheart.

Later that evening, Alix entered her apartment and tossed her purse on the white sofa. Her Ferragamo pumps went off next. "Cal, honey, where are you?"

"In the bedroom," he called back.

Alix headed to the kitchen, which was done in shiny blue and white tile. This was Cal's domain; he loved to cook. Alix poured herself a glass of Chardonnay then went back to the living room.

"Well come on out here and tell me about your day." She hiked up her red skirt to show as much thigh as possible.

Cal strolled out. Six-foot-four, he had wide shoulders that tapered down to a broad chest. His waist and hips were narrow. With skin the color of dark chocolate, he turned heads when he entered a room. He was dressed in a Ralph Lauren

cotton knit shirt the color of sand tucked into olive green
pants. Muscular arms looked more like they were accustomed
to lifting weights instead of wielding T-Fal cookware. Alix
smiled up at him from the sofa. She fiddled with the button on
her silk shantung blouse.

"Alix, we need to talk." Cal wore a sober expression.

"Sure, sweet thing. I like it when you talk to me." Alix
leaned forward to be sure he had a view of her plunging demi-
bra. She gave him a saucy smile.

Cal turned away and clasped his hands together. "Don't do
that. I'm serious, okay? It's about us . . . me."

Something in his tone sent a shiver of anxiety down her
spine. Alix suddenly felt exposed, vulnerable. She hurriedly
pulled her blouse closed. "Sure. Sounds like we both need a
glass of wine." She tried to tease him out of his grim mood.

"Damn right. I'll get it."

She watched him through the pass-through window that allowed a view of the kitchen from the living room. The oak shutters were pulled back. Cal poured himself a glass of wine, drank
from it then filled the glass again. He sighed and walked back
into the living room. Alix set her glass down. Her patience was
wearing thin. For months now she'd played the understanding
woman to his blue moods. After all, they'd been lovers, friends
and confidantes since high school. But she'd reached her limit.

"Cal, what's up with you? If I've done something to make
you mad—" Alix swung her legs from the sofa to rest both
feet on the floor.

"No, no. It's not anything you've done," he answered
hastily then stopped. He raked his fingers through his hair.

"Then what? Look, we've known each other too long. You
can talk to me."

"I don't know where to begin. This is different." Cal
twisted his hands and paced in front of her.

Alix felt tears forming in her eyes, pushing to get out. Suddenly all the distance she'd felt between them made perfect
sense. "You've found someone else."

"It's more complicated than that. I've found me, a different
me than I've ever allowed myself to be." Cal stopped pacing
and looked at her steadily.

She felt a sliver of relief. Alix got up. "An identity crisis?

Baby, everyone approaching thirty goes through that kind of thing." He stepped back when she reached for him.

"Right! I'm coming to terms with being the person I really am, and I always have been." Cal nodded with vigor.

Alix's eyes narrowed. "So, does this finding the real Calvin James Mitchell also include finding another woman?"

"No . . ." Cal pursed his lips for a second then sighed. "It's a man."

"Excuse me?" Alix's heart stopped. "Did you say *man*?"

"I've been struggling with this sexual identity question for years, Alix. And I hope you love me enough to understand. I'm gay, or at least I think I am." The words spilled out in a rush.

"Gay," Alix repeated the word in a dazed voice. The floor seemed to tilt beneath her feet as the walls closed in on her. Her heart began to thump so hard it hurt; she started to hyperventilate.

Cal leaned toward her with a look of concern on his handsome face. "Whoa, honey. Just take slow and steady breaths!" When he reached out a long arm to brace her, Alix jerked away.

"Don't touch me you—*you*," she hissed. Alix fell back onto the sofa like dead weight—she couldn't have lifted her legs if she'd tried. She panted three times then caught her breath. "Oh, God!" she gasped finally.

"I never wanted to hurt you, honey." Cal sat on the sofa, but at a safe distance.

Alix put a hand to her forehead. "Oh, God," she kept mumbling.

"I care about you, Alix, and that's the truth. It's just that I'm tired of denying what I really feel. I've met someone—"

"Oh, God!" Now Alix sprang from the sofa. "Did you . . . while we were . . ." she sputtered.

"Of course not! I'd never do anything to put you at risk or betray you," he said fervently.

"How damn noble of you, Cal! No, I imagine you just started flirting with your future boyfriend. I feel so much damn better knowing how much you care!" Alix shouted as she swung her arms around in crazy circles.

"Honey, calm down. Please," Cal said, his voice shaky.

"Don't call me 'honey' again or I'll throw up all over this freaking white furniture that *you* insisted we buy."

"Hon—Alix, don't. This is hard enough for me."

"It's always about you, isn't it, Cal? This sofa, these stupid prints that I don't even like. You chose Morehouse, so I went to Spelman instead of Howard so we could be together." She tried to think of all the ways in which she'd bent her life to what Cal wanted. Alix looked down at her clothes.

"I dress in red because you like it. You prefer Indian food, so I eat it. You like Aruba, so we go to Aruba. Everything I do is centered on you." Alix walked in circles as she talked.

"Baby, please. Don't do this to yourself."

Alix came to a halt and faced him, defiantly, both hands on her hips. "What about when we made love? You were *pretending* to have an erection?" She seethed.

"Lower your voice, Alix. These walls aren't very thick. You're a desirable, sensuous woman. It's just . . ." He approached her.

"Cal, I'm mad as hell right now. I wouldn't get too close if I were you." Alix's voice shook as tears slid down her face.

"I didn't choose to feel what I feel—I've been fighting it for years. Alix, you mean the world to me. If I could change, and believe me I tried, I'd do it for you." Cal closed his eyes and wiped the tears from his face with both hands.

She turned her back to him. "Now what?" she whispered, her voice hoarse from shouting and anguish.

"I'll move out," he said quietly and went down the hall. Minutes later he came back with two large suitcases.

"Moving in with *him*, I suppose." Alix kept her back to Cal.

"No, I'm going to a hotel. It's not about him, it's about really being who I am for once in my life. Goodbye, Alix." Cal waited. "Please, I know it's a shock but can't we—"

"Leave. Just go." Alix hugged herself tight. She felt as though she were flying apart.

The soft thud of the door closing went through her like a bullet. She collapsed to the floor and sobbed uncontrollably.

*The weekend was hell. Alix wandered around the apart*ment trying not to feel miserable. Every nook and cranny reeked of Cal. In an act of extreme desperation, she'd called Robyn on her cell phone Saturday at midnight and spilled her guts. Ever eager to help, Robyn had ended her date early and rushed over. Well, if you could call three in the morning early. Her loopy style of comfort, lots of fruit juice and deep breathing exercises, had left Alix oddly, if temporarily, calm. Or zonked out on too much fructose and oxygen. Either way it was an improvement. She hadn't retched in over five hours at the thought of Cal's big announcement.

Robyn padded down the hall from the bedroom where she'd slept after their all-nighter. Alix lay curled in a fetal position on her sofa—correction—Cal's freaking pain-in-the-ass-to-keep-clean sofa. She couldn't even lie there and mourn without breathing in the scent of him.

"Did you sleep at all?" Robyn said as she dropped down on the smaller sofa facing Alix. "I must have drifted off at about eight this morning."

"A little I think," Alix said. "What time is it?"

"Wow! It's almost two." Robyn hopped up and pulled back the slate blue draperies that matched the carpet.

"Oh, God," Alix muttered.

"Come on, let's eat," Robyn said in a gentle voice.

"No!" Alix grabbed a large throw pillow and covered her head.

"You've got to keep your strength up. What about a nice sandwich and a bowl of soup?" Robyn's tone was coaxing, like a mother talking to a toddler.

"I can't," Alix howled.

"Okay then I'll fix your favorite." Robyn stood and started for the kitchen then stopped. "Uh, what is your favorite?"

"Robyn, please. Anything I eat would taste like cardboard and poison. Don't mention food again." Alix waved a hand in the air.

"Well, at least have some more papaya juice," Robyn chirped with enthusiasm. "You admitted it made you feel better. And you need something in your stomach, young lady."

Alix tossed the pillow aside and looked at her. "Alright, alright. You and the damn fruit juice," she mumbled.

"What?" Robyn called from the kitchen.

"I said I hope there's still a can of juice left," Alix said louder. She pushed herself up to a sitting position.

"Don't worry. I brought plenty."

"Oh goody," she said then immediately felt guilty.

Robyn came back into the living room with a tray. She'd

poured two small juice glasses to the top. Also on the tray was a plate with two bagels, a small bowl of cream cheese and another bowl of fresh fruit. When Alix frowned, Robyn clucked an apology.

"Just in case you change your mind. Besides, I need more than fruit juice. I worked up an appetite with Steve last night." Robyn sighed with satisfaction and put the tray on the cocktail table between them.

Alix fell back down on the sofa in misery and covered her head again. "Oh God, my life could not suck worse than it does right now!"

"There, there now." Robyn joined her on the sofa. She was patting Alix's shoulder when the doorbell rang. "I'll get it," Robyn answered cheerily.

Alix sat bolt upright and yanked her friend back by the arm. "No, don't! It's him! He's come for the rest of his stuff," she whispered.

"But—" Robyn began in a normal tone.

"Shh, I can't bear to see him. Not this soon. Just be quiet and he'll go away." Alix trembled. The thought of looking into his hazel eyes filled her with dread. The doorbell rang a second, then third time in quick succession.

"Alix, I—"

"If you value our friendship, don't move." Alix gripped her arm tighter.

Robyn pulled against her hold and shook her head with a tolerant smile. "Don't be silly."

"If you value your life, *don't move*!" Alix squinted at her.

The doorbell rang a fourth time, this time followed by Dana's voice. "Open up. Robyn, get the damn door for cryin' out loud."

"Are you guys okay in there?" Carole added in a more sympathetic tone.

"You told them? I can't believe you called the whole world to share my humiliation." Alix glared at her.

"C'mon, Alix. We care about you. The more the merrier. Oh wait, I meant two more heads are better than us."

"Say what?" Alix blinked at her with a baffled expression.

Robyn took advantage of her confusion and darted to the door. "Coming," she yelled.

Alix groaned as she watched her open the locks, then the door. "Here we go."

Carole came in first. "Honey, what a horrible night you must have had here alone." She hugged Alix.

Dana followed, kicking the door shut behind her. "Hey, girl. You know I'm here for ya." She joined Carole by putting an arm around Alix's shoulders.

"Thanks guys. I'll be okay." Alix tried to blink back tears but they fell despite her effort.

"You know we love you. Oh hell, I'm gonna mess up my face," Dana sniffed. She fished out a tissue from her Coach purse and dabbed at her mascara.

"Man, feel the love," Robyn said in a reverent voice.

"Elyssa's coming over too, I think, after Joe leaves and . . ." Dana's voice died when Robyn shook her head vigorously.

"Don't mention men," Robyn whispered over Alix's head.

"I'm heartbroken, not deaf," Alix said and blew her nose. "Besides, you guys can talk about men all you want. I'm through with 'em."

Carole sat next to Alix on the sofa. "I can only imagine what a shock it must have been."

"Shock, disbelief, rage—I've been on an emotional roller coaster since Friday night. Oh, and homicidal. Don't forget that." Alix took a deep breath and let it out.

"I'll fix some coffee." Dana flung her purse down and marched to the kitchen. "Listen, this could be a blessing in disguise, babe."

"Now why didn't I think of that?" Alix wiped her eyes.

"I'm serious. Where's your—nevermind, I found it." Dana went on with her task. "Like I was saying, at least you didn't find out on your wedding day."

"What they mean is there is no good time to find out this kind of thing. But at least he was finally honest." Carole glanced harshly at Robyn and Dana.

"Right," Robyn said.

"For sure," Dana replied over the sound of running water as she filled the coffeepot.

"Maybe I'll be able to see that wisdom later on. Right now it just hurts like hell." Alix rested her head on Carole's shoulder.

"I know, baby. I know." Carole rocked her gently.

"I feel ugly and unwanted," Alix said in a soft voice.

"Don't you even start. Look at you." Robyn spread her arms wide. "Five feet seven inches of perfection with a figure women would die for."

"She's right," Dana agreed.

"Thanks guys." Alix smiled at them fondly. Then she sighed as she looked around the apartment. "I've got to get out of here."

"Hey, come live with me. I've got plenty of room," Robyn said with a grin.

"Well . . ." Alix hesitated.

"It's going to take you a while to find an apartment. I'm neat, don't snore and I promise not to pry." Robyn ticked off each point on three fingers.

Alix sprang from the sofa. "I'll go crazy if I have to spend another night here. Let me throw a few things in a couple of suitcases."

"Fabulous. We can do facials and paint our nails," Robyn burbled.

Alix froze in the act of walking toward their room. She turned around with a pained smile. "Uh, right. Look, Robyn, it won't be for long. I'll start looking for a new place first thing."

"Stay as long as you want. It'll be fun, pal." Robyn winked at her.

Dana exchanged a glance with Carole. "Buckle up, ladies, Robyn's behind the wheel," she quipped.

Chapter 3

Robyn pushed through the door to the Allheart office suite. "You're so nervous lately, Alix. I'm telling you this massage therapist I used to see is wonderful. You remember Don Driscoll?"

Alix came close on her heels. "Robyn, he's in prison for identity theft. Don wasn't really a massage therapist!"

"It was all a big misunderstanding. He's out now." Robyn dropped her black leather backpack on the reception desk.

"He plead no contest," Alix said, waving her arms for emphasis.

"Which isn't a guilty plea, Alix. It means—"

"I know damn well what it means," Alix cut in. "They had the goods on him so he folded like a cheap patio chair."

"No, it means he didn't admit guilt but conceded a few legal points." Robyn spoke clearly as though instructing a student.

"Yeah, like the legal point that he's a crook." Alix waved her arms again.

"Alix, I understand your suspicion of men. Really I do."

Robyn wore a patient expression. If not for the iridescent blue-green nail polish that almost matched her top, she would have looked like a competent young nurse dealing with an unreasonable patient.

"We're talking about a known felon." Alix wagged a finger at her nose.

"Look, you've been tense for days. I'll call Don," Robyn said in a gentle voice just above a whisper. She lifted the receiver of her phone and began to tap on the number pads.

"Argh!" Alix threw up both hands and stomped off to her office.

"Good morning," Dana said as she passed Alix in the hall-way.

"You're half right," Alix snarled back, marching right past her.

Carole approached holding a paper cup from the local cof-fee emporium. "Here, pal. You need this more than I do."

"Thanks," Alix said and took it from her without stopping.

Carole exchanged a glance with Dana and they followed Alix into her office. "Tense today, aren't we?"

Alix set her Bottega briefcase down hard on her desk with a thump. "First, I'm *not* tense—no matter what Robyn told you."

"Your neck muscles look like telephone cables pulled tight, Alix. And you're growling like a panther." Dana leaned against the wall inside the office and crossed her arms. "A very pissed-off panther."

"Who hasn't eaten in days—or had a boy panther to—" Dana stopped when Alix looked at her.

"Don't go there, you won't like it." Alix put one hand on her hip, girlfriend-from-the-hood style.

"I wasn't being literal." Dana held up both palms in a sign of appeasement.

"What's really bothering you?" Carole motioned for her to sit down. Then she took the chair next to Alix's desk.

Alix dropped down into her chair with a groan. "You don't know what it's like living with Rebecca of Funkybrook Farm! She's a sweet kid. But you wouldn't believe the stuff she does."

Dana and Carole looked at each other again and laughed. "Yes we would," they said in unison.

"I'm in the shower, right? I hear the door open so naturally I think it's Robyn, right?" Alix leaned forward.

"Right," Dana said and Carole nodded agreement.

"It doesn't matter to her if I'm reading, on the toilet, in the shower. If Robyn wants to talk, she comes in and starts talk-ing. In the middle of a conversation no less, as though we've been chatting away all along. But don't get me started." Alix shook her head.

"On the toilet?" Dana started to snigger but stopped when Carole shot her a warning look.

"Go on, Alix," Carole said.

"So there I am, in the shower when this male voice says

'Don't freak, I'm just getting some mouthwash.' Then the bathroom door closes."

"So naturally you freak." Dana pressed her lips together to keep from laughing.

"Like I'm on LSD. I'm shaking like crazy thinking about that *Scream* movie." Alix jumped from her chair as though unable to keep still.

"I warned you about watching that crap," Dana said.

"Finally after standing frozen with fear for like ten minutes, I get out of the shower and lock the bathroom door. I then cowered in the bathroom for two solid hours."

"A burglar?" Carole ventured.

"Oh no, that's what happens to normal people. No, it was the guy down the hall. He had overnight guests and Robyn told him to go ahead and help himself to whatever he needed in her bathroom," Alix said. "Normal neighbors borrow sugar. Robyn's neighbors borrow toiletries—while I'm standing there buck naked!"

"She forgot you were in there. It happens." Carole offered her version of a reasonable explanation with a shrug.

Alix waved a forefinger. "No, no, no. She told him 'Alix is in the shower, but go on in.'"

"Well, the shower stall *is* in its own little corner. It's a pretty big bathroom." Dana bit her bottom lip.

Alix marched up to Dana and stood nose to nose with her. "Are you ready to die?"

"Sorry," Dana said in a strangled voice. She turned her face away and struggled not to let out a giggle.

Carole got up and led Alix back to her chair, gently pushing her down into it. "Honey, now you just take it easy. This is an adjustment period."

"One week, and every day has been a fresh hell," Alix wailed.

"At least it's kept your mind off you-know-who," Dana offered. She sat down in another chair next to Carole.

"I'm sure it's difficult for *both* of you," Carole said, both eyebrows arched.

"Are you telling me she had the nerve to complain about me?" Alix sat forward as though she was about to spring from her seat.

"What about insisting on keeping the draperies closed at all times? Or the thousand brands of macrobiotic tofu filling up the fridge?"

"You can't seriously compare that to some of the wacked-out stuff Robyn does," Alix protested.

"My point is you both have . . . idiosyncrasies." Carole held up a hand to forestall another outburst. "And you have to set ground rules and compromise."

"Like don't let psychos into the bathroom when your roomie is naked," Alix retorted.

Robyn stood in the doorway with a stricken expression. "I apologized for that. And Bobbie isn't a psycho. He just collects horror movie memorabilia."

"Alix is overwrought since—you know," Dana said to her.

"She hates me," Robyn said looking at Alix. Her green eyes sparkled with tears.

"No, of course not." Carole reached out and yanked on Alix's arm. "Right?"

Alix let out a long breath. "No, Robyn. You know I don't hate you."

"Then you think I'm an idiot." Robyn sniffed twice more. Dana handed her tissues from a small box on Alix's desk. She blew her nose daintily. "Thank you."

"I . . ." Alix pursed her lips.

"Alix," Carole prompted when she hesitated.

"I think you could use better judgment sometimes. Like whom you invite into the apartment and when," Alix said finally.

"'Kay," Robyn said through a wad of tissue.

"Communication is the key," Dana said.

Guilt crawled over Alix like a spider when she looked at Robyn. She held out both arms to her. "Carole is right. Ever since, *you know*, I have been a real witch. It's not your fault."

Robyn crossed to her and they hugged briefly. "I understand how hard the past week has been on you."

"Thanks, kiddo," Alix said and smiled at her fondly.

"Even though you keep using the wrong knives when you're cooking, I'll just learn to roll with it." Robyn nodded with a look of compassion. "You just don't know what you're doing."

Carole looked at Alix again. "That's what friends are for, to understand and be tolerant of each other's habits."

"Don't forget compromise," Dana chimed in.

Alix squinted at her then looked at Robyn again. "I'll try to remember to use the right knife next time, baby girl."

"See? I told you living together would be good for us both. You're learning about kitchen utensils and I'm learning about . . . life." Robyn beamed at Alix.

"Uh-huh." Now Alix couldn't help but laugh. And it didn't take a thing for Carole and Dana to join her.

"What's so funny? I wanna know too." Robyn blinked at them all.

"Me, Robyn." Alix wiped her eyes. "Maybe I'm on the mend. I can finally see the humor in it all."

"Great!" Robyn smiled again and turned to leave. "Oh wait, hunky Marc Preston is holding on line two. You've still got your phone programmed to Do Not Disturb."

Alix could picture him instantly. She could almost see his full lips curved into a sexy smile and smell his Aramis cologne. "Thanks."

Elyssa walked up at that moment. "Is there a good reason no one is working? You know, like you're busy fighting a forest fire or something?"

"Right, Boss!" Dana did a military about-face and marched off.

"On my way. You know, Elyssa, you could use a good relaxing massage. Maybe I'll call Don," Robyn said before she walked off.

"Uh, Robyn, don't," Alix said.

Carole laughed. "I've got phone calls to return." She shook her head as she left.

"What was that about?" Elyssa looked at Alix.

"You don't want to know." Alix waved a hand.

"You're right, knowing Robyn, I don't." Elyssa smiled. "By the way, you need to meet with Marc Preston today."

"Oops! He's holding." Alix snatched up the receiver and punched line two. "Hi, Mr. Preston. Sorry to keep you waiting." She tingled when his mellow voice drifted through the phone line.

"Get with him soon," Elyssa whispered.

"Lunch?" Alix could see Elyssa nodding as she clicked open the calendar on her Mac. "Sure thing. I'll see you at 12:45, then."

Elyssa gazed at her. "Nice guy. He practically crackled with electricity when you walked in the room the other day."

"Hey, I've been kicked enough for one lifetime." Alix shook off the memory of erotic heat snaking from his solid body.

Elyssa lifted a shoulder in a shrug. "At least you'll have a nice view over your romaine salad."

"I'm not taking the scenic route ever again," Alix said shaking her head emphatically.

"You've got plenty of miles left to travel, my friend. Trust me, you'll start looking."

"I'll stick to my career, thank you very much." Alix squared her shoulders and lifted her chin.

"I saw that teeny tiny gleam in your eye when you first saw him. And that was *before* you and Cal split up."

Alix winced just hearing Cal's name spoken out loud. A fist seemed to close around her heart. "All business, Elyssa. Men are not on my radar screen."

"Hmm, I said that myself once," was Elyssa's only response. She cocked one dark eyebrow at her then walked off.

"I mean it," Alix called out to her.

"Hmm," she repeated over her shoulder.

"I do," Alix muttered to herself, pushing aside the strange mix of memories of Cal and Marc Preston's hot body that flooded her head.

Alix walked into DC Coast, one of her favorite restaurants. She looked around. Waiters hustled back and forth to serve the overflow crowd of diners. DC Coast served equal helpings of the best Creole dishes in town and great music, all on top of a funky, distinctive decor. Wynton Marsalis serenaded the customers via a dynamite sound system.

Marc's choice of restaurant told her much about the man. The dress code and atmosphere here was laid back. No high-powered, pricey place to impress her, though he certainly could afford it. Maybe he wanted her to know more about him. Alix brushed away that train of thought.

"Hi, there," Marc said over her shoulder. "I'm late, sorry."

Alix turned around to greet him as a cool feeling, like a mint oil massage, slid down her back. That voice had supernatural powers. She stuck out her hand in a brisk professional gesture. Arm's length, she answered mentally.

"Only by about five minutes. No problem. Good to see you again." Her smile was just as distant, she hoped.

Marc took her hand with a smile that countered her cool demeanor with warmth. "I feel exactly the same way," he replied.

Alix extracted her hand from the warm, smooth palm that was sending her mad vibes. "Yes, well . . ." She stammered as she tried to get her cool back.

"Table for two?" An attractive woman with ebony skin stood holding two menus.

"Yes, nonsmoking," Marc said.

They followed her and sat down at a table near a window. "Drinks?" the woman asked.

"Water with lemon," Alix said.

"Iced tea." Marc smoothed down his silk tie and settled back against the chair. "So how's your week been going?"

"Not bad," she lied automatically. Not bad compared to being shoved from a plane at thirty thousand feet with no parachute, she mused. Still she managed a polite smile. "And yours?"

"Hectic, but I like to move fast." He smiled back.

Alix cleared her throat and avoided looking in his eyes. Then she made a tactical error in this battle of the libidos—she looked at his chest instead. Broad and firm, not even the light blue cotton dress shirt could disguise the solid flesh beneath. Faint outlines of muscles came through, firing up her imagination. What was wrong with her? She was still in official mourning and here Marc Preston was whetting her appetite for more than food. Alix examined him closely this time with a purpose. Neat fingernails, every hair in place. *Just like Cal.* She went rigid at the thought. The waitress returned with two glasses on a tray and she set them on the table.

"Ready to order?"

"I'll have the Louisiana seafood and chicken gumbo." Marc handed her the menu.

"Bring me a Caesar salad and asparagus soup, please." Alix closed the menu and gave it to her.

"Coming up," the waitress said and scurried off.

"So, where did you go to school?" Alix said.

"Hampton." He sipped from his glass.

No clue there. She'd have to be less subtle. "Oh."

"And you?"

"Spelman, with extra courses in graphic design at Howard once we moved here," Alix added without thinking.

Marc looked up sharply. " 'We' as in husband?" His gaze went to her left hand.

"No, boyfriend. Now ex-boyfriend." She gulped down water to fortify herself.

He smiled and seemed to relax again. "Oh, I see."

Seeing the perfect opening, Alix looked at his hand. "I see you're not married either. Don't tell me, you're driven to succeed with no time for commitments."

"Something like that. More like I never found anyone worth breaking my stride for."

"Which means you've been through plenty of women." Alix studied him for some telltale sign.

"Ah, ah. Don't do an Oprah on me." Marc laughed and shook a forefinger in the air.

"What are you talking about?" Alix smiled back at him.

"You know how she used to have those women on her show dogging brothers out. I haven't left a long line of weeping women behind me."

"I see. So you've been selective." Alix's eyes narrowed as she scrutinized him even closer. "Ever read any E. Lynn Harris novels?"

"Huh?" Marc's brow furrowed as he tried to connect the dots in their conversation.

"I think it's fascinating the sensitive yet provocative way he describes hidden agendas. You know, being gay or bisexual for black men is a real cultural taboo that hasn't been explored." Alix propped both elbows on the table and stared at him hard.

He looked at Alix, a befuddled expression on his handsome face. "I really don't—"

"Here we go!" the waitress boomed, cutting him off. "For the lady, a nice cool salad. For the gentleman, one of our delicious specialties. Enjoy!" She hustled off to another table.

"Thanks," Marc replied with a puzzled look all over his face.

Alix realized just how odd she must be acting. To cover her embarrassment, she changed the subject again. "Looks delicious. Wish I'd gotten that."

Chattering on about food, she diverted his attention with some success. Still he tended to glance at her from time to time with a quizzical frown. They got past the awkward moment when she got Marc talking about himself. Alix followed her mother's advice: compliment men about their performance. Works every time, Mama assured her.

"Some of your ad campaigns have been inspired. That commercial last year with the cute little kid talking about insurance is one of my favorites," she said.

"Thanks. But notice you said a year ago. We've lacked freshness for the past few months."

"What about those billboards around town a few weeks ago? Your team did a bang-up job for La Perla lingerie." Alix lifted her glass of water in a salute.

"You really liked it?"

"Yes indeed. Top drawer," she said.

Marc gave her an appraising gaze.

"That's a helluvah endorsement from a woman with your style."

Alix blushed and cleared her throat. Time to get this conversation back to business. "Very effective in, uh, reaching the targeted consumer."

He leaned forward. "Yes, the vibrant, sexy African-American woman. The kind of woman who can kick butt in the board room while wearing slinky lingerie under her power suit."

Marc's voice rumbled like soft thunder. Alix shivered at the look in his eyes. He seemed on the verge of reaching across and unbuttoning her blouse. She leaned forward in anticipation of his long fingers doing just that. Then he sat back abruptly and broke the spell. Blinking rapidly, Alix sat back, too.

"Right, right. Like I said, you reached the right market." Alix felt scorched suddenly but resisted the urge to fan herself with a napkin.

"You understand exactly where I'm coming from, Alix." Marc fished a succulent shrimp from his bowl of gumbo.

Alix watched him close his lips around it. He chewed slowly, savoring the flavor. "I-I guess so," she stammered then looked away.

Marc patted his mouth with his napkin before he spoke. "Preston and Saks could use your talent. In fact, we're actively looking for a graphic designer right now."

That brought her back down to earth. She sat straight, all

crisp and professional now. "So that's what this lunch is really about. You're trying to get revenge on the cyber world for stealing your talent, huh?"

"I'm trying to get the best talent around. Period." Marc nodded to her.

"I'm flattered," Alix said and sipped from her glass.

"It's a fact. We handle some of the top businesses going. It's a good mix of retail and business-to-business companies."

"I've read up on your agency. You've done work for Pepsi, Fubu, and No-Limit Records. Impressive." Alix was sincere. Preston and Saks were heavy hitters.

"Ah, checking me out," he said with a sly smile.

Alix forced herself not to give him a full body scan. Instead she lifted her chin and spoke in a crisp tone. "Elyssa and I always do our homework. I saw great synergy between your copy and graphics."

Marc took a deep breath then let it out. "Yeah, then we lost three damn good people. Our graphics guy went with a new company that creates online games. It went public and now he's a wealthy man."

"Lucky dog," Alix quipped.

"Tell me about it. A month later we lost two writers. We're doing okay, but we just haven't recaptured that spark that the old team had." He shook his head.

"When it clicks you get magic," Alix agreed.

"Exactly. Which is where you come in. I think we can make magic, Alix." Marc sat forward again with an eager expression.

"I'm happy where I am, Marc. But it's still nice to be asked."

"You've never gotten an inkling, some small sign that it's time for a change?" His expression became intense.

Alix went still as she thought about her love life. She drained her glass then signaled a waiter carrying a large pitcher of water. "Not a clue. Excuse me, may I have some water, please?"

"Sure," the waiter said and filled it to the brim before moving on.

Marc waited for a moment before he continued. "All I'm saying is think about it. I know Allheart is a great place to work."

"It is."

"You could see your designs on television, in national print publications and on the web." Marc's face was full of lively expression.

"The stuff dreams are made of," she said.

"It's how reputations are made, Alix. National exposure brings on incredible opportunities."

"But I've had enough changes lately. A new job . . . I don't know." Alix gazed off, thinking about her future suddenly.

"What changes, Alix?"

She gazed at him. His deep voice seemed to radiate compassion. Could it be that he understood her need to reassess her life, her goals? Cal had been that intuitive, too, seeming to sense every shift in Alix's feelings, sometimes before she was ever aware of it herself. Alix snapped to attention and her eyes narrowed.

"Thanks for the offer, but I'm staying put for now," she said coolly.

Marc seemed to sense a change in her manner. He went with the flow and adopted a professional tone. "At least consider the possibilities. We're willing to pay you very well."

"Money isn't everything. I'm part of the team that helped make Allheart one of the best e-commerce sites around."

"I'd personally help make the transition a smooth one for you. Write your own ticket. Decorate your office before you move, take a few days off before you start, whatever." Marc swept a large hand out to make his point.

"I—"

"Listen, I know how you feel about your boss and about what you've built together. But just how far can you reach there? It's not ingratitude to move up. We both know Elyssa Wentworth is the kind of woman who'll understand. She took that step herself more than once."

Alix looked at him with true admiration. He wasn't at the top of his game for nothing, she mused. Marc Preston was damn good at selling. She was thinking in terms of fresh starts on both fronts now, personally and professionally.

"Let me get back to you. But," Alix said and held up a hand, "don't start redecorating that office yet. Allheart means a lot to me."

"Understood." Marc wore the confident smile of a salesman who's gotten his foot in the door. He picked up his fork again.

They finished lunch without talking about his offer again. Her earlier dramatic suspicions seemed ridiculous. Marc was charming without going overboard. He was funny, intelligent and a jazz enthusiast. The man couldn't have been more perfect if he'd read her mental checklist for Mr. Right. Alix caught herself wondering just how far he'd go if she responded to that sexy smile with an invitation. She quickly discarded the notion. Years spent with one man meant she probably had zero skills at the dating game.

"Well, I'd better get going. I have a two o'clock." Marc extended his right hand. "It's been a real pleasure, Alix."

"Thanks. I enjoyed it too." She held his hand a bit longer than she'd intended. When he broke contact, the warmth from his skin made her palm tingle.

"I look forward to seeing you again." Marc stood.

"Like for dinner?" she blurted out then wondered what idiot had said that.

Marc studied her for a time, a soft yet unreadable look in his dark eyes. "I'd like that very much."

"To talk about your agency. I might as well know what I might be passing up," she stammered.

His smile was wise and sensuous at once. "Of course. I've got deadlines and a business dinner coming up. What about Friday night?"

"Sounds great! I mean okay." Alix cringed inwardly. *Damn, girlfriend! Try to sound a little more desperate.*

They agreed to have dinner at City Lights of China, an elegant restaurant. Alix watched him walk away, a nice sight indeed. He had a sexy stride that turned more than a few female heads. She imagined that sweet combination of power and grace unleashed in the bedroom. For the first time in weeks she got a lift.

"To moving on," she mumured and toasted herself.

Alix had barely gone ten steps toward her office when Dana appeared with Robyn right behind her.

"Spill it," Dana said.

"He's so tasty. Did he ask you out?" Robyn chimed in.

"Don't you people have work to do?" Alix entered her office with them on her heels.

"We're taking a break," Dana said. "Don't change the subject. Tell us about the lunch."

"I think he'll do a great job with the proposal. He's got a solid team behind him. His ads—"

"Skip that junk. Did he make a move? I'll bet he did," Dana rushed on without waiting for an answer.

Robyn peered at her. "She's got a certain glow about her. Yep, there it is."

"It's hot outside. Grow up, why don't ya. This isn't junior high." Alix assumed a woman-of-the-world expression.

"Fine. We're only the friends who nursed you for days, let you cry on our shoulders. Go ahead, shut us out," Dana said.

"Don't even try it. You're junior league compared to my mother. Guilt trips won't work," Alix said.

"I'm beginning to think nothing happened. Darn! And I was hoping you would get some." Robyn wore a disappointed expression.

"Geez, Robyn!" Alix's mouth hung open with astonishment.

"Well it is your lunch hour. You can use the time any way you want," Robyn said.

"I—you—" Alix fell into her chair. "Where do I begin?"

"Maybe she wants to take it slow," Robyn said to Dana.

"Sure. Give it a few more days then jump him." Dana giggled.

"This is unbelievable." Alix shook her head.

"It's so obvious, Alix. You buzz like a honeybee when he's around." Robyn said with a grin.

"Both of you, out!" Alix snapped.

Carole came in. "What's going on?"

"Alix went to lunch with sexy Marc Preston and doesn't want to admit they're hot for each other," Robyn supplied.

"Like it's not written all over her. He walks in and she starts shooting off pheromones like crazy," Dana added.

"I said get out." Alix pointed to the door.

"Can't handle the truth," Dana said in a stage whisper to Robyn. The younger woman nodded as they left together.

"Giving you a hard time, eh?" Carole said.

"Don't get me started. All I want is to concentrate on these new designs. I don't want to think about handsome men with soulful eyes." Alix shuffled through a jumble of sketches on her desk.

"Sounds like you're already doing just that."

Alix looked up to respond but Carole was gone. She would not, repeat *would not* allow Marc Preston to penetrate her shield of protection. Anything that happened between them would be on her terms. Period. Even as she made the vow, her body refused to listen. The tingle remained.

Robyn and Alix were at home engaging in a new ritual: beauty night. At least once a week they selected some way to pamper themselves and indulge in a little girl talk—as if they needed an excuse for either tonight. Alix wore a soothing cucumber facial mask while she lay back on the sofa flipping through a fashion magazine. Robyn sat with one foot propped on the leather ottoman. She painted each toenail carefully with polish that was such a deep red it looked like dried blood. Alix tried not to think of horror movie carnage as she watched Robyn.

"So what's up with you?" Robyn asked without looking up from her delicate task.

"Robyn, we work together, live on top of each other. I think we have few secrets these days."

"You were actually humming in the bathroom this morning." Robyn blew lightly on her toes.

"So?" Alix flipped another page.

"So for the past month you've been a perfect bitch on your best days. And even when you were with—"

"Don't speak that name," Alix cut her off.

"Even before your breakup with what's-it you didn't hum." Robyn examined both sets of toenails with a satisfied expression. "So I repeat, what's up?"

Alix put down her magazine. She picked up a self-help book from the cocktail table and held it up. "I'm well down the path to total healing thanks to Dr. LaWanda Jackson."

"*When Good Women Get Dumped by Chumps*," Robyn read aloud. "Well, at least it's an objective treatment." She giggled.

Alix opened to a bookmarked section. "She's got plenty of

words of wisdom in here. Like this—imagine your ex is covered with painful boils and you get to lance them."

"Oh, that's lovely." Robyn grimaced at the imagery.

"It helps you to exorcise all the anger in a nondestructive way. She's got a section on taking up amateur boxing too."

"Punching people is therapeutic? I don't think so. Besides, you get hit back." Robyn lay back in the easy chair.

"Yeah, I thought about that part." Alix tossed the book aside.

"Bet I know who put a song in your heart. Could his name be Marc Preston?"

"I don't need a man to make me feel worthy—chapter one, section one." Alix pointed to her book.

"Let's get real here. We're smart, accomplished and independent women of the new millennium." Robyn raised an eyebrow.

"Can't argue with that," Alix said.

"But we both know nothing makes us feel complete like having a desirable male respond to us. Admit it. It doesn't mean we're weak, it just means we're alive." Robyn lifted a shoulder.

"Okay, I'm still with you."

"Therefore Marc Preston is the reason you're humming." Robyn gave a sharp nod like a lawyer resting her case.

"Such crystal clear, linear logic. Astounding they haven't hired you away to work for the FBI." Alix made a rude noise.

"I saw the look in his eyes when you smiled at him. That was no act."

"Marc Preston's successful career is based on applying thick layers of bullshit. I know it and he knows it." Alix assumed a sophisticated pose, nose in the air.

"Right, so you're playing his game. Go for it. Get some of that." Robyn clapped her hands.

"Why should men be the only ones having fun? I've had enough of the monogamy thang. If we do click, fine. If not I'll move on." Alix waved a hand.

"To whom?" Robyn blinked at her.

Alix became flustered then tried to recover. "I've got prospects on the line."

"Like that guy in the suit down the hall, the accountant. I

heard him tell you he'd like to total your columns." Robyn nodded.

"Yeah, well," Alix said with a slight shudder.

"Or the guy who handles our web server—what's his name? Andre Townsend. Didn't he send you that very phallic flower arrangement?"

Alix closed her eyes tightly. "God, don't bring that up again. I must give off some kind of hormone-attracting musk."

Robyn tapped a forefinger on her bottom lip while deep in thought. "Then there's that guy who works at the IRS. He—"

"Stop!" Alix groaned and let her head fall back on the sofa. "I'm doomed."

"No, you've got Marc. Believe me that man looks at you with a hungry glint in his eye."

"Sure, he probably wants me to be his freak of the week," Alix retorted.

"I sense it's deeper than that." Robyn's voice dropped.

"Here we go. You've been watching that psychic infomercial again." Alix stood and went to the bathroom down the hall.

"Scoff if you will, but I know what I'm talking about," Robyn yelled at her retreating back.

Alix returned, still patting moisturizer onto her face. "Scoff? Now I know you're crazy." She was about to continue when the phone rang.

"That's him." Robyn nodded sagely.

Alix stared at the caller ID on the cordless phone. "You don't know th—Oh, my God!"

"Told ya."

"Hi, Marc. No psychic powers, just caller ID," Alix said. She waved at Robyn's know-it-all smirk and went into the dining room for privacy. "Sure, I look forward to tomorrow night too. Good night."

Robyn still wore the smirk when Alix walked back into the living room. "Just called to say he was thinking about you."

"Yeah," Alix said in a soft tone.

"How romantic. You two kids make a handsome pair," Robyn teased.

Her words were like cold water in Alix's face. "Hell, that's what people said about Cal and me. We could be the couple on top of a wedding cake, they'd say. I'm not putting my heart out there to get squashed flat again."

"So you've got it wrapped in a bulletproof vest, huh?"

"With a suit of armor on top of that," Alix retorted. "I'm attracted to him sexually, but he's not getting in emotionally."

"I don't see you playing the stone-hearted lovergirl role, Alix." Robyn shook her head.

"I'm going to be the one in control this time. Starting with dinner," Alix said with every ounce of conviction she could muster.

Robyn wore a skeptical expression. "I don't believe it."

"Believe it, baby. 'Cause it's gonna be like that!" Alix stood defiantly, hands on hips.

"Yeah, well I saw the look in your eyes that day too."

"Oh, no. I've got this." Alix wore a sassy smile.

Yet deep down she shivered, thinking of those eyes staring at her. Marc was top grade. She could be playing with fire by testing her new resolve on him—the nerdy accountant might be more her speed. Alix stiffened her spine mentally. Marc was no doubt using his seductive skills to sway her into working for him. It was best she repeat that like a mantra as extra protection.

"*This was the best idea I've had since the Popeye's Fried* Chicken eating contest." Marc grinned at her. His broad shoulder brushed hers.

"Nice place," Alix stammered. *Damn, she had to work on her small talk!*

The ride to the restaurant in his white Jaguar had been a study in how *not* to impress a date. Each time Marc looked at her, Alix had tugged at the hem of her dress like a prim, elderly schoolteacher. Normally the elegant interior of a car would have been soothing. Instead all Alix could think of was how not to make a fool of herself, though she wasn't sure she was having much luck at it. By the time they arrived, she thought she had gathered her strength.

City Lights of China was filled to capacity, which was to be expected, as their Hunan and Schezuan dishes were a local legend. They were led to a table against the wall; Marc pointedly sat next to her rather than across the table. Alix battled with her own reaction to having him so near. Soft lighting and music wrapped them in an intimate mood despite being surrounded by other diners. His cologne combined the best of both worlds, a blend of citrus with a luscious musk fragrance. It smelled warm and spicy at the same time. She was exhilarated and terrified by turns. Marc doubled his assault on her senses with his appearance. He wore a gunmetal gray jacket. Underneath it he wore a white shirt with a rounded collar fastened at the neck with a silver antique-style button. His pants were a lighter shade of gray.

Alix once again glanced down at her simple black skirt and soft pink silk blouse. She wondered if the scoop neckline revealed too much. The sheer black hose might have been a bad idea. Too sexy? While he ordered drinks for them, Alix looked down at her legs for the third time in five minutes. Lord have mercy! Her skirt didn't look that short when she left home.

"You look stunning," Marc said.

Alix glanced up to find him gazing at her. His brown eyes twinkled with a hint of teasing. Still there was something else there. She wasn't so far out of the mating loop that she didn't recognize that look.

"Thanks." Alix cleared her throat and became very interested in making sure the large linen napkin was arranged just right in her lap.

He sipped from his glass of iced tea then set it down on the table. "I'm glad you're not one of those women who doesn't mix business with pleasure."

Her head snapped up. "What's that suppose to mean?"

"Whoa! Don't shoot. I only meant this is a more relaxed way to talk business. That's all. I swear." Marc held up both hands, palms turned out.

"If you think you'll get our account because I'm here—"

"If that's what I wanted, your boss would be sitting across from me." Marc tilted his head to one side slightly.

"True," she conceded grudgingly, then leaned forward with a stony expression. "And I'm not trying to up the asking price on working for Preston and Saks by showing a little leg."

He lifted one dark eyebrow as he looked at her legs for several seconds. His gaze traveled up her body and to her eyes. Alix felt as though he'd touched her in a most intimate way.

"It wouldn't work. Much as I admire those long, shapely

limbs." He lifted his glass to her as though offering a toast to them.

Alix swallowed hard to get rid of the lump in her throat. "Oh," was the best comeback she had.

Marc put the glass down without drinking from it. "Straight up, I'm attracted to you. Hell, that's an understatement." He took a deep breath and sat back against the banquette.

For the first time, the fabulous Marc Preston seemed uncertain of himself. He gazed at her as though he wanted to speak but hadn't a clue how to begin. For a moment she sympathized. Her natural inclination was to relent, cut the man some slack and make it easy. Then the spirit of Dr. LaWanda stepped in. She'd done that very thing with Cal for twelve years of her life and look where it got her. So instead of being the old, sweet, accommodating Alix, the new, sophisticated Alix gave him a composed smile.

"I understand. Let's just deal with it in whatever way feels right." She tossed her hair.

Marc blinked at her. A sheen of perspiration formed on his top lip. He dabbed it with his napkin. "Uh, right."

He still seemed off balance when the waiter appeared to take their orders. Alix calmly scanned the menu and selected Kung-Po chicken. The tables were turned. Take that, Mr. Seduction! Marc held his menu but his eyes had a glazed quality. The waiter tapped his pad with a black ink pen.

"Need more time, sir?" he asked.

"No. I'm, uh, hmm." Marc looked at her then back at the menu.

"I suggest a classic, Schezuan shrimp. It's the best I've ever tasted." Alix affected a guileless expression. "That's if you like it hot."

Marc watched her mouth while she talked. "Yeah, fine, I'll have that."

"Very good," the waiter said in a clipped tone and left.

"What are you doing to me?" Marc propped one arm on the table, the other around the back of her chair.

"What do you think I'm doing?" Alix replied coolly. She lifted her chin and met his gaze.

His deep voice dropped to low, husky timbre. "I don't know what you're trying to do, but I can tell you one thing—I'd like nothing better than to test a theory."

His gaze was fierce enough to burn away the fabric of her clothes. She understood the true meaning of having a man undress her with his eyes.

"What theory?" she murmured. The ball was back in his court.

"That your skin is even softer, more delightful to touch than that silk blouse you're wearing," he whispered, his lips close to her ear.

She melted. Game, set, match. Alix had been too long without this kind of attention. Eyes closed, she let out a long sigh. His fingers brushed her arm lightly and started a fire inside her.

"We've only known each other a few weeks," he whispered again. "But . . ."

Alix gripped his hand. She imagined them caressing her breasts, wondered how his thighs would feel pressed against hers. Her nipples hardened against the satiny bra she wore.

"We could be moving too fast," she mumbled.

"Or too slow," he replied.

The waiter's voice broke the spell. He held a tray with two small bowls of steaming wonton soup.

"Here you go. Your entrees will be out shortly."

Marc moved away from Alix by only an inch or so.

Alix breathed a sigh of relief at the interruption. "Did I mention their soup is excellent also?"

"Best in the city, ma'am. Can I get anything else for you folks?" The waiter beamed at her.

"No, we're fine," Marc said.

Speak for yourself, mister. Alix watched the waiter leave then spoke. "Listen, I'm not—"

"Ready for this?" Marc finished for her.

"Right." Alix twisted the napkin in her lap. Sophisticated Alix jumped ship, leaving the old Alix on her own.

"Know what? I don't believe that. I think you're more than ready for me."

"Am I that obvious?" Alix looked away, too embarrassed to meet his gaze.

Marc took one of her hands in both of his. "No. What I see is a beautiful, desirable woman who deserves tender loving care. I'm just glad your former boyfriend was stupid enough to let you go."

Her temperature spiked again at the gentle, soothing tone

of his enticing voice. Suddenly Alix didn't care if he meant it or not. She wanted—desperately needed—a taste of passion. Almost a month had passed since Cal made his dramatic exit. In reality he'd left her long before that night. Alix had just been too blind to see how long he was in letting go.

It felt so good to hear those words and see the look in Marc's eyes. Yet a sharp pang reminded her of the price for an unconditional surrender. Alix mustered every ounce of strength she had left. Marc seemed to recognize the change.

"You're not going to come with me to my place," he said. It was a statement, not a question.

"No. For one thing, what if I took the job you've made such a fuss offering me? That would be an awkward situation, and that's putting it mildly."

"Well—"

"Not to mention the rest of your staff will be convinced I slept with you to get it. I'm not putting my reputation on the line." Alix shook her head.

"They wouldn't dare." Marc's face clouded.

"You can't control what people talk about twenty-four seven. We both know how a company grapevine works."

Alix sighed. She was being totally logical. What's more, she was right about the effect on her credibility as a professional. Still, regret pricked at her like a sharp needle. That body of his promised delights galore, none of which she would sample. She wanted to feel proud of taking a stand.

"I have a simple solution. Turn me down," Marc said with a wicked smile.

"Excuse me, but I just did," she tossed back.

"I mean the job, damn it."

"I thought you said you need me," Alix asked with a scowl.

"That's exactly the reason I'm not going to hire you after all," he said with intensity. "You're backing away and I don't want that to happen."

"I don't know what to say." Alix almost got lost in his eyes but looked away.

"I'll be honest with you. I'm used to setting the limits with women. When they start to get too close, I get out. This feels different. I want it to be different."

Marc leaned closer with each word until his lips brushed

her ear. One arm circled her, resting on the back of her chair. The other hand settled on her thigh.

"Stop it," she pleaded in a whisper. The strong Alix definitely could not be counted on in a clinch!

"I want to undress you, touch every honey-brown inch of you. Want me back, baby," he whispered hoarsely.

"I think I said stop," Alix panted. She was no longer sure what she was saying and she couldn't move.

"No, not until you tell the truth. You want me as much as I want you, am I right?" Marc demanded.

"Alright, it's true." Alix exhaled long and hard.

"I knew it." Marc nuzzled her neck.

Alix drew away from him. "But I still want to keep all my options open, including the job."

"Uh-uh. Offer withdrawn. I won't give you that excuse to turn me away." Marc gently squeezed her thigh.

Alix firmly grasped his hand and removed it. Still her skin burned from his touch, and it felt wonderful. She ignored her rebellious body. "You'd settle for less and compromise Preston and Saks?"

"Not at all. There are three other excellent candidates to choose from. I believe you know them all. Bill Blassingame, Cheryl Tarton, Hilton Morris," he rattled off the names.

He was right, they were three of the best around. "But they're not me," she said.

"You do have a certain flair, which is why you were at the top of my list. But . . ." He placed his free hand over one of hers.

She drew her hand from his grasp. No way was he going to call the shots in both her personal and professional life. Alix had had her fill of being a passenger. She wanted to be in the driver's seat.

"I might want that job. Now what?"

Marc's expression tightened. He took his arm from around her. "Fine. All business from now on."

Alix allowed herself a few seconds to revel in this small victory over hormones and habit. She cleared her throat. "Look, I'm not being a hardass—"

"Like hell," he muttered.

"I need space to heal. And you agree with me about the job. You'd feel the same way in my shoes." Alix could afford to be generous. She spoke in a reasonable, even gentle tone. Marc seemed genuinely hurt and it was more than male pride.

"Yeah, yeah." He frowned as though in pain from the admission.

"Friends?" Alix stuck out her hand.

Marc gazed at her hand then into eyes. He seemed to struggle for a moment before he took it. "It'll have to be enough. For now."

Alix shivered at the message one touch sent through her body. She pulled her hand away quickly. "Let's eat. All this has made me hungry," she quipped.

"Right." Marc finally smiled back at her.

The rest of the evening went by without a major hitch. Marc relaxed and talked about his agency. He and a college buddy had founded it after they were downsized from two mega agencies in New York. Their contacts and skill had served them well. Within the first three years they'd gone from small business accounts to winning bids with major corporations. Marc hadn't exaggerated when he said she could make a name for herself. Alix marveled at the possibilities.

Their talk turned to her background. He learned that she had grown up in Silver Spring, Maryland, and had one spoiled younger brother. She learned that Marc had grown up in Hampton, Virginia, and was his family's version of the spoiled younger brother. They shared funny stories over an after-dinner pot of hot tea.

"I can't believe I'm spilling my guts to you like this. You must have slipped something in my tea." Alix eyed her small china cup with suspicion.

Marc held up both palms. "Not guilty. Your conscience forced you to confess all."

"Maybe so." Alix laughed and then grew serious. That smile was getting to her again. She made a show of glancing at her watch. "Gee, look at the time."

"I get the hint," he said quietly.

Alix avoided his gaze. Marc signaled the waiter and handed him his American Express gold card. In minutes they were in his car and on the way back to Robyn's apartment. Jazz played softly from the compact disc player. For the first five minutes neither spoke. An alto sax poured from the speakers, wrapping them in a sensual melody. Marc talked about the music and his favorite performers. Alix answered with more questions to keep him talking. She hoped the distraction would help her maintain some control. When they pulled up in front of her building, Alix softly breathed a sigh of relief. Then she made a big mistake.

"I really enjoyed this evening. Thanks for—"

She turned to find his face less than an inch from hers. His lips closed over her mouth before she could react. Resistance was futile—her body wouldn't listen to the feeble voice of protest in her head. Her body relaxed, melted actually, as she yielded to his urgent kiss. Alix trembled when one hand cupped her breast. They pulled away from one another, both breathless.

"Do you really give a damn what people think?" he rasped.

"No."

Alix closed her eyes as he pulled back out into traffic.

Chapter 5

They didn't speak during the drive to his place. Alix was terrified to think where she was headed. He kept his right hand on one of hers as he drove to his apartment in the Heights. He let go of her hand only to ease his Jaguar into a parking space.

"We're here," he announced unnecessarily.

"Yes, well—"

Marc got out of the car quickly. He strode around the rear of the car to the passenger side. The door swung open and he held out his hand. Alix took it with a deep sigh. Each step brought her closer to a new threshold. Her heart pounded so hard she felt sure he could hear it. Before she knew it Marc was putting a key into his front door. When he stood aside to let her go in first, Alix seriously considered running in the opposite direction, but he stood so close her back was pressed against his body.

"Hey, I'm nervous too. This means so much to me," Marc whispered and pressed his lips against the nape of her neck.

Alix suddenly felt sure of where she was, what she was doing. She spun around and backed into the apartment, pulling him with her as she walked. Marc kicked the door shut then bolted it using one hand. He started to speak again but she placed two fingers on his lips to silence him and smiled. He smiled back then made a mad dash down the hall. He was back in seconds.

"I—" He held up the condom.

"Of course," Alix broke in.

The next few minutes were a blur of clothes tossed in every direction. By the time they were down to their underwear, both were moaning with impatience.

"Thank God for modern lingerie," Marc said, his voice muffled against the flesh of her cleavage.

His fingers deftly unhooked the front of her lacy pink bra. He paused to gaze at her breasts for only a moment before his lips closed around one nipple.

Alix gasped as he nipped and licked it then took the other one in his mouth. His hands cupped her buttocks. She wrapped both arms around his shoulders and held on for dear life. Marc stood straight and kissed her mouth hard. A deep animal groan of pleasure rumbled in his chest when Alix grasped his erection. Melded together, they stumbled to the large sofa. He eased them both down and she straddled his lap. They gazed fiercely into each other's eyes as she slowly lowered herself onto him.

"Damn, Alix. Damn!" Marc rasped.

He buried his face between her breasts. Alix cooed and sighed to him, her lips against his ear. She rocked her pelvis to a rhythm that said to take her time, to savor every movement. It was sweet torture. Marc mumbled something.

"What is it, baby? Tell me what you want," she murmured gently.

"Faster, harder," he gasped.

"No," she whispered and continued her slow assault.

Alix dug her fingernails into his taut shoulder muscles. True to her words, she moved with deliberation, determined to possess him. She wanted to drive him insane.

"Alix!" Marc exclaimed and lifted his hips with one strong thrust.

She wiggled faster, unable now to ignore the tigress that roared. Marc said her name over and over as he lifted them both. Alix felt his white-hot explosion inside her. It pushed her into a powerful orgasm that pulsed through every inch of her body.

"More, more," Alix pleaded, her hips moving with a mind of their own.

Alix shuddered as the orgasm subsided. It seemed every ounce of her flesh twitched, a kind of aftershock. With one last sigh, she draped herself over him limply. He eased them both sideways until they lay face-to-face on the sofa.

"So beautiful," Marc whispered. He combed his fingers through her hair.

"Boy, we've done it now." Alix snuggled against him.

"We certainly have," Marc replied with a sweet, sly smile.

"One of us should have exercised some self-control." Alix threaded a few dark curls of his chest hair through her fingers.

"Yeah, Alix. Why did you seduce me? A brother didn't stand a chance," Marc teased.

"You scrub." Alix tugged a few strands in retaliation.

"Ouch! Not the chest hair, baby!" Marc laughed at her scowl.

"Who seduced whom?" She gripped a tuft of curls between two fingers.

"Alright, alright. It was me. No more torture." He kissed the top of her head.

Alix grew serious. "Marc, we've got to think about tomorrow."

"No we don't." He tightened his embrace.

"People will think—"

"We decided we don't care what people think," he broke in.

"My boss—"

"We're not talking about your boss, we're talking about you. What's the real deal?" Marc lifted her chin with one finger.

"I don't want to rush into anything heavy just yet."

"You've been burned and so you want to play it safe." Marc closed his eyes. "I've been there, you know."

"Don't tell me some lady broke your heart." Alix looked up at him. "Marc?" she urged when he didn't answer immediately.

"Yeah, I had one of those forever loves once. Except her definition of forever was a little different from mine." Marc's voice was calm and even.

"What happened?"

"My best friend happened. Old Virginia family, old money," he said tersely. "She wanted status."

"Well, I'll bet she got exactly what she deserved," Alix said in a fervent tone.

"Yep—country estate, a beachfront condo on the Virginia coast, vacations in Europe . . ." Marc chuckled to himself.

"She wasn't the one for you then. You should be glad, eh?" Alix patted his chest as if to console him.

"Glad doesn't exactly describe how I feel, but yes, I agree, she wasn't the one for me. So what about your lost love?" Marc caressed her cheek with his fingers.

Alix squeezed her eyes shut. "God, Marc. Please don't laugh. I'll die if you do."

Marc kissed her lips then stared into her eyes. "Why would I laugh? I want to be your lover, your friend, your champion."

She took a shaky breath. "Cal—the man I loved since high school—has decided he's . . . gay."

"Wow, that must have been rough, baby. I'm so sorry. You had no idea . . . ?"

"Not a clue. I'm pretty sure he didn't have a clue either, though, at least not until very recently. If I didn't still want to choke him with my bare hands, I'd feel sorry for him." Alix sighed. "What a mess . . . I guess I should be glad he was always careful—so you don't have to worry." She gave Marc a halfhearted smile.

"Yes, you should be glad—and so am I." He kissed her again. "Now let's sleep."

"But we should talk." Alix rested her cheek on his chest.

"Later. You wore me out. At least for the next hour or so," he mumbled.

Alix giggled against his skin. She drifted off hoping he wasn't just bragging. Two hours later she discovered he'd been too modest.

Monday morning at the office was a typical day for everyone except Alix. Colors burst around her in a vibrant visual celebration. The smell of fresh-brewed coffee was a delight to the senses. Robyn had pumped her for information all weekend. Alix provided scant details. How could she describe the most incredible night of lust she ever remembered having? Words failed. Robyn would glance at Alix from time to time and let out a low whistle.

Now Alix sat in her office, trying to focus. The images she was staring at didn't help. She was working on a series of draft ideas for a new line of romantic cards. One had a starburst pattern of silver on a midnight blue background. The draft message would read "Last night I touched the stars and was swept away." Last week, this concept had seemed strong to her. Today, however, it felt too tame. She set about sketching a new idea.

"And just where the devil were you until three in the morn-

ing, young lady?" Dana stood in the door of Alix's office with
her arms crossed.

"Robyn can't keep her mouth shut," Alix said, continuing
to draw.

"Are you kidding? As much as she knew, she told." Dana
grinned. She came in and flopped down in a chair.

"Have a seat. It's not like I'm busy or anything," Alix muttered without looking up.

"Hey, I'm your pal. I want a first-person account, not
second-hand scoop. Well?"

"Dana, you should get out more." Alix gazed at her handi-
work. "Hmm, needs to be bolder, a grab-you-by-the-heart
kinda thing."

"So I hear he could put any of those models in *GQ* to
shame. Gray jacket that hung on his fine frame perfectly. A
smile that could melt icebergs. He's—"

Alix flipped the wide sketchpad around so she could see.
"What do you think?"

"Yeah, brilliant. You're the queen. Now about Marc—he's
got a Jaguar. That's the best accessory a gorgeous man can
have." Dana let out an appreciative sigh.

"I was also thinking of maybe a silhouette of a woman
with her arms reaching up toward the heavens." Alix turned
the pad back and looked at it.

"You're not going to talk about him or your date, are you?"

"Not by any stretch of your overheated imagination," Alix
said in an even tone and went back to drawing.

"Damn it! Have a heart, Alix. Let me at least enjoy *your*
love life," Dana blurted out. "Please, just one tiny morsel.
Nothing too graphic, unless you really want to."

"Forget it! I don't kiss and tell."

"To hell with the kissing part. Skip right to the part where
you got naked." She leaned forward with a look of anticipation.

"Not on your life, girlie." Alix's face made it clear the case
was closed.

"Bitch!" Dana spat at her.

Elyssa appeared in the door. "I presume you guys are
working on that new line. I just told the Candy King we had
something brand-new and hot—don't make me a liar."

"We're on it, Elyssa. Not to worry," Dana said smoothly.
Their boss nodded and went on her way.

"You're shameless," Alix said, squinting at her. "Now get over here so we can really get some work done."

"Fine. But this ain't over," Dana said tartly.

"Just shut up and look at this."

Alix held up the picture of a woman reaching for a burst of stars. Dana gasped a little as she took it from her. The woman wore a sheer gown with a low neckline that not only showed generous cleavage; her erect nipples were prominent through the filmy fabric. Her lips were full and parted.

"Whew. This woman has just had some of the best sex on the planet!" Dana stared at the figure.

"Elyssa said 'daring.' The kind of card lovers with few inhibitions would share. New millennium, the Final Frontier kind of sexuality."

"You captured it and then some." Dana fanned her face with one hand.

Alix laughed. "Honey, you're very easy to engage. Look at you, all hot and bothered."

"Hey, don't change the subject." Dana patted a fine sheen of perspiration from her face with a tissue.

"Okay, back to the line then." Alix picked up another sketch.

"No, back to Alix Harris, woman of passion. That is *you*." Dana stabbed a forefinger at the picture.

"Don't be silly." Alix shoved it to the bottom of her stack.

"You don't have to tell me anything now. I see it all clear as day." Dana smiled broadly at her and winked.

Alix blushed. "Grow up."

"You had the most extraordinary night of sexual pleasure since the author of the *Kama Sutra* finished his research. The stuff dreams are made of," Dana said in an awestruck voice. She wore a naughty grin.

"I'm going to slap you in a minute." Alix made a big production of arranging the sketches.

"Alix, it's okay to enjoy it. Let him help you heal."

"Look, all I want is a good time without the hearts and flowers." Alix lifted her chin.

"So, you're going to toy with this man's affections? Yeah right." Dana snorted.

"I'm going to keep it light and easy, stay in control. *I'm* going to set the pace." Alix gave a worldly toss of her head.

Dana looked at her for two seconds then burst out laughing. "Don't look now but you're too late." Dana shook her head slowly.

"What are you talking about?" Alix frowned at her.

"You're already in—"

"Do not use the *L* word," Alix snapped.

"But—"

"No," Alix cut her off sharply.

"You two—"

"Don't make me enforce that order." Alix fixed her with a murderous look.

"Fine, run from reality," Dana shot off her last volley.

Alix ignored her final dig. "Now let's get down to business. You heard Elyssa. We're on deadline."

They worked for the rest of the day without another mention of her night with Marc. Still, the evening was never far from Alix's mind.

Marc ran backward in front of her as she power-walked around the indoor track. Alix was glad to accept an invite to work out.

"Come on, one lap."

"I get the same cardiovascular benefits as you do. Easier on the joints." Alix wiped her brow with her sleeve.

"Chicken," he taunted.

"Your taunts are falling on deaf ears." Alix pretended to hum so she couldn't hear him.

"Alix is scared she can't keep up."

"Hey, I can keep up with you any day, mister."

Marc slowed his pace and fell in step beside her. "Damn right you can."

A tiny jolt of electricity went through her pelvis at the hidden meaning in his words. She needed to stay in control, she reminded herself. "How's the presentation for Allheart coming along?"

"We plan to set up a meeting within the next two weeks. My student interns will finish their reports from six focus groups."

"Focus groups?" Alix glanced at him.

"Yes. We used the demographics of your report and new customers to assemble the groups," Marc said.

"So what did they say?"

"You mean did they like the artwork?" Marc grinned at her.

"Okay, okay, so I want to know. Sue me for being a bit vain." Alix smiled back at him.

"I'll tell all in the presentation," Marc teased then took off at a trot with Alix in pursuit.

"The hell you will, Preston."

She caught up with him just as they rounded a curve on the track. Marc waved bye-bye and shot ahead of her. His long powerful legs pumped with the grace of a seasoned athlete. Alix forgot about chasing him and just watched; he was a thing of beauty. Women on both sides of the gym paused a little to watch him glide by. When he slowed down to a walk, Alix could almost hear a collective female sigh of appreciation.

"Show-off," Alix said as he approached.

"Nah, just doing what comes naturally. I was a total jock in high school." He stretched gently to cool down.

"Let me guess, you ran track." Alix stretched alongside him.

"Basketball in high school. Tennis in college."

Alix winced. Cal had been an all-round athlete in school. "Guess you're still close to those guys, your teammates I mean."

"Yeah, I—" Marc froze. "Hey, we ain't *that* close, baby."

"I didn't mean . . ." Her voice faded. Of course she did. *God, what's wrong with me? My paranoia is showing.* "Sorry."

"By the way, I started reading E. Lynn Harris. Anything you want to know, just ask," Marc said in a calm voice.

"No, no. I'm cool." Alix wiped her face with the towel around her neck to cover her embarrassment. "Gotta get a shower."

Alix ducked into the women's locker room, chiding herself for being so obvious. *Get over it!* Still a part of her said she needed to guard her heart this go round. But, geez, was she going to have to be on guard for such a worst-case scenario for the rest of her life?

Thirty minutes later they met in the reception area of the club. Marc had his suit on again; looking just as splendid dressed to kill as he did dressed casually. *Or undressed*, the lusty little devil in her whispered. Alix silently ordered the devil to hush.

"Join me for a healthy meal." He looked at his Rolex. "It's six. Dinner will be served at seven."

"Look, I've got an early meeting tomorrow."

"So do I. I'll have you home by midnight if you cooperate. Maybe even earlier."

"If I cooperate?" Alix tilted her head to the side, hand on one hip.

"Well, you're the one who keeps me going and going . . . like a sex machine." Marc leered at her playfully.

A nearby group of women stared at them, eyes wide. Two men walking past caught the last sentence just in time. Both raised clenched fists in the air at Marc.

"Go ahead, my brother," a tall ebony man with dreadlocks said. Then both men gave Alix an appreciative glance.

Once they were out the door, Alix punched his arm lightly. "Thanks for broadcasting our business, *my brother*."

Marc laughed and opened the car door with his remote. Alix pretended to be angry, Marc pretended to be contrite. Both were laughing by the time they got to his apartment. Once inside, Marc went into his bedroom.

"I'm going to get comfortable. Come keep me company. Umm, you haven't seen my bedroom yet." His dark eyebrows went up.

Alix blushed at the reference to their hot first date on the sofa. "Right."

She followed him down the hall and entered a cool blue room. The carpet was robin's egg blue. The walls were a lighter blue. Both shades were picked up in drapes that had an abstract pattern with red and antique gold mixed in. A king-sized bed with an oak headboard dominated the large room. An oak dresser stood on one wall. It was a man's room, for sure. Little decoration save for one brass sculpture on the wall next to the window.

"Welcome to the inner sanctum. Have a seat," he said.

Alix started for the bed then sat in an armchair instead. Marc went to a walk-in closet and turned on the light. He set the bag on a luggage holder and took out the contents.

"I'm learning something about you," Alix said. She

watched him methodically place his dirty clothes in a hamper.

"Oh, what's that?" he said, his voice muffled as he changed clothes.

Alix looked around the room before she answered. Everything had a place and there was a place for everything. An oak valet was next to the bed. On the dresser was a tray with spare change and a bold silver bracelet.

"You like things tidy. Everything where it belongs."

Marc came back in the bedroom. He'd changed into a tan cotton knit shirt and olive chinos. "Alix, I'm neat, not gay. Are we going to go through this every time we get together?"

"I wasn't thinking you were gay. But I do seem to keep dragging out this stupid baggage, don't I?" Alix shook her head and covered her face with both hands.

He knelt in front of her. "Baby, you had a nasty shock. And it's only been a short time since he left."

"The whole thing makes me feel like an idiot. Here I am, Alix Harris—walking cliché," she mumbled through her fingers.

"Come here." Marc pulled her hands away and led her to the bed.

They lay down side-by-side, fully clothed, on top of the blue and ivory bedspread. Alix stiffened in his arms at first. He whispered reassurances as he gently stroked her back.

She wanted to trust again, to give all of herself to this compelling man. Strangely, she could have handled it if he'd made a sexual pass right now. But this tender intimacy frightened her more. It threatened her resolve not to let her heart be involved in what went on between them.

"I thought we came here to eat," she tried to sound light-hearted.

"I just enjoy being close to you. We don't have to have sex, baby." Marc planted delicate kisses all over her face.

Alix wiggled free. "This romantic interlude is sweet, but I believe I was promised some food, mister." She sat on the edge of the bed.

"Don't push me away, Alix. Let me show you how I feel," Marc said.

She stood up. "It's too soon. I thought I could handle it but I can't."

"So you're scared too." He folded her in his embrace with

a sigh. "Good, that means I'm not in this thing alone."

"I really should go. There's no way I can think straight right now," Alix murmured.

Marc didn't answer. Instead he kissed her hard and long until Alix sagged against him. His hands roamed all over her body. Her already feeble will to resist vanished. Next thing she knew her shirt was off and he was hooking a finger under the front of her satin bra and opening the front clasp. He bent his head and kissed each bit of exposed flesh as he pushed her bra off her shoulders. Alix cried out by the time his tongue rubbed a nipple. She gasped and guided his hands to her hips.

Her pants were already halfway down her thighs. She kicked free of them and deftly yanked Marc's shirt off. His hand snaked down her belly and into her panties. His fingers drove her insane.

"Hmm, nice, wet, hot," he mumbled against her skin.

She pulled him down onto the bed atop her. Marc kissed her breasts and stomach. Then he stood to gaze at her as he took off the rest of his clothes. Moments later, their eyes locked as he eased himself inside her, inch by inch, until their hips touched.

"Sure you don't want to get serious?" His voice was husky with emotion.

Alix moaned but kept her eyes open. "Trust me, Preston. I'm real serious right now," she whispered.

His answer was a sharp thrust that made her call his name. Then he moved in a slow, steady rhythm that drove them both to a frantic pitch. Alix came first with a shudder that started deep within and spread until her mind went blank. Marc soon followed her over the edge. Alix clung to him, savoring every sweet tremor of his hard muscles. Their waves of pleasure subsided until they lay still, bathed in sweat and gasping for air.

"We can take it as slow as you need to." Marc pressed his cheek against her face as he spoke. "Just don't push me away. Please."

Alix stroked his dark curls. "Okay," she whispered, "I won't push you away." *As if I could,* she thought with a sigh of resignation.

Chapter 6

A week later Alix squirmed under the steely-eyed scrutiny of Elyssa Wentworth. Her flinty gaze could send grown men fleeing in terror. Elyssa rocked back in the chair behind her desk. Alix felt as though she were in the principal's office.

"The line of romantic cards you designed is extraordinary," Elyssa said.

Alix relaxed and smiled. "Thanks. Dana and I worked hard on those."

"The artwork is magical. There's a subtle eroticism that blows me away. That goes for everyone I've shown them to."

"We were aiming for that effect." Alix thrilled at creating art that provoked the emotion she wanted.

"So what's this I hear about you and Marc Preston?" Elyssa's dark sweep of hair shimmered as she tilted her head.

"We're dating," Alix clipped off the words then pressed her lips together. "It shouldn't affect—"

"It didn't. We met with him and his associates Tuesday as you know. His presentation was brilliant. He and his people seemed to know exactly what I wanted. The campaign is young, hip, but not too trendy. He's going after generations X, Y and even Z, not to mention boomers."

"Sounds fabulous."

Elyssa nodded. "It is. No wonder they're the most successful African-American ad agency in town. One of the top agencies in the country actually."

"Marc has a talented group of folks working for him," Alix said.

"He's weak in the graphic arts department though. He has only one designer left."

Alix cleared her throat. "Yes, well . . ."

"He's courting you, isn't he? And I'm not talking about romance," Elyssa added with a pointed stare.

"He did, uh, mention it a few times." Alix flushed. They had hardly wasted time during their last two dates discussing work.

"By the look on your face, I'd say you've been taking care of business in more ways than one." Elyssa's dark eyebrows formed twin arches.

"Marc isn't trying to use me if that's what you're thinking," Alix said defensively.

"I wasn't, but you obviously have been." Elyssa made a quick intuitive assessment, a trait for which she was well known.

"You think our relationship will in some way compromise his work for us? It won't. We're both professionals." Alix lifted her chin.

Elyssa's diamond-studded watch sparkled when she waved her left hand. "I know that. First, on a personal level, I'm glad you found someone."

"It's nothing serious. I'm just taking this dating thing on a test ride," Alix said hastily.

"Alix, you're not the type to play the field," Elyssa said in a dry voice. "So drop the sophisticated lady act."

"Maybe I was naive once, but not anymore. I'm not putting my heart out there again. At least not so soon." Alix marveled at her own performance. It was easy to sound so cool without Marc's soulful brown eyes gazing at her.

"Uh-huh," Elyssa said with a look that clearly showed she wasn't convinced.

"I mean it," Alix said firmly. She did too. Somehow she'd have to maintain this same resolve when he was close to her.

"Whatever. Now let's talk about the professional side. I'm going to top whatever he's offering by, let's say, seven percent. It's not much but—" Elyssa sat forward.

"The money isn't why I listened to his offer." Alix blinked hard.

"Soon we'll be advertising on television, in major print media, even movie shorts in theatres and videos. You won't have to leave Allheart to get the challenge you want or the chance to grow."

Alix sighed. "I admit that lately I've been thinking about change. I guess this breakup with Cal was the catalyst."

"That's normal," Elyssa replied, then waited.

"I sensed it was over between us for months. The reason, though, was one helluva shock, but still . . ." Alix looked away briefly. "I guess I've been holding on to what I know because it feels safe."

"You think it's time for a challenge, a new direction," Elyssa said.

"Maybe. I honestly don't know." Alix shrugged.

"I'd hate to lose you, but I totally understand. I wouldn't be able to pass up a ticket to the big time." Elyssa smiled at her.

"Thanks, Elyssa. You're the best." Alix got up to leave. "And don't start planning my going-away party. I haven't decided anything yet."

"Good. I'm going to fight Preston hard to keep you." There was a competitive gleam in Elyssa's eyes.

"I'm counting on it." Alix grinned at her then left. She got only a few steps down the hall when Robyn and Dana rushed up behind her.

"Are you leaving for that hunky Marc Preston?" Robyn said.

"Better ask when, Robyn. She hasn't said no to the man in weeks," Dana said.

"I think eavesdropping is a federal offense. Now if you'll excuse me." Alix marched ahead of them into her office and shut the door before they could react.

Undeterred, Dana barged in. She planted her feet apart and crossed her arms. "Now listen here, Harris, tell us what's going on."

"Yes, we have a right to know." Robyn craned her neck to peek over Dana's shoulder.

"Since when?" Alix stared at them hard.

Robyn glanced at Dana for guidance. "Well . . ."

"Since we've become more than colleagues. We're sisters. We've been a bridge over troubled waters for each other." Dana glanced at Robyn who nodded with approval.

"Yeah, what she said," Robyn chimed in.

"I hope the copy you have for that new line of friendship cards is better than *that*." Alix rolled her eyes.

"Okay, so it needs work. But the sentiment is sincere. We love you, please don't abandon us." Dana affected a forlorn expression.

"I'd never leave you guys. You're so charming, so respectful of my space. You never pry into my personal life or barge into my office to grill me." Alix walked over to them as she spoke. She planted both fists on her hips.

Dana looped her arm through Alix's. "Listen, babe, let's get serious. I know Marc has the goodies between the sheets."

"Dana, I'm warning you." Alix jerked free.

"Come on. We can always tell the morning after. You glow like the White House Christmas tree," Dana said with a wicked grin.

"Let's stop talking about sex for crying out loud!" Alix burst out.

Carole strolled in. "Damn, I came too late. Give me a quick, titillating recap, Robyn."

"Alix is getting way more than her share, and I think Dana's not getting any," Robyn promptly supplied then grinned. "I'm a happy medium."

"Gotcha." Carole grinned back.

"Ha-ha." Dana scowled at them both.

"So what's this I hear about—" Carole started to go on when Alix cut her off.

"I haven't decided to leave Allheart and I'm not madly in love with Marc Preston," Alix announced.

"Wow, this is better than CNN news. No lengthy back story, just sensational headlines," Carole wisecracked.

"Alix isn't being completely honest, Carole," Dana said.

"Yeah. I saw Marc hand you his card the first time he came to the office." Robyn pointed a finger of accusation at Alix's nose.

"And I told him I was happy right here. So much for your big news, Miss Can't-Keep-Her-Mouth-Shut," Alix said.

"But you're going out with him. So either you're considering his offer or . . ." Dana shrugged.

Robyn spoke up like a tag-team partner. "You're hot for him or both. Either way you haven't fooled us."

"Right." Dana nodded.

Alix sighed with resignation. "Yes, I've thought about his offer."

"Which one?" Robyn quipped then winked at Dana.

"The job, smart-ass," Alix snapped.

"And?" Carole asked.

"It's got me thinking, I mean really thinking, about my career goals. Where do I want to be in five years? How do I define success and am I working to get there?" Alix sat down abruptly. The questions were overwhelming.

Robyn shook her head slowly. "Wow. I thought this was all about Marc."

Alix shook her head slowly. "Hardly. I planned my future around Cal. Big mistake. He walks and I'm lost because I haven't thought about my future without him."

"I think you're discovering inner strength, grasshopper." Carole gave her an affectionate smile.

Alix laughed. "I'm not sure how strong I am, but I appreciate the sentiment."

"All kidding aside, you go, girl. If accepting Marc's offer is good for you then do it. We shouldn't be selfish and lean on you to stay," Dana said.

"Yes we should," Robyn blurted out. She walked over and hugged Alix. "Allheart can take you to the top. Besides, we need you more than Preston and Saks does."

"It's nice to be needed and wanted," Alix said, her eyes misty.

No matter how nice a distraction Marc Preston had been, watching Cal walk away had left her feeling neither for weeks. It was a painful wound that she still felt as if it had happened yesterday.

"You're part of the original Allheart sisterhood. Can't beat that! We're a lean, mean, creative machine." Dana grinned.

"No matter what you decide we're behind you. Right, Robyn?" Carole eyed the youngest sister of the group.

"Well, okay. I do want you to be happy." Robyn nodded.

"Great. We've shared the love. Now everybody out. I've got to get moving on the new fonts." Alix waved at the door.

Carole and Robyn stood, but Dana's voice stopped them from walking out. "Not so fast. You haven't said anything about you and Marc," she said.

Robyn did an about face and looked at Alix. "Yeah."

"You almost pulled it off," Carole said with a grin.

"Well?" Dana pressed.

"I don't know yet," Alix admitted.

Truthfully she didn't. When she was with him, it seemed crystal clear. Yet away from the heady experience of really being romanced for the first time, doubts rushed in.

"And that's okay. You've got all the time in the world." Carole smiled her wise, reassuring smile.

Alix took a deep breath. "Yeah, I guess. Plenty of time to be confused."

"Walking around in stupor—sounds like love to me." Dana smirked at her.

"Your office is close by, go to it," Alix shot back.

Carole laughed. "I've got a meeting. Talk to you guys later."

"There is a stack of work out there with my name on it too." Robyn waved goodbye and sailed off.

"I can take a hint. Just keep me posted, please," Dana said.

"*Goodbye*, Dana." Alix scooted her out of her office and closed the door firmly.

Alix concentrated on work for the next several hours, but Dana's question nagged at her. Where was she headed with Marc? The answer was uncertain. Alix had been used to the comfort of knowing exactly where she was going with a man. Despite what she'd said to Carole, something inside her said it wasn't okay. She craved the security of being loved. Why push it away? By lunchtime the need to call him consumed her. The lines and graphics in front of her would swim out of focus then seem to meld into Marc's face.

"Just do it so you won't keep daydreaming," Alix muttered to herself.

She punched in his number while her pulse rate jumped. After giving her name, his secretary put her through.

"Hi. Nothing important, I . . ." Alix stumbled over what to say.

"You couldn't stand being away from me and just had to call."

A tidal wave of foreboding pulled her under in a split second. She was doing it again! The same thing she'd done with Cal. Here she was on the brink of losing herself in a man. Alix pulled her shoulders back.

"I think we shouldn't see each other for a while."

"What?" Marc said sharply.

"How about we see other people and give each other some space."

"There's that word again, *space*." He sighed. "Where did this come from?"

"Things are getting too . . . intense and I'm not ready for it. I'm sorry."

"See other people," he echoed in a strained tone.

"Yes," Alix replied and bit her lower lip.

"You're sure?" Marc seemed to put every nuance of heated emotion in those two words.

"Yes, Marc, I am," Alix said in a firm voice.

"Just like that, all cold-blooded."

"I don't mean to be. But yes, I think this is right for me."

"Then I'll have to accept it. Next time we meet it will be all business. And I definitely want you to consider coming to work with us."

"I'll be in touch one way or the other. Goodbye."

Alix hung up the phone with a sigh. She'd played it safe and smart, her head told her. Her body complained about being deprived of the best lover she'd ever had. Her heart chimed in too. Yet Alix went back to work by sheer force of will.

The phone rang and she picked it up. Marc started talking before she could speak.

"At least have the guts to tell me to my face," he said then waited. "Well?"

"No," Alix said vehemently.

She'd never be able to tell him goodbye face-to-face. She'd be working against his amazing eyes and smile and her resolve would melt like butter.

"You're wrong about this, Alix."

"I'm sure of my decision."

"Then goodbye."

A click and a dial tone. That's all there was to it. Alix tried to feel good about being the one who took control. Yet she sat holding the receiver for several minutes. When a sharp beep signaled that the phone was off the hook too long, she put it down gently. Work was a gigantic struggle from that moment on.

After one of the most unproductive work weeks she could remember, Alix had brought work home in the hopes of jump-starting her creativity. It was Sunday night. She'd been staring at the screen of her laptop for an hour and nothing. No inspiration. That she had to create romantic images for a line of love notes seemed like a cruel joke. The cursor on her Mac seemed to mock her. Maybe if she stretched her legs. So Alix got up to walk around the living room. She stopped in front of the art deco mirror that hung on the wall and stared at her reflection.

"Mirror, mirror on the wall, who's the biggest chump of all? Don't say it," Alix snapped at herself.

"What are you doing?" Robyn peered over her shoulder.

"Oh, just having a little insanity break. Nothing to worry about." Alix pressed the heels of her hands against her eyes for a second. When she took them down, she faced Robyn with a weak smile. "I'm fine."

Robyn grasped her shoulders and turned her back to the mirror. "You've been in a daze for the past week. Look at those bloodshot eyes. No sleep."

"I'm sleeping very well, thank you." Alix gently shrugged Robyn's hands away and went back to the sofa.

"Really? Then your twin is sneaking in here every night to pace the floor," Robyn retorted.

"One night, it was, that's all. And I was thinking about a new line of Christmas cards." Alix avoided looking at Robyn.

"Yeah, right. Look, you ought to call him. You'll feel better." Robyn grabbed the phone and held it out.

Alix recoiled as if it were a snake. "I will not!"

"Yes, you will," Robyn insisted. "I'm tired of living with a lovesick zombie roommate."

"I'm not lovesick!" Alix's eyebrows gathered together in a fierce scowl. "Marc and I clicked for a minute but it wore off. End of story."

"Oh yeah?" Robyn tilted her head to one side.

"Yeah," Alix shot back with a hard edge to her voice.

"Okay," Robyn said with a shrug.

Robyn hummed to herself as she went into the kitchen. Alix pretended to be engrossed in her work on her laptop. Robyn came back with a diet soda, plopped herself down at the other end of the sofa, and began flipping through a magazine. The only sounds for several minutes were the *snick-snick* of Alix's computer keyboard as she worked and the occasional snap of a page from Robin's magazine.

"So I guess you don't care if, say, he dates some tall lingerie model," Robyn said casually without looking up at Alix.

A sick feeling clutched at Alix's stomach. "N-no. I mean, he's a free man and so am I."

"You're a free *man*?" Robyn pursed her lips snidely.

"Very funny. You know what I mean." Alix glared at her.

"Right, right." The pages of the magazine rustled as Robyn continued to turn them.

Alix stewed for a time until she just couldn't stand it anymore. "To what lingerie model are you referring?" She tried to sound nonchalant.

"Hmm?" Robyn flipped another page, pretending not to hear her.

"Not that it matters. In fact I might go out with that accountant. He's a nice guy," Alix said in a defensive tone when Robyn gave her a look.

"If that's your taste these days—number crunchers." Robyn rolled her eyes before going back to her magazine.

"I mean, Marc probably can't turn around without tripping over some gorgeous model. Advertising is his business."

"Maybe that's what it was, business," Robyn said in a vague tone.

"Did you see Marc with another woman?" Alix clamped her lips together too late. The words had slipped past her internal barricade.

"You set him free to date, remember?" A little *touché* flickered across Robyn's face.

Alix felt a painful thud in her chest. "Right."

Robyn went back to the story she was pretending to read. Alix tried to concentrate on the group of images she was trying to lay out in an arrangement. She stared at the screen until the art grew blurry. All she could see was a picture of Marc giving *that smile* to someone else.

"So who was she?"

Robyn did not look at her. She flipped another page. "Who?"

"The model, damn it!" Alix dropped her laptop onto the coffee table with a thud.

"Oh, I don't know. All those tall, beautiful supermodels look alike to me." Robyn lifted a shoulder.

Alix twisted her hands together. Unable to sit still, she got up and walked around the room. She glanced at the phone lying on the end table three times. He'd moved on and now where did that leave her? Ten agonizing days would turn into a month, then a year.

"To hell with it. I survived Cal and I can damn well live without Marc Preston," she mumbled to herself.

"What was that?" Robyn stared at her.

"Nothing," Alix said firmly. "I've got work to do."

She sat down and concentrated on shoving Marc Preston to the back of her mind, where he belonged. When the phone rang, she didn't look up as Robyn answered it.

Robyn grinned as she held out the cordless phone. "It's Kismet!"

Alix gasped then collected herself. "Okay," she said with a deep breath meant to steady her nerves.

She carefully saved the file she was working on then took the phone. She spoke quietly into the phone, careful to keep her voice just low enough that Robyn couldn't hear her.

After a few moments, Alix hung up the phone. Aware Robyn was staring at her, she avoided returning her gaze.

"Tell me now or I'll scream!" Robyn blurted out finally.

"He wants to talk. So I'm going to meet him at his office around four." Alix couldn't stop the feline smile of satisfaction that spread across her face.

"Wow, he really wants you." Robyn tossed aside the magazine.

"I guess."

"Don't play cool with me. You're crazy about the guy." Robyn squinted at her. "Confess."

"I really like him, yes." Alix felt relieved just to say it out loud.

"Then stop pushing him away. Next time he might not come back," Robyn said and returned to her magazine, this time for real.

Alix only nodded as she considered Robyn's warning. There was no doubt she looked forward to seeing Marc again, despite the send-off she'd given him a few short days ago. Now what? Alix had to decide where she wanted to go with this thing.

She couldn't just keep jerking herself back and forth on it, and Robyn was right—she couldn't expect Marc to keep going along with her manic about-faces. After a few more minutes of pretending she could concentrate on work, Alix headed for her bedroom.

"I'll help you," Robyn said, jumping up to follow her.

"Help me what?"

"Do your hair, nails and pick out just the right day-to-evening ensemble." Robyn looped her arm through one of Alix's. "I say the deep-red skirt with your white silk blouse with the blouson neckline. You can wear a jacket, then take it off for the evening."

Alix stopped short. "I didn't say—" She broke off at the look Robyn gave her. "Good idea." They both giggled like teenagers planning for the prom and raced each other to Alix's room.

Alix walked into the offices of Preston and Saks with her head up. She felt calm and fully in control. "I'm here to see Mr. Preston," she told the receptionist.

"Ms. Harris, isn't it? Right this way." The lithe brunette led her down the hall and past Marc's office.

"Excuse me, where are we going?" Alix said.

"To the conference room."

The woman strode forward and opened double doors. Alix smiled when she saw Marc standing at one end of a highly polished oval oak conference table. One look at his magnificent body draped in an expensive Italian suit and she melted. She dropped her purse on a chair and headed straight to him without hesitation.

"Baby, I'm so glad you blinked first. I was such an idiot. I'm so hot for you right now." Alix was about to wrap both arms around his neck when his wide-eyed expression stopped her.

"Ahem, Alix, this is my partner, Jamal Saks. And uh, this is our design team." Marc stepped back and nodded as he looked beyond her toward the startled group of people at the other end of the room.

"*God, tell me you're joking,*" she whispered hoarsely.

"No," he whispered back, pressing his lips together in an obvious attempt not to grin. "But it's nice to know you care."

Alix risked a look over her shoulder then faced him again. "I'm going to strangle you, Preston!" she hissed low.

"In front of witnesses?" Marc said softly, a twinkle in his brown eyes.

Then in a normal tone, he addressed his colleagues. "Guys, this is the talented lady I was telling you about. My partner, Jamal Saks." Marc pointed to a tall, athletic-looking man.

Alix turned and faced the four people at the other end of the long room. They each held a cup of coffee. And they all stared at her with various expressions of frank curiosity. The one woman among them pursed her lips in judgment, and this wasn't good from what Alix could tell.

"You need a moment alone?" Jamal Saks said with a significant look at his partner.

"No!" Alix and Marc said in unison then exchanged glances.

"What I mean is, uh, I'm Alix Harris." Alix stuck her hand out and marched across the room with a forced smile.

"Hello," Jamal Saks said. "Nice to finally meet the notoriously talented Alix Harris." His smile said he might be considering talents other than those related to graphic design.

"Hello," Alix said stiffly.

"This is Cora Lee, our graphic artist. Ted and Wayne write copy for us," Marc said.

"How nice to meet you," Alix said then turned sharply to face Marc again. "So, you wanted to talk?" she said in a tight voice, one eyebrow arched.

"About the job," he said with a cool smile.

She looked toward the foursome again. The three men smiled back. Cora merely stared, a slight frown on her light brown face.

"We agreed our next meeting would be all business, didn't we?" Marc queried.

"I said I'd be in touch," Alix said tartly, then forced another smile for appearances' sake.

Marc smiled back at her calmly. "Yes, well, we need to move fast. We've acquired two more major accounts in the past week."

Jamal crossed the room to stand close to her. "We really need to expand our team, Ms. Harris. May I call you Alix?"

"Of course," Alix said in a composed tone. When Marc pulled out a chair, she sat down hard. He sat next to her.

"We have two dynamite account executives—us." Jamal pointed to Marc and himself with a grin.

"But we can't risk bringing in more business than we can manage. You're our first choice to hire as our new graphic design manager," Marc said.

"I'll tell you right now, there's no way I can make a decision today." Alix said.

"We understand," Jamal said smoothly. "We wanted to give you the grand tour and let Cora tempt you with what you'd be working on. But first, let's talk about this agency's vision."

For the next hour, Jamal and Marc talked about the state of the advertising business for minority firms, market share and the competition. Cora and the other two men added their own comments from time to time. Alix nodded, even managed to pose coherent questions in the right places. Still she felt a bit dazed. She tried to not think of how big a fool she must have looked to them all when she first walked in.

After a good long debriefing about Preston and Saks, Marc suggested Alix split off and spend a bit of time with Cora in her office.

"Here are some of my designs, a little of what I learned working in LA. So, I understand you're doing greeting cards." Cora, dressed in a mustard-yellow suit that fit her curvy figure well, folded her arms across her chest.

"Allheart.com," Alix said with a nod as she looked over the drawings and color designs. "These are good. Crisp lines on this one, perfect really."

"Yeah, the client, Taylor Office Supply, has fifteen stores

in the Southeast. You've done ad work before?" Cora studied her critically.

"Yes, in Atlanta and for a New York firm briefly before I moved to Washington." Alix gazed back at her steadily.

"I see," Cora said in dry voice. "I worked in New York for five years right out of school. Handled some pretty big assignments."

"Sounds like great experience. It shows," Alix replied mildly, not rising to the bait.

Marc and Jamal came in. "You can see Cora has her hands full. She's been working long hours to keep up," Marc said.

"Sleeping and eating are overrated," Cora quipped with a grin at Marc.

"Let's head to Marc's office for a wrap-up sales pitch—one we're hoping you can't refuse," Jamal said with a charming smile.

He led the way down yet another hallway to his office. Next to the double doors leading to Marc's larger office, a short, plump woman sat in a small office with the nameplate "Lorise Ricker" on the door.

"Fresh coffee waiting, Mr. Saks," she said as they approached.

"Thanks, Lo," he said briskly then stood aside and let Alix go in first. "Here we are."

They approached the seating area, forest green leather chairs around a small rosewood table. An insulated carafe filled with coffee sat on a tray along with coffee cups. Cora joined them after a few minutes. Marc served everyone.

"So, what do you think? Is Preston and Saks a place you'd like to be?" Jamal asked.

"As I've told your partner," Alix said, not trusting herself to say his name; she was afraid it would come out sounding intimate in spite of herself. "I'm very happy at Allheart. We're growing fast."

"Have you heard of Pepsi? No Limit, Inc.? How about Magic Johnson's string of movie theaters?" Jamal leaned toward her slightly.

"Of course I have," Alix said with a slight smile.

"You could be on the team that takes their message to urban, upper-middle class and wealthy black and Hispanic consumers," Jamal said.

"I've been tempting her with our client list for a couple of weeks now." Marc sat down next to Alix and took a sip from his cup.

"And I'm still not sure," Alix added quickly with a sideways glance at him. "Listen, I appreciate all the time you've taken to . . ."

"Seduce you?" Marc said.

Jamal stared at his partner with an expression of male admiration. Cora's eyebrows shot up.

"Um, right," Alix replied and cleared her throat. "But I'm not ready to make a commitment."

Marc turned to her. "So you keep telling me. We don't have to get engaged right off the bat. Let's date first before you say no."

Alix's mouth went dry. "What?" she managed to choke out.

"I think you'll see we're a good match if you just give us a chance, Alix." Marc kept a straight face, but his dark eyes called to her in a very unbusinesslike way.

"That may be, but I have to be ready. And I'm not sure I am," Alix replied. She swallowed hard.

"Then I'll just have to keep trying," Marc said insistently. No one spoke for several moments.

"Yes, well . . ." Jamal stood and extended a large hand to her. "I'm expecting an overseas call in ten minutes. Again, it was a pleasure meeting you. I hope we'll, er, hook up with you, Alix."

She blushed as she shook his hand. "Thank you for the tour."

Jamal headed for the door, but stopped and looked back at Cora. "I'll need that layout for the Baker account," he said firmly.

"What?" Cora looked at him with a slightly befuddled frown. When he cocked his head to one side, she sprang from the chair. "Oh, right. The Baker account sketches. On my way. Nice to meet you, Alix."

"Nice to meet you too, Cora," Alix mumbled.

She strode past Jamal standing in the open door. He nodded to Marc and followed her out. The moment the door closed, Marc held up his hands as if in surrender.

"Don't hurt me." He leaned way back to put distance between them.

"Give me one good reason not to." Alix glared at him.

"You're crazy about me?"

"Try not to be so modest!" Alix snapped.

"Calm down, babe." Marc became serious. "I wanted to see you and thought a business offer was the only way."

"You were purposely vague on the phone, I assumed . . ." Alix pressed her lips together.

Marc's handsome face relaxed into a soft expression of desire. "You want me as much as I want you. Admit it."

"I'm going to—"

"Kill me? Then I'll die a happy man if you give me one last kiss," he said in a voice like smooth mocha crème.

Marc came toward her, took her by both hands, and pulled her to her feet. He cupped her chin. Alix watched in strangely detached fascination as his full sensuous lips came closer and closer. The feel of his lips on hers sent hot and cold shivers down to her toes. His tongue teased its way into her mouth, tasting sweeter by the second. Her anger evaporated and was replaced by a familiar hunger. They kissed for a long, delicious moment. Both were panting faintly when they finally parted.

"Damn, I missed you," he said as he stroked her back with both hands.

Alix moaned and rested her cheek against his. "You're not playing fair, Preston," she said.

"All's fair in love and war. And this is war, Harris. I'm not letting you run out on me."

"I have got to get my act together before I can go down this road again."

"Okay, so leave," Marc said quietly yet tightened his embrace.

"I can't and you know it," Alix said with a sigh.

"Then come to my place and we'll talk."

She pushed free of his hold and looked up at him through narrowed eyes. "And who's going to be there this time, the entire city?"

Marc laughed. "Just you and me, baby. I promise." His smile faded. "Are you going to trust me, Alix?"

She studied every angle of his face. The strong jaw that gave him a determined look at times now gave him an intense expression. He stood very still, waiting for her answer.

Alix sighed and nodded. "Okay, but no more tricks—or else." She pointed a finger at his nose.

Marc held up one hand. "I swear by all the rules of mating as set forth in the *Brothers Plotting to Get Some* official manual."

She gave his arm a playful slap. "There you go, living up to the stereotype."

He twirled a tendril of her hair around a forefinger. "Seriously, baby. I'm glad you said yes."

"So am I," she said quietly and touched his cheek with the tips of her fingers. "I have to go back to work for a late meeting. Elyssa sprang it on me as I was leaving the office to come here." Alix picked up her Louis Vuitton purse.

"How about eight? That'll give me time to set my trap—I mean, prepare a sumptuous meal." He wore a devilish grin.

"Be careful you're not the one caught, mister." Alix grinned back.

"I already am," he said, his voice low and sexy.

Alix kissed his cheek and strode out quickly. She wasn't sure she could trust herself not to rip his clothes off and take him right on that fancy desk of his.

"Don't be late," he called after her.

"No way," she called back over her shoulder.

"*Welcome,*" Marc intoned in his deep voice. He opened the door to his apartment wider.

Alix couldn't help but feel like a lamb wandering into a lion's den. She walked into the room, once more admiring the view from his living room window. Streetlights shone through the deep green leaves of the trees outside. They sat down on the sofa. Marc pulled her close and kissed her.

"Hi. How have you been?" she asked.

"Lonely without you."

She raised an eyebrow at him. "Really?"

"Really." Marc smiled, stood and headed for the kitchen. "So, I'm going to ply you with good food and wine and change your mind about everything."

Alix followed him and perched on a bar stool to watch him work in the kitchen. Marc poured them both a glass of wine. She sipped the smooth Chardonnay and wondered at the ease with which he prepared the food.

"Smells good. What are we having?" she asked.

"Wild rice and roasted garlic, Cornish hens, French-cut

green beans. And for dessert, apricot-kiwi sorbet. Tempted?" Marc said over his shoulder.

"Totally." Alix traced a finger around the rim of her glass and studied his broad, muscular back for a time. "You were lonely, huh?"

Marc turned to her purposefully. "Very."

"A certain lingerie model filled that empty space, from what I hear," Alix said, forcing what she hoped was a casual, lighthearted tone.

"No, she didn't. Fact is, she lost patience with me by the end of the evening. My mind kept wandering and she figured out why."

"Sorry I spoiled your date." Alix smirked.

"No you're not," he said with a soft laugh. "You look beautiful."

"Thank you," she said softly.

"Now turn that mad sex appeal down a notch so I can cook," he quipped.

Alix tossed her hair and affected a pose. "Dahlink, I'll try."

They shared a laugh and a steady stream of chatter as he served up their dinner. At the table, they talked easily; Marc listened with interest as she talked about her work, something Cal seldom did.

The urge to throw herself into being with Marc was strong. She enjoyed watching his mouth as he talked and the way he titled his head to one side when he asked a question. A little voice told her not to hold back. Marc stopped in the middle of a sentence and gazed at her silently for a time. He put down his fork and took her hand.

"What are you thinking?" he asked.

She didn't answer immediately. "About us," Alix said finally. "About that job you keep dangling in front of me."

"Let's start with us." Marc lifted her hand and brushed his lips against the back of it.

Alix shivered at the warm contact on her skin. "I can't think clearly if you keep this up."

Marc turned her hand over and kissed the palm. "Keep what up?" he murmured.

She closed her eyes and let go. He leaned close and planted light kisses all over her face. Then he traced a line of fire down her neck to her cleavage with the tip of his tongue. Between each kiss, he whispered her name. Alix moaned and buried her fingers in the soft dark curls of his hair.

"We can have dessert later," he mumbled, mouth brushing against the top of one breast.

"We'll have that dessert now," she said huskily and pulled him from his chair.

They undressed each other in fits and starts as they stumbled down the hall to his bedroom. They made love hard and fast, whispering passionate endearments in a kind of call-and-response pattern. She came, shuddering from the impact of the powerful orgasm. He followed her over the edge, his strong thrusts pushing her into another climax. When they both stopped, they were exhausted and covered with perspiration.

"Damn, that was so good," Marc whispered between deep breaths.

"Hmm," was all she could manage. Alix sighed as he rolled off her and onto his side.

Marc closed his eyes as he stroked her hair gently. "So, you've decided you want to be with me?" he asked softly.

Alix gazed at him. "Yes."

He smiled with satisfaction. "Good. And we'll make one helluva team too."

"I'm sure we will." She smiled and snuggled against his chest.

"We'll get to see each other during the day and at night, all night," Marc said sleepily as he kissed the top of her head. "It'll be great."

Alix's eyes popped open. "What?"

"At the office, we'll get to see each other—"

"I didn't say I was going to take the job, Marc."

He opened his eyes in surprise. "But I thought . . ."

"Yes?"

"Why fight it, baby? You want me and the job." Marc ran his fingers up her right forearm, causing goose bumps to pop out.

"I'm still considering my options, on both counts." Alix pushed his hand away. Still she watched his muscular chest rise and fall, hypnotized by the motion.

"Really? I'd say you made a decision some time ago." Marc cupped one breast, leaned close and ran his tongue over the nipple.

"Cut that out." Alix shook her head to clear it.

"Come on. We're compatible on so many levels," Marc murmured between taking gentle nips at her flesh. "When you took my card that first day we met, I knew."

His confident tone pierced through the fog of lust that filled her head. "Is that right?"

Marc pulled back to gaze into her eyes. "You're a passionate woman. I'm a passionate man. We're also both very ambitious."

"I see."

"Look, I got you over to the office knowing you'd stop playing hard to get. We're going to make magic together, Alix." He smiled at her softly. "You and I."

She pushed up on one elbow. "So, this is just an extension of the job interview?"

"Not exactly. I mean—"

"Not exactly?" Alix sat upright and crossed her arms over her chest.

"Baby, you know it's more than that." Marc reached for her, but she slapped his hand away.

"Don't make assumptions about me, Marc Preston. I'm not that uncomplicated." Alix got out of the bed. She searched around and found her underwear buried in the folds of the comforter.

"Give me more credit than that," he pleaded. "I think we can reach the top of the world, Alix." He grabbed her bra and tried to tug it from her hand.

"Your ambitions now include me. How flattering," she retorted. Alix snatched the bra from his grasp and put it on. Then she bent over to put on her panties. "As good as you are, and you're damn good."

He stared at her body hungrily. "My pleasure."

Alix put her hands on her hips. "But your skill in bed didn't completely scramble my brain."

She *had* been wonderfully mindless, but there was no need to mention that now.

"Okay, I've been a bad boy and I deserve to be punished. So spank me." He grinned then turned over. The sheets slid away to reveal his firm, brown buttocks.

"This isn't a damn joke, Marc!" Alix yelled, her voice trembling as she tried not to cry.

Marc turned over and sprang from the bed. "Alix, listen to

me. We're both young, smart, good-looking and on our way to the top. What's wrong with that? The agency—"

"The agency, huh? You seem to want a neat package, a top-notch graphic designer who will sex you up whenever you want it." Alix grabbed his bikini briefs from the floor and threw them at him. "I don't think so!"

"Baby, wait," he said as she stomped out of the bedroom.

Alix found her panty hose and put them on. She was buttoning her silk blouse by the time he came into the living room.

"Can't we talk about this rationally?" Marc walked in, a vision in nothing but the navy blue briefs.

She forced herself not to stare at his muscles, which rippled as he moved. "Right now I'm not capable of rational discussion. I might do something drastic," she snarled.

Marc winced and took a step back. "We'll talk when you've calmed down then."

"I don't plan to calm down ever again if it means letting you or anybody else walk over me. Good night." Alix tucked her blouse into her skirt and marched to the front door.

"If you let me explain—" Marc held up both hands when she whirled around and faced him with a scowl. "Just be cool, baby."

"Don't call me 'baby.' And I am cool. In fact I've just had a cool, refreshing shower of reality. Thank you, Mr. Preston."

"Baby—Alix, wait a minute."

"Remember when you gave me that bird's-eye view of your ass a few minutes ago? Well, that's where you can stick your job offer, corner office and all."

Alix jerked the locks open and slammed the door hard on her way out. Surprisingly, she did not cry as she rode the elevator down to the lobby. Even the drive home was dry. She eased her Honda Accord into traffic and turned up the radio. A blast of Mary J. Blige came through the speakers.

"Girl, I think maybe you're on the mend." Alix said to herself, giving all thoughts of Marc Preston an unceremonious shove right out of her head.

Alix walked into the Allheart conference room the next day with her head up. She gave Marc a stiff smile then sat down between Dana and Carole. Jamal beamed a megawatt smile at her.

"Good seeing you again, Alix."

Elyssa's perfectly arched eyebrows went up a notch in a pointed glance at Alix, but she said nothing.

Carole leaned close to Alix. "What's up?" she said with an almost imperceptible nod toward Marc.

"Later," Alix whispered, rustling several notepad sheets to mask her response.

Dana glanced from Marc to Alix. "Me too," she mumbled close to Alix's ear, then flashed a smile around the table.

Elyssa introduced her staff to Jamal Saks then got down to business. "I'm very happy with your ideas for the Allheart campaign, gentlemen. So where do we go from here?"

"You've submitted a few changes and additions you'd like us to make to our plan. Let's go over those to make sure we understand each other," Marc said.

For the next hour, they bounced ideas off each other with Marc taking copious notes. Jamal seemed to be the big-picture man, while Marc payed attention to the details.

Alix studied Marc. He behaved as though they had never spent those fiery nights clawing at each other. She wondered at the man, hot in bed but a cool operator in the boardroom. He looked at her with a composed expression, betraying nothing. Alix hoped she was just as serene as he was on the outside. Mentally, however, she was replaying their last night together. How juvenile stomping out like that, she admonished herself over and over.

"Your staff did an excellent job integrating our logo into those graphics, Marc. It's the kind of branding we want," Elyssa said.

"Thank you. Of course Alix put us on the right path." Marc glanced at Alix briefly.

"It seems her work with the Preston and Saks team was a seamless fit," Elyssa said mildly, a slight smile on her face.

"I only gave them a few suggestions. They did the work," Alix answered quickly. "Obviously they didn't need much from me." A short, pregnant silence fell, which Jamal broke after a few seconds.

"Allheart's blend of sexy, contemporary cards will hit the twenty- and thirty-something market right where they live, Elyssa. You ladies know your stuff," Jamal said smoothly.

"Thank you," Elyssa said with a nod.

They finalized plans for print and web advertising and the meeting drew to a close. Jamal and Elyssa stood aside talking while Robyn, Carole and Dana headed for their offices. Alix meant to follow them when Marc put a hand on her arm.

"A few loose ends to tie up about the graphics we discussed, remember?" he said.

Jamal and Elyssa paused imperceptibly in their exchange of Beltway gossip to glance at them. Alix studiously avoided looking at her boss.

"Of course, come to my office," she said.

Marc turned to Jamal. "Technical stuff, minor details, that's all. I won't be long."

"Take your time," Jamal said blandly. "We want to get the little things right."

Alix smiled weakly then walked out of the conference room ahead of Marc, acutely aware of two sets of sharp eyes gazing at them with intense interest.

Chapter 8

After they went into her office, Alix closed the door and faced him. "Try to be a bit more obvious next time."

"Don't be angry with me, Alix. I know I sounded like a complete fool the other night." Marc swept both arms outward.

"I agree," she said in a frosty tone.

"What I meant, in my clumsy way, was I'm happy you're in my life." Marc took a cautious step closer to her.

Alix stood, legs planted apart and arms crossed. "Go on."

"I was excited by the idea of us burning up the twenty-first century at work and play." He moved still closer. "We're an awesome team, baby. C'mon, tell me I'm right."

Alix stared at the way his mouth curved into a sensuous confection of brown sugar. She remembered just how sweet his kisses were, all over her body. A shiver started at her shoulders and shot down to her hips.

"Don't make me suffer through another lonely night without all this," Marc said softly, his gaze flickering over her.

"Maybe I overreacted," Alix finally admitted. She tilted her head back, hoping he'd take the hint. He did.

With a deep-throated sigh, Marc grazed her cheek and neck with his lips. "The job is yours if you want it. Whatever—I'll take my cue from you. But there's no need for us to be apart, is there?" he whispered.

"I guess not," Alix said, savoring the feel of his strong arms closing around her.

"Guess?" His kisses grew more insistent.

"I mean, yes," she said between short breaths.

He brushed her lips lightly then stepped back. "I'd better stop or I'll have you on that desk in a minute flat."

Alix took a deep breath to steady herself. "Right, Jamal is waiting."

Marc dabbed traces of her lipstick from his mouth with a linen handkerchief. Then he straightened his tie and smoothed down the lapels of his Armani suit jacket.

"Let's have dinner tonight at Blue's Alley."

"Pick me up at eight," Alix said with a sigh.

He blew a kiss at her and left.

Alix waited until the door closed behind him before she sagged against her desk.

Five minutes later there was one quick knock before her office door opened. Dana and Robyn came in. "Well?" they said in unison.

She tucked her hair behind one ear and went around her desk. "You two have a lot of work that's going undone. Dana, I need copy for six cards."

"You're not going to dodge us, Alix," Dana said with a squint.

"And Robyn, what about those travel arrangements to the trade show?" Alix cocked a critical eyebrow at them both.

Robyn waved a hand. "It's already done. Now tell us what he said."

"Said, hell! I didn't hear voices through the door. I want to know what they were doing!" Dana dropped down into a chair and crossed her legs. "From the top, Harris."

"Yeah, every juicy bit," Robyn agreed with a wide grin.

Alix rolled her eyes. "You won't give me a minute of peace, will you?"

"Nope," Dana retorted.

"Okay. Marc apologized. He's not going to assume I'm an easy catch. End of story." Alix nodded to them curtly and sat down at her desk.

"Aw, c'mon!" Dana protested.

She pursed her lips for a few moments, letting them squirm in suspense. "Well, the man *could* start a fire with his tongue!" Alix blurted out.

"I knew it. More, more." Dana leaned forward eagerly.

"His apology was old-fashioned-sweet and a huge come-on at the same time." Alix hugged herself like a teenager.

"So, all is forgiven. Well, well, well." Dana slumped back in the chair, shaking her head.

"It's so romantic, Alix. And to think you wanted to crawl into a hole after what's-it left," Robyn said.

"I think I can finally say that that's in the past. Marc is the future." Alix rocked back in her swivel chair. "I was so wrapped up in Cal that I never thought about *me*, what *I* wanted."

"And you're not going to make the same mistake with Marc, huh?" Dana asked.

"I set him straight, girl. You would have been proud of me." Alix extended both arms and flexed her muscles playfully.

"So what's next?" Robyn said.

"Marc's taking me to dinner and then probably to his place for a little nightcap." Alix smiled widely. "A *lot* of naughtiness."

"As much as the poor man can handle," Robyn quipped. "Dana, a monster has been set loose upon the city."

Dana stood. "You're pissing me off again, Alix. First you had Mr. Perfect—"

"Except it turned out that my Mr. Perfect was looking for *Mr. Right*," Alix said with a grimace.

"Well, now you've got the *real* Mr. Perfect. Tall, dark, handsome, rolling in money and giving good love." Dana heaved a melodramatic sigh. "Some women have all the luck."

"You and Marc," Robyn said cheerily as she stood to leave. "Looks like things are back to normal for you. A steady guy, no guesswork on the mating scene."

Alix faltered. "I, uh—"

"I'd better get to work. See ya later. Have a good time tonight with the new Mr. Perfect." Robyn waved her fingers at her as she and Dana left.

"Yeah, right." Alix sat deep in thought, a frown on her face.

The next few weeks with Marc were a whirlwind of romantic dates. He sent her flowers, Allheart love notes via email and called her on those few nights they didn't see each other. And Alix enjoyed every minute of it. Even better, Elyssa had nothing but praise for the way Marc was handling their advertising campaign. Their web traffic increased six percent within a week after new banner ads were up at selected websites. Six new companies bought ad space at Allheart.com. Fun and funky print ads in the slick women's magazines definitely pleased their investors. All was right with the world. Almost.

Another workday ended with Alix and Marc spending the evening together. First, an idyllic dinner at a restaurant with a breathtaking view of Washington Harbor. Then lovemaking hot enough to melt steel.

Alix lay in Marc's arms while soft light from scented candles cast shadows on his bedroom walls. They lay spoon fashion, her back against his chest. Marc sighed contentedly and tightened his embrace, cuddling his hips closer against her buttocks. She had every reason to be outrageously pleased with herself. And yet . . .

"What are you thinking?" Marc whispered, causing Alix to jump in his arms.

"Nothing," she said quickly. "I mean—"

"You mean you can't think straight. I've blown your mind with good love." Marc laughed, his voice a sensuous rumble from deep in his chest.

"And so humble too," Alix joked.

"On the real side, baby, I'm the one who's in a daze." Marc kissed her shoulder. "I can't believe how lucky I am."

Alix turned in his arms and looked into his eyes. "You mean that?"

"Damn right." Marc brushed her hair tenderly.

"I'm not crowding you or anything? I know how men are about that kind of thing." Alix studied him.

"No way."

"Cause, I mean, we don't have to get all intense if you don't want to . . ." Alix's voice trailed off.

"I'm cool, Alix." Marc's dark eyebrows came together. "What's up?"

"I just don't want you to think I'm pushing you into this thing," Alix said with a weak smile.

Marc gathered her into his arms again. "I think I see where this is going, baby."

"You do?" Alix said, her cheek pressed against his chest.

"Yeah. You're waiting for me to show my male colors . . . you know, run from commitment, right?"

"Well, I . . ." Alix fumbled for something to say.

"Look, I *want* to be with you. Period. There's no rush to

meet each other's parents just yet, but eventually . . ." Marc trailed off.

"Right. No rush."

Meet his parents? *Oh my God!* Alix's mind reeled. She was on a runaway train that *she* had put in motion.

"No," Marc went on. "We're going to spend some quality one-on-one time together for a while. Then we'll do the family thing."

"Yeah, I guess," she murmured.

"We're both swamped with work right about now. Did I tell you about this new account we just got?"

Marc's deep voice droned on, telling her about the agency's latest coup. Alix lay thinking of how comfortable this felt. And familiar.

"Hey, I put you to sleep." Marc smiled at her.

"No, no. I was listening." Alix smiled back at him. "That's great, Marc."

"Every little bit helps. We'll be lying on the beach in St. Kitts before you know it." Marc sighed and closed his eyes.

"St. Kitts?" Alix looked at him hard.

Marc yawned. "You'll love St. Kitts. It's my favorite island." His words became muffled as he drifted off to sleep.

Alix thought hard for several moments about herself, him and them. He was making plans. She shook her head. She should be thrilled. Here she was in the strong arms of an undeniable hunk. Dozens of women would kill to be here. Instead of having doubts, she should be happily counting her blessings.

"Yes, I'm sure I will," Alix said softly.

"What's that, sweet thing?" Marc murmured drowsily.

"Love St. Kitts."

"Sure you will."

Alix lay awake in his arms for a while listening to his steady breathing. She finally drifted off with a vague feeling of unease that troubled her sleep.

Three days later, Alix was in her office working on a layout for new cards that would be enclosed with lingerie. She saw a movement from the corner of her eye. "Put the copy on my desk, Dana. I'll be through in a minute and then we can get together."

Dana closed the door. "We've got bigger problems than this deadline."

"Oh really? You must have forgotten how Elyssa gets when we're behind," Alix tossed back and kept drawing.

"It's nothing compared to the coming explosion from Mount Elyssa. I just heard—"

The door swung open suddenly. "Alix, we need to talk," Elyssa said with a sharpness in her voice.

Alix glanced at Dana who bit her bottom lip. "Sure. Is there a problem?"

"Come to the conference room." Elyssa strode off without waiting.

"I'll just go back to my office now," Dana whispered and scurried to safety.

Alix followed Elyssa to the conference room. Carole was already there. Alix was surprised to find Marc there too. Elyssa sat down across from Marc and rested her elbows on the table.

"Okay, from the top," she said to Marc, her tone curt. "Explain to me why the hell three of our sponsors are threatening to pull out on us."

"What?" Alix sat down hard next to Marc.

Marc turned to Alix. "One of the ads pushes the envelope a little. We thought it fit the Allheart brand."

"I approved the ad with a softer touch. Not this S and M crap!" Elyssa said waving a sheet of paper.

"Let me see." Alix caught the offending item as Elyssa slid it across the table with one sharp motion. She stared at it, then blinked hard. "Is that black leather and a . . ."

"No," Marc said. "It's only meant to suggest . . ."

"Suggest, my ass," Elyssa snapped. "I sure as hell would have remembered *that* in the proposal."

Alix winced then tried to smile. "Well, those cards we call 'Love Taps' are pretty hot. Maybe our customers will find it funny."

"Our sponsors don't and neither do I." Elyssa glared at Marc.

Marc leaned forward. "Your image is hip, sexy and edgy. That's what you want to project, right?"

Elyssa's eyes narrowed. "Yes, but—"

"Don't freak just yet. Wait and see how the customers react. The sponsors won't care once their sales continue to climb." Marc smoothed down his silk tie.

"First, this is about more than the sponsors. You had no business changing that ad without checking with me. Second—"

Robyn appeared in the open door. "Elyssa, Ms. Collins of Petals is on line three. She's kind of upset about the new ad."

"Uh-oh," Carole said quietly.

"I couldn't make out everything 'cause she was talking kinda fast. Something about women being depicted as objects for violent sexual exploitation." Robyn looked at Alix and mouthed a silent message.

"Good Lord!" Elyssa sprang from her chair. She hurried from the conference. "I'll be back. I want to see how you're going to fix this," she said to Marc, pointing a finger at him.

"Uh-oh," Carole repeated then looked at Marc expectantly.

"Cora and Dave got a bit carried away working late one night and decided to jazz up the ad," Marc said with a sigh. "It's not really that bad."

Alix held up the ad. "Marc, I'm no prude, but this is a bit over the top."

The picture was a silhouette of a man built like a wrestler standing over a woman. The woman was lying on a long chaise lounge, legs apart. The man appeared to be touching himself with one hand. The copy said "Allheart Cards—Your Sentiments Exactly."

Carole stared at the ad. She tilted her head from left to right to see it from different angles. After a few seconds she shook her head. "No, it still looks like he's about to . . . you know."

"I think maybe we should wait a few days and see how it shakes out," Alix said faintly.

Elyssa came back to the conference. "So far we have six sponsors screaming bloody murder and three tickled pink." She looked at Marc. "Well?"

"Why don't we all take a deep breath and have a meeting with my team? This afternoon at three is good." He looked at Elyssa without flinching.

Elyssa glanced at her watch. "Fine. That will give you five hours to come up with a reason why I shouldn't sue you." She stomped out without another word.

Carole stood. "I'll see you this afternoon." She gave Alix a quick glance then left.

"What the hell were you thinking?" Alix burst out the moment they were alone.

"We were on a tight schedule. I really think your boss is overreacting." Still, Marc frowned and rubbed his chin.

"Yeah, well you better come up with satisfactory answers by three or your ass is gonna be ground meat."

Marc patted her arm then stood. "Talk to Elyssa before the meeting this afternoon, okay, babe? Get her to calm down."

"I don't think—"

He gave her a light kiss on the lips. "You'll be there?"

"I'm not sure," Alix said.

"Then offer to come. We're on a roll with this campaign. If we all stay calm, we can keep the momentum." Marc flashed his signature dazzling smile. "Admit it, you like that ad."

"Well . . ." Alix glanced at the open door.

Marc leaned down until his face was close to hers. "Just talk to her and we'll be fine. See you at the meeting."

Alix accepted a second kiss. "Okay."

He waved goodbye and strode out. Alix watched him walk away, his long-legged stride graceful and athletic. Carole came back into the room, catching one last glimpse of Marc before he rounded the corner heading for the lobby.

"This afternoon should be interesting," she said in a wry tone.

"Yeah. Marc said maybe Elyssa is being a bit too touchy." Alix looked at the ad again and shuddered.

Carole nodded. "It gets worse the longer you stare at it. But the good news is we've got ten new potential advertisers."

"See, Marc was right," Alix said with a hopeful expression.

"The bad news is they're porno sites."

"Oh my God! Please don't tell Elyssa that!" Alix pleaded.

"She already knows," Carole said with a grimace. "What did Marc have to say for himself after we left?"

Alix sighed. "He expects me to help fight the fire on my end."

"Oh," was Carole's cryptic response.

"Don't give me that. I'm not a pawn here," Alix tossed back.

"All I said was—"

"Okay, okay," Alix said with a wave her hand. "Lately I've been having déjà vu all over again," she retorted.

"The Cal Syndrome." Carole's eyebrows arched.

Alix let out a guttural moan. "Did everyone but me know I was a total wet dishrag in that relationship?"

"I wouldn't say that exactly."

"I would," Alix said. She threw her shoulders back. "But no more. Let him deal with his own mess."

"Right," Carole said with a nod.

"And I don't even want to go to St. Kitts!"

Carol blinked at her. "Huh?"

"Never mind. The immediate problem is this crisis. I assume our new partners know about this little bump in the road?" Alix looked at her.

"You betcha. Elyssa's having to deal with them too." Carole's dismal expression suggested it wasn't pretty.

"Excuse me while I find a deep hole," Alix pushed back her chair and stood.

"Elyssa isn't that bad, Alix. I mean really," Carole said with a smile. Just then they overheard Elyssa loudly barking a string of instructions to Robyn. Carole's smile vanished. "Wait for me."

They hustled to their respective offices. Alix tried to finish work on the sketches in front of her and not think about the meeting.

"*Elyssa, I can assure you things are not as bad as they seem.*" Jamal wore a charming smile that did nothing to soften Elyssa's expression.

They were seated in the elegant conference room of Preston and Saks. Cora Lee sat between Marc and Jamal, a trace of defiance in the set of her jaw. Alix sat on the end with Carole between her and Elyssa.

"Tell that to six sponsors. One of whom is the president-elect of the local NOW chapter," Elyssa snapped.

"I've seen your cards. They're very sensual," Cora, the agency's graphic designer, put in.

Elyssa swung her chair around to face the young woman. "We don't feature cards with prone women with men standing over them holding sticks." Her voice cracked across the room like a whip.

"He's not holding a stick. It's merely suggestive of—"

Marc glanced at Cora sharply, sending a clear silent message she should be quiet. "The bottom line is we made a professional decision to be daring."

"Two people not afraid to explore their sexuality," she muttered, determined to make her point.

Elyssa sat forward with a hard stare. "Make editorial statements about sexual expression on your own time."

"Ahem, I think the point is our customer isn't happy," Jamal put in smoothly.

"A huge understatement," Elyssa put in.

"Cora has done a series of new layouts for your approval," he continued calmly. He nodded and Marc passed the drawings to Elyssa.

For the next hour Alix and Elyssa sorted through the drawings. Alix made several suggestions. They used a computer in the conference room to make changes, compare color schemes and change fonts. Jamal and Marc went to great lengths to please Elyssa, while Cora worked on the changes, never wavering from her tight-lipped expression.

Finally Elyssa signed off on the changes. "These are perfect," she said, pointing to four thumbnail pictures on the computer monitor.

"That should do it then. We can upload these right now," Alix said.

"Carole and I are going back to the office. We've got a lot of kissing up and apologizing to do. We'll see you later, Alix. Goodbye," she said curtly to the others.

"I'll be in touch about the advertisers and sponsors," Carole said to Marc and Jamal as she followed Elyssa out.

"I think I can put these on the web without help," Cora said in a short tone. She didn't look at Alix as she gathered up her notes and sketches.

"I'll give them a quick check before I leave," Alix said firmly. Cora threw her a haughty glance then walked out. "Miss Attitude has a lot to learn about pleasing clients."

"Cora doesn't take criticism of her work well." Marc shrugged.

Jamal stood and straightened his suit coat. "I'll talk to Ms. Collins. She sits on the local arts council with my mother. This will blow over. By next week we'll be laughing about it over drinks at J. Paul's."

Alix watched him stroll off. She shook her head slowly. "He's about to learn a hard lesson. Elyssa is not going to laugh this off. She's an old-school feminist."

"I think reality is somewhere in between, babe. It may take a while, but Elyssa will cool off." Marc came around the conference table and sat next to Alix.

"Maybe," Alix said with a skeptical frown.

He draped his arms around her shoulders. "It's not all that bad, Alix. Six sponsors out of twenty are a bit upset. It's totally fixable."

"Five are a bit upset. Ms. Collins is livid." Feeling his solid muscles around her, she relaxed for the first time that afternoon.

"My biggest concern is that we regain your boss's trust." Marc wore a slight frown.

"Well, you responded quickly and removed the ad." Alix smiled at him. "Elyssa will consider that once she gets over the joystick thingy."

Marc winced. "Please don't remind me. I honestly didn't think it looked that bad."

"Marc, tell the truth."

"Okay, we'd all been working late into the night. Around ten o'clock Cora showed me the sketches. I was exhausted. I'd been in the office since seven that morning."

"So, you plead guilty by reason of insanity—from overwork that is." Alix gave him a playful nudge in the ribs with an elbow.

"That'll teach me. No more making decisions on an empty brain," he quipped.

Cora walked back in. She glared at them for a moment before she spoke. "I've got the first picture up if you want to see it."

"Sure. I'll take a quick look then I've got to head back to the office." Alix left the warmth of his embrace reluctantly.

"I'll call you later. I've got to get ready for a meeting in about an hour," Marc said.

"Okay." Alix smiled at him then followed Cora to her office.

Once there, Alix and Cora took turns fiddling with the graphics. Ten minutes had turned into over an hour but finally they had it just right. Alix stretched and looked up toward the knock on the door.

"Hello, Sharlene," Cora said with a sideways glance at Alix. "*This* is Alix Harris. She's with Allheart. Alix, Sharlene Thomas."

The tall, lithe woman smiled and extended an expertly manicured hand. Her skin was the color of honey. She wore a smart, sexy red suit jacket and navy skirt. "Nice to meet you."

"Sharlene is with the accounting firm of Nelson, Braitwaite, Ellis and Connors. We handle their advertising too," Cora explained.

Alix returned the woman's cool smile as she shook her hand. "Hello. I can get with you later if you've got a meeting," she said to Cora.

"I'm here to see Marc," Sharlene said. Her smile lengthened into a feline smirk of satisfaction. "We go way back."

"I see," Alix said.

"So he's handling your account too?" Sharlene took a seat and crossed her long legs. The hem of her short skirt rose to reveal firm thighs.

"Yes." Alix pressed her lips together.

"I've known Marc since college. We have this regular thing where we get together. Business, mostly." Sharlene rolled her eyes and laughed.

"How nice," Alix said in a clipped voice. She picked up her leather briefcase then looked at Cora. "I've got to get going. I'll take a look at—"

"He's good at what he does," Sharlene said. She tilted her head to one side. "Don't you agree?"

Alix paused for a beat. She felt a familiar sinking sensation in her midsection. Still she forced an impassive expression. She turned slowly to face Sharlene.

"Yes, he is."

In the silence that followed, Alix and Sharlene sized each other up. Cora seemed not the least bit uncomfortable. In fact, she glanced from one woman to the other as though watching a tennis match. Then Marc walked in.

"Cora, I—" Marc wore the expression of a deer watching an oncoming car on a rural country road. "Uh, Sharlene, aren't you early? How long have you been here?" he stammered and glanced at Alix.

"A few minutes. I just came back to say hello to Cora."

Sharlene followed his gaze to Alix. "I had a chance to meet your new . . . *client*."

"Excuse me. I'll let you two get to whatever it is you do," Alix said with an icy smile. "I'm on my way out." She went past Marc without looking at him.

"I'll walk with you," he said and followed, closing the door of Cora's office behind him. "Alix, wait a minute."

"For what?" she said over her shoulder.

Marc grabbed her right forearm and held on. "Stop. Is there a problem?"

"No. Now if you'll excuse me," Alix tried to pull free, but he held on.

"It's not what you think."

Alix looked at his hand then at his face. "What do I think?"

"Okay, knowing Sharlene she probably mentioned we had a thing. Had, past tense."

"Really? Until about what, a month ago?" Alix said, an eyebrow raised.

"Well, maybe a little longer." He blinked rapidly as her eyebrows went higher. "Definitely longer than a month. Much longer. Did she tell you we—"

"No, you just did," Alix said with a grim smile.

"Baby, it's over. Sharlene and I were never serious." Marc walked up close to her and lowered his voice. "There's no comparison. It's different with us. You're a different kind of woman to me."

Alix gazed up into his dark eyes. The scent of his cologne, warm and spicy, was like an invitation to surrender. Marc was counting one too many times on his masculine charm. Yet she wasn't angry. She touched the fingertips of her left hand to his face.

"You're right, baby. I'm a very different woman," she said softly. Alix let a slow, sultry smile curve her lips up at the corners.

"I knew you'd understand. I'll call you later." Marc brushed three feathery kisses on her forehead. He stepped back, a self-assured smile on his face.

"Yes, you do that." Alix waved the fingers of one hand at him flirtatiously and left.

* * *

Robyn pressed the Off button of the cordless phone. She muttered an oath and marched down the hall to Alix's bedroom. When she pushed open the door, Alix glanced up only briefly.

"Girl, will you please call that man back? I'm tired of being caught in the middle," Robyn said. "Ten messages in two days."

Alix lounged against fluffy pillows and flipped through a magazine. Her small color television was fixed on a shopping channel.

"Hmm," was her bland reply.

Robyn dropped down on the foot of Alix's bed. "What if he stops calling?"

"Then he stops calling."

"Cut the hardass act." Robyn bounced on the bed to get her attention.

"It's not an act." Alix sighed and dropped the magazine. "I'm just finally learning my lesson. I gave myself to a man so completely, I lost my identity. It was like I became a big amorphous glob called 'Cal and me.' I'm not doing it again."

The doorbell rang and Robyn sprang from the bed. "I don't believe you're going to give up Dr. Feelgood."

"Believe it," Alix called after her as Robyn darted off. Minutes later she came back with Dana at her heels.

"I agree with you, honey," Dana said without preamble as she came in and sat on the bed. "To hell with him and his number-crunching bimbo."

"Don't listen to her, Alix. You and Marc were good together." Robyn said and ducked when Dana tossed a throw pillow at her.

When her phone rang, she picked it up without thinking. "Hello? You're where?" The doorbell chimed again.

Robyn and Dana exchanged a glance. "He's here!" they said together.

"I'll let him in," Robyn said and started to stand.

Alix grabbed her T-shirt and yanked her back. "Move toward that door and I'll drop you with one kick."

She stood and adjusted her clothes, a lavender casual pant set of soft terry cotton. Moving quickly, she went to the closet and put on a pair of silver sandals.

"At least let us say a quick hello, then—" Dana started.

"Forget it. Stay here," Alix warned, giving them both a deep scowl before she turned to go.

"Okay, but we expect a full report later," Dana tossed back. "Hey, did you hear me?"

Without answering, Alix pulled the bedroom door shut behind her with a firm thump. She willed her heartbeat to slow down. With one last breath for courage, she unlocked the front door and opened it.

"Well hi there," she said mildly.

"Very cute, Alix. Some punishment."

Marc slipped the slim cell phone into the inside pocket of his jacket. Once inside the apartment he spun around to face her just as she closed the door and leaned her back against it.

"I don't know what you mean." Alix said, regarding him with her head to one side.

"What's with the teenage stuff, not returning my calls or emails?"

"I've been busy," Alix said with a shrug. She went around him and sat on the sofa.

"Bull!" he said through clenched teeth.

"It's true. I've had mad deadlines in the past few days and—" Alix threw an arm across the back of the sofa.

Marc's frown softened as he sat next to her. "Baby, if this is about me and Sharlene, don't waste more time on it."

"I'm not really worried about that," Alix said in an unruffled tone. Something in her voice must have convinced him.

He blinked at her, a slight frown of worry on his handsome face. "So what is it?"

"It's just as much my fault as it is yours, Marc," Alix said in a serene tone. "I needed someone and you were there."

Marc's mouth fell open. "Damn! You saying you used me?"

"No, not exactly." Alix wore a gentle expression of fondness as she took his hand. "Look, Marc, I'm staying at Allheart."

"To hell with the job offer. This is about us," he said passionately.

"I've thought about it, and I really don't want to get serious. I mean it this time." Alix did mean it. She wanted him but on her own terms.

"I want you, Alix Harris," Marc said and pulled her into his lap.

"Hey!" she yelped.

Alix fell against his broad chest, surprised by his fast move. Her face was less than an inch from his. She breathed in and was enchanted by the scent of cologne on his warm brown skin.

"I want you," Marc repeated louder this time. "I don't care who knows it. Damn it, I'm going to change your mind."

"Think you can, Preston?" Alix grinned a challenge at him.

"Let's go to my place so I can start my campaign," he whispered hoarsely, his mouth close to her ear.

"You guys okay in here?" Dana called out as she came into the living room, Robyn close on her heels. They stared at them.

"Everything is just fine," Marc replied without taking his gaze from Alix's face.

Alix gazed back at him for several heated seconds then said, "We're going out."

"Uh, okay," Robyn said and nudged Dana with an elbow.

"Drive careful, kids," Dana quipped.

They left without speaking again. The drive to Marc's apartment took too long. They kissed at red lights during the trip until horns honked. When they arrived at his apartment building, Marc parked and they walked quickly inside to the elevator. Alix wrapped herself around him and kissed him hard before the doors whisked shut. By the time they arrived at his front door, Marc was in a fever. He fumbled with the keys and Alix took them from him. With a cool grin, she unlocked the door. When it closed behind them, Alix took off her blouse and tossed it aside.

"So, I guess you got me where you want me," Alix said, knowing she was exactly where *she* wanted to be.

"I'm the one going down for the count," Marc murmured.

"You better believe it," Alix answered with a satisfied sigh.

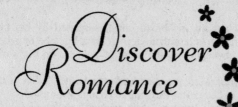